ARTICLE 109

A Novel

Peter Gregoire

Set in Beijing and Hong Kong, **ARTICLE 109** is a high-octane, page-turning thriller. A young solicitor, investigating the suicide of his former colleague, unravels a conspiracy to cause chaos on the financial markets by instigating the downfall of one of Asia's richest tycoons. ARTICLE 109, Joint-Winner of the Proverse Prize 2011, lifts the lid on Hong Kong's fragile status as an international financial centre and the role it plays in China's unrelenting march towards becoming the most powerful global economic superpower.

Born in the United Kingdom, **PETER GREGOIRE** moved to Hong Kong in May 2003. Currently the head of the legal department for the Hong Kong subsidiary of one of the world's largest general insurance groups, Peter has also worked for the regulatory authorities in Hong Kong and as a private practice commercial litigation lawyer in the City of London. During his career, Peter has been responsible for implementing anti-money-laundering and anti-fraud compliance systems, dealing with ICAC investigations and litigating complex financial frauds through both the English and Hong Kong courts.

Peter has been writing fiction since 2006 and his stories have been published in a wide range of anthologies. His short story 'Dispute Resolution' won the senior category prize in the 2008 Standard/RTHK competition and a consultation with Pan Macmillan.

ARTICLE 109, a fast-paced financial-crime thriller in which Peter draws on his inside knowledge of working in the financial services industry and his experience of the subtle political and economic relationship between Hong Kong and China, is his first full-length novel and Joint-Winner of the Proverse Prize 2011.

Peter currently lives with his wife, Isa, his son, Luke and his oversized basset-hound, Dumbo, in Hong Kong.

Proverse Prize Winner 2011

ARTICLE 109

A Novel

Peter Gregoire

Proverse Hong Kong

Article 109
By Peter Gregoire.
2nd pbk edition published in Hong Kong by Proverse Hong Kong,
December 2015.
Copyright © Proverse Hong Kong, December 2015.
ISBN: 978-988-8228-19-5
Printed by CreateSpace

First published in pbk in Hong Kong by Proverse Hong Kong, 20 November 2012.
Copyright © Proverse Hong Kong, 20 November 2012.
ISBN 978-988-8167-33-3

Pbk distribution (Hong Kong and worldwide):
The Chinese University Press of Hong Kong,
The Chinese University of Hong Kong, Shatin, New Territories, Hong Kong SAR.
Email: cup@cuhk.edu.hk Website: chineseupress.com
Tel: [INT+852] 3943 9800; Fax: [INT+852] 2603-7355.
Distribution (United Kingdom): Enquiries and orders to Christine Penney,
Stratford-upon-Avon, Warwickshire CV37 6DN, England.
Email: <chrisp@proversepublishing.com>

Distribution and other enquiries to:
Proverse Hong Kong, P.O. Box 259, Tung Chung Post Office, Tung Chung,
Lantau Island, NT, Hong Kong SAR, China.
E-mail: proverse@netvigator.com; Web: www.proversepublishing.com

The right of Peter Gregoire to be identified as the author of this work has been asserted
by him in accordance with the Copyright, Designs and Patents Act 1988.

Cover design by LOL Design Ltd.

British Library Cataloguing in Publication Data.
A catalogue record for the 1st edition of this book
is available from the British Library.

To Isa and Luke,

the two lights of my life.

PROLOGUE

Deputy Controller Liuming sensed the threat as soon he opened the door into the ornate meeting room, his political antennae responding the same way his arthritis did on a frigid Beijing morning.

"We started without you, Deputy Controller," said Secretary Wu, a bookish man with an unemotional manner that belied the power he exercised as a direct-line report to the Minister of Security on the Politburo Standing Committee. Wu was highest ranked of the three men in room. Any decision today was his and his alone to make.

Liuming slowly seated himself. "I thought we were starting at eleven-thirty."

"Eleven-fifteen!" snapped General Zhao. "Your office obviously passed you the wrong message."

Liuming nodded, the army commander's abruptness causing the dawning realization that he had just walked in on another military power play. Another attempt to grab influence in the name of national security. "If the Third Bureau's staff is to blame, General, then I apologise. Perhaps, you could tell me what I have missed."

Zhao snorted into his moustache and puffed out his immaculate uniform. "We are here to discuss the special administrative region of Hong Kong and to address the latest embarrassment it has caused our government"

"The General is referring to the incident involving Rupert Kwan and the Lantau Island container terminal," Wu added. "It was a matter of some concern for the Minister, so I'm keen to hear both your recommendations."

"The Minister's concern is fully justified!" Zhao continued. "Trying to sell the container terminal to a Singaporean conglomerate was disgraceful behaviour. Typical of what we've come to expect from the Hong Kong tycoon class. That terminal accounts for seventy percent of the airport's through-put. If it had fallen into foreign hands, it could have done untold damage to the country. And all because that spoilt tycoon brat, Rupert Kwan, wanted fast money!"

Liuming rested a liver-spotted hand on the tabletop and took a moment to collect his thoughts. "The Minister knows the Third Bureau will deliver its briefing on this matter next week?"

"Next week?" Zhao snapped. "This matter is urgent!"

"Perhaps," Wu moved to mediate, "you can provide a summary of your conclusions today, Deputy Controller, since the General has already raised the issue with the Minister."

"As you wish," Liuming conceded. "But as this is the General's meeting, it would be discourteous not to allow him to present his recommendations first."

Wu nodded.

General Zhao cleared his throat. "Well it's clear this incident shows a complete lack of control in Hong Kong. The place is run by business interests, tycoons who think nothing of China. Rupert Kwan is the worst of them! Never done a hard day's work in his life, but here he is selling strategic parts of Chinese territory to foreigners. We must make an example of the Kwan family. Confiscate their wealth, limit their movements. Send a strong message to the entire tycoon class that they don't run Hong Kong. We do!"

Liuming wondered how many times he had heard this plaintive cry from the military, trying to grab power on the pretext of keeping the nation safe. As ever, it would be up to his Third Bureau to provide the counterbalance. China's continued path of progressive development demanded it.

"In the end the container terminal was not sold to Singapore, I believe," Secretary Wu said. "It stayed in Chinese hands."

Zhao laughed disdainfully. "It was Cyrus Kwan, Rupert's uncle, who made the purchase, Secretary! So ownership stays with the rich tycoons. Pah! It doesn't even leave the family. An uncle bails out his nephew, the threat to Chinese security remains and we are a laughing stock in the media. You saw the international press? Pure nepotism, they called it!"

"Perhaps I could shed some light on the matter?" Liuming said. Zhao's eyes flashed with anger, but Wu signaled for Liuming to speak. "The Third Bureau is responsible for intelligence operations in Hong Kong, Macau and in the special economic zones. It is our task to identify threats to Chinese security in these places. Any failure in this respect therefore lies with us and I answer for it." Liuming placed a frail hand on his chest, then addressed himself to Zhao. "General, the sale of the container terminal was a matter brought to our attention as soon as the non-disclosure agreement between the parties was signed. Our assessment was the same as yours; that it was in the strategic interests of the nation for the terminal to remain in Chinese hands. Our options, however, were limited. Nationalisation was out of the question. According to the Foreign Ministry, it would have damaged relations with the Singaporean government and at the broader regional level. So a private sector solution was needed. Thankfully, one materialized when Kwan Holdings made the purchase."

Secretary Wu's brow narrowed in thought. "It seems a solution rather left to chance, Deputy Controller? What if no Chinese buyer had come forward?"

"In this instance, Secretary, the appearance is" – Liuming seesawed his fingers – "deceptive. As soon as the Third Bureau learned of the Singapore bid, we set up a back-channel approach to Cyrus Kwan, to ask if Kwan Holdings would consider bidding against the Singaporeans."

"You mean the Third Bureau engineered the purchase by Cyrus Kwan?"

"We merely suggested it to Cyrus Kwan as an option to consider. The ultimate decision lay with him. So you see, not only did the Third Bureau identify the threat, but we encouraged a solution that disguised government involvement and avoided damaging China's relations with its regional partners. This is all set out in our report, which, as I say, is due to be delivered to the Minister next week."

The room was doused into a taut silence. General Zhao had been out-manoeuvred. But he wasn't ready to surrender just yet. "You had to promise Cyrus Kwan something for his co-operation, I assume?"

Liuming nodded slowly. "Cyrus Kwan was the lead representative for the Hong Kong Chamber of Commerce during the negotiations on the Cooperation in Services Agreement. As you know, the CSA is being unveiled this week. Mr Kwan merely asked that we see to it that the treaty is implemented effectively. The Finance Ministry was happy for us to make this promise."

"China shouldn't have to make deals with tycoons to preserve its security!" Zhao said. "Why, it's as if the Kwan family has held us to ransom! For all you know, Cyrus Kwan orchestrated the whole thing. The nephew offers the container terminal to foreigners just so the uncle can step in, save the day and extract high-level favours."

Liuming felt all his seventy-years bearing down on him. "There was no such conspiracy here, General, I can assure you."

"Can you?"

"General, please..." Secretary Wu felt obliged to intervene.

Liuming raised a hand to Wu. As Deputy Controller of the Third Bureau of State Security, he was still able to fight his own battles despite his age. "General, since it was set up, the Third Bureau has built a secret surveillance network in Hong Kong which has gone unnoticed. Why? Because it is part of Hong Kong society; a developed, fast moving society filled with subtleties far more numerous than we here can ever imagine. The Third Bureau has developed an intimate knowledge of the individuals and relationships that make Hong Kong function. The very suggestion that Cyrus Kwan conspired with his nephew Rupert ignores the underlying dynamic of that particular blood tie." Liuming turned to Secretary Wu. "If you would permit me to explain?"

"Please."

"Rupert Kwan is the only son of Cyrus Kwan's younger brother who died of lymph cancer when Rupert was only six years old. Since then, Cyrus has been responsible for Rupert's upbringing. He has indulged the boy: an expensive education in the United States, start-up capital for his first business, leverage of the Kwan name. Yet as Rupert has grown up, so their relationship has become strained. The Hong Kong media continually portray Rupert as a spoilt child with nothing to offer but his uncle's backing. This, Rupert resents and he has made it his ambition to assert his independence by proving himself to be the better businessman. Unfortunately, Rupert is not blessed with his uncle's acumen. All his ventures so far have been unmitigated failures, the container terminal being the latest. Yet Rupert Kwan is still associated with his uncle. So any failure of Rupert's is also perceived as a failure of Cyrus."

"I see," Wu understood. "You are saying that Cyrus Kwan had an incentive to bail out his nephew to protect the Kwan family name?"

"Indeed, Secretary, which is why we knew the back-channel proposal to him to purchase the container terminal would find favour. You see, to Cyrus Kwan, his nephew is both a great responsibility and his greatest curse. Their relationship is crucial to our understanding of Hong Kong. That understanding has kept the Lantau terminal out of foreign hands."

General Zhao's jaw set hard. A safe retreat would have been the sound option, but Liuming knew obstinacy in the face of the truth would be the General's response. "I remain firmly of the view that control needs to be established over the entire tycoon class in Hong Kong. The consequences of not doing this poses great risk."

"General!" Liuming couldn't let that comment ride. "The kind of crackdown you are recommending would do untold damage to China's path of economic development which has been thirty years in the making. Businessmen like Cyrus Kwan must be left to do what they do best. When they benefit, the whole of China benefits. Their investment lifts people out of poverty and the Cooperation in Services Agreement provides the next step in that process. It will harness the entrepreneurship of men like Cyrus Kwan for the benefit of the nation. Your iron fist, by contrast, would only serve to turn back the clock to darker days in our country's history."

Zhao reddened with rage, but Secretary Wu had heard enough.

"General, I am grateful to you for calling this meeting. I understand the reasons for your recommendations, but I am going to go with the Deputy Controller and the Third Bureau on this occasion. Their approach has worked thus far. I see no reason to change course." Then Wu addressed Liuming. "Deputy Controller, I look forward to receiving your report next week, but I will first pass on the highlights to the Minister. He wants to ensure that the forthcoming Cooperation in Services Agreement proceeds without any problems. This must be your main priority over the coming weeks. Please ensure that the Third Bureau remains vigilant to any potential threats."

"As you wish, Secretary," Liuming said.

Wu was about to get up, but General Zhao wasn't finished. "I would like to make clear, Secretary that should any further threats materialize in Hong Kong, my people will be able to move quickly, should you decide a more decisive approach is needed."

Wu let the cold comment hang a moment. "Thank you, General. Should the situation change, I shall revisit your recommendation. For the moment, however, I'll leave it to the Third Bureau to handle." As Secretary Wu got up to leave, Liuming looked over at Zhao and saw a glint in the military man's eye, which set his political antennae fluttering again. Something told him this wasn't the end of General Zhao's powerplay.

He was right.

CHAPTER ONE

Half an hour before the past walked in the door to send his life hurtling back towards a black abyss, Scott Lee was on the phone chewing out his opponent. "Are you kidding me, Vincent? Your clients have had all the time they need to produce the documents! If I don't get them tonight, I'll see you in court tomorrow!"

Scott slammed down the phone, hit divert and let rip with a heavy, frustrating sigh.

Hong Kong was the most modern city in the world with hundred-storey sky scrapers rising from every street corner, built on nothing but filled-in waterfront. Its transport system sparkled clean, was never late and cost little to use. And yet its court system allowed solicitors like Vincent Tang to get away with running cases at the speed of a tortoise with indigestion. Just another of the many contradictions which made Hong Kong tick: east versus west; communism versus capitalism; the most efficient society in the world pock-marked with pockets of recalcitrant inefficiency. A city wound so tight, moving at such a high-octane pace that it left Scott either exhilarated or frustrated, but nothing in between.

"Problems?"

Scott looked up. Philip Yip – his boss and best friend – was leaning against the door frame.

"Nothing a few tequila shots wouldn't solve."

Yip lifted an eyebrow.

"I was kidding, Phil. Remember jokes? Or is a sense of humour transplant a precondition to being senior partner these days."

"We need to talk."

Scott sighed again, sensing the tidings about to be delivered could only be ill. It had been one of those days after all.

Yip sat, crossed one tailored trouser leg over the other and knitted his fingers over a knee-cap. It reminded Scott of their law school days together, Yip pulling up the next door library seat and asking for advice with assignments. Back then Scott had been the one destined for partnership, his tuition fees picked up by his then future employer, international law firm Jackson, Weiss, Macdonald. Philip Yip was just another Hong Kong brat being force fed an English education before joining the safe haven of the family firm, Yip & Siu.

Ten years on and a lot had changed. Philip Yip was Yip & Siu's new go-getting senior partner. Scott Lee, after pushing the self-destruct button on his career at Jackson's, was a man in need of a job. The temporary consultancy Yip had offered Scott was supposed to have been only for a few months. Two years on, Scott was still here, but now he was hoping to turn the short-term position into something more permanent. Judging by the look on Yip's face, though, his hopes were about to take another beating.

"The Law Society called," Yip said wearily.

"Don't tell me. They want to make me President."

Yip gave him flat eyes.

"Come on Phil, now that was funny."

"You have another complaint. Esther Lai says you contacted South China Bank without going through her. That true?"

Scott looked skywards. "Maybe," he said coyly.

"You can't contact an opponent direct if they have a solicitor on record, Scott."

"I can if the solicitor in question is incapable of passing on simple messages to her client," Scott jumped on the caveat. "Phil, if I'd waited for Esther to pass on that settlement offer ...."

"So you didn't even tell her! You just picked up the phone to the head of legal at South China Bank and did it your way. Always the same! Scott Lee knows best, screw the rest!"

There was a knock at the door. Polly, Scott's secretary, a petite fifty-something who acted like she owned the place, stood in the doorway carrying more than just a bad attitude. "This just arrived for you." She dumped the huge fruit basket, dolled up in cellophane and ribbons, on Scott's desk, mangling a set of pleadings in the process. "They're from Mrs Wu. She's received her money from South China. Rang to say she's very happy with the settlement."

Scott craned his neck over the top of a pineapple. "Least someone is."

"Polly, would you give us a moment?" Yip said.

"Don't forget you have a twelve o'clock," Polly told Scott.

"I do?"

"Someone from a company called Prontofit."

Scott unscrewed his fountain-pen and noted the name on the nearest scrap of fruit-free paper. "What's Prontofit?"

"Don't know," Polly pouted. "Will you be finished by then or do you want me to push it off?"

Scott looked at Yip for an answer. "We'll be finished," Yip said.

Polly was about to leave, but stopped half way. "Oh yes, and Vincent Tang has called twice. Thinks you're trying to avoid him."

"Yeah, he'd be right about that."

Yip shook his head as Polly shut the door.

"Is there any lawyer in Hong Kong you treat with a shred of respect?"

Scott picked an orange from the basket, tossed it in the air and let it smack his palm. "You were commenting on my unprofessionalism regarding the settlement I got for Mrs Wu!"

Yip got up and thrust his hands into his pockets, every inch a Hong Kong big-shot in the making, from the coiffeured hair to the hand-made shoes. Image was everything in this city and Yip sure knew how to play the game. He'd come a long way since law school. Scott tried not to roll his eyes. "You got a decent settlement out of South China. No one's denying that, Scott. It's just the way you did it.... We have rules to play by...."

"Come on, Phil, Mrs Wu almost lost everything! If you think I'm going to let bending some rules, get in the way of going after...."

"That's exactly what you're going to do if you want a partnership here, okay!" Philip Yip snapped out the interruption. Scott leaned back, smiled wanly. He knew what was coming. "We can't keep having this conversation, Scott! Bloody hell, the vote's next Friday! Do you get that? Next Friday, we vote on whether you become a partner at this firm! At this rate, I'm going to have difficulty keeping you on the pay roll! Stop stepping out of line!"

"Even if it's for the good of a client?"

Philip Yip sighed with resignation. "Even if it's for the good of a client."

"Come on, this is Gordon talking, not you, Phil!"

Gordon Siu was Philip's father's old partner. He contributed the 'Siu' in 'Yip & Siu' along with a steady stream of minor personal injury cases from his cousin's transport company which made Siu, nominally at least, the firm's top biller. It mattered little that Siu's legal skills were inversely proportional to the chip he had on his shoulder about any lawyer in a younger generation who thought they knew better. Gordon Siu brought in money. That was the only equation that mattered. Period. Scott placed the orange back in the basket. "You know that old bastard sends his assistants in here to ask me to re-draft their letters so he can sign something that looks half-way respectable? And he thinks I've got a problem being professional?"

Yip shook his head. "Gordon's a partner, Scott. You're not. You want to be one, he has to say yes! And since you haven't got a client base, he's already got enough difficulty with this decision. So stop giving me a hard time."

"Ouch!"

"Come on Scott, you know how it works."

"And if I don't I've always got you there to remind me, right Phil?" Scott regretted the words as soon as they had left his mouth. He raised his palms in apology. Philip Yip had been the one person who'd looked past the screw up which had cost Scott his Jackson's career. He had tugged Scott back to the surface when failure and booze had threatened to pull him under. Other lawyers Scott had no problem being obnoxious to. Not Philip Yip. He deserved better.

"What if I had my own client base?" Scott asked.

"Then you can have as many complaints against you as you like and still expect me and Gordon to kiss your arse. But until the vote next Friday...."

"Yeah, yeah. Play nicey, nicey with Esther."

"Charm offensive, rather than just plain old offensive."

Scott twisted his face like he'd just bitten an apple with toothpaste on his gums.

"What, you're the only one here allowed to be funny?" Yip opened the door and made a gun with his fingers. "I'll catch you later."

After Yip was gone Scott got up, stretched his back and hitched up his trousers. Since quitting drinking he'd been exercising more, the physical activity helped exhaust the craving.

But it came with side effects. His suits all hung loose now, not that Scott cared too much for fashion. A fifty buck hair cut and a shoe shine up the trouser legs did him fine. He worked a checkered tie under his collar then looked at his watch. Only fifteen minutes until his meeting with Prontofit. He sat back down and googled the name.

Turned out Prontofit was an up-market interior design company run by a man named Barrie Ho. Ho, pictured on Prontofit's home-page, had a toothie grin and a penchant for black polo-necks. There were photos of numerous Spartan white empty spaces from luxury Peak apartments which Ho had...uh.... 'designed'. Scott didn't get it. The closest he'd ever come to interior decoration was the poster of the West Ham team circa 1986 on his study wall. Anybody who'd watched the re-run of their four-nil demolition of Chelsea at the Bridge that year would understand, but Scott doubted Barrie Ho fell into that bracket. He phoned Polly. "This Prontofit thing, did they ask for me specifically, or am I just on the rota?"

"*She* asked for you."

Scott frowned. "Did *she* give a name?"

"No. Just said she was from Prontofit."

He rang off. What did a woman from a high-class interior design company want with a tainted insurance lawyer like him? A case of mistaken identity, perhaps? Scott had heard it happen before. A prospective new client rings up, asks for the lawyer who has been recommended, the receptionist mishears, puts them through to someone different who just plays along and snaffles the instruction. Careers had been made on such opportunism.

Scott looked down at his rumpled tie, the creases in his shirt, the fading sheen on his belt buckle. Interior design savvy he was not, but he could wing it with the best of them. Counter-cultural that's what you got with Scott Lee as your lawyer, someone different, someone creative. He liked the way the image sat and imagined his entry in next year's law list: Scott Lee, partner, Yip & Siu, specialist in insurance litigation and interior design law....

The phone snapped off the day-dream.

"She's here," Polly chirruped. "I've put her in meeting room two."

Scott put on his jacket, checked his hair in the computer screen, pushed a hand through his fringe and reached for his legal pad. It was show time.

The black abyss was moments away.

She was standing with her back turned when he walked in the room.

Scott fixed his Matt Damon smile – disarm and charm, Yip had said – and shot her his killer opening line.

"Good afternoon."

As smooth as the fur on a freshly groomed chihuahua.

When she turned, a vague sense of recognition snagged. Her face was pretty with the right amount of sweetness. She had wavy black hair down to the tops of her shoulders. Round her neck hung a small silver cross, below which a mauve blouse tapered to a tight waist. But it was her eyes that grabbed Scott; rounded wells of dark melancholy fixed on him with discomforting intensity. The distant memory remained agonizingly out of reach, however. Just nature's way of reminding him he was the wrong side thirty-five.

He pointed for her to sit and asked whether the glass of water on the table was adequate. As he settled himself opposite, the scent of jasmine perfume caught his nostrils, strong enough to be noticed but at the same time alluringly subtle. He handed her his business card and waited for her to reciprocate, but her hands stayed on the table-top. The nagging familiarity turned the heat up on his impatience, so he got straight to it.

"Have we met before?"

"Yes, Mr Lee, we have. Once. A long time ago."

As answers went, it wasn't overly helpful. Scott added her Hong Kong accent into the mix, tried to wring out the memory. Still nothing. "I'm sorry, but I can't remember exactly how...." He said it in a self-deprecating, half-embarrassed way, a la Hugh Grant in *Four Weddings*.

"You worked with my elder sister at Jackson, Weiss, Macdonald," she said after a beat.

Scott stiffened at the name of his old employer; a hair-trigger response, like the nervous twitch of an almost-famous golfer re-living losing the Open on the final green. But the jolt finally freed the memory. "You're Kimmie Yang's younger sister? It's Sally, right?"

She nodded.

Scott let out a slow sigh. Kimmie Yang's younger sister. He could see the resemblance now. The round eyes hungry to know more, the perfect cheek bones.

"I was still at school when Kimmie brought you home for dinner that one time."

"Right." Scott clicked his fingers. "And you used to wear glasses."

Okay, so that was about as cool as Cliff Richard in a cardigan.

"Lazer surgery," Sally Yang said.

An awkward silence fell between them. Scott moved to quell it. "You're in interior design, now. Prontofit, right?" He made a show of checking his legal pad. Potential clients liked to know their lawyers did their research. "Barry Ho's quite a name in the industry, I hear."

"You know Barry?" She asked as if it was hard to imagine someone like Scott occupying the same stratosphere as the minimalist designer extraordinaire.

"I know *of* him." As if that explained anything. Scott quickly changed the subject. "So how's Kimmie doing these days?"

Sally Yang's answer, when it came, was unwavering. "She's dead, Mr Lee. Kimmie is dead."

The room powered into a numbing hush. Scott became conscious of his jaw dropping, buzzing filling his ears. Then it started; the spiral towards the black abyss, like a car moving up through the gears as it headed towards a cliff edge. Salt flushed his taste buds, turning his mouth to syrup, white heat igniting behind his eyes. He reached for the water glass. It went down in one, a wayward trickle lurching out the side of his mouth. Water instead of alcohol. A poor replacement on this occasion. He told himself to breathe in slowly… then out.

"Are you okay?"

"I'm sorry." His voice was a heavy whisper. "It's just…I… I had no idea."

He took a moment to gather himself, then asked Sally when it had happened.

"March this year. On the sixteenth."

Scott's throat thickened. It was October now. Six months and he had no idea. *Kimmie! Dead!*

"How?" He blurted out.

Sally bowed her head. The sight of her tears made Scott brace himself for an answer which he instinctively knew was going to hit like a sledge hammer.

"She killed herself, Mr Lee. Kimmie committed suicide."

CHAPTER TWO

The apartment was thick with humidity, the air so heavy it weighed on Scott's heart as soon as he stepped through the door.

After dropping the bombshell of her elder sister's suicide, Sally Yang had asked if she could take Scott somewhere. She wouldn't say where and stayed silent during the taxi ride which saw them cross Hong Kong Island to Kowloon. As they drove through the fluorescence of the Cross-Harbour tunnel, Scott felt a numbness descend. He settled back and let it bed itself down as the string of lights on the tunnel ceiling sliced hypnotically through the top of the windscreen. By the time they hit daylight again his defences were locked down, his emotions compartmentalized away from that cold rational part of his brain which had moved front and centre.

But when the door opened onto the shoe-box apartment in the district of Hung Hom, Scott felt the dense sadness immediately envelop him. It couldn't have been more than five hundred square foot inside. The living-room-dining area they'd walked into was a small rectangular space, elongated by Ikea storage units stretching down the walls. The units were stuffed with books, CDs, travel guides and shoes. Clothes were draped on an exercise bike. To the right was a two-seater sofa within touching distance of the flat screen TV, now heavy with dust. To the left was a tiny blue-tiled kitchenette with just enough room to turn around in. There was a closed door, white, opposite the front entrance.

"This is where Kimmie lived, Mr Lee," Sally said, but he'd guessed that already from the *Hello Kitty* stuffed-toys and *McDull* pigs lining the back of the sofa. Kimmie used to love them, he remembered. The loose leaf volumes of *Tolley's Company Law* stuffed in the storage units were another give-away.

Scott let the melancholy wash through him like a penitential ritual. Suddenly his gazed hovered over a photo frame on a shelf above the television. The photo inside was obscured by a sparkling maelstrom of necklaces and other trinkets draped across the top frame. The whole thing looked like a make-shift jewelry tree.

Scott leaned over for a closer look.

The necklaces and trinkets were souvenirs from places which Kimmie had visited around the world. He remembered how she loved to travel, whenever and wherever she could. Kimmie had never been one for package tours, not like most Hong Kongers. No, she had always done her own thing, made her own way. And here were her memories. A silver dolphin necklace from Turkey; a bracelet with tiny sea-turtles and turquoise oyster-shell beads from Thailand; numerous pendants from Japan and a leather-tie with a tasteful jade carving the size of a thumbnail hanging from it, probably Chinese. At one time or another, he had seen Kimmie wearing each of these.

The memories flickered through his mind like fireworks.

He reached out, hooked his fingers round the collection of trinkets and felt as if he was taking a life full of experiences into his hands. A life that was no more.

He moved them to one side so that he could see the photo in the frame.

There she was. Kimmie. On the day of her admission as a solicitor down at the High Court. The black robes and white neck bands had done nothing to dull her beauty. Her smile reached out from the picture and tightened round his ribcage. Flanking Kimmie were her parents. They stared at the camera through tired eyes, etched with the shadows of the years of hard work which had got them to that day; the day of their daughter's triumph.

"My grandfather had a carpentry business in Guangdong province before the war, Mr Lee," Sally looked at the photo over his shoulder. "He and my grandmother left everything behind when the Japanese invaded. They arrived in Hong Kong with nothing and were given a piece of land to squat on, no bigger than a bed. My grandfather started selling cigarettes to street kiosks to feed the family. My father grew up always knowing what it was to worry where the next meal was coming from. He saved and saved until he had enough to open a little grocery shop. He and my mother worked every hour of the day in that shop, just so Kimmie and I could have the opportunities my grandfather had dreamed about when he came here. That day," she reached out and tapped the frame, "was one the proudest days of all of our lives."

Scott wasn't sure what to say, so he went with nothing. He moved his hand carefully away, shifting the collection of turquoise, silver and jade necklaces back across the picture, as if he was entombing the past.

Then he turned to look at Sally Yang. Her complexion was a gaunt alabaster. She could have been only in her early twenties, but already her face carried signs of life's bitterness. "Kimmie bought this place three years ago," she said, her eyes moving slowly round the room.

"I remember," Scott's voice came out in a heavy whisper. "It was just before we lost touch."

"Kimmie told me once that you and she were...." She began, but then checked herself, as if unsure whether to continue. "That you two were more than just friends. Is that right?"

Rippling fingers played down Scott's neck at the question, his emotions straining against the walls of their compartment. "We were together for a short while, yes. A long time ago. But we stopped before it developed into anything solid."

Sally considered his answer. "Do you mind if I ask why?"

The truth was that he did mind. This wasn't a road Scott wanted to go down, but he'd already talked himself along the first few steps, so what the hell. "Kimmie and I were colleagues in a small branch of a big law firm. We worked long hours together and enjoyed each other's company. We became close and the truth is it could have developed into something more. But careers and relationships aren't a good mix, Sally. We both realized that in the end." He gave a rueful shrug. "You always end up having to choose one over the other."

Sally's mouth became a flat line, one hand delicately fingering the silver cross round her neck. "Do you ever regret the choice you made?"

The question caught Scott like a blunt left hook, forcing him to adjust and cover. He swept his hand back through his hair, mussing in the sweat beads bursting on his forehead.

"It was the right decision. At the time, anyway."

A heavy silence hung between them for a moment.

"But why didn't you and Kimmie keep in touch after you left Jackson's?"

Scott felt himself smile, the kind of smile that went with the memory of a time he was glad was a part of the past and long done away with. "I was in a bad place back then. Up here I mean," he tapped his temple. "I needed to get my head together so I took some time away. Then when I came back I was offered a contract at Yip & Siu. After that, work seemed just to get in the way again. I guess that's how it's been for these past three years."

Scott sensed Sally Yang was working up to something. He decided not to push it; let her get there in her own time.

"Kimmie said you were the best lawyer she ever knew. 'Scott Lee always knows the answer', she used to say. 'He always knows what to do'. When you left Jackson's, I know she missed you."

He smiled at the compliment. "I missed her too, Sally."

Her gaze drifted to the window which looked onto the flat in the neighbouring block. A Filipino maid was bending down to load some washing into a machine. "She told me about your problems with Charles Conrad. That's why you left Jackson's wasn't it?" she asked.

The comment stung like vinegar on an open wound. Charles Conrad. For three years, Scott had worked hard to erase the name from his memory. He wormed his tongue round his mouth as the salt taste started to pump again, but this time he staunched it before it got into gear.

"Sorry, I was being intrusive."

"It's okay," he parried. "That wasn't an easy period in my life."

The sound of a car changing gear and accelerating up the road drifted up from the streets below before disappearing into nothing, The flat was quiet again. "Why have you brought me here, Sally?" Scott asked after a while.

She continued to gaze towards the window, arms folded, fingers nervously tapping her elbows. "I wanted to ask you something," she said, then paused for a moment, again unsure whether to continue. Slowly she turned towards him. "My parents always used to tell Kimmie and me that if we worked hard we would be successful. That here in Hong Kong anything is possible with hard work. That's what we grew up believing."

Scott wasn't sure where she was going with this.

"He never liked politics, my father," she continued, "but he hated the starvation and chaos in China when he was growing up. He used to tell us about it. The famine, the riots, the Red Guards. It scared him. He believed our way of life here was so fragile, that with all the chaos just across the border, Hong Kong could easily change. My father always worried about the future. Even thought of taking us to Canada before the British gave Hong Kong back so we could be away from it all. But then one day, he went across the border to Shenzhen. He saw China had changed. 'They think as Hong Kong does now' he told us after that. So we stayed."

Scott was well enough versed in Chinese history to understand what Sally was telling him. The Communist triumph in China in 1949 had brought an end to years of miserable civil war and instability. But the ensuing disaster of Mao's Great Leap Forward and the pandemonium of the Cultural Revolution had left the world's most populous nation completely shattered. Against this chaos, the example of the booming economies of neighbouring Japan, South Korea, Taiwan and, most of all, the British colony of Hong Kong on its doorstep, could no longer be ignored. So Deng Xiaoping, Mao's successor, had forced China to embrace the path of capitalism, even though politically it was to remain autocratically communist. Getting rich through hard work was no longer a sin and the special economic zone of Shenzhen – as it was declared in 1980 – just across the border from Hong Kong, became a shining example of Deng's new message. The past had made many people fearful of what would happen when Hong Kong returned to China in 1997. But even though many did leave, those fears had proved to be unfounded. Hong Kong remained as pure a capitalist society as there existed in the world.

"Kimmie listened to my father," Sally said. "She worked hard for what she wanted and she achieved it. Becoming a lawyer meant everything to her. She loved her job more than anyone I know."

"I remember," Scott said.

"She made my parents so, so proud. And this place," Sally cast another slow gaze round the flat. "It was what my father always wanted. To see his children work hard, own their own property and be successful."

Sally's mouth started to crease into a smile, but before it reached its full extent something darkened, as if a shadow had passed over her lips tugging the corners down under the weight of a bad memory. "But then something changed in Kimmie. She went from being this wonderful, outgoing, hard working person, to someone..." – she swallowed, her eyes filming with tears – "...someone capable of taking her own life."

Cold fingers closed round Scott's heart.

"I keep asking myself how this could have happened" Sally's voice had ticked down to a quavering whisper, "I have thought back to every conversation I ever had with my sister. And I know the answer. Such a simple explanation. Yet none of us did anything about it."

She threw Scott a look which drew his curiosity to the surface. "Tell me," he said.

She bit her lip. "It was him, Charles Conrad! He broke Kimmie's spirit. He took away the joy she got from work. He put so much pressure on her that she couldn't take it any more!"

Scott's breath caught in his throat. "I don't understand."

"After you left Jackson's," Sally continued, "Kimmie became Conrad's main assistant. That was the turning point. He gave her no guidance, no help, not like you did. She had it all on her shoulders and no matter how hard she tried, it was never enough. Not for him." Her hand went into her left sleeve and came out with a tissue. She dabbed her eyes. "She would get home after midnight completely exhausted. At weekends she just worked or slept. She never had any time for herself or to enjoy this place. But she never complained, not once. Just kept on taking it, until...." Her voice cracked.

Below Scott's calm exterior, a weird mix of emotions had shaken loose from their confines. Brutal sadness blended with disbelief that was fast turning into anger.

"There must have been an inquest?" He pushed carefully.

"That was a useless process," Sally spat the words. "It told us only what we already knew."

Once again, the flat powered into silence. Scott looked around him. Six months ago Kimmie Yang had killed herself and here was her apartment, sagging under the dreariness of disuse and the promise of the agony that clearing it out would bring.

"Why have you brought me here, Sally?" Scott asked for the second time.

Her eyes moved to his feet then back to his face.

"My parents tell me it is useless to apportion blame; that we need to come to terms in private with Kimmie's death, as a family, together. They are shadows of the people they once were. Just ghosts walking around in their skins. They know nothing except pain now. Being alive is their torture."

"I'm sorry," Scott whispered, but she continued as if she hadn't heard him.

"So because of Charles Conrad, I have lost my entire family! And he is still earning money in his big law firm as if nothing has happened! He has no idea of the pain he has caused!" After a moment her face softened. "But what can I do? I must obey my parents' wishes. I am all they have now. They need my support, so I have to let go of this...this burning." She held a fist to her chest, signalling the source of the furnace. "But, I can't let go, not until I ask someone to make things right! That is why I invited you here, Mr Lee."

Scott felt the heat of her intense gaze. He swallowed down his discomfort. "Sally, I'm really not sure if I can do anything...."

"Please," she cut him off and something in her face told him the moment had arrived. The reason why he was here.

She stepped over to the closed white door on the opposite wall. It made a sucking sound as it opened. She stepped in, signaling with her head for Scott to follow.

The hard acidic smell of fresh paint assaulted Scott as he went into the empty white-walled space. Sally did a slow circumference, her heels echoing off the wooden floor.

"This is where it happened, Mr Lee. This is where my sister took sleeping pills to knock herself out, while charcoal burned. This is where Kimmie died."

Scott's eyes widened with fright as a strange terror started to take hold. He opened his mouth, but no sound came out. He looked down at the piece of floor where he guessed the bed would have been, the image of Kimmie lying there, alone, her eyes closed, her skin going cold in the fug of the fumes....

He felt Sally's hand touch his elbow.

"I remember what Kimmie told me about you, Mr Lee," she said. "You always know the answer. You always know what to do, she said. I trust my sister's judgement, Mr Lee. And I trust you to do what I cannot do."

He heard her footsteps recede back to the living room. But Scott didn't follow her, not just then. He stayed where he was. In the room where Kimmie Yang – his Kimmie – had died.

Letting his anger ignite into a slow burn.

CHAPTER THREE

The Financial Secretary reached the climax of his speech, his teeth glinting in the spotlights of the main conference hall in Hong Kong's Convention Centre.

"....the Cooperation in Service Agreement – the CSA – cements Hong Kong's financial system as a fundamental part of China's business apparatus. Hong Kong financial service companies can now establish subsidiaries on the Mainland with lower start-up capital and fewer exchange controls. In short, ladies and gentlemen, the CSA gives our businesses a competitive advantage over New York, London, Tokyo, Singapore," – he paused dramatically – "and the rest of the world."

Applause rippled and the audience stood in unison to witness the choreographed handshake between the speaker and his Mainland counterpart. Photographers scrimmaged on stage, the explosion of flash-bulbs leaving no one in doubt what tomorrow's front pages would herald.

Three rows from the back of the hall, Leopold Chan waited for the sycophantic piece of political theatre to exhaust itself. A nauseating civil servant ingratiating himself with the public was not something he wanted to waste time on, especially when everyone in the hall knew the Financial Secretary had had nothing to do with the CSA negotiation. As with everything in Hong Kong, the CSA was the result of a businessman's efforts, and not just any businessman. Yet as Leopold watched Cyrus Kwan applauding politely in the second row of dignitaries on stage, he wondered if the treaty's real architect was put out by the man absorbing the plaudits.

As the flash-bulbs died out, the audience was ushered through to another spacious hall and met with drinks and dim-sum-style canapés. Mingling circles quickly formed and soon the place was buzzing with gossip and tinkling glasses.

Leopold stayed out of the way; being stuck with the wrong group of bores was the last thing he wanted. On a side-table he spotted a pile of brochures for today's event. Recalling that his marketing director had made a contribution to the sponsorship, he leafed through a copy to see what value his money had bought.

AsiaRisk's familiar logo, promising to provide for 'your every insurance need', was in on page twelve. A disappointment, Leopold thought, but at least his corporate photograph showed him off at his Napoleonic best, chest puffed out, head glistening imperially, his 'trust-me' eyes steely and assured. "Our grateful thanks go to Mr Leopold Chan, Managing Director and Chairman of AsiaRisk, for his contribution to today's event," read the caption.

Leopold placed the brochure back on the pile. It was time.

Back in the heart of the hall, he searched for the man he had come to see.

There he was, Cyrus Kwan, dispensing words of wisdom to an impromptu audience, like a king holding court. Leopold politely sidled his way into the group and listened.

Cyrus Kwan had shabby white hair and an academic appearance and looked like someone ill at ease in the commercial world. Nothing could have been further from the truth, however. In Hong Kong, Cyrus Kwan was *the* businessman, his rags to riches story so widely known it had become part of Hong Kong folklore.

Originally from Fujian Province, Kwan had illegally immigrated to Hong Kong as a teenager, found a job in an electronics factory and worked his way up to become a senior salesman. Whilst selling the factory's wares he had absorbed himself in every aspect of the business and, through the contacts he made, eventually raised enough finance to branch out on his own. Cyrus Kwan's first venture was manufacturing a hand-held electronic tennis game called *Pintec*, named after the sound it made whenever a ball was hit. *Pintec* became an instant hit and made Cyrus his first fortune, which he used to diversify into shipping, IT, property and banking.

Today, Kwan Holdings, the conglomerate Cyrus Kwan had built, was the most popular company listed on Hong Kong's Hang Seng Index after the HSBC Banking Corporation. Owning shares in Kwan Holdings was like owning a piece of Hong Kong itself.

As Leopold watched Cyrus Kwan, he was struck by the complete absence of any trappings of wealth. Kwan's suit wasn't tailored, his sallow face showed no hint of the fine dining he could so easily afford. Yet the way he weighed every word and flipped so confidently from subject to subject betrayed his shrewdness and intelligence. Here was a man whose utterances could dictate whether the Hang Seng Index finished in positive or negative territory on any given day.

Leopold moved his gaze to the people lined up at the tycoon's shoulder. Three to the right stood Cyrus's nephew, Rupert Kwan, reveling in the trappings of wealth which his uncle rejected. Rupert wore a pink shirt and Windsor knotted tie. His hair was imaculate, his chiseled face that of a film-star. In business, Rupert had proved as reckless as his uncle had proved shrewd. The Hong Kong press was still on his back for his disastrous attempt to sell the Lantau container terminal to foreigners. Rumour had it that Cyrus was furious at having to purchase the terminal himself, just to prevent damage being done to the family name. And judging from Rupert's coyness that evening, the rumours were correct.

Cyrus Kwan continued to field questions from the crowd, but after a little while a photographer arrived and everyone lined up to have their photograph taken with the tycoon; a treasured memento which could be displayed to jealous friends.

While Leopold waited his turn, he noticed Rupert surreptitiously wandering off, hands clenched hard behind his back in seething frustration.

Interesting, Leopold thought; this was setting itself up nicely.

A camera flashed, Cyrus Kwan offered some parting words to the lady ahead of Leopold in the queue. Leopold fixed his smile and stepped forward.

"Mr Kwan!" Leopold held out his business card in both hands, the traditional Hong Kong business greeting. Cyrus Kwan, a good head taller than Leopold, took the card and read it. Leopold saw recognition flicker on the tycoon's face.

"And what business is AsiaRisk in?" Kwan asked, gesturing for Leopold to move into the line of the camera lens.

"Insurance," Leopold said. "We do commercial lines; motor, life and some marine."

"Insurance is well placed to take advantage of the CSA, I understand."

"We already have some representative offices on the Mainland," Leopold said confidently. "Just marketing operations, but we're hoping to expand on them soon. Does Kwan Holdings have plans to get into the insurance business? You seem to have fingers in every other pie."

Kwan chuckled. "Who knows, I might be tempted one day."

The photographer took his shot. And with that, Cyrus Kwan turned to the next person in the queue.

The encounter had been brief, but it had meant a great deal to Leopold. This was the beginning, the moment the hunter looked into the eyes of his prey.

The chase was definitely on.

Out in the corridor Rupert Kwan blew air through his lips and eased out the humiliation pounding through his chest. The nightmare of the last seven days had culminated in the showdown which had taken place in his uncle's office that morning.

"This is the last time, Rupert!" Cyrus had berated him from behind the desk as Rupert stood opposite, head slightly bowed like an errant school boy taking his punishment. "Have you any idea of the damage you would have done by selling to Singapore?"

"They were offering a sound price, uncle, and I needed liquid funds to keep the banks at bay. Anyone in my position would have done the same thing."

"No one with any sense would have leveraged himself the way you did to buy that terminal in the first place! What were you thinking? Didn't I teach you anything about risk?"

"That's all very well with hindsight, uncle. But at the time the container terminal represented a tremendous opportunity. And with the IT upgrade I was planning, it would have generated a significant return on equity...."

"You couldn't afford it, Rupert!" Cyrus Kwan slapped his hand on the mahogany table-top. "I've seen your budgeting; your projections. They were totally unrealistic! You cannot do business that way!"

"Then why are you buying it off me, if it's such a bad idea?"

And that was when Cyrus Kwan had erupted. "You dare ask me that? After what your stupidity has done to this family!" The old man's face had trembled with rage. "If he were alive today, your father would be disgusted with you!"

A moment passed which seemed like an age, before Cyrus Kwan felt able to look his nephew in the face again. "From now on, you work as an analyst in the investment team....."

"An analyst! You've got to be joking...."

Cyrus cut him off. "You will learn how to invest money and quantify risk properly! You want funds from me again, you will earn my trust!"

In the end Rupert had no choice but to agree and, after the meeting, had resigned himself to his new role of playing the prodigal nephew by acting subserviently towards his uncle in public until such time as he could convince the old man that he could be trusted with money again. How difficult could that be?

Six hours on and feeling the strain already, Rupert had his answer. He was born to be on a big stage, not be part of life's background.

Wandering up the corridor, Rupert nodded politely to delegates exiting the function early. He found a men's room. Thankfully it was empty. Cooling his palms under the cold tap, he tried to lower the temperature in his mind and body. He checked his Rolex. It was still early, but he was restless to prove his manhood. Shirley, his girlfriend would still be at work, thankfully. They'd been together six months. Rupert wanted to dump her, the initial thrill had long worn off. She just bored him now with her incessant talk of restaurants and holiday destinations. Just another ripening fruit which, once bitten, had turned rotten and begun to smell. But Cyrus liked her, so Rupert had decided it was politic to hang on for a bit longer.

Tonight, though, he needed the kind of sex which Shirley couldn't offer. Forget tender and sensuous. He needed dark and brutal. The escort agency number was in his speed-dials. Rupert called and asked for a Thai girl called Yvonne. Leaving the men's room, he headed for the nearest exit, salivating at the prospect of relieving his pent up tension....

"Rupert, I need a quick word." The voice came from over his shoulder.

Rupert gave a half glance backwards. "Actually, I'm in rather a hurry...."

"It won't take long."

Rupert bit down his irritation and turned round.

A man, bald and stocky, came towards him with a confident deliberation that made Rupert step back.

"Your uncle's still upset with you, I see," the man said, his eyes glinting in the dimness of the corridor.

"What?" Rupert's face contorted with confusion. "Who are you?"

The man held out his card for Rupert to take. Rupert refused. The man gave a nonchalant shrug; then reached up and slipped the card into Rupert's top pocket. "Take it, Rupert. You'll want to hear my proposition."

"Proposition?"

The man stared. "... My proposition to get you back in your uncle's good books, Rupert." He said it like it was the most obvious thing in the world.

Rupert's mouth dropped open. The man's steely gaze unsettled him.

"I'll be in touch shortly," the man said; and with that, he walked away, leaving Rupert Kwan flushed with confusion.

Leopold headed out into the humid Hong Kong evening. His driver Terrence O'Rourke was waiting. He opened the rear door of the black Mercedes and gave Leopold a nod.

Inside the car General Robert Zhao sat staring straight ahead, as if frozen by the frigid air-conditioning. Leopold slipped in next to him. O'Rourke gunned the engine and smoothed them into the full frustration of Hong Kong traffic.

"What time's your flight?" Leopold asked.

"Ten past eight," Zhao said.

"Sure you don't want me to upgrade you to business class?"

Zhao's head swiveled like an automaton. "It's more discreet this way. ... How did it go this evening?"

Leopold stifled a smile. Thirty-five years had passed since Robert Zhao had last been part of his life, but Zhao was still the same old ascetic revolutionary Leopold had first encountered as a student in London. Back then, Zhao had headed a Chinese student organization acting as a front for recruiting young British born Chinese at the beginning of their professional careers to become lifelong sources of intelligence. The recruitment method was as crass as it was effective: monetary assistance towards tuition. What impoverished student could resist? Zhao's remit was to recruit sources for the People's Liberation Army. Even back then, he had been a dogmatic bore, a man bereft of ideas but ruthlessly efficient at execution; destined for an army career, in Leopold's opinion.

"It went as I planned it," Leopold said.

"You've made contact with the Kwans, then?"

"Yes."

"That is pleasing." A typical Zhao compliment. Delivered with the emotion of an ice cube. "Your plan is bold, Leopold. If it works, China will owe you a significant debt of gratitude. It's not often one comes across someone willing to make a sacrifice like this."

"It is no sacrifice when you compare it with the achievement it would bring." Leopold layered his words with the right amount of nobility. He could see Zhao was pleased.

"You have come a long way, Leopold. The contribution we made to your education all those years ago has certainly paid dividends. Even though it has been a long time, I knew you were the right man for this task. Your ideas were always the most...creative."

The compliment sat comfortably with Leopold.

"The Kwans are a danger to China and deserve to be crushed," Zhao continued. "Unfortunately, there are some elements within our government who are incapable of seeing that. They prefer the light approach, rather than the strong hand which is needed."

"Don't concern yourself, Robert," Leopold said. "When I'm finished with Cyrus Kwan, everyone will see him for the corrupt snake he is; you have my word on that. Your confiscation and detention orders will have the support they need. Hong Kong will be under your control soon enough."

A beat of silence.

"How can you be sure Kwan will take the bait?" Zhao asked.

"Because I'm going to present him with the kind of offer that he would be a fool to refuse. And whatever his other faults maybe, Cyrus Kwan is no fool."

The military man visibly relaxed.

When they pulled up outside the the glass monolith of Chek Lap Kok airport, Zhao got out, took his briefcase, and signaled for Leopold to walk with him along the pavement, out of the lights and into the shadows.

"This is where we say good bye, Leopold." He spoke with a finality which Leopold understood. "No one must ever know about our involvement. You are not to contact me until it is done. If things do not go according to plan..." his voice tailed off.

"I know how this works," Leopold said.

There were no handshakes. Just an exchange of nods.

The doors to the terminal hissed open. General Zhao went to catch his plane.

*

"Home or office?" O'Rourke asked.

Leopold checked his watch. "Office, please Terrence."

As they crossed over the Tsing Ma Bridge, Leopold gazed into the glittering night, at the black outlines of the mountainous islands, lit by the public housing developments clinging like limpets to the rugged slopes and reaching to the heavens. It had been a strange day, one in which his past, in the form of General Zhao, had collided with the present to give Leopold what he had been searching for all his life: the next challenge.

Challenge had always been Leopold's driving force; risk his opiate. That same combination had made him willingly accept Zhao's offer of recruitment thirty-five years ago. And it had driven his subsequent rise in the insurance world.

Today the wheel had come full circle. Zhao was back in his life, posing Leopold a challenge too irresistible to let pass. And the timing was perfect; it was as if the fates had aligned themselves to present Leopold with his shot at immortality.

"I shall be calling on your skill set in the coming weeks, Terrence," Leopold told his driver.

O'Rourke's eyes flicked to the rear-view mirror and darkened with pleasure. "Happy to oblige, boss."

Terrence O'Rourke had been with Leopold for three years. They had first met when Leopold's previous driver had retired and the agency had sent this brute of a man to fill in until someone more suitable was recruited. But after a few awkward conversations with the taciturn giant, Leopold had O'Rourke's measure. Foreigners like O'Rourke ended up in Hong Kong either to secure their financial future, or to escape a sorry past. O'Rourke fell into the latter category for sure, having been forced to leave his native Northern Ireland in a hurry, for what reason Leopold had never discovered; but given that province's troubled history, it was easy enough to guess. There was a harshness about the Irishman that impressed Leopold. Hiring O'Rourke permanently had been an easy decision, one Leopold had never regretted.

"How was the thing at the Convention Centre?" O'Rourke asked.

"Nothing special," Leopold said. "Although I did have my picture taken with Cyrus Kwan."

O'Rourke's eyebrows creased into a frown. "I know that name."

"Cyrus Kwan, founder of Kwan Holdings, Terrence. One of the richest men in Asia."

"Cyrus Kwan...right."

Leopold drummed his fingers on his knees and then after a moment said, "You know, last year Kwan Holdings actually tried to take over AsiaRisk."

"What?" O'Rourke shook his head slowly. "Bastard!"

It had only been a rumour, but it oozed credibility and had all the hallmarks of a Cyrus Kwan move. Well-placed stories in the media about Kwan Holdings looking to acquire an insurance arm; speculation as to the intended target; a spike in share prices across the insurance sector. But then Leopold had received a call from a journalist asking him to comment on the rumour that it was AsiaRisk which was top of Kwan's shopping list. Leopold had beaten away the suggestion, but the logic of it made perfect sense. Being one of the few private insurers left in Hong Kong made AsiaRisk prime Cyrus Kwan territory.

In the end, nothing had happened, but that didn't make the rumours any less true. And the glint of recognition Leopold had seen flicker in Cyrus Kwan's eyes that evening had confirmed it for him. The old fox knew exactly who Leopold and AsiaRisk were and, in all likelihood, Leopold's company was still on Kwan's hit list.

"Not like you to take something like that lying down, boss." O'Rourke said as they turned the corner.

"Oh don't worry, Terrence," Leopold stifled a yawn. It had been a long day. "I'm going to teach Cyrus Kwan a valuable lesson."

"Yeah?" O'Rourke said. "What?"

Leopold peered out of the window at the surrounding traffic. "That sometimes the prize you covet the most can turn out to be your worst nightmare."

O'Rourke nodded. "I like the sound of that."

"Me too, Terrence," Leopold settled back into the comfort of the leather seat. "Me too."

CHAPTER FOUR

Joel's Place styled itself a 'café-bar-restaurant' as if desperate not to give passing trade an excuse to say they were in the mood for something else.

"Please come in," the white-shirted fat man standing out front said to Scott, as he wandered by in the early evening heat. It sounded like a plea for help, which, judging by the empty tables and chairs, the fat guy – Joel, Scott guessed – needed in spades.

"Why not," Scott shrugged and Joel almost fell over in shock. Scott asked for a coffee and a Perrier and took an outside table by the walkway so that the pedestrian traffic from Central Plaza would pass straight by him. It was ten before five and the sun was off its height, but the humidity was still unforgiving for October.

His drinks arrived. Scott went for the coffee first. He'd had a restless night. Every time his eyes had closed, all he saw was Kimmie Yang standing at the door at Jackson's Hong Kong office on his first day at work eight years before. He'd been jet-lagged and felt like hell that day, but right then, pow, that was the moment her beauty had taken hold of him and refused to let go.

But love wasn't why Scott had come to Hong Kong. It wasn't part of the plan and didn't fit in with his image as part of the 'brat pack', a group of six Jackson's assistants earmarked for early partnership. His boss back in London had come up with the idea of a stint in the Hong Kong office, which was ailing under the leadership of Charles Conrad. The partnership committee would look kindly on it, Scott was told, and the fact that he had a Chinese background through his mother made him perfect. So a couple of years in Hong Kong, then back to London and partnership; that was the plan. Falling in love had never entered the frame. But then, neither had Kimmie Yang.

Kimmie was two years Scott's junior. Her work-ethic and eye for detail gave her the makings of a good lawyer. Only a certain flexibility was absent, but the more she worked with Scott, the more he had managed to hone that skill. Keeping his true feelings subdued was easy, as Charles Conrad's lack of interest in doing any work meant there was more than enough to absorb Scott's full attention. Yet there were times when Scott had been vulnerable. One time in particular.

He and Kimmie had been working late and went out for drinks at the Blue Virgo on Wanchai's boulevard of sin. A Tuesday night, Scott remembered; the music was turned down low and the clientele sparse. Back then, he still drank; and after a while a collection of empty beer bottles had gathered on their table.

"Why does becoming a partner matter so much to you?" Kimmie had asked him, knocking him off-balance with her bluntness like always.

Scott tried a parry. "What, you don't want to be a partner?"

"Sure I do," she shrugged, "but not like you do. It's like you need it." Her words were like a screwdriver easing under a lid. "Like you need to prove something. Is that it?"

With anyone else Scott would have ordered another drink and pivoted to a more vacuous topic. But Kimmie's eyes held him in fascination, drawing him in, picking at his veneer. She pushed a swirl of black hair behind her ear and toyed with her necklace – one of the souvenirs she'd picked up on her travels. Then she leaned her head on her hand and waited out his answer.

"You don't have an elder brother do you?" Scott said after a while.

"No."

"I do. His name's John. He's a doctor, an oncologist at the John Radcliffe hospital in Oxford."

"Impressive."

"Yeah, that's John all right. Mr Impressive."

Someone put on James Blunt's *Back to Bedlam*. The singer's haunting pitch wafted ethereally through the bar.

"Are you close?"

Scott shook his head. "We're different. John's like my dad, built like a rugby player. Celtic features. Me, I'm more like mum. She was local, you know, born and bred in Hong Kong, grew up in Causeway Bay in fact. She only moved to the UK after she married dad back in the sixties. Makes me and John real mixes. That's why people double-take when they first meet me, they're struggling to work out where I'm from. But John's different, doesn't look like he has one ounce of Chinese in him. At school no-one ever believed we were related. John was popular, clever, good at sport; you know the type. Me, I was just...." Scott stopped himself.

"What?" Kimmie encouraged.

"I didn't like school much. I was glad when it came time to go to university."

"Where'd you go?"

"Durham."

"Good school. Did John go there?"

"No. He went Oxford. I tried for it, but..." Scott shrugged. "You see, I've always been second-best in my family, Kimmie. Sport, school, even damn universities, John has always been better. I don't resent his success and mum and dad never treated us differently, but for me it was...well brothers, you know."

A moment later Kimmie said, "So getting a partnership means you get to be best at something for a change?"

She was right. To be recognized as the best in his own profession would wipe away all those plaguing doubts. A once and for all cure for all the times he'd ever felt different and inferior.

"Don't you, like, feel you're missing out on so much else?" Kimmie asked.

Scott looked up at her. "What else is there?"

They stared at each other for a long moment. Then Kimmie said the words that were now coming back to haunt him. "Don't waste your time, Scott. It's not worth it"

And at that moment, Scott did what he was supposed to do. He leaned over and kissed her and she kissed him back, her soft lips unsure at first, but then responsive. There was nothing awkward in the silence that followed, in the way she slipped up close next to him and cradled her head into the crook of his neck. They stayed like that, swaying gently, listening to the music and when it was over Kimmie drew her lips to his ear and whispered, "Take me home."

That night, they made love tenderly, sensitive to every reaction and after they had reached the summit of their mutual passion, they lay in each other's arms until the sun came up.

When Scott woke, Kimmie had just finished showering. He helped towel her hair and over breakfast they had the conversation they needed to have."Last night was kind of unexpected," Kimmie said.

"But good 'unexpected', right?"

"Oh yeah," she smiled as if reliving the memory. A moment went by.

"I'm not that kind of guy, if that's what you're thinking...."

"I know." She shut him up. "But let's take things slow, okay?" She must have seen the disappointment in his eyes. "I live with my parents, Scott. They might have a problem with me spending nights away. Last night we went straight to stage three. Mind if we spend some time going through stages one and two?"

It was relieving to hear her talk like that. He gave her a peck on the cheek.

During the next few weeks, though, they lost their way. Taking it slow meant going out for the odd meal and saying good night at the end of it; and as the weeks and months passed everything ground to a halt. Even after Kimmie bought her own place nothing changed, as if they'd reached a mutual unspoken decision to keep things as they were.

Don't waste your time Kimmie had told him, but that's exactly what Scott had done. And after he had resigned from Jackson's, he compounded the mistake by breaking off contact with her altogether because he needed space to get over the destruction of his stupid career. Instead he should have beaten down Kimmie's door and told her the time for taking it slow was over.

And now it was too late.

"Another coffee, sir?" Joel's question broke Scott away from his stream of consciousness.

"Make it a decaff."

Joel scuttled off like a cockroach. Scott looked at his watch. It was coming up to five-fifteen. Evening shadows were lengthening towards nightfall in the sky. The walkway remained empty, but Scott knew that, in about fifteen minutes, the offices would start emptying out and he would see the first signs of people starting their commute home.

His eyes drifted two hundred yards south. The Central Plaza building rose defiantly from its podium into the sky. Seventy eight-floors of black glass and neon tapered into a transluscent skyroof, topped by a spearhead mast, like a gigantic rocket ready to blow. Central Plaza had been the tallest building in the world when it had opened. Now it was only the third tallest in Hong Kong itself. Looking up at the edifice, Scott felt a stab of nostaligia. Jackson's offices were on the sixty-second floor and had the most impressive views of the harbour he'd ever seen. When he'd walked out of the door three years ago, part of him knew that was as good as it was ever going to get for him.

Joel returned with the coffee. Scott killed time by scribbling out a to-do list for the following day. When he got down to item number ten, the ink in his fountain-pen began to fade. He clipped the lid back on, pocketed it and turned back to the walkway. People had started to appear along the path, early-shift secretaries and admin boys done for the day. Joel was back out front searching for custom.

Countless times, Scott had walked this way to work. Since leaving Jackson's though he had deliberately avoided it because....well he wasn't sure why.

Just then, a man turned the corner into the walkway and Scott felt something clunk in his chest. Recognition was immediate. No question, it was him.

Scott got to his feet, but held fast in the shadows until the man was only yards away. Then Scott stepped into walkway and used his stance to form a barrier across the path.

Charles Conrad looked up and froze.

"Hello Charles," Scott said. "You've got time for a drink with an old colleague don't you?"

Charles Conrad hadn't changed a bit.

His stomach bulged a Ralph Lauren shirt into a distended tautness. The built-in shoulders of his suit aimed for gravitas but missed by a country mile. Scott led him to a table further away from the walkway and watched him sidle into the seat against the wall. Without being asked, Conrad ordered a Jack Daniels and Coke and made a show of absorbing himself in his Blackberry. When the drink arrived, he took a hefty sip. Only then was Scott given some attention. "This is a nice surprise," Conrad's manner was false and hearty. "Didn't know you were still in Hong Kong. How long's it been?"

Scott was about to reply when Conrad's eyes were fish-hooked by stilettos clacking on the walkway and the promise they brought.

"Three years!" Scott said.

Conrad turned his pudgy face slowly back and shrugged a lascivious naughty-school-boy apology. Clammy fingers ran down Scott's back.

"So how're things going, Charles?"

"Busy," Conrad shrugged. "Got a decent flow of instructions coming in, enough to keep London happy anyway. Means having to keep up the momentum on the cocktail circuit, though; it's all I ever seem to do nowadays. What firm are you with now? Would I have heard of it?"

Scott almost burst out laughing. *'No, please Charles let me think about that one ... wait ... .I get it. You're looking down on me, right?'*

"Yip & Siu."

Conrad's eyes went skywards. "Oh, right."

Then Scott hit him with it. "I heard what happened to Kimmie Yang."

Charles Conrad's Adam's apple bobbed in its fleshy encasing. He lifted his drink, unsteadily and supped a larger gulp than intended, his face twisting at the alcohol sting. "A sad business," he said. "Kimmie must have had a lot of internal pain we didn't know about. If we'd known she was the type to ...." The comment tailed off into a shrug.

There it was, Scott thought: the passing-buck, the finger-point elsewhere, the move to avoid blame. As predictable as the Hong Kong Chief Executive's election.

"The type to what, Charles?" The question was like a judo throw in the way it hurled Conrad off-balance.

"Well, I mean..." Conrad scrambled to reply. "Kimmie obviously had.... psychological issues."

"You're saying Kimmie Yang had psychological problems?"

"Explains what happened, doesn't it."

Scott unscrewed his Perrier and took a sip. "Was Kimmie under any pressure at work?"

"Not more than usual...."

"But she was under pressure ... of the usual sort."

"Well I'm not sure that's anything to do with...."

"Was she working long hours, Charles?"

Conrad's eyes narrowed into pips of blackness. He wet his thin lips with his tongue. "Why are you asking these questions, Scott?" They held each other's glare for a moment.

"Kimmie's younger sister, Sally, came to see me," Scott said. Conrad stiffened in his seat. Scott still wanted him to talk, so he moved to defuse things down a notch. "Not in a professional capacity. I've known Sally from way back. She wanted to talk, that's all." Conrad remained on guard so Scott decided to move gently. "The Yang family is having difficulty coming to terms with what happened, Charles."

He waited for Conrad's response. "It's tragic, I know."

Scott gave a slow nod. "Sally told me that Kimmie was putting in some long hours at work. Jackson's can be a demanding firm, we both know that. You can see how Kimmie might have had difficulty coping."

"She never said anything," Conrad said a little too quickly. "I've always made it clear that if you're over capacity, you should tell me...."

"Come on, you know what Kimmie was like, the last thing she'd ever do is admit weakness to you!" Scott decided it was time to make his request. "There are no rights or wrongs here, Charles. Just a family in pain at the loss of their daughter. And you can do something to help them."

"Me?" Conrad gave him a skeptical look.

Here went nothing. "Write a letter to the Yangs, Charles. Say you're sorry for what happened to Kimmie. It's a small act of humanity that will cost you nothing, but would mean everything to them."

Conrad screwed his eyes. "I can't do that ... risk management, our professional indemnity insurers, they won't allow it. You know what it's like."

Scott stiffened at the knock-back. He had tried with the carrot. Time for some stick.

"You could see it as doing Jackson's a favour," Scott said. "Bitterness left to fester too long can lead to unnecessary lawsuits and that's in nobody's interests. A letter to the Yangs saying you're sorry for their loss might help nip things in the bud."

Conrad shifted uneasily in his seat, sweat collecting between the folds of his chin. "Are you threatening me?"

"I'm asking you to do the right thing by the Yangs."

"Really? You're sure you're not looking for a bit of pay-back because of what happened three years ago?"

Scott felt his eyes go into slits. "That's not what this is about, Charles!"

The air between them became lead with tension.

"Then why don't *you* write that letter!" Conrad went on the attack. "Apologise for walking out on Jackson's! When you left, it was your workload Kimmie had to pick up. So if you want to blame someone, look in the mirror, Scott!" He slugged the rest of his drink in one, then leaned in close. "And if I ever get wind of your trying to help the Yangs sue Jackson's, I'll make sure you never get another job in Hong Kong again!"

An electric current of rage crackled through Scott's veins. As Conrad got up, Scott shoved the table hard, slamming its edge into his erstwhile boss's heafty midriff, sitting Conrad slap back down and pinning him to the wall, a wheezing, eye-bulging mess.

"Is there a problem, sir?" Joel was over like a shot.

The question snapped Scott out of the red mist. He released the table. After a moment he handed Joel a pair of one hundred notes. Then he got up and walked away before Charles Conrad had the chance to regain his breath.

CHAPTER FIVE

The cough exploded like a fire cracker in Leopold Chan's throat emitting pain to every crevice of his rib-cage. Gasping for air, he fumbled open the container and forced pills into his mouth. The bitter taste flowered on his tongue. He counted to three, swallowed and waited for the agony to ease. It had been six hours since his last dose. Far too long.

"You okay, boss?" O'Rourke's head came in the door.

"Another of my little episodes, Terrence," Leopold wheezed, his voice a cheesegrater. "Come in, I want to talk to you."

O'Rourke seated himself opposite the vast desk. Leopold took a moment to regulate his breathing and wipe away the tears. He swivelled his chair round to the window.

There it was, Hong Kong harbour shimmering in the night fifty-floors below. From up here Leopold could make out the lights from the Star Ferries dancing their slow tango across the inky shipping lane which separated Central pier on the island from Tsim Tsa Tsui on the Peninsula. Nothing else in the world could match the sight of that sliver of water. It represented Hong Kong's soul, its heartbeat, constantly working, constantly in flux, its existence often threatened by reclamation and pollution down the years, but each time it had reinvented its passage and returned stronger, just like Hong Kong herself. Seeing it from this height, from the office building he himself owned, always restored Leopold's spirits to a better place. "Your monthly visit to Benny Wang is coming up tomorrow, isn't it Terrence?"

"Just need the cheque, then I'm good to go," O'Rourke said.

Leopold swiveled the chair back around, steepling his fingers at chest-height. "I'll be joining you tomorrow. Benny and I have something to discuss."

The skin on O'Rourke's muscular jaw flickered. "Mind if I ask you something, Mr Chan?"

"Please," Leopold said.

"Why don't you let me cut off Wang's fingers and have done with it? Five minutes with me, I promise you'll never have to pay him another cent."

Leopold didn't react. Not immediately anyway. Then his lips turned into a smile, then the smile into a chuckle. O'Rourke stayed deathly still.

"I'm sorry, Terrence, but do you honestly think Benny Wang is blackmailing *me*?"

O'Rourke's eyes narrowed. "I just assumed...you're paying money every month to a man like Benny Wang ...." His voice tapered off, as Leopold shook his head.

"Benny isn't blackmailing me, Terrence, so there's no need for you to er...remove any of his digits. Those cheques are payments which he is due."

The room lapsed into silence.

After a while Leopold said, "I guess I can tell you the truth about our arrangement. You've certainly proved yourself trustworthy enough. You realize don't you, Terrence, that Benny Wang makes his money from ... how best to put this ... less than legitimate means."

"You don't say." O'Rourke deadpanned.

Leopold smiled. "Selling pirate DVDs, untaxed alcohol, Ketamine and other soft drugs. That's Benny's bread and butter. And he turns a nice profit from it, I'll give him that. But success has its problems. One problem in particular. He has too much cash."

"That's my kind of problem!"

"Quite," Leopold nodded. "But it's true, Terrence. You see, a few years back Benny found that the more cash his business generated, the more difficulty he had in spending it without attracting attention from the police. So he had to find a way of laundering it, otherwise – frankly – it was worthless. And that's how our paths first crossed. You see, Benny once tried to launder his money through AsiaRisk."

"You're kidding!" O'Rourke said.

"I'm not, I'm afraid. You'll find, Terrence, that men like Benny have the subtlety of a wrecking-ball. A few years ago he made all his staff members purchase AsiaRisk insurance policies in cash. Then the following week, they all tried to cancel them expecting me to refund their money in nice clean legitimate cheques. But I knew what was going on, so when Benny turned up to collect, I refused to give him his money back. He didn't like that one bit. Started banging the table, threatening me, so I threatened to call the police and he soon calmed down."

"I take it you didn't call the cops," O'Rourke asked.

"I thought about it, Terrence, I really did. But in the end I did something different."

Leopold let his mind drift back to the frisson of excitement which had passed through him the moment he had taken the decision which had changed his life forever. "I decided that if Benny Wang wanted to launder money, I'd show him how to do it properly."

The rhythmical twitching in O'Rourke's jaw stopped.

"It made perfect sense for me, Terrence. Insurance is the business of taking on and managing risk and I've been doing it for over thirty years. When Benny walked into my life, I'd already achieved everything there is to achieve as an insurer. AsiaRisk was doing well and I could easily have slid off to a comfortable retirement. But that just isn't me. I love challenges. I love the stimulation of risk. And that's what Benny Wang was offering."

It was true. Risk was the drug for which Leopold had strived after all his life. The concerns which kept people awake at night were the very commodity he packaged and traded at vast personal profit. His company, AsiaRisk, stood as one of the last privately owned insurers in the Hong Kong market, and success had fuelled his appetite for more. He had no family to be concerned about. Trixie had long since left him, the silly bitch had never been able to satisfy his intellectual restlessness and it was no wonder she had opened her legs for any man willing to make her feel wanted. The banking sector offered little appeal. Securitization, CDOs, credit-default swaps, they were just insurance by another name, certainly insufficient to satisfy Leopold's craving. He needed something more, something that went beyond the line which his peers ever dared to cross. And he had found exactly what he was looking for in the world to which Benny Wang gave him access.

"So those cheques I deliver each month. They're funds you've laundered for Wang?" O'Rourke asked him. Leopold nodded. Again surprise flickered on the Irishman's brutal face.

"It's just another form of business, Terrence," Leopold explained. "Of course, when I started, I was a complete novice. But that was an advantage. I was like an artist with a blank canvass." He pushed himself off the chair and started pacing, his breathing back to normal, his mind alive with the memory of where it had all begun.

"I started with the problem – Benny's need to convert criminal cash into legitimate money. To do that, we needed to get Benny's illegitimate cash into a bank account, but that was virtually impossible because of the amounts involved. You see, transactions over a certain limit have to be reported by bank tellers to their superiors. You can't just walk into a branch with a suitcase of cash and make a deposit. So I needed a more subtle means of depositing the money without raising suspicion."

Leopold paused at the bookshelf on the other side of his office and ran his fingers down the spines. "At first I sent members of Benny's staff round to different branches, each one depositing small amounts under the reporting limits. Smurfing, they call it. But that was too labour intensive to provide a long term solution. So I had to come up with something more comprehensive. And that's when I had some luck. Do you remember the SARS pandemic back in 2003, Terrence?"

O'Rourke snorted disparagingly. "You mean when everybody was afraid of catching a cold."

"I'd hardly call SARS a cold. It shut down Hong Kong for six months!" Leopold fell back into his chair and let his mind drift back to that bitter period in Hong Kong's history. People still shuddered at the memory of Severe Acute Respiratory Syndrome – SARS, as it was known – a disease which had killed almost three hundred people across the territory. But it was the economic impact which had left more lasting scars. Tourists fled, the property and share markets nose-dived. The once vibrant streets emptied out and Hong Kong became a ghost town, the whole world questioning its future.

"Every crisis brings opportunity, isn't that what they say? All those bars, restaurants, jewellery shops facing bankruptcy, they were a dream come true and we were able to invest in them at basement prices. It took me a while to convince Benny though, he always was a stubborn brute, but eventually he realized it made sense. And the businesses were all too happy to take

Benny's money; it was the only thing standing between them and closure, after all. They were cash businesses, you see Terrence. Every day they sent someone into a bank to deposit takings and no bank teller batted an eye-lid because they knew the business was legitimate. All we had to do was mix in Benny's cash with the legitimate takings and it slipped into the banking system like oil through engine. The businesses updated their books to reflect an increase in turnover. Nobody was any the wiser."

"So those cheques for Benny are from those businesses?" O'Rourke asked.

"In a round-about way, yes," Leopold continued. "But that's only how we load the machine, how we get the money into the banking system. After that, Benny's portion is wired to other accounts, in small enough amounts to avoid detection, of course. Then it goes through my spin-cycle."

"Your spin-cycle?" O'Rourke asked.

Leopold nodded. "A network of accounts I've set up in Panama, the British Virgin Isles, Belize, St Lucia, St. Kitts" – he listed them off on his fingers – "places which guarantee shareholder secrecy. The accounts are in shell company names. All I do is mix the money around the accounts, in different amounts, at different times, until the trail's so complex no one will bother following it. Then it all gets wired back to Hong Kong and passed through AsiaRisk's accounts as claim payments on legitimate insurance policies which I make Benny Wang pay for. Those claim payments, Terrence, those are the cheques you deliver to Benny each month."

O'Rourke pulled his lips tight in concentration. "I get it," he said after a while.

Leopold chuckled to himself. "You know the funny thing is, all those policies I've sold to Benny Wang to make the payments look legitimate, they've been brilliant for AsiaRisk's turnover. Done my dividend payments no harm at all."

Leopold turned his chair back to the window and the serenity of Hong Kong harbour below. Risk. Challenge. That was what Hong Kong was all about. It was funny to think that, in 1842, the British had sent in their gun-boats to enforce their right to sell opium to the Chinese on the pretext of free-trade, taking this barren rock in the process and then transforming it into the world's greatest trading entrepot. And here was Leopold, centuries later carrying on that legacy by washing Benny Wang's drug money through the giant sink which Hong Kong's beautiful harbour represented. Just another challenge Leopold had faced down, grappled with and overcome.

And now it was time for the next one, one that would be Leopold's greatest challenge.

And his last.

CHAPTER SIX

Scott bolted from his restless sleep and knew immediately he was heading over the edge tonight.

Cold sweat had pooled in the crevices of his torso and cascaded down his front as he sat up. Salt flooded his mouth. His head was a cyclone of thought too fast for him to get a grip on. He flipped out of bed, hit the floor and started doing push-ups until his arms and chest burned, but the exercise didn't stem the craving, not this time He needed a drink, a real drink.

The clock looked down on him in judgment. It was almost one in the morning. Noises from sporadic car engines floated up from the streets of Happy Valley punctuated by the 'ticker-ticker' of traffic-lights turning from amber to green and the echo of the external air-conditioner from the flat upstairs dripping onto his window sill. Sounds of the night in this claustrophobic, twenty-four hour city.

To hell with it!

Scott threw on some jeans and a lumber shirt, rode the lift to the ground, hailed a taxi,and was in Wanchai in fifteen minutes. Striding impatiently down the neon spectacle of Lockhart Road, he ignored the catcalling Mama-sans trying to entice him into clubs called 'Pussy Cat', 'Bunny' and 'Paradise', which offered their own sort of relief. But not the kind that Scott needed tonight. The bar he wanted – 'the Handover' – was tucked away down a side-alley like a forgotten memory. The sprinkling of regulars didn't bat an eyelid when Scott walked in the door. A juke box pumped out The Knack's *My Sharona* at an apologetically low volume. Scott chose a corner table and signalled the Filipino waitress over.

While the first San Miguel was on its way, a chink of sanity made him dash off his safety valve text message – it had been a while since he'd used it – but the madness returned as soon as the waitress came back and glass met beer mat. It was the weight of a pint that Scott missed the most; that just-so heaviness of a sweating beer. He supped his first taste of alcohol in over a year. Pure Nirvana. His tongue absorbed the sharp taste like a sponge.

But that had always been his problem. He had never been able to have 'just one beer'. Drinking for Scott Lee meant drinking until he could drink no more, the first pint dulling his self-control; then after that it was a one-way ticket to hell. Whether that made him an alcoholic or just obsessive, Scott had never been sure, but either way abstinence was his default option nowadays, for the most part anyway. Most days he drowned the craving in exercise rather than at the bottom of the glass. Sometimes, though – like tonight – physical activity was no substitute.

With the third pint, Scott felt the buzz taking hold. His mind moved like a runaway train to an inevitable destination he didn't much like, but it was impossible to avoid.

He settled back and let the painful memory take its course.

One phone-call.

That was all it needed. One phone-call and 'boom', Scott Lee was no longer a contender. He was an also-ran. One phone-call on a piece of advice that wasn't his from a department he'd never worked for.

Project Claret. A dumb name for an acquisition, but the corporate boys loved their mystery labels, like they were some secret society that rolled up trouser legs and sacrificed chickens. Claret was the brainchild of Richard Denham, the head of corporate at Jackson's London, a man whose blood pressure was as high as his bank balance, both of which were outdone by the shortness of his temper. Denham's client was buying a warehouse in Hong Kong, part of an acquisition of a global wine business linking the vineyards of France to the high rollers of Shanghai. Hence, Project Claret.

An international law firm like Jackson's prided itself on its cross-border expertise, and Claret involved teams from the London, Paris and Shanghai offices billing big multi-currency fees. The Hong Kong branch's role was miniscule, what else could have been expected from Conrad's three-lawyer outfit? Denham only needed advice on one issue of Hong Kong law. One damn discrete issue which even a trainee could have got right if they'd bothered to do the research. But when the request came in, Scott's work-load was through the roof and Kimmie was on leave; so either the work had to be referred out, or Charles Conrad had to roll up his sleeves.

Conrad, like the idiot he was, had decided to do it himself. Never mind that he didn't know anything about corporate law, he banged out the letter of advice on his dictaphone during the course of a morning, without opening a single text. Off-the-cuff, gut-instinct, analysis-is-for-wimps, that was Conrad's way and if he had only signed his own letter, Scott would have been in the clear. Instead, though, Conrad put the tape on his secretary's desk and rushed out for his golf game. His secretary typed the letter and passed it to Scott.

Not checking it. *That* was Scott's mistake. But with three deadlines to meet that day himself, London screaming for the advice and Conrad being a partner and supposed to know what he was doing, Scott just penned his signature and sent it.

A week later came Richard Denham's voicemail message. Scott Lee was to be at his phone at midday to wait for his call. That's when Scott checked the letter and found the nugget of problematic advice in the last paragraph which read: *'In our opinion the deed passing legal title in the Warehouse from the vendor to the purchaser has been executed in accordance with Hong Kong law.'*

A copy of the deed was on file. Scott hoped to high heaven Conrad had known what to look for, but when Scott read the execution clause and saw only one director's signature, a cold tingling rippled down his spine. Scott downloaded the vendor's articles of association from the Companies Registry website and flipped through the pages. When he found the right section a tidal wave of panic hit him.

To execute a deed the vendor needed the signatures of two directors. A perfectly standard requirement, one Conrad should have known. One signature was sufficient only with a board resolution authorizing it. In Conrad's file, there was no such resolution, nor was one listed in the documents mentioned in the letter. That meant only one thing. The deed was invalid. Denham's clients hadn't got good title to their warehouse and Conrad's letter, the letter that Scott had signed, was negligent.

When Scott picked up the phone at midday Richard Denham was eating red meat. Scott quickly admitted the mistake but it was an easy fix, all he needed was half an hour to draw up a resolution and...Denham cut him dead. The vendors had used the mistake to pull the plug on the deal leaving his clients – and Scott remembered Denham's exact words – 'with their dicks out pissing into a shit storm.'

That was supposed to have been Scott's year, when it all paid off, the endless billable hours, the lack of a social life, the stress, the commitment, the early mornings hung-over after binge-drinking with clients the night before, because that was what it took to become a Jackson's partner. Years of dedication. And finally Scott had his appointment with the partnership selection board that September. An assistant came up for consideration only once, everyone knew the score. One chance, and you were in or out.

But in the end Scott was denied even that. Richard Denham made sure of it. Scott was finished at Jackson's.

One phone-call and it was all over.

"Another one?" the waitress asked.

"Sure," Scott slurred.

She took away the empties.

Scott smiled vacantly, recalling the inevitable reaction from Charles Conrad when he had learned the advice in the Claret letter was wrong. *"It was only a draft, Scott! I wanted you to check it, that's why I asked Bonnie to give it to you. I didn't mean for you to just send it out!"* It was bullshit, of course, but Conrad was a partner and when the accusations started to fly, partners closed ranks to protect their own. Scott's career at Jackson's was over.

In retrospect, resigning without having another job to go to was stupid. People jumped to the wrong conclusions and interviews were hard to come by. Scott tried to keep in contact with his old clients, taking them out for after-work drinks, but they would make their excuses after the first round, leaving Scott to find solace at the bottom of several more glasses on his own. Soon his phonecalls stopped being answered, leaving him to embark on a two-month blitzkrieg of booze and self-pity which only ended when an old law school friend stepped in to drag him back to the surface.

Scott's phone vibrated in his pocket. He looked at the number. *Speak of the Devil*, he thought and opened the phone.

"Which one of these holes are you in?" the voice said.

"The Handover," Scott shouted above the music.

"I'll be there in a minute. And I'm going to kill you!"

The next pint arrived. Scott took a long pull, then went to the toilet. When he returned Philip Yip was standing there in pressed khaki slacks, pink Dunhill shirt, blue blazer and low-cut loafers, looking as out of place as a male stripper on a stag night.

"The Glee Club's missing its top falsetto, I see." Scott chuckled. Yip strode over and put his hand on Scott's arm. "I'm driving you home, right now!"

"The hell you are!" Scott pulled away hard, sat back down and lifted his drink.

Yip stared at him. Then, realising argument was useless, he clicked his fingers at the waitress and ordered an iced tea. The waitress raised her eyebrows. Scott gave her a 'what-can-you-do' shrug.

"I thought we were past these midnight cries for help!" Yip said. "And by the way you woke Maxine up. Big mistake!"

"Nice girl, Maxine," Scott stifled a yawn. "Don't know what she sees in a fraud like you!"

"Oh, you're welcome by the way."

Scott wiped a hand over his face and felt the stubble springing up on his chin. INXS's *New Sensation* cut through the bar. He bobbed his head in time.

"Fine! Don't tell me why I'm here," Yip continued. "Nothing I like better than being dragged out of bed at three in the morning to watch you act like a selfish, spoilt, superior brat."

"Selfish. Spoiled. And Superior," Scott counted the words off on his fingers. "That's like poetry, man." Then he added in his best Mr Myagi a la Karate kid voice, "Grasshopper learn to insult well, make master proud."

Yip checked the table-top and leaned an elbow onto a dry spot. "Scott, the meeting to decide whether you get partnership is next Friday! If Gordon Siu walked through the door now..."

"Phil, if Gordon Siu walked through the door of *this* bar at *this* time, I'll admit you have the fashion sense of Versace!" Scott paused. "Actually, you know what, it wouldn't surprise me if

Gordon did walk in. The old bastard's probably next door right, with his head buried in some girl's chest."

"That's my fellow partner you're talking about."

"A lawyer that lies," Scott shrugged. What are the chances?" Then his tone suddenly sharpened. "You think, because you're a partner, you're better than the rest of us, Phil? Well let me tell you something. Gordon Siu, Charles Conrad – they've got where they are through blind luck, no brains, and treading on anyone who gets in their way!"

Yip gave a slow nod. "Charles Conrad! I figured he'd be at the root of this. So what was it this time? You saw his name at the bottom of a journal article and felt a pang of regret? Well boo-hoo, so you got screwed by Jackson's. That was three years ago, buddy. Get over it already."

"I got over it, *buddy*! I left the past behind." Scott snapped. "Just didn't bank on it waltzing in the door again and slapping me in the face!"

Yip's face showed concern. "Why, what happened?" The ice tea arrived. Yip took a sip, screwed his mouth in distaste.

Scott let the strains of Michael Hutchens die into nothing. Then he told Yip about Sally Yang's visit, Kimmie's suicide, Sally's request for help and how this had prompted a renewal of acquaintance with Charles Conrad.

"I'm sorry to hear about Kimmie," Yip said. "I know you two were close."

Even through his alcohol addled mind Scott appreciated the sincerity. Philip Yip had always been there to help pick him up the pieces ... Scott took another heavy gulp. A small belch followed, leaving a vinegary taste in his teeth. Beer sloshed in his gut. He was blind drunk and the tank was full. Binge over.

"Mind if I offer some advice?" Yip asked.

Scott held out a flat palm.

"Appealing to Charles Conrad's better instinct was the wrong move."

"You think?"

"You want to harm Conrad, hit him where it hurts."

"And where's that, oh wise one."

"In his partnership takings."

Scott laughed. "Tell me Phil, instead of porn do you use balance sheets?"

"I'm serious," Yip protested. "The likes of Charles Conrad and Gordon Siu are safe in their positions because they have clients who bring in money. That's all that matters in this game. So if you want to undermine your old boss, steal his clients away. Or at least *try* to do it. When Conrad finds out, he'll shit bricks. Then you may find him more amenable to negotiation."

Scott thought for a moment, then signalled for the bill. "Your MBA philosophy's making me nauseous."

But the truth was, much as Scott hated to admit it, Philip Yip had a point; and through the alcoholic haze, an inkling of an idea was already starting to form.

"I know that look, Scott. What are you up to?"

Scott didn't answer. He paid the tab, left a generous tip and played with the idea some more. They left the bar. Yip put Scott in a taxi and told him to show up for work on time.

All the while the idea took on further shape and by the time Scott stepped out onto the quiet streets of Happy Valley, it had morphed into a full-blown strategy which he was just dying to implement.

Soon Hong Kong would be waking up to a new day. Old men and women would be doing tai chi in the park, school kids packing their schoolbags and financiers checking Wall Street's over-night performance. At around the same time Scott expected his hangover would be kicking in like a mule with a bad temper.

But that didn't matter.

He had a plan now and he was just itching to get started on it.

CHAPTER SEVEN

'Accessories X' was the shop's name; fashion with an edge the idea behind it.

Leopold Chan stared up at the offensive lightning-bolt lettering with distaste and pride. Distaste because this glorified second-hand handbag franchise represented the worst of the frenzied consumerism Hong Kong had to offer. Pride, because Accessories X was his creation. Through the shop window a *mêlée* of sharp elbowed females were jousting for position. "Feeding time at the zoo," Leopold muttered.

"Sure you want to go in there, boss?" O'Rourke was at his shoulder. "Looks kinda dangerous. Benny can meet us somewhere else."

"We're here now, Terrence. Might as well get on with it."

O'Rourke's reticence amused Leopold. He knew the type of action that Terrence O'Rourke was capable of, yet here he was, flinching at a shop full of Hong Kong women.

They crossed the road together. O'Rourke pulled the door open and an unwelcoming cackle spilled in. Taking a deep breath, Leopold bulldozed through the mayhem, ignoring the cries of 'aiyaaah', 'gaau cho' and tuts of annoyance.

At the main counter stood Joey Yan, a callow youth whose thin frame appeared about to succumb to a single waft of air. His hair was unkempt – that was, Leopold understood, the fashion these days – and he was peering through thick-rimmed glasses at the stitching on the Gucci purse which one of his customers was trying to convince him was worth the full trade-in price.

Leopold tried to gain Joey's attention with a polite 'ahem'.

"Oi!" O'Rourke bellowed when that didn't work.

Joey turned with a look of annoyance, but his face changed when when he saw it was Leopold. "Mr Chan, Mr Chan," he flitted his customer away like unwanted dust, "please come this way."

Joey ushered them through a door which led them to the back of the shop and the relative tranquility of a musty stock room. In single file, they picked their way through piles of designer handbags still in their original wrappings and emerged into a cramped stairwell which led them up to the first floor. Along a short corridor, Joey stopped at the second door on the right. He knocked, went in, and motioned Leopold and O'Rourke to follow.

If Benny Wang was annoyed by the interruption, it didn't register on his ample face. He was slumped oafishly behind his desk, studying the racing pages for that evening's card at Happy Valley. The office stank. Cigarette smoke layered the single shaft of natural light stretching down from the small window. Benny didn't get up. Even if he'd had the manners, there was no room.

"Please sit!" Joey pointed Leopold to the foldable chair tucked in at the door side of the desk.

Leopold and O'Rourke exchanged glances.

"I'll wait outside," O'Rourke said and left them to it .Joey asked if Leopold wanted anything to drink.

"No thanks, Joey. Business seems good."

"Oh, it's going brilliantly, Mr Chan. We are *so* busy. There's a sale on at the moment. Please excuse me. I should get back."

When the door closed, Benny Wang looked at Leopold with tired, unfeeling eyes. "That stupid idiot still has no idea." His voice had the phlegmy rasp of nicotine. Benny was referring to Joey's continued ignorance of the Accessories X franchise being another of Leopold's creations; a self-contained mini-money launderette adjunct to the main machine which Leopold had built.

What Leopold particularly loved about Accessories X was how it fed off Hong Kong's consumerism. After all, where else in the world did women feel the need to change their handbags faster than it took the Star Ferry to do a roundtrip across the harbour? At Accessories X, Hong Kong girls could trade in their old bags in return for a discount on their next purchases, provided those next purchases were made from the shop's own range of stock and payment was by credit card. It was an attractive proposition, particularly as Leopold saw to it that Accessories X always stocked the latest offerings from the best boutiques in town, by handing out cash to Benny's staff. with instructions to unleash their girlfriends on the classiest shops in Central and Admiralty. Once the cash had been converted into the latest Louis Vuitons, Chanels and Guccis, the bags would then miraculously appear, still in their original packaging, on the shelves at Accessories X for sale to the next Hong Kong girl who walked through the door with her trade-in bag and credit card at the ready. The trade-ins fetched a good price too, so there was little in the way of leakage. Dirty money turned clean, with a little help from Ms Hong Kong. It was masterful.

"Why did my daughter ever marry that idiot?" Benny had never liked the thought of the unmacho Joey for his son-in-law. "Still he does his job, so what should I care, hey Leo?"

"Quite," Leopold said, not wishing to become embroiled in Benny's family affairs.

Benny Wang was a hideous sight. From the mole on his fleshy cheek – the hair on which he refused to trim – to the tattoos snaking round his flabby forearms, there was nothing likeable about the man. Every time they met Leopold had to reassure himself this was a marriage of convenience.

"So why did you want to see me?" Benny croaked.

Leopold pulled out a cheque from his pocket and passed it across. "For you," he said.

Benny unfolded it. "Four point seven million dollars!" A shred of life glittered in his eyes. "Nice, but we have couriers for this!"

Leopold steepled his fingers. He knew Benny hated it when he did that. "I also have a proposal for you."

"What proposal?" Suspicion laced Benny's voice, sending a frisson of excitement through Leopold.

Another challenge....

"It's time we took the system I built to the next stage," Leopold said.

"The next stage?" Benny was instantly put off by the idea of change.

Leopold knew how to handle this. "That cheque I just handed you is for four point seven million dollars. The one last month was for a similar amount. Next month, it will be the same."

"So what's the problem?"

Leopold dangled the bait. "What if I told you we could be increasing those payments to a hundred million or more?"

Benny pouted his lips into a tight 'o' and whistled. "A hundred million a month? I don't need that kind of money washed! I don't make anywhere near that much. Remember what they say, Leo: 'Snakes shouldn't try to swallow elephants.'"

Leopold disliked Benny's penchant for using Chinese proverbs to guide commercial decisions. "My dear Benny, the first rule of business is 'never be complacent'. If you're not moving forwards you're moving backwards. And before you know it," Leopold snapped his fingers, "you're standing in the way of progress. You become the problem for which the likes of Joey downstairs will need to find a solution."

Tension lines deepened in Benny's face. "Think I need to worry about that fairy? I could squash him with my thumb!"

"Joey's young and ambitious, Benny, just like you and I were at his age."

Benny took out a pack of cigarettes, drew one out with his lips. Leopold waited for Benny to puff away, letting him play with the thought of his son-in-law as a potential threat, allowing the paranoia to filter through his psyche.

"And it's not a question of whether you need to launder more money; you're looking at this all wrong." Leopold leaned forward and made like he was letting Benny in on a secret. "We can use the laundering operation to expand your business."

"What are you talking about?"

"You have competitors, Benny. Not just in Hong Kong, but regionally too, in the markets you're trying to break into!"

"Competition is part of business," Benny shrugged.

"What if I told you that the new facility I have in mind could launder both your own money and your competitors' money?"

"What?" Benny made a face. "Why would I do that?"

"Because if you control your competitors' money supply, you control them. You get to turn off the tap whenever you like. Then they have to pay tribute to you, otherwise you stop the supply and before you know it, you control them. Simple, really, when you think about it."

Benny's bottom lip folded in under his teeth. Slowly but surely Leopold could see him convincing himself. The suspicion eased out of Wang's eyes.

"What have you got in mind?"

Leopold readied his ace. "Something similar to the current system. We still look to control interests in legitimate businesses and run your money through their books, just like we've been doing. Only instead of handbag shops and restaurants, we go for something much bigger." Leopold cleared his throat. "We gain control of a listed company."

Benny let out a cross between a laugh and a belch. "You want me to play the stock market? Oh, Leo, I already stir-fry shares. Me and the rest of Hong Kong."

Leopold grimaced. Maybe he'd come at this too quickly. "I'm not talking about just buying shares, Benny," he soldiered on. "I'm talking about gaining control."

Benny's heavy breathing paused. "Do you have a target in mind?"

Time for the Ace.

"Kwan Holdings," Leopold said.

Benny's face froze. Leopold nodded slowly in answer to the subliminal request for confirmation.

"You want me to take over Cyrus Kwan? Tell me you're joking, Leo! Tell me this is you making me laugh."

"When it comes to business, you know I don't joke."

Benny's eyes narrowed to black pips as he assessed the idea. "Cyrus Kwan. You know that man almost ruined me when he bought the estate I lived on and turned it into apartments?"

Yes, Leopold knew. The poverty stricken Tai Koo Wan Estate; where Benny had grown up and learned his trade. Built in the sixties, Tai Koo Wan had been a place for the government to house all society's dregs, its criminals, its drug-dealers, its illegals. Out of sight out of mind, that was the idea. But within a decade, the social experiment had gone wrong. Tai Koo Wan became a breeding ground for triad activities, a no-go area for the police, and a place where the young Benny Wang had plied his business with impunity. And it would have continued, had it not been for Cyrus Kwan's offering to buy the estate from the British government and turn it into affordable middle-class housing. The British had jumped at the offer, seeing it as their last chance to clear away an embarrassing blot on the otherwise unblemished landscape they were handing back to China in 1997. So overnight the police moved in, forcing the likes of Benny Wang from their beds and from their homes. Sure, they were given compensation and a roof elsewhere. But it did nothing to compensate Benny for the loss of his business, which was shut down overnight. All thanks to Cyrus Kwan.

"I'm aware of your personal opinions on Cyrus Kwan," Leopold said. "Which is why I thought you might enjoy this opportunity. He shut your business down. Now you get the chance to control a piece of his."

Benny's hang-dog features remained still. Then, slowly, his lips sloped upwards into a reluctant smile, revealing a hotchpotch of yellow teeth.

Leopold Chan felt a shiver of excitement pass through him. *Another challenge overcome.*

O'Rourke snaked the Mercedes across lanes, accelerating into gaps as they revealed themselves, ignoring the irate honks of the taxis and mini-vans who felt he was encroaching on their territory. After being dropped off outside his AsiaRisk building, Leopold rushed for the lift.

"Has Credit sent up the delinquency list I asked for?" he asked, breezing past his secretary into his office.

"It's on your desk, Mr Chan," she bustled after him, "and this was left for you at reception."

She held out a brown envelope. Leopold took it. His name was written in blue ink in the centre under the words "private and confidential". There was no courier stamp, which meant it had been hand-delivered. Leopold put it to one side to deal with later, and turned his attention to the inch wad of paper front and centre on his desk: the delinquency list. But his secretary was still hovering. "What is it?" he asked.

"Daniel Wong of Lambert Brothers wants to speak to you urgently," she cowered.

"Have Yan deal with him!" He waved her out. "And no phone-calls!"

As soon as the door closed, Leopold removed the bulldog clip and caste his eyes down the columns of figures. "Who's not been paying up this month?" He muttered to himself.

Under the terms of every AsiaRisk insurance policy, AsiaRisk reserved the right to cancel coverage if a monthly premium payment was missed. Usually Leopold showed lenience with late payers. Standard practice was to cancel coverage only after payment had been delinquent for three months, and after four written warnings had been served and ignored. But it was important to keep a record of late payments and the delinquency list did just that.

Ignoring the section on consumer policies, Leopold flipped to AsiaRisk's delinquent commercial policyholders. He ran his finger down the columns displaying each business's turnover and sums insured, circling in red the ones which fell within the parameters he wanted. Those circled were then narrowed down further, based on their location and business type. He repeated the process to make sure no obvious candidates had been missed. When he was done, he had exactly what he wanted: a single company which met his desired criteria. A warm glow of satisfaction rose in his chest. He rang the extension number for the AsiaRisk executive handling the account.

"Kevin Choi," a voice answered.

"Kevin, it's Leopold Chan, I understand you're handling the Chow Mei account."

Pause. "That's right Mr Chan."

"Bring me Chow Mei's latest report and accounts straight away, please."

Within five minutes Kevin Choi, a sickly man with a moustache that didn't do anything for his looks, was standing before Leopold. Leopold told him to sit, while he read the financial statements of Chow Mei Paper Limited.

Chow Mei was a toilet paper manufacturer; its factory sited on an industrial estate outside Shatin in the New Territories. Not the most glamorous business in the world – and, judging by the figures, not the most profitable either. Chow Mei was a company on the brink. Its profit margin had ebbed away to nothing in the last five years and was now encroaching upon negative territory, despite a series of cost-cutting measures which had left its operations sheered to the bone. No wonder it couldn't afford its insurance premium. It could hardly afford to retain staff.

It was perfect.

"Ever had any problems before now?" Leopold asked Choi.

"No, Mr Chan. They've always passed their annual inspection, and apart from a few minor liability claims, the overall loss record is good."

"Yet we have received no premium this month."

"A temporary cash-flow difficulty, I think. I'll chase for payment next week...."

"Don't bother," Leopold handed back the accounts. "Cancel the policy please."

Kevin Choi's mouth dropped open. He cleared his throat. "The broker may not like it, Mr Chan. We have a good relationship. He brings us other business and...."

"We can't let broker relations get in the way of sound underwriting decisions, Kevin. Any fool can see Chow Mei is on the verge of bankruptcy. We're better off cutting ties now. See to it, please. I want the cancellation notice on my desk for signature by close of business today, understood?"

Leopold smiled at the sight of his deferential employee scurrying out of the office. It had been a good morning's work. As he re-secured the delinquency list, his eyes caught the envelope which his secretary had handed to him earlier. A private and confidential letter, delivered personally. Leopold picked it up and stared at his name, spelled out in handwritten fountain-pen ink. Odd. Very odd. Easing a finger nail under the adhesive, he worked it across the join until the opening was enough for him to see the contents. Inside was a folded piece of paper and a business card. Leopold drew out the business card and looked at it. Neither the person nor the business name meant anything to him. Then he unfolded the single page letter and read the one sentence it contained. He looked up blankly. Then read the sentence again.

Leopold Chan started to laugh at the writer's sheer bravado, whoever the hell he was.

He called for his secretary to come in and passed her the business card.

"Arrange a time for this fellow to come in would you?"

CHAPTER EIGHT

Huang Yi sat down on the park bench, allowed his heavy eyelids to rest closed and fell into a deep meditation under a grey Hong Kong sky.

Concentrating on his breathing – the coolness of the air going in through his nose and its transformation into a warm outward gust through his mouth – Huang Yi began to drift out of himself, and in his mind's eye made a mental audit of the physical toll which the years had taken on his body. – Years which he had dedicated to his country, to the detriment of all other aspects of his life; his marriage, his family and now even his health. – All of it he had sacrificed to the Third Bureau, because that was what this job demanded.

Eyes closed, Huang Yi mentally visualized himself sitting there with a Buddha-like detachment. He could see how the jet black hair of his youth had given way to a salt and pepper mop, how worry lines of experience sprouted like scars across his forehead and under his eyes. But it was the growing curvature of his spine which concerned Huang Yi the most. Recently he had been developing the stoop of a man who was old long before his time.

And yet there was still his duty to perform.

Always his duty.

With that thought, slowly Huang Yi allowed the world to drift back in, becoming conscious first of the lilt of the birdsong in the trees, then the swishing of the traffic on the roads surrounding the park. The traffic was Hong Kong's constant soundtrack and how Huang Yi hated it. As a country boy from Sichuan, he had long since grown tired of this city and its constant pressure-cooker life-style. It was only his ability to meditate deeply, to find that part of himself that the Third Bureau would never be able to take away, that kept Huang Yi going.

Opening his eyes, Huang Yi looked down at his hands, still tucked together on his lap. He was holding his jade laughing Buddha, rubbing it unconsciously between his forefinger and thumb. Huang Yi had developed this habit long ago, using the Buddha as part of his meditative ritual, as a way of reaching the restful meditative oasis when it all got too much. Nowadays his Buddha trinket served him like a set of worry beads served a Greek. Huang Yi kept the silver key-ring, to which the Buddha was attached, constantly hooked on his finger like a wedding-ring. The coolness of the jade against his touch somehow offered comfort and strength whenever Huang Yi needed it, reminding him of why, ten years ago, he had given up his home and family in Sichuan and come to Hong Kong.

The thought stopped hard and fast, as Huang Yi sensed the presence of another human entering his personal space. It was nothing more than a disturbance in the air around him, but still Huang Yi was attuned to it.

"Thank you for being on time, Recruiter Huang Yi," a voice said.

It had been a long time since Huang Yi had heard someone address him by his official Third Bureau title. He looked up from the bench. A man was standing three feet to the left in front of him on the concrete path. He had a mobile phone pressed to his ear and was pretending to speak into it. As soon as Huang Yi saw him, the man's other arm dropped down to his side with a speed designed to draw attention.

A Jade laughing Buddha – a replica of the one on Huang Yi's own keyring – dropped down from the man's fingers and dangled there on a thin piece of red thread.

The symbol of the Third Bureau. Contact had just been made.

Within seconds Huang Yi took in the man's features. Medium height, soft build, dressed like a father on a day off on his way to pick up his son from school. Not unlike Huang Yi himself, or at least like he had been before the years of constant stress under the demands of the job had taken their toll. Yes indeed, the man was Mr Average. Totally non-descript. A Third Bureau operative through and through. "Welcome to Hong Kong," Huang Yi said.

"I bring urgent instructions from the desk of the Deputy Controller," the man replied abruptly, still pretending to speak into the mobile, a false smile now playing on his thin lips. He waited a beat before continuing, as if expecting the reaction from Huang Yi that his comment deserved.

Huang Yi didn't move, however. *Urgent instructions from the desk of the Deputy Controller.* They were words he had heard so often down the years, their effect had been dulled.

"Recruiter Huang Yi," the man continued, "you are to cease all other existing projects and immediately focus your resources on escalating surveillance activities to Code Blue."

Huang Yi swallowed and calmed his breathing. This was not what he wanted to hear. "We have just come off the Code Blue alert for the container terminal incident. Our other projects are already backed up. There are matters which I need to address urgently for the sake of the Third Bureau's future here! Does Liuming know how limited my resources are?"

The man stiffened at Huang Yi's use of the Deputy Controller's name.

"The Deputy Controller is aware of your situation, Recruiter Huang Yi. He is appreciative of the hard work you are putting in. Resourcing issues are being looked at. I can assure you of that. But this Code Blue is necessary, right now! The Deputy Controller insists on it!"

Huang Yi felt himself nodding slowly. Liuming had trained him personally for the role he was performing in Hong Kong. Back then the old buzzard of Chinese Intelligence had imbued Huang Yi with a sense of the importance of his work here. This wasn't just a job, according to Liuming. It was a mission, one which it was vital for Huang Yi to believe in, precisely for moments like now when it all seemed too much to cope with. Belief in the mission would always give Huang Yi the strength to carry on, Liuming had told him.

Huang Yi looked down at his Jade Buddha.

"Recruiter Huang Yi, are the orders I have given you clear?" The man seemed anxious for confirmation.

Huang Yi gave a heavy sigh. "Very well. I will approach my network and activate another Code Blue. But you must remember we are stretched to the limit and these people do not get paid for what they do. You must let Liuming know that. If the Code Blue throws something up, it may be difficult for us to cope. There is only so much I can do."

"I shall pass back the message."

And with that the Third Bureau operative ambled away, pretend-laughing into the phone as if he had not a care in the world.

Huang Yi sat perfectly still wishing he had time for another meditation.

But it was time for him to get to work.

CHAPTER NINE

Scott Lee sat in AsiaRisk's reception area reading the pristine pitch document he had pulled together in a twelve-hour adrenaline-fueled blitz the previous day. Not a bad effort, given the hangover from hell he'd been suffering from. Revenge sure had a way of sharpening the focus.

Now Scott was here, however, his nerves were starting to roil. He took it as a sign that he was near the top of his game, entering that zen-like state of readiness where anything was possible. Or maybe it was just his body's way of telling him how bad an idea this was. A successful pitch required charm and flattery, according to Yip, neither of which had ever been a big part of Scott's repertoire. Still, there was always more than one way to get under a potential client's skin and today Scott intended to play to his strengths.

"Mr Lee," the receptionist's voice jerked his attention. "Please come this way!"

Straightening his tie, he followed her down a lushly carpeted corridor. The walls on either side were adorned with panoramic photographs of infrastructure projects at different stages of development. 'Don't let the address fool you', those photographs said, 'this company isn't afraid to get its hands dirty'. Scott took the message on board.

He was shown into a meeting room possessing a large veneer table, black leather chairs, a flip chart and a view to make your jaw go slack. The receptionist asked if he wanted a drink. He asked for water and when the door closed headed straight for the window.

It was disappointing. Outside the air was thick with a billion poisonous particles. Some days the smog sat in beautiful layers of reds and oranges which made you think it wasn't bad for you at all. Today wasn't one of those days, however. Today there was no mistaking the toxicity in the white blanket which hung like mosquito gauze over the city.

A blue-suited amah came in with the water and some glasses. Scott thanked her and placed his pitch document on the table. Then he began to pace, the activity kicking his adrenalin up a gear. This was the equivalent of an actor's first night nerves, that little bit of something which added an edge.

Scott paused at the window again. Down below figure-like worker-drones fought for space on crowded pavements. On his way here he'd seen a Maserati stuck in traffic, burning petrol just so its driver could enjoy being looked at. The only show of interest had come from a tough old street lady pushing a trolley full of discarded cardboard and newspaper which she hoped to exchange at the recycling depot for the price of a meal. She threw the Maserati driver a toothless smile as she pushed on past him. Just one of those beautiful only-in-Hong Kong moments.

The door opened then and a tall westerner entered. Scratch 'tall'. This guy was colossal, although he seemed to glide with the grace of a sportsman, holding the door open for the next entrant.

A beat later, in walked Leopold Chan. In the wake of the giant preceding him, an understated entry could have been forgiven, but Leopold Chan evidently didn't do understated. He moved with the speed of a man whose time was limited, seating himself at the table, pointing his power-lifter pal into the next-door chair. Only then was Scott's presence registered.

"You don't mind if my assistant Mr O'Rourke joins us?" Chan spoke like he was used to being listened to, his head held high like Caesar's, chest puffed out in the pose of a nobleman sitting for a portrait. Less than ten seconds he'd been in the room. Already he owned it.

Scott slipped into the opposite seat, slid a business card across the table to the hulk identified as O'Rourke, turned back to Chan and fixed the Ol' Matt Damon smile. "Thanks for taking the time to see me, Mr Chan."

"How could I not, after such an attention-grabbing note?" Leopold Chan drew out a piece of paper and read from it. "'If you want Jackson's to stop robbing you blind, you'll want to hear my pitch'.Your business card came with this, Mr Lee. I assume you wrote it?"

"I did."

"Then no doubt you have an explanation for accusing my lawyer of" ... glancing back down at the note ... "'robbing me blind'."

Scott took a moment to clear throat. Here went nothing.

"My explanation, Mr Chan, is that it's true. What Charles Conrad is doing constitutes theft. I know this because I used to work for Jackson's. I don't any longer, let me say that up front and, no, I don't especially like Charles Conrad much. But it doesn't make what I have to say any less true. Charles Conrad in my view is robbing you blind. And you need to know that."

A small smile crossed Leopold Chan's face, not one of amusement. More quizzical. Wary. Curious to know more. "Okay. I'm listening. But I warn you, Charles Conrad has been my lawyer for some years now."

"I understand that," Scott said. "He handles AsiaRisk's litigated claims, right?"

Chan nodded.

"Well next time you get an invoice from him, have a look at it carefully. I guarantee you'll see the following." Scott counted them on his fingers. "Conrad's charge-out rate is five thousand an hour when partners in other law firms handling insurance claims only charge three thousand if they're lucky. He charges travel time in full; other firms don't. But the real slap is the fifteen percent mark-up he adds to the bill. No other lawyer in Hong Kong would dare charge a mark-up on litigation work." Scott let his words sink in. Then he went for the kill. "But that's not the worst of it."

Chan's head went back in surprise. "There's more?"

Scott flicked a glance to O'Rourke then turned back to Chan. "The worst thing is Charles Conrad himself. He's a bad lawyer. In fact 'bad' doesn't do it justice. He isn't worth the title of 'solicitor'. The examiner must have been drunk the day he marked Conrad's papers." That got a chuckle from O'Rourke. Scott took it as a good sign. "Despite the amount he's charged you down the years, I'm guessing you haven't had much legal advice from him. Check your files, Mr Chan. I bet they're filled with letters that contain no legal analysis, no liability assessment and no solid recommendations."

Knowing amusement gave way to serious consideration on Leopold Chan's face. Scott could see he was hitting some pressure points. He opened his mouth to continue, but stopped himself as Leopold Chan started coughing. Short, staccato, breathy coughs at first; but they soon gave way to long, painful rasps.

"Are you okay?" Scott asked, but he was cut off quickly.

"Don't worry about it." They were the first words O'Rourke had uttered. "Sit tight for a second." He reached for the water and filled half a glass.

Chan continued to dissolve in convulsions, his face a beetroot hue. Struggling for something in his pocket, he pulled out two yellow medical containers. O'Rourke took them, measured out the requisite dosage and held them out for Chan to take.

Not wanting to embarrass the man, Scott played oblivious to Chan's painful rasps. He took out his pen and began making notes on his pad. For want of anything else to write, he jotted down the names of the medicines Chan had just swallowed, the containers for which were sitting there on the table. 'Prednisone'. 'Percocet'. They meant nothing to Scott, so he moved on to sketching out bullet points for a letter he needed to write when he got back at the office.

Slowly the coughing subsided. When Scott looked up, Chan's face was still twisted in agony, but the worst of it appeared over.

"Sorry about that, Mr Lee," Chan said, his voice heavy with phlegm. "The last vestiges of a nasty cold." He drank some water, took a breath, then looked at Scott with concentrated eyes. "That was a very direct .presentation. I take it you're not sharing these thoughts out of the goodness of your heart. Tell me. What do you want?"

Scott clicked the lid back on his pen and placed it carefully on the table.

"You know, Mr Chan, we Hong Kong lawyers have a pretty bad reputation," Scott said. "Ask any one, they'll tell you we cost too much and provide too little. Personally I think that's an exaggeration. Hong Kong has a lot of top-class lawyers who dispense quality advice and look after their client's interests. I happen to believe that's vital in a place which advertises the rule of law as one of its main business attractions. But when someone like Charles Conrad reaches the top of the profession, even the good lawyers out there get maligned. So in answer to your question, no, I'm not doing this out of the goodness of my heart. I want you to instruct me instead of Conrad. I'm asking you to do this because I'm a better lawyer. I'll do a better job for you at half the price. You want references, I'll provide them. But the fact that I'm here to sell doesn't make what I've said about Charles Conrad any less true. The proof you need is in your files. Go look for yourself, I guarantee they'll bear out everything I've said."

Chan let his eyes drift to O'Rourke before turning back to Scott. "Well, you've certainly given me a lot to think about." He started to get up, signaling the meeting was over. They shook hands. O'Rourke opened the door.

Half way across the thresh hold, however, Chan paused. He looked at his watch, then turned back into the room. "Actually, I have a few minutes before my next meeting. Perhaps you wouldn't mind if I asked you a few questions, Mr Lee...may I call you Scott?"

"Of course," Scott said. In his mind he was punching the air in victory. The door closed. All three of them stayed standing. Chan pinched at the edges of his mouth with his forefinger and thumb and started pacing the carpet.

"How long have you been in Hong Kong, Scott?"

"Eight years."

"You're from London?"

"Yes, I used to work for Jackson's there."

"But you're not..." Chan stopped and rephrased. "Where are you from originally?"

Scott smiled. It wasn't the first time people had looked at him and wondered. "My mother was from Hong Kong, my father's English. Makes me part Chinese by race anyway, but I was born and brought up in the UK. I came out here only because Jackson's sent me."

"Yet you decided to stay." Leopold stopped by the window and looked out. "Tell me, are you optimistic about Hong Kong's future? Or do you share the view that our days are numbered, that it's only a matter of time before we're overtaken by Shanghai?"

Scott weighed his thoughts. "I believe Hong Kong's future is fragile, yes. But that fragility is this city's biggest strength."

Leopold frowned curiosity. "Why do you say that?"

"Because it's always been that way," Scott shrugged. "Under the British it was a ticking time-bomb counting down the days until it was handed back to China in '97. That date was seen as Armageddon or supreme righteousness, depending which side of the political divide you were on. But even with all the political uncertainty hanging over it, Hong Kong became an economic success story. Why? Because everyone was in a rush to make money before the dreaded day came. And since the Handover, nothing's changed. Hong Kong's still on the brink, trying to find a new role as part international finance centre, part gateway to China, before Shanghai or Singapore overtake it. So the whole place is running to stand still, because it's constantly under pressure. But pressure produces results. It has done before and it will do so again."

Leopold Chan appeared to absorb every word like a professor in a tutorial. "Interesting," he said. He paced back round to the door side of the table. "Might I then place you under a bit of pressure by asking you a question which has always intrigued me?"

Scott's heart beat faster. "Please."

"Article 109 of the Basic Law," Chan said. "Do you know what it says?"

Scott swallowed. This was a test. All the references in the world about how good a lawyer he was would amount to squat if he couldn't give an answer.

Chan let out a sly smile. "Perhaps it's unfair of me to be so a specific. But it's a provision of our constitution that has always fascinated me ..."

"Article One-O-nine requires Hong Kong to be maintained as an international finance centre, right?" Scott interrupted.

Chan's smile broadened. "Very impressive, Mr Lee! But don't you find this fascinating? Our constitution mandates that Hong Kong must be maintained as an international finance centre. What happens if one day Hong Kong loses that status because the financial world has changed? Does that mean Hong Kong would automatically cease to exist because it can no longer comply with the law which governs its existence?"

Scott was puzzled by the comment. "It's a pretty unique provision to see in a constitutional document, I grant you. But being unique sums up Hong Kong, don't you think Mr Chan? That's why, after eight years, I'm still here."

Chan checked his watch again and tapped its face. "Ah! I'm afraid Hong Kong isn't the only one running out of time. Thank you for your time, Scott. It's been most interesting."

As he shook Chan's hand, Scott had an idea. "Next time you see Charles Conrad, why don't you ask him the same question about Article 109? See what he has to say on the subject."

A chuckle resonated in Chan's throat at the audacity of the request.

But he didn't say 'no', Scott noted. It was definitely game on.

CHAPTER TEN

5.30pm, Leopold and O'Rourke settled down on a sofa in the empty Club-level Lounge bar of the Renaissance Harbour View hotel. O'Rourke grabbed the bowl of complimentary olives and used a toothpick to guide them into his mouth.

"Order some food if you want, Terrence," Leopold said.

"I'm all right. I'll stick with these."

Leopold marveled at the man's discipline. O'Rourke worked out every day; an hour in the morning, an hour every evening, immersing himself in his private world, channeling out the aggression that lurked below the surface. A man with tree-trunk arms delicately popping olives in his mouth made for an incongruous sight. "So what did you think of Scott Lee?" Leopold asked.

O'Rourke shrugged. "Lawyers are all gobshites, if you ask me."

Leopold laughed and relaxed into the sofa, the soft lighting making it hard not to drift off. "I thought he was quite impressive. Especially his knowledge of the Basic Law."

"What's all that about anyway?"

"Come now, Terrence," Leopold said, "you must have heard of the Basic Law? It's Hong Kong's constitution. It contains the fundamental rights of every Hong Kong citizen and sets out the structure for the government's role in society. Article 109, the provision I asked Lee about, is very odd though. It makes it the government's duty to maintain Hong Kong as an international financial centre. Strange, don't you think?"

"Suppose so." O'Rourke clearly wasn't interested.

Leopold might as well be talking to a brick wall, but he enjoyed his unilateral debates with O'Rourke all the same. It gave him a chance to think out loud. "It actually requires Hong Kong to be an international finance centre. Makes you wonder what would happen if it wasn't. – If one day the whole financial system came crashing down. – Can Hong Kong exist if it can't even comply with the law that governs its existence?" Leopold looked out at the purpling sky. The smog was clearing. The Chinese characters on the neon advertizing hoardings across the harbour sharpened into focus.

"Mind if I get some more olives?" O'Rourke signaled to the waiter.

"Really, Terrence, have you no interest in the place you call home?"

"This isn't my home!" The Irishman said with a sudden sharpness. "I already lost that to the Brits. Count yourself lucky they gave you this place back!"

Leopold lifted an eyebrow. "Actually, that's an interesting comparison you make, Terrence. You consider Northern Ireland can exist only if it's part of a united Ireland?"

"Too bloody right."

"And so long as its part of Britain, it isn't your home any more. Belfast isn't your Belfast. Well don't you see? We have a similar situation here in Hong Kong. If the law says Hong Kong can exist only if it's an international finance centre, then as soon as it loses that status," Leopold snapped his fingers, "no more Hong Kong."

The waiter came over with the olives. O'Rourke continued to guzzle. "Bloody stupid law if you ask me. Bet the Brits thought that one up, the bastards!"

Leopold wondered for a moment how the conversation would have proceeded if it had been Scott Lee sitting here instead of O'Rourke. Debating issues just for the intellectual challenge of it wasn't something practiced very much in Hong Kong. Using one's brain power for anything other than career advancement was considered anathema, which made for monumentally sterile discussions at the functions Leopold attended. Share tips, the property market, business opportunities, and holidays were all anyone ever seemed interested in.

But Scott Lee, he was cut from a different mould, Leopold could tell. Here was someone with the kind of intellectual curiosity Leopold respected. Why else could a lawyer quote virtually verbatim from the Basic Law? It had nothing to do with insurance, Lee's professed area of expertise. No, Leopold knew that today he had met someone interested in things beyond the confines of his own career, a rare trait in Hong Kong. And if things had been different, dropping Charles Conrad in favour of

Scott Lee would have been an easy decision. But right now, Conrad's lack of talent was exactly what Leopold was banking on.

"Here's another one of them, boss," O'Rourke nodded towards the stairs leading up the lounge entrance. "Bloody lawyers!"

Leopold looked over and saw Charles Conrad standing there hunkering his shoulders in a way that had never inspired confidence. Leopold signaled Conrad over.

"Do what that lad said, boss!" O'Rourke said mischievously before Conrad was in earshot. "See if buggerlugs here knows anything about that Basic Law stuff!"

"Evening Leopold," Conrad said. "Terrence." He ordered an Asahi and sat down in the armchair next to the sofa. "Sorry, I'm late. Conference call with London ran on a bit."

Conrad's penchant for letting people know how busy he was had always irritated Leopold. It smacked of an inflated sense of superiority. Leopold decided to give it a prick.

"Do you know what Article 109 of the Basic Law says, Charles?"

"Sorry?"

"Article 109 of the Basic Law. What does it say?"

Conrad puffed his rosy cheeks. "In what context?"

O'Rourke snickered.

"In the context of you being my lawyer and me asking you if you know what Article 109 of the Basic Law says."

Conrad sipped his beer, swallowed deliberately and slowly placed the glass back down on the coaster. "Why don't I call you tomorrow once I've had time to give it some thought?" Leopold rolled his eyes at O'Rourke. "Now, what did you want to see me about?" Conrad pushed on. "I'm on a bit of a deadline this evening. Got a bit of a domestic crisis brewing."

"Cathy not getting the full servicing she deserves?" O'Rourke perked up. "Say the word, I'd be happy to step in and do the business."

Anger flashed in Conrad's eyes. He looked like he was about to say something, but then thought better of it.

"That's enough!" Leopold decided to put a stop to things before they got out of hand.

"Bet that's something Cathy's never said to you," O'Rourke continued to goad.

Conrad was out of his seat. "Why don't you just...."

"Enough!" Leopold snapped.

The bartender glanced in their direction. Conrad sank back down, humiliation etched on his face. O'Rourke winked at him.

"Terrence, please wait for me in the lobby," Leopold ordered.

O'Rourke paused for a moment before getting up to leave. As he passed Conrad's chair he patted the lawyer on the shoulder and leaned down. "Next time you try getting all aggressive with me, buggerlugs, I'll rip off your bloody balls."

Charles Conrad's face drained white. When O'Rourke was gone, he sank his beer to calm his nerves. "I don't see why you keep that psycho around!" he said to Leopold.

"He has his uses," said Leopold. Not an answer designed to put Conrad at ease. Leopold let a moment pass. "A lawyer called Scott Lee came to see me today."

That revelation seemed to shake Conrad more than O'Rourke's threat.

"What did he want?" Conrad asked cautiously.

"He said he used to work for you, Charles, and then proceeded to list off a number of reasons as to why I should instruct him instead of you."

Conrad swallowed nervously.

"He seemed very bright, I must say. When did he leave Jackson's, Charles?"

Beads of sweat blossomed on Conrad's forehead. "About three years ago."

"Then it's a little strange, him coming to see me out of the blue like this, don't you think?" Leopold waited for Conrad to respond, but Conrad remained quiet. "Tell me Charles, when was the last time you had contact with Scott Lee?"

"Actually," Conrad glanced at the floor, "we ran into each other two days ago. He started asking me about Kimmie Yang." He paused. "Blamed me for her suicide. Probably thinks stealing you away as a client is a way of getting back at me, or something."

Leopold let the news slip through his mind. "And you saw fit not to tell me about this?"

"I didn't think it was relevant."

"It's not up to you to think!" Leopold spat. "You do what I tell you, understand!"

A beat of silence.

"I'm sorry." Conrad said.

"Does he know anything?"

"No way, he hasn't been in contact with anyone at the firm since he left."

Leopold stared hard for a moment, then leaned back in his chair and pondered how to deal with this new situation. Scott Lee posed a potential threat. Not a huge one. But a threat all the same. "The things that Lee said about you, Charles. They weren't very flattering, I must say. Not flattering at all in fact."

"You can't believe anything he says, Leopold. He was forced out of Jackson's because..."

"I'm not interested in your firm's politics!" Leopold interrupted. "I'm only interested in ensuring he doesn't get in the way of any of our plans. Do you understand?"

Conrad nodded.

"So here's what I want you to do." Leopold reached into his jacket pocket and pulled out the note that Scott had used to effect his introduction. He handed it to Conrad and gave him his instructions.

Slowly, Charles Conrad's lips turned into a cautious, bitter smile.

After finishing up with Conrad, Leopold went to the lobby and found O'Rourke sprawled on a couch, glancing through the sports pages of the *South China Morning Post*.

"Where to now?" O'Rourke asked.

"I have a dinner appointment at the restaurant upstairs. I'll make my own way home after that, Terrence. No need for you to hang around."

The Irishman shrugged 'fair-enough' and sauntered off. Leopold headed for the lifts.

The restaurant on the seventh floor was French and one of the few in Hong Kong to have been awarded a Michelin star. Its interior was pure modern art, clearly the handiwork of a designer limited neither by imagination nor budget. Strange fountains were juxtaposed against cubist black-and-white murals. Set-designer lighting toyed with running water and shadows. It was all very effective, Leopold thought. Precisely the type of place which Rupert Kwan would love to be seen in.

The younger Kwan was already seated, sipping a gin and tonic and leering at a curvaceous waitress. So enchanted was Rupert with the girl, in fact, that he failed to notice Leopold sidle into the opposite seat.

"Please keep your brains above trouser level for the duration of this dinner, Rupert. Otherwise I'll take the offer I am about to make elsewhere."

Rupert's face snapped round and started to darken with anger.

"Not used to being spoken to like that, eh?" Leopold cut Rupert off before he said anything. "Well, get used to it, Rupert. If you want a quick and effective way of repairing your relationship with your uncle, that is."

"You know nothing about me and my uncle!" Rupert hissed.

Leopold leaned forward and intertwined his fingers on the crisp white tablecloth. "Your father died when you were six. Since then your uncle has made it his duty to raise you. In return you have thrown away every opportunity he has given you. He paid for you to go to Duke, you failed to come away with a degree. He gave you capital for your first business; you lost the lot on some misconceived start-up internet venture. When he fed you more funds to get you back on your feet, you used the Kwan name to put together a syndicate to purchase one of Hong Kong's main container terminals even though you have absolutely no experience of transportation. Needless to say, you overreached yourself and in a desperate attempt to liquidate your funds, you attempted to sell the terminal to a Singapore company, thus compounding your stupidity. The press has labeled you a traitor to Hong Kong and China and your uncle's reputation risked being smeared by association; so once again he was forced to bail you out. Now, understandably I would say, he's had enough and you've been relegated to a desk in his investment department until you've learned your lesson. Have I missed anything?"

Rupert Kwan's eyes exploded.

"Ambition in youth is admirable, Rupert. But exuberance needs to be harnessed, to be worth anything in the business world."

"Sounds like something my uncle would say. Tell me, are all old men full of crap?" The cleverness of his come-back seemed to please Rupert, but Leopold was quick to pop his bubble.

"Only when it concerns spoiled conceited brats who can produce only crap!"

They sat in silence for a moment, Leopold using the pause to deepen Rupert's humiliation, until he was drowning in it. "Make no mistake, Rupert. Your reputation is not why I am sitting here."

"Then why are you here?"

Leopold picked up the menu. "We'll get to that after we've ordered." He signaled the waitress back and noted with satisfaction that Rupert Kwan's attention wasn't distracted this time. The waitress didn't seem to take it as any great loss.

"Did you do any research on my company before turning up this evening?" Leopold asked after they had ordered.

"I had someone prepare me a note and pull some numbers," Rupert shrugged, still playing the big tycoon. "AsiaRisk's an insurance company. You own it and run it. You're doing alright."

It was hardly insightful.

"Did your note tell you that last year Kwan Holdings wanted to buy AsiaRisk?" From the look on Rupert's face, the answer was 'no'. "You see Rupert, it's salient facts like that which you might want to pay a little more attention to!"

"So what? You want me to tell my uncle to lay off your company?" Rupert appeared amused by the idea.

"Rupert, I own AsiaRisk myself. I don't need your help in getting anybody to 'lay-off'." Leopold added the quote marks with his fingers.

"Then what do you want from me?"

Leopold leaned forward, made sure he had Rupert's full attention, and then spent the next twenty minutes outlining his proposal, paying particular attention to the incentives he had carefully crafted to hook the younger Kwan's interest. When he was finished, the look in Rupert Kwan's eyes told Leopold that he was sold on the plan. But Leopold gave him a confirmatory nudge all the same. "Your uncle will be impressed if you can pull this off, don't you think?"

The starters arrived and this time Rupert Kwan didn't even cast the waitress a sideways glance. "Okay," he said. "I'll do it."

Leopold smiled. It was all going like clockwork.

CHAPTER ELEVEN

"Polly, if anyone needs me I'll be out by the library!" Scott brushed passed his secretary.

"The where?"

Scott stopped, turned back. "The bookshelves in reception."

"Oh, I thought those were just for show?"

He rolled his eyes. It had been a sad day for the legal profession when online case law repositories like LexisNexis and Westlaw had done away with the need for books.

"Some of us still do our reading on paper."

Polly gave him a 'whatever' shrug and turned back to her web-based gossip columns. She was right, however. The books in reception were there only to impress clients who still liked to think of their lawyers searching through dusty tomes for the answers to their problems. Anyone who looked closely enough could see that the blue-spined All England Law Reports ended at 2002. After that, Yip & Siu had sold out to the online revolution, which now enabled legal research to be done by key-words and search engines; another skill-set sacrificed on technology's altar.

Sometimes, however – like today – Scott found a use for the old way of doing things. That morning, Philip Yip had passed him a new instruction, a favour for the mother of one of Yip's friends, who was trying to claim compensation from her home contents insurers, for the loss of the engagement ring given to her by her late husband. The old lady hadn't worn it in over a decade, her fingers were too gnarled with arthritis, but it still held sentimental value and its loss had cut deep. Not that her insurer was big on sympathy. When she told the loss adjuster she couldn't remember seeing the ring in the last three weeks, he rejected the claim on grounds of late notification.

Yip decided his friend's mother needed the type of lawyer who would show no mercy. The papers were waiting for Scott when he got in that morning and by the time he'd finished reading them, his guns were ready to blaze. All he needed was some case law to make sure the bullets did the maximum damage, which was where the books in reception came in. Scott remembered a case he'd read about once in an outdated version of *Chitty on Contracts*, the book sitting second shelf from the top. Its spine crackled as he opened it, the smell of aging print leaping off the pages. If knowledge had an odour, then this was it. Scott checked the index, located the paragraph and felt the bloom of satisfaction when he read the reference. It was exactly on point. Hurrying back to his office, Scott enjoyed the moment.

He'd been on a high since leaving AsiaRisk's offices two days before, certain that he'd impressed the hell out of Leopold Chan. One chance he'd been given and, bang, he'd nailed it. Confidence was a strange beast. When it was with you, the world played out in sync. Even Gordon Siu had cast a pleasantry in Scott's direction in the lift that morning. Now it was Friday, the end of an emotional rollercoaster week in which Scott had learned of Kimmie Yang's death, confronted Charles Conrad about his part in it, fallen off the wagon big-time and hauled himself upright to pitch to AsiaRisk. Next week, there would be the partnership vote to worry about. But that was next week's problem. For now, all Scott wanted to do was finish up and close down his mind for a couple of days.

But not before he'd ruined that damn loss-adjuster's weekend.

Back at his desk, Scott pulled up a new document on his computer and started framing out his letter-before-action, politely introducing himself as the solicitor of record, pointing out the tenuous legality of the loss-adjuster's declinature and giving the insurance company a chance to do the right thing before the dogs of war were unleashed. He read it through and was pleased with the result. All he had to do now was fax it, go home and forget about things for two days.

But Polly had other ideas. She was standing in the doorway when Scott looked up. "Mr Yip wants to see you."

"Perfect timing, Phil, as always," Scott muttered to himself.

Figuring it was about this new case, he printed the letter and headed over to Yip's office.

When Scott saw that Yip's door was closed, a pang of tension jarred through him, his newfound confidence, fragile mistress that it was, chinking with doubt. Philip Yip never closed his door.

"Phil wanted to see me?" Scott said to Yip's secretary.

"You can go in," she replied flatly

Scott wavered a moment, but pushed the negativity aside and knocked.

Yip's office was what you'd expect a senior partner's to be. Aircraft-carrier desk, virtually paperless. Family photos arranged in wall-cabinets with precision. A welcoming settee, armchair, coffee-table combo. Fresh cut-flowers tinged perfectly temperatured air. Somewhere a stereo played Yo-Yo Ma's ethereal cello at low volume. The only blip in the scene was Yip himself. He was standing with his back to Scott, hands deep in his pockets, cufflinks removed, shirt-sleeves half way up his forearms, staring vacantly out of the window, but not seeing beyond his thoughts.

"You wanted to see me, big guy?" Scott said.

Yip turned round. "Hey...Scott... take a seat!" He pointed to the settee, grabbed a remote control and switched off the stereo. Whatever was going down, he didn't want Yo-Yo interrupting.

Scott sat but didn't relax. He leaned his elbows onto his knees keeping the weight over his feet. "I've done a letter on your friend's mother's case," he said handing Yip the letter. "Should make 'em sit up and take notice."

Yip read it, smiled, put it on his desk with a "thanks", then came round and took the armchair. "I need to talk to you about something."

"Yeah?"

"I've just come back from the Law Society. There's another complaint against you."

"What? I haven't spoken to Esther Lai all week..."

"It's not Esther this time. Or Vincent Tang."

Scott made a face. "Then who is it?"

Yip gave him a rigid stare. "Charles Conrad."

All the sound in the room died right then, except for the thrumming of Scott's quickening heartbeat. "Conrad?"

"Did you do a pitch to AsiaRisk, Scott?"

"You know I did, you suggested it in the bar the other night. I wanted to pinch Conrad's one and only client. Teach him a lesson. Is that what this is about? Come on Phil, there's no law against poaching clients."

Yip was already shaking his head in disappointment. He screwed up his eyes, his face etched deep with tension lines in a way Scott had never noticed before.

Ice picked at the back of Scott's neck. "Phil, what's going on?"

"Conrad's complaining about what you said to Leopold Chan."

"Conrad wasn't even there, how could he possibly..."

"Leopold Chan told him!" Yip said sharply.

Scott's discomfort clicked up three notches. He tried to run it through. Leopold Chan had told Charles Conrad about his pitch. Not what he had expected, sure, but then again it didn't explain Yip's level of concern. "What's the big deal, Phil? I told Chan that Conrad was an idiot who charges too much and..."

"Damn it, Scott!" Philip Yip banged his fists on the chair arms. "I saw the note you wrote! The President of the Law Society showed it to me! He gave me a copy!"

Yip stood up, went to his desk, opened a drawer and pulled out a piece of paper: "'If you want Jackson's to stop robbing you blind, then you'll want to hear my pitch'," he quoted. "What the hell were you thinking?"

Scott didn't like where this was going. "Look it was a short sharp shot in the arm to gain Chan's attention..."

"Scott, you've gone down in writing accusing another firm of robbery. It looks like you're blackmailing one of their clients into giving you work!"

Silence.

"That's not what this is about," Scott kept his voice even. "This is Charles Conrad desperately trying to hang onto AsiaRisk..."

"Gordon Siu came with me to the Law Society!" Yip interrupted. "He's had enough, Scott. I warned you!"

Scott felt his lungs fill with lead. This was history repeating itself. This was Richard Denham chewing him out down the phone-line three years ago. He knew what was coming, but was frozen in the headlights bearing down on him.

Yip walked back to the chair, sat down. "A mistake like this could kill us, Scott. I've got people's livelihoods to think about. Conrad said Jackson's was thinking of suing."

"That's bullshit! Conrad wouldn't have the balls to tell the London office, he'd have risk management crawling all over him."

Yip shook his head. "I'm sorry Scott. Gordon's had enough. He wants you out."

Scott's stomach tightened into nothing. "No way!"

"I've talked him out of terminating your contract straight away," Yip held up a placatory palm. "But you're going to have to be suspended on no pay for a while, just until I can talk him round. A couple of weeks, maybe a month that's all we're talking about. Let Gordon see how much we miss you and need you; then we can start again...."

"This isn't happening!" Scott was up and heading for the door. "Not again, no way! I'm sorting this out right now!"

"Scott, don't..." Yip called after him, but the door slammed shut before he could finish the sentence.

So much for his quiet end to the week. One minute Scott was winding down to two days of nothing, next he was a ball of fury ready to lash out hard, fast and terrifyingly at any one who stood in his way. Friday evening and the whole city was breathing a sigh of relief it seemed, even the concrete on the buildings appeared to relax, releasing the heat they had spent the day soaking in. It multiplied Scott's frustration as he bobbed, weaved and jaywalked his way through the pedestrian throngs.

Outside the entrance to AsiaRisk's building, Scott paused a moment and tried to tether his ire. Two days ago he'd made a connection with Leopold Chan. There was no reason he couldn't sort this mess out with one rational face-to-face conversation.

Having straightened himself out in the lift, Scott went straight up to the reception desk where the girl who had shown him to the meeting earlier in the week was sitting, wearing the same insipid smile. Scott caught a caustic waft of nail varnish and let his eyes drift left and right until he saw it. The scarlet vial of liquid was tucked away behind her phone. It gave him an idea.

"Hi there, I came to see Leopold Chan on Wednesday? I just need five minutes of his time to follow up. The name's Scott Lee."

"Do you have an appointment, Mr Lee?"

"No I don't, but...."

"Then I'm afraid it won't be possible. Mr Chan's diary is full today. Would you like me to ring his secretary and make a time for you next week?"

The nice guy routine wasn't working. Time to give nasty a go. Glancing over at the waiting area, Scott saw a smartly dressed couple wrapped in deep conversation over an open laptop. He turned slowly back to the receptionist and let a little of the pent up aggression leak out.

"See those two over there?" He thumbed to the seating area. The receptionist craned her neck and as she did, Scott reached over and grabbed the bottle of nail polish.

"Hey!" She snapped through clenched teeth.

"You can have this back after you've told Leopold Chan I'm here to see him."

"But…"

"If you don't, I'm going to walk over to those two and shower them with this!" He held up the bottle. "People are going to wonder where I got it, don't you think?"

Her eyes darted between Scott and the other clients. He knew what she was thinking.

"It's ten metres," he said. "Think security would stand any chance of stopping me?"

He made a dramatic show of unscrewing the lid.

She picked up the phone. Hushed instructions were exchanged in urgent tones. She got up. "This way!" she said. No 'please' this time, Scott noted

He handed back the polish and followed her along the same lushly carpeted corridor he'd walked down two days before. This time the photographs of the infrastructure projects held a ruthlessness he hadn't previously noticed. 'There's no mercy in business, kiddo' was the lesson they told today.

Leopold Chan and Terrence O'Rourke were waiting for him in the meeting room. Their presence threw Scott slightly off his stride. The receptionist shut the door with a sinister click and silence hit like a bed sheet snapping taut.

Leopold Chan smiled like he was everybody's favourite granddad. A dark hand clasped round Scott's rib cage. The only way Conrad could have got hold of his note was if Chan had given it to him. Which meant Scott had seriously misjudged this man.

"I came here in good faith the other day, Mr Chan," Scott made his play. "I thought a man like you would appreciate some straight talking for a change. Now I've got Charles Conrad and the Law Society on my back and my employers aren't too pleased about it. All because I came here and told you the truth."

Leopold let out a smidgeon of a laugh. "Come now, Scott, it's no use trying to play the martyr. You came here because you wanted my business and you were prepared to rubbish Charles Conrad's reputation to get it. You knew that Charles and I had worked together for years, but you still went ahead and made your accusations. Don't you think it's fair that I let Charles know what you said about him? Isn't that what you lawyers call 'the reasonable course of action'?"

Heat prickled down Scott's back. "Everything I told you was true, Mr Chan. Did you look back at your files like I said? Did you check Jackson's invoices?"

Leopold Chan clasped his hands behind his back. "What you did, Scott, was question my ability to manage AsiaRisk. Do you honestly think I would have let Charles Conrad do to me what you are suggesting? How dare you!"

Scott stepped back. This wasn't how it was supposed to go. He had horribly misjudged Leopold Chan. Back-tracking was his best tactic now. "In which case I apologize...I was wrong to have come here, I admit that. But I'm asking you, Mr Chan, to ask Charles Conrad to withdraw the complaint. I don't deserve this."

Leopold Chan faced Scott. "You have talent. I can see that, Scott. But some lessons just have to be learned." He turned away and opened the door. "Terrence will see you out," he called over his shoulder as he began back down the corridor.

Scott thought about chasing him down, but O'Rourke was already looming over him like a tower block.

"You heard the man," O'Rourke said brusquely. "He told you to leave."

CHAPTER TWELVE

"Breathe in for me. Now hold it. Okay, breathe out again. Good." Leopold Chan winced as the doctor's stethoscope pressed into his flesh. Such a distasteful procedure, invasive and humiliating. The doctor moved round behind him and they went through the same routine. "You're sounding congested," Dr Adam So concluded.

Leopold put his shirt back on. "That may have something to do with the cancer, doctor."

Dr So wasn't amused. He signaled Leopold into the chair by his desk. The same chair Leopold had sat in four months ago when So had told him that the tumours showing up on his X-rays were not good news.

Not good news. It was an oddly understated way of telling someone they were dying. Yet Leopold had greeted it with the same ruthless equanimity he approached everything in his life. He hadn't felt angry, numb, or even scared; only the frisson of another impending challenge. Here he was with the clock ticking down on him now, free to use whatever time he had left to push back the boundaries. And with General Zhao's reappearance, fate had given him the biggest stage on which to play out the last act of his life.

"Have you thought any more about chemotherapy?" Dr So asked. "It can work wonders these days. Cancer can be managed and controlled. You could prolong your prognosis considerably."

"No!" Leopold tried to keep the annoyance out of his voice. Every time So would try on this good Samaritan act. "It's just putting off the inevitable, Doctor."

"What about your family?"

"Don't worry. My wife left me years ago and I have no children." The thought of his ex-wife, Trixie, caused Leopold's mood to darken. She'd be the last person to mourn his demise. Their mutual affection had long since evaporated, Leopold finding solace in AsiaRisk, Trixie finding it in a string of lovers willing to give her the attention she craved.

"Well if you change your mind..."

"I won't."

"Well if you do, ring my receptionist and make an appointment."

They sat there in cold silence. Part of Leopold admired the medic's persistence, but the conventional thinking so irked him. Death couldn't be avoided, so why bother expending so much effort trying to do so? Leopold intended to embrace his date with destiny. The news of his impending death had put true immortality in his grasp. He was no longer confined by the laws and regulations of a world he would soon depart.

"Is there anything else I can do?" the doctor asked.

"Something to lessen the frequency of these dreadful coughing episodes would be helpful. And some more painkillers."

"We'll increase your dosage and see how we get on." The doctor tapped out instructions on his computer and clicked 'print'. Within moments there was a knock on the door.

"Yes doctor?" It was the surgery nurse.

"Please fill this prescription for Mr Chan."

"You can pick them up from reception in about five minutes, Mr Chan," she said, the epitome of surgical efficiency.

Doctor So's face was etched with the concern of someone not fulfilling his hippocratic obligations.

"Don't worry, Doctor," Leopold reassured him. "This is what I want."

"Well it's your choice, I suppose."

"Yes it is. But I appreciate everything you are doing for me."

After that, Leopold turned the conversation onto other topics, feigning interest in how the doctor's two children were getting on. Both, it seemed, were meeting their father's expectations, although they needed to work a bit harder at their Mandarin studies and he was looking to increase their weekend tuition. Such was the lot of Hong Kong youth these days.

Silence returned.

"Tell me doctor, do you follow the stock market?" Leopold asked after a while.

Adam So's face brightened. "Well I dabble. Do have any tips?"

Leopold thought for a moment. "Sell."

"Sell? Sell what?"

"All your Hong Kong shares. Sell them."

"What?"

"I believe we've reached the top of the cycle. Things are about to turn."

"You bears are always the same!" Adam So waved a hand, no longer the concerned doctor. "The economy's doing well and look at this Cooperation in Services Agreement! The Mainland wants to do business. It's good news."

Leopold twisted his mouth. "Things can change very quickly in this market, mark my words."

The nurse called in to say Leopold's prescription was ready. He went out to pick it up.

After arranging the date for his next appointment, Leopold wandered out into the heat of Ice House Street. He called O'Rourke, but the Irishman was stuck in traffic on Queen's Road East and wouldn't be there for another fifteen minutes. Leopold decided to wait rather than get a taxi. But even time spent waiting was time that could be used for forging ahead with his plans.

He took out the two-page summary of the Chow Mei factory's financial highlights that he had prepared that morning and began to study it. The information confirmed his decision. Chow Mei was a company on the brink. Costs were as low as they could be and it was still operating at a loss.

Now AsiaRisk had just cancelled its insurance. Yes, the Chow Mei paper company was in its death throes. It was time to put it out of its misery, Leopold believed. He pressed the speed dial on his mobile and called Benny Wang.

1.30am, Monday morning.

Terrence O'Rourke leaned back on the car bonnet. Five hours he'd been parked up on this dusty ridge. He closed his eyes and took a deep breath, enjoying the taste of air which hadn't already been circulated through a hundred other people's lungs. The silence of the New Territories was a beautiful thing, almost ethereal in the way it delicately hung in the night.

Below, the Chow Mei Paper Factory sat like an offensive blot on the landscape, its brick monolith set in a compound of wire-fencing resembling a torture victim begging to die. The place was virtually empty, the last bus having ferried the skeleton Sunday staff away just after eleven. Only three geriatric security-guards remained. Enough to satisfy minimum legal requirements; but they wouldn't have stopped a toddler with a water-pistol.

The guards had patrolled from eleven to midnight. After that they'd lost interest and settled in for the night in a shack which served as their common room. They weren't supposed to. But breaking the rules tonight was probably going to save their lives.

O'Rourke had the flask of Jameson's whisky in his jacket pocket, a tradition that went back to his days in the old country. *A nice slug of the Jameson's and a night of havoc for the British scum. What could be finer?* He put the flask to his lips, drank greedily and for a moment he was back in his homeland watching the mist rise over the lush rolling hills of God's own country.

Almost 2am now. The guards' bio-rhythms would be at their lowest ebb, their response times like treacle. But O'Rourke was a professional. He wasn't taking any chances. He lifted the jerry-can and tested its weight. Its contents slopped around, but it was steady enough. The earth slope down to the wire fence at the compound's edge was twenty metres, he judged. Looking up, he saw a dim light in the window of the guards' shack. No sign of movement inside.

With the dexterity of a gymnast O'Rourke vaulted the road barrier and zigzagged down the slope, his footsteps quick and light, burying his shoulder into a tree at the bottom to halt himself. Leaves shushed in the branches above him. He waited for the sliding debris on the slope behind him to calm, then he glanced over to the guards' shack. Still nothing moved.

Bloody amateurs.

Keeping one eye on the shack he edged up to the fence, slid the jerry-can underneath and stepped through the top two wires. He was disappointed, this wasn't even a challenge. What he wouldn't give for a couple of RUC to come sprinting out of the night, blasting their H&Ks.

He picked up the jerry-can, clasped it to his chest and, keeping low, jogged across the compound to the back of the factory, until the entire building was between him and the security-guards. He rested for a moment, calmed his breathing. Then he went to work.

The flat expanse at the factory's rear formed a loading-point for the heavy-goods vehicles which transported the toilet paper. Two trucks were parked, up off to O'Rourke's left. Up against the back wall were three industrial skips stuffed full with paper cut-offs. O'Rourke shook his head. This place was an arsonist's dream, he probably didn't even need the petrol. But it always paid to make sure; experience had taught him that.

He unscrewed the lid on the jerry-can and slopped its contents liberally over the skips. Then he doused the rest of the back wall, making sure the windows got their fair share. With what was left, he traced a trail from the skips to the two trucks, then tossed the empty can into the skip.

He loved the smell of petrol; always had done. Compared to the old days this mission was basic, like going back to the stone age. No incendiary devices, no semtex. Yet there was a certain pleasure in its simplicity. Destruction was an art form, from which technology had taken away much of the creativity. Well, not this time. Easy though it might be, a professional's touch was needed to reap maximum damage with only a jerry-can and a Zippo lighter.

O'Rourke pulled out the pack of cigarettes he had bought at a Seven-Eleven on the way up. Pealing off the cellophane, he threw it into the night, then put one of the death sticks in his mouth and lit up.

Jesus, these things are bloody disgustin'!

He flicked the lit cigarette into the skip, tossed the packet in after it and waited while the fire caught.

When all three skips were smouldering, he jogged back the same route he had come, across the compound, through the fence, back up to the ridge. There he watched the orange glow develop. Before long a column of smoke was angling into the dark sky, dispersing white clouds into the heavens. Still no movement came from the guards' shack.

"Amateurs," O'Rourke said to himself.

The path of the fire spread just like he'd planned. The skips were a furnace, the flames licking up the side of the factory's north wall, caressing the bricks with their soft tongues and easing in through the windows. In the opposite direction, the flames wandered temptingly towards the trucks. Slowly and patiently it unfurled, like a brilliant piece of music, with the overture sitting nicely on the ears, promising more and building slowly to a devastating crescendo. "Come on, come on," O'Rourke whispered excitedly.

Now the flames were swirling underneath the first truck. A thing of rare beauty was unfolding. It was if he could choreograph the countdown.

Three.

Finally movement came from the guards' hut.

Two.

The door opened. One of the old buggers was out, scratching his head and shouting.

One.

Cries turned to panic, as the flames hit the truck's petrol tank.

O'Rourke smiled.

Boom!

CHAPTER THIRTEEN

Eva Chow stared in disbelief at the burned-out shell of her factory. Two generations of hard graft gone in a matter of hours.

A sodden ash stench hung like a blanket; smoke and steam layering the humid dawn sky. Three fire-engines were parked in triangle formation, jets of water hosing down the blackened brickwork like an afterthought. Firemen with charred faces swapped war stories.

The fire had started at the waste skips out the back, the police had told Eva. They shouldn't have been so close to the factory... just an accident waiting to happen. Eva seethed at the accusation. Those skips had been there for years, causing no alarm at the fire inspections Chow Mei underwent every quarter. She enforced a strict non-smoking policy throughout the premises and there had never been any hint of a problem. But what was the point of arguing now when her entire business lay in ruins?

Her father had bought the factory back in 1977 when he had found enough backers willing to give his idea a chance. Toilet paper. It wasn't glamorous, but it was necessary and therein he had found his niche. But the old vulture had never got over not having a son to inherit the business. Eva, his daughter, was his last resort. He had always hated the idea of handing her the reins, but he had had no choice and when, ten years ago, the time had come, he had continued to plague her from his sick bed, barking orders and belittling her for not living up to expectations which her sex made it impossible for her to fulfill. His grave lay half way up the hill overlooking the factory. Good Feng Shui, he had said when he had chosen the site, but Eva knew it was just his way of continuing to torture her even in death.

Deep down she hated that factory. Her entire life, it had been a millstone round her neck. The time she had spent trying to keep the place afloat when all she wanted was to be rid of it... but selling had never been a realistic option, the goodwill was minimal, the machinery only good for parts, the land of no interest to developers. Other manufacturers had long since transferred their businesses to the Mainland where labour was cheaper. Chow Mei couldn't compete with that. So instead it was death by a thousand cost cuts.

The fire should have been a blessing. Several times it had crossed Eva's mind to end it in this way herself, but maybe her father had been right? Maybe she did lack a man's courage to do the one act that would have saved her such heartache?

Eva hugged herself as the fatigue chilled her bones. She had nothing now. She had never married; her pig-like features had made that impossible. She lived alone and had never found comfort in her colleagues who resented the way Daddy's little girl had become their boss.

She cast a forlorn glance at the hillside where her father's remains were buried and wondered if he was happy, now that the fates had conspired to cause the one thing he was proud of in his life to burn to the ground, only forty-eight hours after the insurers had cancelled coverage. The old vulture had been wanting his daughter to screw up. *Well Bah-bah you finally have your wish.*

She drove the two-mile stretch back to the sales office where she had asked the admin staff to gather. When she walked through the door, twenty desperate faces greeted her. Eva felt their eyes, judging this to be her fault. She gave her instructions quickly and cruelly like her father would have done. Liquidators would be appointed, she didn't know when. They would decide who to keep and let go. The factory workers needed to be told not to come in until further notice.

"What about pay? They will want to know," one of them asked.

"They will be paid for the work they have done," Eva said matter-of-factly although she wasn't sure whether that was a promise she could make. "Okay, get on with it please." She walked into her office and closed the door.

If she had her time over again, she would have told her father to go to hell and pursued some other career outside his influence, rather than spending the best years of her life nursing the poisoned chalice bequeathed to her. She gripped the top of her nose between a thick forefinger and thumb. A migraine was working its way in through her sinuses. Bankruptcy was her only option now. Swapping one set of shackles for another.

Her eyes fell on the cancellation notice from AsiaRisk sitting at the top of her in-tray. A single piece of paper which had done more damage than the devouring flames. Usually they were lenient with late payment, but this time some over-eager bean-counter had stuck to the letter of the contract. No doubt he would get a promotion for saving AsiaRisk millions, while her staff lost the means to support their families. One person's stock rises; that of fifty others falls. Fate held a dispassionate cruelty.

A knock at the door.

Eva wasn't in the mood to see anybody, but she knew she had responsibilities. All her life, responsibilities. "Come in."

The door opened. It was a man. A man she didn't recognise. A mountain of a man with tree-trunk arms and snake tattoos poking down below his rolled shirt sleeves. It took a special effort to tear her gaze away from the tattoos. "Who are you?"

The man manoeuvred his great bulk into a seat, checking to see it was stable enough to hold him. His breathing was as heavy as a horse's and filled the room with sinister, steady huffing. "So you don't know who I am?" he said, when he was ready.

"No."

"Good." His smile revealed yellow teeth. "It's better that way."

"What do you mean?"

He chose not to hear the question, just looked round the office with distaste.

Eva hunkered into her chair. This man reminded her of her father, the way he elected to notice her only when it suited. "What do you want?"

The man knitted his thick fingers on top of his belly and glared. "I am sorry to hear about your factory, Ms Chow. I would like to help. Tell me, was your factory insured?"

The question stunned Eva. Instinctively her eyes flashed to the cancellation notice in the in-tray. The man followed her gaze. He reached across, read the letter for himself and sniffed pure contempt.

"I will help you," the man said. It was no longer an offer, Eva noted. "I will pay you five million dollars in cash as an investment in your factory. I will ensure the staff that you need are paid for the next month. In return, all you need do is pay me any money which your insurers pay to you after you have submitted your claim."

Eva wasn't quite sure if she had heard him right. "But the insurers have cancelled the policy."

"That is a risk which I am willing to take. Now do we have a deal?" He looked at her, waiting for an answer, but Eva didn't respond. "Your choice is simple, Ms Chow. You can accept my offer and walk away from this disaster with five million dollars. Or you can walk away with nothing."

The migraine throbbed to the front of Eva's skull. "I...I need to think."

"No you don't!"

Heavy breathing filled the room.

Eva blinked, trying to make sense of the last three hours. Then the realization of what this man was hit her. A bloodsucker, a man preying on people's misery to obtain what he wanted. A criminal. But he was also a man who, right then, was offering her five million dollars for something worthless. It wasn't redemption. But neither was it to be ignored.

"I agree," she said. The two words tasted rotten.

The man showed his yellow-toothed smile. "You will have the money today," he said and got up to go, like a large walrus awakened from its hibernating slumber. Then he turned back to Eva. "One last thing, Ms Chow."

This was it, Eva thought. The moment when the joke was revealed, when her stupidity would be laid bare for the world to enjoy.

"You are to tell nobody about this. Nobody, do you understand?" His voice was laced with menace.

Eva nodded. As the door shut, guilt rocked through her like a thunderstorm. Guilt that told her that she had just made a deal with the devil.

CHAPTER FOURTEEN

Sunlight knifed through the curtains into his skull. Scott groaned with pain, flopped an arm over his eyes to block out the unforgiving rays and let the first question of the day filter through.

What the hell had happened?

He'd got drunk again, that's what. The whole weekend, in fact. Numbing his senses on Friday night in Lan Kwai Fong, then hitting the Wanchai bars on Saturday, ending up in a twenty-four-hour joint called The Castle which pumped out dance music and shuttered the windows to mask the passage of time. Ten o'clock Sunday morning, Scott had staggered into daylight feeling like a sports sock at the end of a marathon, headed home via MacDonalds and crawled slug-like into bed. Now it was Monday morning and time for work – only not for him. He'd been suspended without pay. His whole life was one damn mess. Again.

Coiling his tongue in his mouth, Scott scraped off a gluey membrane of dehydration. The arid taste forced him awake and to his feet. Around his cramped flat, unwashed clothes draped off the back of cheap, expendable furniture. The air was tepid and stale.

His eyes rested on two picture-frames leaning on the wall. One held a gushing letter of thanks from a former client – an engineer whom Scott had successfully defended in a law suit – the win saving the engineer's future and the livelihoods of his staff. The second frame held a photograph of Scott's parents. There was dad, silver haired, broad shouldered, craggy faced, the very image of the strong patriarch. Next to him Scott's mother looked wan and frail by comparison, the illness having taken hold of her by then, although none of them had known it.

Funny how a picture could get reality so wrong. The only thing Scott had inherited from his father was a weakness for alcohol. His mother had given him ambition, drive and a desire to fight everything in his path. The opposing parental traits had combined together in him to produce a self-destructive cocktail.

Scott missed his mum. Ten years she'd been gone and not a day went by when he didn't ponder what she'd think of how his life had turned out. Right now, she'd probably be ripping pieces off him. 'You've no right to feel sorry for yourself, something like this happens you just pick yourself up, keep on going, keep fighting'. He could almost hear the staccato rhythm of her Hong Kong accent, sparking like gun-fire from beyond the grave.

He needed coffee. Staggering through to the kitchen, he put on the kettle, then searched out his mobile phone. Four missed calls and an unopened text, all from Philip Yip. The text read simply: "U okay?"

Last night, Yip playing friend again would probably have flipped his rage switch; so Scott was glad he hadn't picked up the text till now. Phil wasn't to blame for this. This wound was purely self-inflicted.

And Scott knew what he had to do to sort things out.

Pitching to Leopold Chan had been the wrong move, at the wrong time, for the wrong reasons. What the hell had he been thinking? Pure selfishness had made him link his desire to take down Charles Conrad with advancing his own partnership ambitions at Yip & Siu.

But this should never have been about Scott Lee. This was about Kimmie Yang.

Scott had already been stupid enough to put his career ahead of going after her and building a relationship that could have been the finest achievement in his life. Now Kimmie was gone; her death visiting tragedy on her family. Being alive was her parents' torture now, Sally Yang had told him. A living hell of guilt and regret.

Scott felt something twist inside him at the thought, but instead of unleashing anger, a strange state of grace descended. He had his mission now. And, with his suspension from Yip & Siu, he had time to complete it. This time for the right reasons. This time, for Kimmie.

He made coffee and drank a cup, let the caffeine work into his blood-stream. The plan he'd hit on in the small hours, when the chink of sobriety had finally broken through mist, came back to him right then. But before Scott got started on the plan, there was one phone-call he felt he had to make. He found the number and dialed.

"Hello?"

That voice. That one word twisted regret deep through Scott's gut. *Kimmie*. Only it wasn't.

"Sally, it's Scott Lee."

Two beats of silence.

"Mr Lee ... are you okay? ...You sound like you are ill."

Scott realized his throat was still thick with dehydration. The coffee hadn't helped on that score. He pulled the phone away and coughed into his fist.

"Sally, don't worry about me, I'm doing just fine. Are you at work?"

"I am, yes."

He could picture her in his mind, sitting over one of those sloping design work-boards. In looks Sally was very different to Kimmie, but Scott had seen the familiarity. The way Sally had tucked the curl of black hair behind her ear. The headstrong manner in which she had come to see him out of the blue to obtain his help, taking him to Kimmie's apartment to make sure her request had its full impact. Her round eyes, etched with the experience of someone much older.

"Mr Lee?" she said after the pause had become too awkward. "Are you sure you are okay?"

The prompt snapped Scott to the point. He took a breath and said what he had to say. "Listen Sally, I'm phoning because I felt I had to tell you something," he said. "Kimmie was very special to me. In the last few days, since you told me what happened to her, it's hit me how special she was. You said the other day that you trusted me to do what you weren't able to do. I'm not sure what that is yet." He swallowed hard. "But I promise you that I'm going to find out and do it, whatever it is. Because this should never have happened to Kimmie. She had too much to live for."

He heard the sound of her breathing go shallow. Then the hitching sobs started.

"Thank you, Mr Lee," her voice quivered, "thank you."

Scott stayed on the line for a while and rang off only when the moment felt right. Afterwards, he spent ten minutes gathering himself together, rolling his shoulders out, then hitting the floor for press-ups to get the blood pumping.

He still felt like hell, but now he was ready to begin.

He phoned Yip.

"Where the hell have you been?" Yip snapped it up on the first ring.

"That's you being concerned, right?"

"I've been trying to get hold of you all weekend!"

"So here I am...at home by the way, not some seedy strip club or the police station or the hospital, so stop wetting yourself." A beat went by. "I need a favour, Phil."

"What?"

Scott told him what he wanted. When Yip asked why, Scott said it was best he didn't know. They went back and forth for a bit; so Scott sprung a guilt trip on the back of the suspension Yip had fed him. Yip backed down after that, but not without a parting shot. "Just make sure you stay out of trouble. – If that's possible."

Scott hung up. Part one was complete. Part two needed another phone- call. Staying out of trouble hadn't done him much good so far. It was time for a step into the unknown. He composed himself, then dialled his mobile.

Someone answered, "Jackson, Weiss, Macdonald."

Scott pretended he was smiling; then made his play.

Carmella Lo was six foot tall, single, the wrong side of thirty and – if that wasn't a tough-enough hand for a Hong Kong girl to be dealt – she had the fashion sense of a marine corp sergeant. Her hair was done up in a functional clasp, she wore practical shoes and was one of the few people for whom contact-lenses weren't an improvement. But what Scott liked the most about Carmella was that she didn't give a damn.

Scott spotted her outside the Pacific Coffee shop on the Sanlitan walkway where they'd arranged to meet, puffing a Marlboro Light.

"Hey, Carmella!"

She turned. One arm crossed her stomach, hand cupping the opposite elbow. Quizzical eyes moved from Scott's face to his feet to his face again. "Hey," she said flatly.

He hadn't been expecting hard-to-contain enthusiasm, but something more seemed somehow appropriate. They hadn't seen each other in three years.

"You want coffee?" he asked.

"Sure."

Scott went in, placed the orders, picked them up at the end of the bar. Since his phone-calls that morning he'd been busy. A four-mile run. A penitential routine of more push-ups, pull-ups, sit-ups and stretches. The exercise had sweated out the toxins and cleared his mind. He felt sharp and with it. The coffee was a bonus. The coffee-shop bar was quiet but he was catching Carmella in a smoke-break, so he took the coffees outside and suggested they walk and talk.

They started to wander, sipping occasionally, pretending to enjoy the view over Wanchai Pier where ferries were loading up. Straggling passengers shouted and broke into a run before the gates closed.

Scott wondered how to play this. Carmella would know something was up, he figured. Eight years ago when he'd joined Jackson's Hong Kong office, she was the court clerk, working her law degree part-time at the City University. Court clerks were the life-blood of any law firm. A lawyer could prepare the best case in the world, but if it got listed at the wrong time in front of the wrong judge, it didn't stand a chance. That's where the court clerk came in. Every day Carmella would go to court, talk to the officers, get a feel for the lists, where the gaps lay; and through charm or downright manipulation, she would squeeze a case in front of whichever judge a lawyer wanted. The experience was to serve her well in her next role, which opened up only because Scott and Kimmie had pushed Charles Conrad into it. Carmella Lo had become Jackson's newest trainee solicitor. That was just before Scott had left the firm, three years ago.

Now here he was phoning her out of the blue. Yeah, Carmella would know he wanted something, and the only questions on her mind right now would be whether it was something she could give, and what she would get in return. Once a court clerk, always a court clerk.

"You must be qualified now?" he decided to lead with.

"Got admitted six months ago."

"Congratulations."

"Thanks."

"So, let's see the new business card."

She took one out of her breast pocket, handed it over. He made a show of being impressed.

"How's it all going?"

Carmella shrugged. "It's challenging." The way she said it suggested the words 'but not in a good way' should have followed close behind.

They reached a part of the walkway overlooking Gloucester Road, one of the busiest arteries dissecting Wanchai and joining it to Admiralty and Causeway Bay on opposite sides. The mid-afternoon sun trapped the pollution, which was quite low that day.

"I heard about Kimmie," Scott said. Carmella nodded, took a slug of coffee. "Her sister, Sally, came to see me...you ever meet Sally?"

"No."

"Nice girl. She told me Kimmie had been putting in some big hours just before it happened. That true?"

Carmella stiffened. "Not more than usual. But the usual was already a lot."

The answer gave Scott something to run with. "I guess you're having to do it all now. I mean you're the only one left, that Charles can dump the work on. Someone in her first six months of qualification. Seems unfair, if you ask me."

Carmella Lo walked over to a bin and stabbed her cigarette in the ashtray on top. "What do you want, Scott?"

"I need a favour, Carmella. A big one."

She said nothing, kept her gaze steady, her face giving nothing away.

"Sally Yang asked me to check out a few things about Kimmie on behalf of her parents," Scott continued.

"Like what?"

"They're looking for some answers, that's all. Reasons why Kimmie did what she did, so they can try to get past it." It wasn't strictly true, but as lies went it felt comfortable enough.

Carmella cupped her elbow. "And you think I can help?"

Scott nodded. "I need to get into Jackson's offices and look through some of Kimmie's old files. I'll be in and out in an hour and I won't take anything other than a few photocopies. No one needs to know."

She let out a short breath. "No way! If Conrad found out, I'd be fired. Struck off too! You know how hard I've worked for this? I have debts. I have my parents to support."

Scott tented his cheek with his tongue. "It's been a long road for you, I know. But remember the part Kimmie and I played in you getting there. We fought your corner when Conrad wasn't too interested...."

"And that earns you a lunch, not assistance breaking and entering!"

A man walked by talking on his mobile phone. He threw a glance in their direction when Carmella raised her voice. Scott gave it a moment then tried a different tack.

"You like working for Conrad?"

"I need the job."

"That's not what I asked."

She took out another cigarette, lit it, sucked it, turned her face away to blow smoke. "Scott, my parents are retired and my brother couldn't hold down a job if his life depended on it. I'm our only income. I need the job!"

"You could always find another one."

"Not a lot of demand for six-month qualifieds out there."

"So you've been looking then?"

She looked disappointed letting that slip. "I keep an eye out. Who doesn't?"

"But like you said, with only six months qualification, your CV isn't going to make it past the HR department. So you're stuck with Conrad for at least another – what – two years?"

"I need the job," she said again.

"Of course – and I'm just thinking outloud here – if you could just get an interview I bet you'll blow their socks off. Your court-clerking experience alone means you're already the equivalent of two years qualified, and they only have to pay you newly-qualified rates. All you need is the chance. Otherwise, it's two more years of working for Charles Conrad."

She gave him a sideways glance, her eyes forming slits as she blew smoke away from Scott's direction. "What's your point?"

A minute passed. Traffic sounds wafted up from Gloucester Road. Somewhere out in the harbour a claxon sounded.

"Yip & Siu want to interview you," Scott said.

Interest sparked in her eyes before she caught herself and clicked them back to stone.

"When?" Her voice was laced with suspicion.

Scott liked that she wasn't taken in by vacant promises. He had his mobile out and up to his ear. "Hey," he said into the mouth piece. "She's right here. Wants to arrange a time to come in and meet." He held out the phone for her.

Carmella looked at it like it was a murder weapon he wanted her fingerprints on. After a moment's calculation she took it and said her name into the mouthpiece. Scott stepped away and let Philip Yip take it from there. He looked at Carmella's face. Yeah, this was the senior partner, not some HR minion giving her the brush off.

She hung up the phone when she was done and said nothing, letting her mind debate pros and cons, risks and benefits. She handed Scott his phone back. "Charles leaves work round six o'clock," she said. "As soon as he's gone the secretaries clear out. I'm always the only one left for the evening. I go down for a smoke and something to eat at eight." She wet her lips with her tongue. "That's when you go in. Tonight. I want it over with."

He had nothing else planned. "What about the door?" he asked.

"If you forget to pull it properly shut, the lock doesn't click. Guess I'll be forgetful tonight."

Problem solved.

"I'll be back at nine," she said. "You be out by then, okay?"

Without another word, Carmella Lo turned and walked away.

Scott realized he was smiling. Day one of his new found unemployment was proving busier than expected.

CHAPTER FIFTEEN

Scott checked his mail-box.

A pizza flyer, a skin-care advert and an electricity bill. Whoopdee damn doo!

Someone on the twenty-fifth floor was holding the lift, so Scott killed time by practicing his Cantonese on Kinson, the old security-guard on duty.

"You eaten yet, Kinson?"

"Yes. Congee. You ever eaten congee before, Mr Lee?"

"Of course, I've lived in Hong Kong for a long time-la."

Kinson let out a chuckle. "Mr Lee, I forget you are a Hong Kong person now."

Kinson couldn't have been a day under sixty. He carried an arthritic stoop and looked as robust as a piece of plasticine in a furnace. But he was a good guy to banter in Cantonese with, especially when it came to his favourite topic.

"Did Man-U win on Saturday?" Scott asked.

"Of course-la. Against Wigan. Three-one."

"And West Ham?"

"Ah useless! Can only draw two-two with Fulham. Going down this year, I think."

"You're talking rubbish Kinson. Typical Man-U fan."

"Come to me in May and see who talks rubbish!"

Premiership football: the one enduring legacy of British colonialism which had permeated through to the grass roots. Kinson probably couldn't put a name to the British prime minister, but ask him to list out Manchester United's squad and he'd turn into a walking Encyclopedia. Politicians would probably bemoan it as a chronic example of Britain's declining role on the world stage. But Scott wasn't sentimental. So long as he could catch a West Ham game on the odd Saturday night, what did he care?

The lift eventually arrived. Scott rode it up to his flat on the seventeenth floor.

It was six o'clock. He had two hours to prepare.

His first dilemma was what to wear. Black combat trousers, polo-neck and balaclava was Hollywood's take on a burglar's uniform, but it wasn't appropriate for what Scott had in mind. He was walking into Jackson's through the front door, not abseiling through the air-conditioning vents. So, like any other day of the week, he went for the first suit and tie out of the closet, with briefcase and fountain-pen accessories.

After dressing, he checked himself in the mirror. Something was amiss. He was too pressed, too first-thing-in-the-morning. He loosened his top button and ruffled his hair. That was more like it. Just any exhausted businessman irritated by another late night at the office.

At seven, he set off, took a taxi down to Time Square in Causeway Bay. Ten minutes of walking got him to the MTR subway. Two stops later, he was in Wanchai's business district, riding the esclator back to the surface.

Outside, the city had transformed into neon and black. Scott walked against the strong tide of commuters heading home, several times getting battered by handbags and off-the-shoulder ruck-sacks in a way that anywhere else in the world would have led to a face-off and fists. In the hustle of Hong Kong, however, accidental assault had to be tolerated as part of life. Personal space meant nothing here. Everyone was used to living constantly on the simmer.

Glancing up, Scott saw the colossal Central Plaza lit up like a three-sided light saber. The building had numerous entry points, most of them from interconnecting walkways that shot out from its first-floor podium, like legs from an octopus. Scott chose a walkway in from the harbour side and pretended to window-shop till it was three minutes to eight. Then he headed over. The Central Plaza lobby was a split-level marble extravaganza, about the size of two football pitches in width, and one in height. Two long escalators connected the ground-level taxi-stand to level one and then level one to the mezzanine. Level one, where Scott was standing, housed two fake palm trees – why, he didn't know – and a gold-plated mirrored mural monstrosity which was equally baffling. Think tastelessness squared. In a city where space was at a premium, this was a colossal waste of it.

Scott waited until he saw two men and a woman, all in business suits and looking like they belonged, coming up the escalator from the taxi level. As soon as they hit level one, Scott fell in step behind them, staying close on the escalator up to the mezzanine. As they stepped off the top he asked the lady in front for the time. She told him what he already knew, that it had just gone eight o'clock, but to the receptionist it looked like he was part of a group of four colleagues, deep in discussion, heading back to the office.

After that, it was simple. An ear-popping lift-ride to the change-over lobby on the forty-sixth floor, then a second lift up sixteen more floors. By the time the doors opened on sixty-two, Scott's nerves were wound tight, his heart going like horses' hooves against his rib-cage. He stepped out into the quiet and took the familiar right-turn down the corridor.

There it was: the sign announcing Jackson, Weiss & Macdonald's, Hong Kong branch. Sweat beads pulsed through his skin. He ran a finger round his hot collar and took a moment. This was it. He was about to cross a line he thought he never would. Dirty his hands in a way that would never make them truly clean again.

Inside the glass door, lights were on. He rang the bell and readied his lame cover story of 'just being in the building and thought he'd pop by to say hello to some old friends' if anyone came. No one did. He gave the door a nudge. It jarred open, just like Carmella had promised.

He looked down at the threshold which at that moment marked the line between legal and illegal. Once over, there was no going back.

"For Kimmie", he told himself.

It was 8.10pm.

Charles Conrad paid the taxi driver, watched him pull away. Then worked up the courage to walk through his own front door.

Jackson's had rented him the generously-proportioned two thousand square foot house on Bowen road, a peaceful pedestrian pathway that snaked the edge of Hong Kong Island's rugged north face, in a district known as Mid Levels because it stood half way between the pinnacle of the Peak and the concrete jungle of Central District below. Most Hong Kongers would never know this kind of luxury.

But for Cathy it wasn't enough, nothing Charles ever did was, and every night she would find a way of letting him know it. Sometimes she'd scream for no reason. Other times it was a subtle manipulative guilt trip. Always, Charles Conrad would head to bed feeling less of a man.

His key in the lock triggered the sound of gruff barking and tiny claws rattling across a wooden floor. When the door opened, a West Highland terrier sped towards Charles offering the kind of unqualified welcome only a dog can provide.

"Hello, Flo!" Charles scratched her ears. "What mood's she in then?"

Flo stuck her tail in the air and scurried off.

"That bad, huh?" Charles threw his jacket over the chrome banister and was just about to go through to the living room when Cathy's shrieking voice pierced his ear-drums.

"How many times have I bloody told you not to wash this blouse in the machine! You've ruined it, you stupid girl!"

"Is okay, Mrs Conrad. Can wash by machine!"

"Don't argue with me!" Cathy roared.

Another fight between Cathy and Maria, the maid, Charles gathered. He considered letting them duke it out on their own, but Maria had been with them only three months, two months longer than the last one. He didn't want the hassle of re-hiring again, so went to intervene. "Hi, I'm home!" He called out, keeping it light and social.

Cathy gave wild-eyes, her bottle blonde hair tied up so it looked like her head was on fire. "This little bitch has ruined another blouse! Take it out of her wages!"

"Is okay!" Maria pleaded. Next to his wife she looked tiny and half Cathy's age, even though he knew there were only a few years between them.

"Look, why don't we just have a drink and calm down…"

"That's your answer to everything isn't it!" Cathy shrieked. "Don't you realize what it's like for me out here?" She ran out of the room. Heavy footsteps clattered on the stairs. A door slammed.

Charles sighed. She would be on the phone to her mum in Milton Keynes for the rest of the night now, telling her how terribly he treated her. He rubbed the pressure out of of his eyes.

"I not do anything wrong, Mr Conrad. I promise," Maria said.

"I know you didn't, Maria. But just try to do what she says in future."

Maria nodded. As she bent down to pick up the offending blouse, Charles couldn't help but admire her supple tight figure. He hadn't given into temptation yet, although heaven knew why not. Cathy hadn't let him anywhere near her in months, lying in bed with her face mask on and reading *Hello Magazine!* until he was asleep.

They were into their second decade of marriage. It was a miracle it had lasted this long. Back when they had met, he had been the fat, freckly senior associate looking to break into the Jackson's partnership. Cathy had recently divorced her childhood sweet heart, a mechanic called Derek who had given her everything his meagre income could buy. But that hadn't been enough for Cathy. She wanted more; and in good old comfortable Charles, she thought she had found her meal-ticket. A woman like Cathy – blonde, big-chested, mischievous glinting eyes – had always been out of Charles's league and he should have known better. They met at a party two weeks after her divorce and she had screwed him that night, screamed her head off authentically enough for Charles to believe he was in love. But the love had lasted as long as the wedding ceremony, before declining into a mutual companionship which Charles thought he could have lived with.

But his partnership at Jackson's changed everything. Cathy loved the money, sure, but not the attached strings it came with. Charles got posted to Hong Kong and after the move she had turned into the bitch from hell. She wouldn't divorce him though, that wasn't Cathy's style. She needed someone to feed off, not just materially but emotionally. So Charles knew he was stuck with her, because with her breasts heading south and her looks giving way to an unattractive hardness day-by-day, the chances of her finding someone else to leach off were becoming thin.

Maria continued to wander about the kitchen in her tight yellow T-shirt and knee-length jeans. Such a simple outfit but one which, Charles thought, made her look oh-so delectable.

The sound of his mobile snapped him out of it.

"Hello."

"Charles, it's Leopold."

Charles felt his stomach lurch. What the hell did he want? "Leopold, how are you?"

"I have an urgent instruction for you. There's been a factory fire out near Shatin. It's one of AsiaRisk's insureds so there's a big claim headed my way. It's got settlement written all over it, so I want you to get moving on the documentation. We can fill in the figures once it's all sorted out."

Charles checked his watch. It was eight-thirty. Half past midday in London. "I'll have to send round a conflict check."

"I know that!" Leopold hectored him. "That's why I'm ringing you now. Send the conflict check round tonight. Your London office can consider it overnight and you can let me know first thing in the morning."

Charles shut his eyes. "Shouldn't be a problem."

"Good. Speak tomorrow." The phone clicked off.

Charles's mood darkened. God, how he hated being beholden to that slanty-eyed bastard. He let the anger pass. Playing the game had always been his way and this was just another part of the dance.

"Maria have you seen my Blackberry?"

The maid looked up at him. "You lose it in taxi yesterday, Mr Conrad?"

"Damn, I forgot." He was always doing that. He hated technology, despised his job and detested Leopold Chan most of all. But he reminded himself that five more years was all he needed at Jackson's, then he'd be free. Five more years. Right then, with Cathy upstairs screaming to her mother and Leopold Chan crunching his balls, it seemed like an eternity.

"I've got to go back to the office," he said to Maria.

"You want me to tell Mrs Conrad."

Charles shook his head as he picked up his keys.

Cathy wouldn't give a damn where he was.

CHAPTER SIXTEEN

It was just like Scott remembered. Jackson's name was spelled out on the wall amateurishly in shiny metallic lettering, as if stuck on while the first clients were waiting outside. Beside the sign was a windowless conference room. This made up the public part of the office, which clients were supposed to see. Scott hurried through to the functional guts: a grey partitioned open-plan area with three secretarial booths and a photocopier. Fee-earner offices were dispersed around it, Charles Conrad's the colossal ego-stroking room at the end, Carmella Lo's the hutch on the left.

The room Scott wanted – the reason he was making his breaking-and-entering debut that evening – was off to the right. In the six months since her suicide, Kimmie Yang's room had been transformed into storage space. The metamorphosis seemed somehow disrespectful. Scott shoved the thought aside. The clock was ticking. Carmella had given him till nine pm.

He opened the door and went in.

Dust and polish assaulted his senses. He flicked a switch and doused the place in depressing fluorescence. Blinds covered the windows, their metal slats turned vertical. The desk stood empty. This was a pale shadow of the place Kimmie had made her own. No sign of the holiday paraphernalia and the stuffed toys she used to have all over the place, the Mcdull pigs, the mouthless Hello Kittys, a pink-tongued Goofy.

"Don't those things get in the way?" he'd once asked her.

"No," Kimmie had pouted, picking up Goofy and doing her best doofus voice. "It's not me who's in the way, it's that rubbish." Goofy's hand had pointed at her in-tray.

The wall-cabinets to the left still burgeoned with lever arch files. Scott went over and ran a hand down their spines. Each file was labeled with case name, number and client, a familiar referencing system he hadn't thought of in an age.

Scott flopped a random file open and went to work. It was full of correspondence from *Hanel v Barista Coffee (HK) Ltd.*, a late delivery of goods dispute, the documents arranged chronologically back to front, conforming to Jackson's colour-code: white for letters, faxes and emails, pink for telephone attendance notes, yellow for copy-invoices. Scott measured out a half-inch section of paper falling between two invoices. Flagging the invoices with post-its from his brief case, he took out his fountain-pen to make notes.

The pen made Scott pause. It was his leaving gift from Jackson's. He still used it. His fingers felt the initials 'SL' engraved on the black barrel. The gold highlighting had faded, but it was still visible on careful inspection.

He shifted his focus back to the file. The documentation between the two invoices he had flagged represented the work-product billed by Jackson's in their November invoice last year. Scott paged through it, paying attention to the copy advice letters and author references. The letters were concise, the advice robust, persuasive and impressive. The pink telephone attendance notes were detailed too, meticulously kept and justifying every minute of time billed. Each document was coded 'KY', meaning that Kimmie Yang was the author. Kimmie and Kimmie alone.

But the November invoice itself revealed the existence of a parallel universe, one where all this work had been done in tandem with Charles Conrad. Not a speck of his presence was evident in the file, not a peep. But still Conrad had racked up thirteen hours and twelve minutes in the month. Pure bullshit, just like Conrad's outrageously unspecific time entries on the bill. *"Internal discussions with KW – 24 mins"* one read, *"Giving input to KW – 12 mins"* was another. Kimmie's entries for the same days were, by contrast, detailed and tellingly held no mention of her receiving any input from Conrad. So one of them was lying and it didn't take a genius to work out who it was.

Scott paused a moment. He had chosen a single random file. One random file from a cabinet-full and here was evidence of how Charles Conrad was screwing Jackson's clients by charging fees for work he'd never done. The guy was a lawyer joke without a punch-line and for too long he'd been getting away with it. Well, not any more.

Scott's plan was simple. A Law Society complaint had led to his own suspension from Yip & Siu. Now it was time to turn the tables by sending evidence of Conrad's outrageous billing habits anonymously to the Law Society and letting the formal investigation process take its course. But the Law Society was just the start. Once word reached London, Jackson's risk management would be out to Hong Kong like a bullet from a gun and that's when the fun would really start. The full rubber-glove treatment they'd give Conrad, every breach in the last ten years dredged up, documented and reported back. At worst, a truck load of aggravation was headed Conrad's way. At best he'd be retrenched to London and shown the door within twelve months.

Bolstered by his initial success, Scott took down another file from the shelf. The same pattern quickly emerged: Kimmie doing all the work; Conrad inflating the bills with his fictionalized input. The man was scum without a conscience.

Scott shuttled to and from the photocopier, collating the material he needed. Soon he was done for the night, his first illegal entry, a complete success.

Before closing the door on Kimmie's office, he allowed himself one last look round. The sadness moved through him like a cold mist. What had once been alive was now just an empty casing.

The thought stopped hard and fast when his eyes snagged on the letters scribbled in blue marker ink on one of the storage boxes piled high against the glass interior wall. Two letters: 'AR'. AR...as in AsiaRisk.

Scott glanced at his watch. 8.44 pm already. He'd be cutting it fine, but seeing the box right there... ten more minutes, he decided.

Shutting the door, he lifted the 'AR' box onto the desk and took off the lid. Inside, green manilla files were piled high. Green for accounting, according to the colour-code, which meant the files held copies of all the invoices dispatched and other expenses billed on a case. These were accounts files for Jackson's AsiaRisk cases. Conrad had always insisted on handling the AsiaRisk cases personally, his way of clinging onto his one major client, Scott guessed, by making sure no other fee-earner got a look-in.

Scott leafed through the top file and soon felt a mixture of satisfaction and outrage thunder through him. Here was proof of everything he had told Leopold Chan. Insurance cases like this were simple stuff. A policyholder makes a claim, AsiaRisk declines to pay, citing some technical breach of the policy, the policyholder appoints a solicitor to sue, some back and forth negotiation follows, then the matter settles out without getting near a court. All Conrad had to do was document the terms of settlement for AsiaRisk – effectively, fill in the numbers on a precedent. But the simple nature of the work seemed to be ignored when it came to the fees Conrad had charged. AsiaRisk was paying for Conrad to research areas of law a first year law student should have known, along with reams of unnecessary amendments. Conrad had also classed each case as "urgent", and charged a fifteen percent uplift. Money for nothing, quite literally.

Scott photocopied the whole file and did the same with the next one out of the box, which repeated the pattern. The next four files, he didn't need to bother with. But the last file made Scott pause. At two inches thick, it contained far more than the others.

Scott looked at the spine. "Uramay Limited", it read. He opened it on the desk. First up was a copy invoice. Made-up Conrad time-entries leapt off the page with another fifteen percent uplift – nothing unusual in Charles Conrad's world.

The next page, however, severed the pattern. It was a copy of an email Kimmie had sent to Conrad. Scott read it carefully:

To: Charles Conrad
Sender: Kimmie Yang
Re Uramay Limited

Charles, after you left last night, I took a call from Trevor Long from accounts in London regarding the captioned case. The cheque requisition form you sent him for a HK$400,000 payment to AsiaRisk had the wrong reference. I found the right reference in the accounts file, but I wanted to raise another issue before I revert to Trevor.

The HK$400,000 represents a refund of what is left of a HK$500,000 payment AsiaRisk made to us on account of fees. Since we have only billed AsiaRisk HK$100,000 on this matter, the overpayment of HK$400,000 needs to be returned.

According to our Anti-Money-laundering Guidelines, an overpayment of this size qualifies as a Suspicious Transaction

(STR) and should be reported to the firm's Money-laundering Officer (MLRO). Would you like me to report it?
  Happy to discuss. Kimmie

Scott pinched the sides of his mouth. Kimmie was right. A transaction like this needed to be reported to Jackson's MLRO. Client overpayments were a classic laundry mechanism; every solicitor who had been on the compulsory training course would have known that. Judging from his reply a few pages on, Charles Conrad must have slept through it.

Kimmie, AsiaRisk is a well-known client, so there's no need to follow the guidelines in this case. Thanks for your assistance, but in future any query on AsiaRisk should be referred directly to me first. Cheers. Charles.

Typical Conrad. Arrogant, patronizing, plain wrong. Scott flagged the emails and wrote exclamation marks with his fountain-pen on the post-its. This was pure dynamite. If Jackson's risk management got wind of Conrad blatantly ignoring money-laundering protocols, they would ...
  The thought was cut dead at the sound of the main office door opening.
  Footsteps approached. Scott froze statue-still.
  A gruff male voice echoed through the silence.
  Charles Conrad. He was in the office.

"Carmella?...Carmella!" Conrad grunted at the lack of response. The lights were on, which meant she was still around. Typical of the Chinese, they seemed to live for work. "Carmella?" He went into her room. Her computer was on, the screen-saver waving across her monitor.
  Probably buggered off for a smoke, Charles figured. Her absence grated. If he was going to be here at this time of night, he wanted someone to witness it. Tramping moodily into his own office, Charles logged onto his computer, waited an age for Lotus Notes to boot up. At the top of his in-box were two jokes from his mate in Dubai. Conrad chuckled lasciviously before forwarding them on. Then he turned his attention to the reason he was there.

Pulling up a new message, he tapped the key-board with opposing forefingers. Fifteen minutes later he had sketched the conflict-check email. He made sure he'd got all the relevant details down... fire at the Chow Mei factory ... potential claim against AsiaRisk under Chow Mei's insurance policy... any conflicts to him by close of business London time. There wouldn't be any conflicts, of course, there never were. AsiaRisk had no connections in Europe and there was no way a toilet paper factory in the New Territories could cut across the lines of any cases Jackson's were currently working on worldwide. This was an exercise in pointlessness really, but at least it afforded an opportunity to remind the rest of the partnership of his existence.

Charles decided to spice in a few more details to make it look like he was rainmaking work in from the Far East. When he was done, he read it through again, making sure there were no typos, changing some words to ones he was a hundred percent sure he could spell. This was going to 'Jackson's-All' so he wanted to avoid looking like an idiot. He pressed 'send'. The electronic envelope swirled across his screen into hyperspace. 'Out of office' replies came flooding in. Ignoring them, Charles printed out his email to put on his secretary's desk. Hopefully she'd notice the time he'd sent it. If she didn't he would point it out to her tomorrow. Here he was beyond office hours, earning money to pay her wages. He printed a second copy to give Carmella, show her what it meant to be a partner ....

Then he heard it. A loud ding of metal on metal.

What the bloody hell was that?

"Carmella?" Charles called out. The printer behind him whirred and spat out the two conflict-check copies. "Carmella!"

No response.

Picking up the print-outs, he went out into the open-plan area. Nothing stirred. Carmella's office was still empty. *So where the hell had the noise come from?* He hadn't imagined it, he was sure. Come to think of it, it hadn't come from Carmella's office at all. It sounded more like....

Charles' eyes came to rest on Kimmie Yang's room. The idea of the dead girl's office giving off nocturnal sounds set his heart racing. Something appeared to be different. The boxes stacked up inside against the window wall. Had they been like that earlier in the day? Had someone moved them?

Come on Charles. Buck up man!
Only one way to find out.
Charles Conrad stepped over to the door and reached for the handle.

As the handle started to turn, Scott cursed his stupidity.

All he had to do was stay down, wait for Conrad to leave, but could he do that? Oh no! He had to go and push 'self-destruct' again. He couldn't help it, it was as if he had Tourrette's.

Face down on the floor, his heart pile-driving the walls of his chest, Scott had heard Conrad shouting for Carmella. But then Conrad had disappeared into his office, a move which had bought some time for Scott to think.

Staying put was Scott's first idea. Wait for Conrad to leave. Then he could make his own exit. But in the darkness with his cheek pressed to the floor and dust playing in his nostrils, his brain had set to work dredging up worst-case-scenarios and before long Scott had himself convinced that doing nothing was his worst option.

Rolling onto his back, he reached into his top pocket for his mobile phone and into his trouser pocket for his wallet. In the wallet he found Carmella Lo's business card. He typed her a text ...*Conrad here, come back now*.... He pressed 'send'. It allowed him some hope. Carmella was a sensible girl. She'd be moving quickly now, for her own sake as much as his. She'd find a way of talking Conrad out....

Then Scott saw it. Above him, stretching over the lip of the desk was the corner of the file he'd been looking through just before Conrad had made his inconvenient entrance. What was the name? Urumay, that was it.

His mind went into 'worst-case scenario challenge' mode again. The open file presented an eye-catching double spread of A4 just waiting to be spotted through the glass window wall. A file open on a desk in a room that was supposed to be in disuse. A dead give-away.

Which was when brilliant idea number two hit. Scott could hear the pedestrian tap of Conrad's key strokes and pictured his old boss, tongue poked through his lips at his computer.

Slowly Scott reached his arm up to the desk above. His fingers pincered the edge of the file. He slid it across the desk, being careful not to go too fast, pausing when he sensed its spine nearing the edge. Reaching his other arm up, he made a V with his fingers and thumb for the spine to fall into. Slowly does it now... he tugged... slowly... slowly... the spine came across. The file fell. Into his palm. Perfect. Phew!

He began to retract his arm like a crane transferring a load back to base, but as he did so the file rocked and tipped, something sliding off the top.

His fountain-pen.

Damn, he'd forgotten it!

Tipping the file back, he tried to equalize the balance, but the see-saw motion took its own course, jettisoning the pen off the bottom edge. The pen spun through the darkness, the gold top flashing as it caught the light. Scott moved a leg to try to cushion its fall in the material of his trousers, but being the idiot he was he caught it square on with his foot, kicking it hard just before it hit the floor. The pen torpedoed off his toe towards the metal cabinets. *Clang!*

Scott's heart stopped.

Cuddling the file to his chest, he prayed that Conrad hadn't heard it. The thin hope evaporated when he heard Conrad calling for Carmella again, his voice laced with suspicion. Footsteps came closer. Shadows of shoes appeared under the gap in the door.

Terror seized Scott, as the door handle started to turn.

CHAPTER SEVENTEEN

Kwan Tower jutted up from the heart of Central like a shaft of light, its one hundred and twenty floor structure a monument to the Hong Kong entrepreneurial spirit. Hideous, Leopold Chan thought as his car pulled up outside the ostentatious entrance. The two ear-popping lift journeys only served to heighten his distaste. This was self-aggrandisement brought to extremes, the type you get with third world dictators who build statues of themselves at every major intersection.

When the lift doors opened on floor one hundred and twenty Leopold was greeted by a woman who looked salon fresh even though it was past nine pm. She wore a practised smile and took delight in announcing herself as one of Mr Kwan's personal assistants.

One of his assistants....

"How many does he have?" Leopold asked.

"Four."

Leopold shook his head.

A Ghurka in khaki uniform and red beret ushered them through a glass door. The beige-carpeted corridor muffled the woman's heels. Photographs of Kwan Tower in all its glory adorned the walls on either side.

"Those were taken by members of staff." – Kwan's personal assistant had evidently mistaken Leopold's yucking under his breath for a display of interest. "Mr Kwan runs a competition which he judges himself. The winners are exhibited here."

"How gracious of Mr Kwan."

The sarcastic bite did enough to end any further attempt at conversation. Leopold was quickly deposited in a meeting room and informed that Cyrus Kwan would be along shortly.

It was a corner room and had a cosy feel to it. The leather arm-chairs, veneered side-tables and table lamps made it seem almost homely, yet the pervasive air of importance was unmistakable. Leopold imagined the mega negotiations that had taken place within these four walls. He wandered over to the head-to-ceiling windows and was stunned to see that he was level with the Peak Tower, an upside-down glass smile on struts that stood on the rugged mountain-top to the south of him, a must-see for any tourist. He then turned to the adjacent window and peered down through the candy-floss clouds below, searching out the chopstick masts on top of the angular Bank of China building next door. It was said that those masts brought bad Feng Shui as they resembled a pair of joss sticks on a tomb. Still, the trio of the Bank of China, Kwan Tower and the inside-out HSBC building, which Leopold couldn't see from here, had long defined the Hong Kong skyline.

There was a knock at the door.

Leopold readied himself and turned. Anti-climax thudded in his chest as Rupert Kwan crept into the room. Rupert's handsome face was etched with nerves, his handshake weak and sweaty.

"You'll be joining us, I take it?" Leopold asked.

"I know how to handle my uncle," Rupert said.

Leopold tried not to laugh.

Another knock. This time it was the man himself, Cyrus Kwan. The contrast with his nephew's lack of bearing could not have been more pronounced. The elder Kwan wore an open neck shirt, black slacks and tassled shoes and moved like a man who bore his huge responsibilities with ease and grace; his handshake was firm and confident, his smile welcoming and designed to put any recipient at ease.

"We met at the Cooperation in Services Agreement celebration only the other day, Leopold," the old tycoon said. "Please sit. I apologise for the late hour. There never seems to be enough time to fit it all in these days." Cyrus settled into an armchair to Leopold's right and signaled for Rupert to sit opposite. "So tell me. How's AsiaRisk doing? Busy, I expect. Probably gearing up for when the CSA comes into force?"

Leopold smiled. He realized this whole performance – the personal assistant, the plush room on the top floor, the personal knowledge of when they had met last – were all designed to convey a single message: that although this meeting had been set up by Rupert, it was Cyrus who was in charge.

Time to give things a little stir.

"Let's stop pretending shall we, Cyrus," Leopold said. "You know full well how things are going at AsiaRisk! In fact, there's

125

probably very little you don't know about *my* company, isn't that right?"

Cyrus Kwan flinched. He glanced over at his nephew, then back at Leopold.

"You've lost me." The response was delivered with a perfect mix of patronizing amusement, quizzical intrigue and threatening bite.

"What Leopold means is...." Rupert tried to intervene but Leopold let fly his next salvo.

"I know AsiaRisk was on Kwan Holding's shopping list last year. So why don't we forget this false bonhomie for the moment and clear the air?"

Cyrus Kwan sat up, his eyes narrowing defensively. It was just how Leopold wanted him; and now having made his point, he decided to swing things in a different direction, keep Kwan off-balance, soften him up. "Don't think I'm here to give you a hard time, Cyrus," he said. "I wish we could have had this discussion sooner. If Rupert hadn't told me about your interest in AsiaRisk, I would never have believed it."

Again, Cyrus Kwan's eyes shifted between the two men, fast trying to grasp what was going on.

Leopold gave him a bit more. "It's a shrewd boy you've got there, Cyrus. He knows his numbers and recognizes a good return on equity when he sees one. Which is exactly what AsiaRisk represents, by the way. That's why Rupert suggested we meet tonight. Cut straight to the chase and see if we can hammer out a deal face-to-face, he said. Isn't that right?" Leopold smiled broadly at the slack-jawed Rupert Kwan.

"Well I...." Rupert stammered, "I thought it might be sensible to get you two together...."

Silence bloomed. Cyrus Kwan's eyes continued to move from Leopold to Rupert searching for tells, waiting for them to fill the awkward quiet with further explanation. Leopold said nothing and was thankful that, for once, Rupert shut up. After a while it was Cyrus Kwan who was forced to to probe. "So let me see if I understand this. Rupert raised the issue of Kwan Holdings potentially acquiring AsiaRisk with you?"

"That's right. When we met at the CSA launch," Leopold said confidently.

"And....you're not hostile to the idea?"

"Hostile?" Leopold shrugged. "Why should I be? It's just the opportunity I've been looking for."

Kwan's eyebrow arched, nothing more than that, but the astonishment portrayed by that one facial tick told Leopold that he was in. "Look, Cyrus. AsiaRisk is my life's work, I won't deny that, so giving up control isn't an easy decision for me. Yet at my age I've got to get the right succession plan in place. I'm not going to go on forever and I have no children, so my options are limited. My current management team is very capable and any one of them could pick up where I leave off. But somehow that doesn't seem enough. I'd prefer to have someone in charge who is .... how do I put this," Leopold tapped his forefinger on his chin, "someone who is sufficiently experienced to take the company forward and fulfil its potential."

Standing up, Leopold turned to the windows. He thrust his hands in his pockets and rocked back on his heels, as if wallowing for one last time in his present glories before he allowed them to become part of his past. "I'm not a romantic man, Cyrus, but I like to think that the product of my career will last longer than I do. I know it may sound like wishful thinking, but I genuinely feel that if I passed the management on to someone internally, AsiaRisk would continue to be profitable, sure, but it wouldn't fulfil the potential that I see for the company. I look today at the position AsiaRisk finds itself in. We're at the forefront of opening up in China, we have several rep offices in the Mainland that are already making the right contacts. I want to pass the company onto someone who will be able to exploit that. With the right investment and the right drive, it is my view that AsiaRisk's Mainland business alone could start turning a decent profit in eighteen months. Five years on, the picture looks even better. At my age, though, I don't have the stomach, the energy or the time." Swivelling round, he looked Cyrus Kwan straight in the eye. "But if AsiaRisk is part of Kwan Holdings, then I have no doubt it would fulfil its potential. Especially with someone young and dynamic, like Rupert, at the helm."

Throughout this rehearsed speech, Leopold noted Cyrus Kwan's face remained fixed with intent. Behind the unflinching façade, though, Leopold could see the old man running sums, weighing pros with cons and, most of all, questioning why this gift had landed in his lap.

Leopold decided to nudge him a little. "I tell you, when Rupert told me about your interest, everything made sense. Selling to Kwan Holdings is an ideal succession plan as far as I'm concerned and I can't thank him enough for setting up this meeting. So here I am, Cyrus. One businessman talking to another, ready to make you an offer which I, as the owner, and MD of AsiaRisk have full authority to make."

A while passed. Then Cyrus Kwan, offering Leopold a tight smile, said, "Such frankness in this day and age is unusual. You will appreciate, however, that you....and Rupert.... have caught me off guard with this. It's true that Kwan Holdings has been looking to get into the insurance sector. But there's a world of difference between showing interest and being able to agree to buy your company. For one thing, I would want to assess your financial reports, market potential, projections and business plan. Fundamentals do have to be adhered to. Then, if it was something I felt I could recommend, I would have to take it to my board of directors. And of course, quite apart from that, an appropriate price would have to be negotiated."

Leopold tucked a hand into his pocket, drew out a folded bit of paper and held it out between two fingers. "I anticipated you might say that, Cyrus. I think you will find this price to be reasonable enough without having an army of analysts or investment bankers pour over it."

Cyrus Kwan unfolded the paper and read the figure. Shock and surprise sparkled in the old entrepreneur's eyes.

"Some may say this is a little on the light side," he said.

For someone like Cyrus Kwan, that was quite an admission.

"It's a fifty percent discount on book value," Rupert Kwan piped in with the information Leopold had fed him.

"I think the word that you are searching for Cyrus, is 'bargain'." Leopold sat back down and readied for the questions that were sure to follow.

"Forgive me for asking, but why are you doing this?" Although the question was put with trepidation, Leopold could tell that Cyrus Kwan was hooked. "You said yourself that AsiaRisk is the result of a life-time of work, Leopold. Yet here you are prepared to part with it so cheaply. As your intended purchaser, I am a little....how should I put it.... curious."

"I'm not selling you a pup, Cyrus, if that's what you're afraid of," Leopold said with a nonchalant wave of the hand. "And I don't expect you to take my word for it. I'm looking for an expeditious sale, yes, but I recognize the need for you and Rupert to do your due diligence and I offer you total transparency, provided we can keep up a good momentum. Sale processes can be unsettling for staff and customers, so the sooner we get it done, the better."

Cyrus placed the piece of paper down on the side-table to his right and smoothed it flat. "That is very reasonable of you, but again I ask the question: why at this price?"

Leopold let out a low sigh. "It's not about the money, Cyrus, you've probably guessed that. If it was, I would appoint an investment banker, open it up for tender and sell to the highest bidder. One of my competitors would probably end up with AsiaRisk. Then they would strip out the profitable portfolios and assets and shed the staff. For sure, I'd be richer than I am now. But everything I'd spent my life working for would have disappeared. I am proud of the AsiaRisk brand, one that promises personal service, with security for its customers. That's not something I want to see disappear. I'd like to think that, long after I'm out of the picture, AsiaRisk will continue to adhere to those same principles as it grows and develops. And I can see it doing just that as the new insurance arm of Kwan Holdings. That's why, if Kwan Holdings was to buy it, I'd be willing to take a significant discount on the price."

Not for the first time that evening, Leopold felt he had hit the right note.

Cyrus Kwan looked down at the price again and took care in folding up the piece of paper, as if it was a sign of respect. "You mentioned you wanted an expeditious sales process," he said. "Do you have a specific deadline in mind?"

"I've had other interest," Leopold said cautiously. "I can hold them off for the moment, but I think it would be sensible to get the deal completed before the CSA comes into force."

"That's next week?" Cyrus Kwan was taken aback, so Leopold turned up the heat.

"Well, I'm not sure how long the other potential buyers would be prepared to wait."

It did the trick. Cyrus Kwan nodded, got up and held out his hand.

"Give me a day to think about it. Then I'll get back to you with an answer. How does that sound?"

"Perfect," Leopold said. "Just perfect."

CHAPTER EIGHTEEN

This wasn't good.

Getting caught red-handed by Charles Conrad in the middle of a criminal foray was not supposed to have been on the agenda that evening, but as the door-handle continued its slow descent Scott felt there was a certain inevitability at play here. Bad karma, Yip would have called it, in that annoyingly calm demeanour of his.

Scott shook off the thought. This was definitely not the time for reminicences.

In an instant, Scott made his decision. He wasn't going to plead with Conrad; that wasn't how this disaster was going to end. He was going to let rip, release those pent up years of frustration through his fists. The worst that could happen was already happening, so what was the point of holding back now? As the door started to move inwards, Scott realized he was smiling. He was ready to take his punishment. Readier still to dish out some of his own, to spring to his feet, tuck his head and lead with his shoulder ....

"Charles, what are you doing here?"

The voice sliced through Scott's stream of consciousness. Was he imagining it? Was this just some sort of residual wishful thinking breaking through?

The door immediately pulled shut, the handle shooting back to its closed position.

"Bloody hell, you frightened the life out me!" Scott heard Conrad say.

"Sorry." It was Carmella Lo. "I didn't expect to see you here. I just went out for something to eat."

"Yes....well...." Conrad puffed, "Listen, in future when you're the last one here, you should really lock up and alarm the place when you go out for periods of, say, more than fifteen minutes."

Through the sweet elixir of relief, Scott rolled his eyes on Carmella's behalf.

"Yes, of course. Sorry about that," Carmella played the admonished assistant to perfection.

In the silence which followed, Scott sensed Conrad's hand still on the door handle. He held his breath.

"You must be busy?" Carmella said to Conrad, clearly playing for time. "To be in here at this time, I mean."

That was true enough. The presence of Charles Conrad in the office past six-thirty was as rare as a solar eclipse. Scott imagined Conrad bristling at the comment.

"I had to send a conflict check round on a new AsiaRisk case we've just been instructed on," Conrad's voice was full of self-congratulation. "Looks like it could be a biggie. Here, have a look. I was going to leave it on your desk. We can talk about it more tomorrow, I've got to get home now. Remember to lock up."

"I will," Carmella said. "'Night."

Scott breathed again as he heard the descending arpeggio of Conrad's computer shutting down and heavy footsteps receding into the distance. The front door to the main office opened and closed.

Silence.

"You can come out now!" Carmella called. Scott gave it a moment, before getting slowly to his feet, rolling his shoulders, letting the relief take hold. Only then did he notice he was still clutching the Urumay file to his chest. He closed it and stuffed it in his briefcase along with the other photocopies he'd taken. Then he put the lid back on the AsiaRisk box and placed it back against the window wall. The door opened, light slicing through the gap, the shadow from Carmella's tall figure spreading diagonally across the floor.

"Thanks," was all Scott could muster.

"Get out of here," she responded abruptly, her arms folded, her face etched with worry and hostility. He understood. She had just put her whole career on the line for him.

"Consider me gone." Scott headed for the front door. But then something made him stop and turn back. "What was that conflict check Charles was just talking about?"

Carmella bit her lip then handed him a piece of paper. "Here," she said. "See for yourself, but please just go now before anyone else comes back."

She wasn't happy with him. There was nothing Scott could do about that now, so he just nodded a thanks and left. Five minutes later he was striding out of the Central Plaza, the humidity bathing him in relief. The Wanchai streets were cramped, crowded and annoying, but right then they made Scott feel alive and free and back from the brink. He wallowed in it, his mind latching onto things it would normally ignore: the leafletters still at work at this time of night, the lights on the walkway and their dusty metal wire protectors, traffic sounds snarling below him, the bitumen scented air. Right then it all seemed sweet, a reminder that he had been out to the edge and made it back.

By the time Scott made it home, however, his adrenalin had nosed dived to nothing and tiredness was taking hold. For his first day of unemployment, it sure had been busy. He set his briefcase down on the floor and took off his jacket but felt the piece of paper in his inside pocket catch against his shirt. He drew it out and read the conflict check which Conrad had come back into the office to send out.

To: *JACKSON'S, ALL*
From: *Charles CONRAD*
Subject: AsiaRisk/Chow Mei (HK) Limited – Conflict check
Is there any reason why we cannot accept a major new instruction from AsiaRisk to represent them in a HK$200 million plus claim by paper manufacturer Chow Mei (HK) Limited. All conflicts to me by lunchtime tomorrow. CHARLES CONRAD

'Major new instruction', 'HK$200 million plus claim'. It was typical Conrad, blowing his own trumpet with nothing but hot air. Right then Scott found it more amusing than annoying.

He went to the bathroom, washed away the day, then lay down on the bed for some thinking time; but the combination of cool air-conditioning and exhaustion soon conspired to send him drifting off to sleep.

As Scott lost consciousness, he thought of Kimmie Yang and her wasted life.

It was an awkward image to go to sleep on.

CHAPTER NINETEEN

Unemployment Day Two was proving no less industrious than Day One had been.

Scott woke early and spent most of the morning sweating at the desk in his spare room. Tranquil sun rays filtered through the cheap turquoise curtains generating a sticky temperature and drowning the room in the green hue of an unwashed fish tank.

Scott had already gone through the documentation he'd liberated from Kimmie's office several times and found enough in there to prove that Charles Conrad over-billed his clients disgracefully. Certainly there was enough to give the Law Society something to sink its teeth into. But somehow that no longer seemed sufficient.

Scott kept coming back to the email exchanges he had found on the Uramay file. They seemed to have changed everything; blown this whole thing into something different; something that merited far more that just getting Conrad's wrists slapped.

In the first email, Kimmie had politely reminded Conrad to report an overpayment received from AsiaRisk as a potential suspicious transaction to the firm's MLRO. The second email was Conrad's testy reply, reminding Kimmie that AsiaRisk and Leopold Chan were his oldest clients and that his vouching for them was enough.

If it had ended there, Scott would probably have just glossed over it as a minor spat between colleagues. Good prejudicial stuff that would have had Jackson's risk management crawling all over Conrad if they ever found out. But Kimmie hadn't left it alone. She had responded to Conrad's petulant rank-pull. And then some.

Speaking out didn't come with the territory of being an assistant solicitor in a big law firm. Power resided in the hands of the partners and every assistant knew that if they wanted to join their hallowed ranks, it was more than their career was worth to start questioning decisions. But then there was that one-in-a-million assistant who put doing the right thing above personal ambition. That was Kimmie Yang all over. A person of integrity in an industry full of sharks.

Regret wormed in Scott's gut as he re-read her response:

Charles, the Rules are unambiguous. AsiaRisk's overpayment must be reported to the MLRO. It is for the MLRO to decide whether or not the payment should then be notified to the Financial Institutions Crimes Unit. There are no exceptions, this was made clear to us at the training. I'm in court tomorrow, but after that I'll speak to the MLRO in London and get the process started. Happy to discuss. Kimmie.

Kimmie Yang had always been a stickler for the rules; Charles Conrad was a man who never even knew what they were. Looking back, a collision of wills had probably been inevitable. But in a collision between a five-year-qualified assistant and a partner of over ten years, there was only ever going to be one winner. Kimmie may have had right on her side, but sooner or later she would have been the one looking for another job, Conrad would have made sure of it.

If, two days after sending the email Kimmie Yang hadn't committed suicide.

And there was the rub; the shove which, as far as Scott was concerned, sent this whole damn thing spinning off its axis. But wrong conclusions were easy to jump to and he didn't want to fall into that particular trap, not with something this important.

He ran a hand through his hair, plastering in the sweat. His mind was awash with implications that didn't sit well. He went through to the kitchen, poured some water, downed it; then went back to his desk to take another swing at the documents.

Cold, hard objectivity was what he needed. Gut instincts were a distraction, a road to pernicious conclusions which were preconceived and plain wrong. But how the hell could he be objective with this? –The girl he had once loved and the scumbag who had ruined his career. Involvement didn't come more personal.

Rawness stung Scott's eyes, the result of extended concentration. Light flashed under the lids as he massaged them with his fingers. *Treat it like any other case*, he instructed himself. Cold. Rationale. Objective. A few minutes passed. He shook out his shoulders and started the process over, scanning the trio of emails for an eighth then a ninth time. Slowly his brain moved up the gears. He needed to construct a fuller picture to understand the context in which these emails had been drafted. He needed to add texture and depth.

Kimmie had been working long hours, Sally Yang had told him that and Carmella had confirmed it. Scott's own experience had taught him what that could do to the psyche. Pressure and exhaustion loosened emotional control; anger and depression followed. Add in a boss like Conrad, a man prepared to milk his assistants for all they were worth, and you had a devastating recipe. Sooner or later, breaking point would have been reached.

Maybe that's what had happened, Scott mused; maybe this last email had signaled Kimmie's breaking point? Her last hurrah, standing up to Conrad, before she walked out on her career. And on her life.

The scenario fit the facts. But there was one fatal flaw, which, Scott realized, rubbished the whole thing.

The language.

Kimmie's email was exact, too matter-of-fact, the spelling and punctuation perfect. She had ended it 'happy to discuss', the way most internal emails in Jackson's were tailed, a nice chatty way of demonstrating one's commitment to the team. Certainly not the words of someone at the edge of an abyss.

Scott rubbed his chin with the flat of his palm; oily bristles scratched his skin. He needed to cast the net wider, see what else he could turn up, to portray events in the right hue. Glancing through the other papers from Kimmie's office, he concentrated on the collection of documents that came from the AsiaRisk box. Scott scanned their contents twice, trying to spot patterns. Most of it seemed straightforward billing information; but after a while salient facts started to emerge.

Like the fact that each instruction which AsiaRisk sent Conrad was of very limited scope. In each case, all Conrad had to do was document a settlement reached between AsiaRisk and the policyholder. Scott also noted how each case followed a similar course; AsiaRisk refusing to pay a claim, the policyholder threatening to sue. Then a settlement would be negotiated and Conrad was asked to document it. All easy, standard stuff.

Beyond that, however, there was nothing linking one case to another. Each time it was a different policyholder; they weren't even in the same industry, and each was represented by a different set of solicitors.

Scott leaned back and gently tugged his lower lip. Something was still amiss. It took him a minute to figure out what it was – a nagging question, which didn't apparently have an answer, but could explain a hell of a lot.

Why Jackson's?

That was the question. Of all the law firms AsiaRisk could instruct, why had it chosen one of the most expensive? In Scott's experience insurance companies like AsiaRisk were the most tight-fisted of clients. No matter how good a result a lawyer achieved, insurers begrudged every penny they paid in legal fees. Yet here was AsiaRisk, a local insurer, instructing a partner in an expensive international law firm.

Scott toyed with the thought some more. Reputation was one possible answer. In litigation, choosing a lawyer was as much about making a statement of intent as getting the right expertise. Turning up with a firm like Jackson's on your side would make opponents think twice, that was a common belief. A law firm's reputation could serve as both a powerful sword to strike with and an immovable shield behind which to conceal a weak negotiating position. Or something even more sinister. Like a crime, may be.

Scott let out a sudden gushing sound through his teeth, put his hands to his ears and shook his head in self-chastisement. He was speculating on a conclusion without having the evidence trail to back it up. "Come on!" he told himself.

He decided to switch perspectives. So far he'd been looking at this from the Jackson's and AsiaRisk viewpoint. But what did the claims look like from the perspective of the policyholders? Perhaps that would shed some light.

He flicked through the papers again, looking for the names of the solicitors who had represented the policyholders, to see if they sparked anything. When he came to the papers on a claim made by Dragon Transport, he paused.

Dragon Transport was, as its name suggested, a road haulier which had threatened to sue AsiaRisk when the insurer had refused to pay out under a cargo policy. The claim had eventually been settled for a discounted amount and Charles Conrad, on behalf of AsiaRisk, had documented the terms. Lo, Tse and Hamilton had represented Dragon Transport throughout. Scott knew the firm well. He found their number in his directory, dialed it and asked to speak to Aloysia Tse.

"Who shall I say is calling?"

Scott thought for a moment. "Tell her it's her old tea boy."

"Her old tea boy?"

"Yup."

He was routed to classical music. Before the orchestra had managed to complete a bar, a voice cut in.

"Scott Lee, is that you?"

"The one and only." Scott pictured Aloysia Tse admiring her finger nails, searching the internet for weekend breaks in Phuket and generally avoiding doing any work. Back when they had been colleagues at Yip & Siu, every afternoon Scott had refilled his coffee and brought back a mug of tea for Aloysia on the way. A nice interlude in both their daily routines.

"So who brings you tea, now I'm not next door?" he asked.

"Anyone I want. I'm a partner, remember."

That made Scott laugh. Aloysia's father was the 'Tse' in Lo, Tse & Hamilton. He had always wanted his only child to follow in his footsteps and take over his lucrative practice. Aloysia had obliged, not because she liked the law particularly, but it paid to keep daddy happy. For Aloysia, practicing law had always been a distraction from her social life.

"Don't tell me I've got a case against you?" she asked.

"No, nothing like that. I'm hoping you can help me with some information on a case your firm handled, though."

"Sure, what was the case?"

"Dragon Transport versus AsiaRisk Insurance Ltd. Settled about a year ago? Jackson's was on the other side. You know it?"

"Not one of mine, I'm afraid," Aloysia said. "I'll have someone check the database and ask the case handler to give you a call. How's that sound?"

"Peachy," he said.

"What's your interest anyway?"

"Oh, just idle curiosity," Scott didn't want to go into details.

A girlish chuckle emanated down the line. "Nothing to do with the rumours I've been hearing about why you left Yip & Siu?"

That made him hesitate. "Bad news travels fast in this town, I see. And for the record, I haven't left Yip & Siu. I'm taking unpaid leave."

"Wanna fill me in?"

"Not really."

She clicked her teeth in disappointment.

"Well maybe over lunch sometime," Scott reneged. He wanted to keep her sweet. "My treat."

"So long as I get to choose the restaurant. Not having you palm me off with some cheap *tsa-tsan-teng*."

Same old, same old Aloysia.

Charles Conrad let rip a breathy curse when he saw it was only 11.30am.

Time was moving like a turgid morass of quicksand today. Work hadn't been high on his agenda that morning, not after coming into the office the night before to do Leopold Chan's bidding. When he had finally made it home, Cathy had treated him to one of her Typhoon signal number ten rages. Every time he'd ventured near the bedroom, an airborne implement or a squawking tirade had forced a retreat and, not for the first time, he had spent the night in the spare room, a refugee in his own home. So today Charles was in self-pitying mood, cursing what Hong Kong had done to his life, turning his wife into an unbearable harridan, rendering his marriage loveless, and reducing him to Leopold Chan's whore.

Five more years, Charles tried to console himself. That was all he needed from this ghastly place. Five more years, then he could abandon Jackson's and its Hong Kong office forever and start again with Cathy back in England, where they belonged, with English people doing English things. Spending summers watching cricket, going to the pub, walking the dog through green fields. Cathy could be with her friends and close to her mother; that was all she really needed. Their marriage could settle down to a respectful relationship, rather than the spiteful co-existence they were living now.

Five more years. Today, it seemed a lifetime.

Another five minutes ebbed reluctantly by, like the last drips of water being rung from a damp dish cloth. Charles could stand it no longer. The walls of his office were pressing in on him; the air stifling. His breath quickened, panic taking hold. He had to get out.

Plucking his jacket from the doorhook, he swept past his secretary, muttering some excuse about an urgent meeting.

"Mr Conrad?" she called after him.

Charles stopped, turned and snapped, "What is it?!"

She shot back a withering glance. "I only wanted to ask if you'd lost this."

Something in her hand glinted under the glare of a desk lamp. "What is it?"

"A pen. Looks quite valuable. The morning cleaners found it. You were working late last night, so I guessed it might be yours."

Charles took it and inspected it closely. The shiny black barrel was cold against the sweaty pads of his chubby fingers. A satisfactory click sounded as he removed the lid. The nib, gold and silver was slightly smeared in black ink. A vague familiarity caught. Slowly the memory evolved. His birthday, a few years back, Cathy had bought him a pen. It had taken him fewer than twenty-four hours to lose the damn thing and a whole month of pretending to his wife that he was faithfully using it every day at the office, until she stopped asking him about it.

Now here it was, after all this time, rescued by a cleaner. A good omen for things to come, perhaps? "Yes, I think this is mine. Thanks!" Charles slipped it into his jacket, left the office and rode the lift down to ground. He jumped into a taxi which sped off at maniacal speed.

The Hong Kong Club was his one oasis of sanity in this city which had become his curse. He headed up the spiral stair case to the library. The oak paneling and lush claret carpets made it feel like he was stepping back a century. Deep leather armchairs were loosely distributed around, paintings of members past adorned the walls in heavy frames. An old duffer with a military moustache and a hospital-issue, rubber-handled walking stick sat staring vacantly out of the window enjoying a pre-lunch sherry. He was a permanent fixture here, Charles couldn't remember his name, but apparently he had once been a high court judge, or something of that ilk. Now he was nothing more than a waxwork, old and alone in a country that was no longer his own.

Five more years, Charles reminded himself.

Charles went to the DVD section and looked through the BBC box sets. Names like *Brideshead Revisted, The Miss Marple Mysteries* and *Last of the Summer Wine* threw him back twenty years to when he had first started out in London, every Sunday night ironing his shirts in front of the telly, regretting the end of the weekend. Life had seemed so much simpler back then, before Cathy, before Hong Kong. Before bloody Leopold Chan.

He settled on a series of *Only Fools and Horses,* the one with the episode where Delboy sold a job-lot of fluorescent paint to the ignorant proprietor of a Chinese takeaway. That evening, Charles was going to lose himself in classic British comedy.

Down on the ground floor at the borrowing counter, the clerk asked Charles for his card. As Charles pulled it out of his wallet, the fountain-pen his secretary had just found clattered across the counter, the clerk catching it and handing it back.

"Thanks," Charles said and examined the troublesome implement as the clerk busied himself with the DVD.

The pen was a Cross, nicely balanced and perfectly weighted. Charles was surprised. Cathy's tastes didn't usually extend to such understated elegance. Her clothes, her hair, her voice, all had an overt quality. Once he had found it seductive, now it was just plain off-putting. Many were the times he'd found himself having to apologise because her mouth had engaged before her brain and....

The thought stopped fast as Charles's thumb pressed into some scratches on the side of the pen barrel. He drew it up to his eyes and inspected the damage.

Not scratches. Engraving. Squinting, he focused on the faded lettering.

"S....L...." he muttered to himself. "Scott Lee."

Wrong pen. Wrong memory.

When the clerk turned round to hand over the DVD, Charles Conrad was gone, the rotating exit doors slowly swinging to a halt.

Lunch for Scott had been microwaved shrimp dumplings smothered in soy sauce, washed down with a Coke. He felt tired and bloated with MSG and caffeine, his back and neck were tense, his research going nowhere. Aloysia Tse hadn't rung back about Dragon Transport yet. Typical Aloysia. Nice girl, but reliability not a strong point.

Meantime Scott had done some more digging, looking into the ownership of the policyholders which AsiaRisk had insured to see if it revealed anything about the cases Conrad was handling. Using the Companies Registry online service, he discovered that Dragon Transport, the company which Aloysia Tse's firm had represented, was a wholly owned subsidiary of Dragon Holdings. Dragon Holdings had its registered office in Shatin and was in turn wholly owned by a company called Rich Qing. Rich Qing was incorporated in the British Virgin Islands.

The offshore jurisdiction had been Scott's first dead end.

So he moved on to another AsiaRisk case, a computer software company called Harlotex claiming indemnity from AsiaRisk for flood damage, AsiaRisk denying the claim for *force majeure*. Harlotex had threatened to sue, solicitors' letters had been exchanged, posture and counter-posture in correspondence had followed until eventually it had settled at fifty percent of the original claimed amount. Harlotex was, according to its Companies Registry filings, wholly owned by another Hong Kong incorporated company named Coral Ventures which in turn was owned by Wang Enterprises. Wang Enterprises was incorporated offshore, this time in the Cayman Islands.

Dead end number two.

So now what? Scott stared blankly at his laptop. Doubts began to fester through the haze of fatigue. What was he really doing here? Salving his conscience? Looking for closure? What the hell gave him the right? Kimmie's family were the ones who had to live with this everyday. Best thing for him was to leave well alone and stop risking prolonging their agony.

He thought back to the promise he had made to Sally Yang, and the thought of walking away suddenly lost its appeal, as did the thought of cracking open a beer to numb his senses. Most of his life both options had been his default setting whenever things got tough. And where had it got him? Half way round the world with a career in tatters. Walking away, trying to forget; they were only ever short-term fixes. The past was never done. It was a living organism, constantly reverberating, rippling through to the present, catching you unawares, sending you off-balance. Just like Sally Yang walking back into his life ten days ago.

Scott shook it off, refocused and immersed himself back in the Companies Registry information he'd just downloaded.

Dragon Transport and Harlotex. Both of them were policyholders of AsiaRisk, both of them involved in cases handled by Charles Conrad. Beyond those obvious links, however, there were no connections between the two companies. The claims had been made years apart, the policyholders represented by different solicitors.

But then here was the Companies Registry telling him that Dragon Transport and Harlotex had ownership structures which ended in the dead end of offshore jurisdictions. And that gnawed at Scott.

Like a nagging itch begging to be scratched.

CHAPTER TWENTY

The mens' changing room was at the top of an iron grill spiral staircase. A thick fug of aftershave and hair gel almost overpowered Scott as he entered. That smell summed up Fong's Gym. Here, fitness was about looking good and not much else. Exercise for pure vanity's sake. No surprise then that the most congested area of the changing room was by the mirrors, where a ritual of posing and preening was going on.

Scott gave it a wide berth, found a corner locker, changed into a T-shirt, running shorts and trainers, and grabbed a towel on the way out. Back down the staircase, he weaved through weight-machines and personal trainers putting their charges through pain-ripping work outs. Dance music blared, aiming to encourage effort but missing by a mile.

Thankfully, the speakers were muted in the studio Scott wanted. The "psshhh, psshhh" of the six-foot-two blond giant shadow-boxing in a roped off corner offered the only soundtrack. Scott watched as the boxer, his arms jabbing like pistons, pummelled an imaginary opponent into a pulp. "Hey, Larson!" Scott called out.

The boxer turned. "Scott! Dude! I was beginning to think you'd wimped out."

Larson Twain bore the definition of the über-healthy. He held out a bearish paw for Scott to shake. "Wanna warm up?"

"Let's just get it over with."

"Hey! It's not going to be that bad, man."

Scott craned his neck. "You should see it from where I'm standing."

Larson Twain laughed like only a Swede could laugh, punching Scott's shoulder with a wrecking ball fist. Hard to believe this fitness-freak beach-boy was a tax accountant who spent his days helping rich expats get richer. Every evening, though, Larson put in a hellish two-hour gym routine which occasionally, when he could find an opponent stupid enough to step into the ring with him, included some boxing sparring. So five three-minute rounds was the price the big Swede had extracted from Scott that evening in return for some free advice. They stretched, strapped on helmets, slipped on gloves, then, after a hearty "ding, ding" from Larson, they began.

Being a good head shorter than his opponent, Scott knew what he had to do: move forward and try to get under Larson's guard. But Larson's superior reach and precision jabbing swatted Scott off like a mosquito. For three rounds Scott chased around like a blind man punching air. In the fourth Larson added injury to insult by landing some heavy hooks, which, by the end of the round had Scott on his backside, heaving lung-fulls, and praying for the end to come.

"Looking tired, dude!" Larson bounced over him mercilessly. "Come on. One more. Let's go."

Scott levered himself to his feet. Nodded.

"Ding, Ding,"

Immediately, Larson feinted with his left and landed a sledgehammer right, spinning Scott away from him like a rag doll. Scott grabbed for the ropes, stars bursting in his vision, the world going wobbly. Blinking himself steady he felt a white heat ignite, as if the punch had flicked a switch. Past frustrations poured in like a deluge and when he turned it was no longer Larson Twain standing there. It was Charles Conrad. It was Richard Denham telling him to forget his partnership. It was the ginger kid at school who'd relentlessly teased him. Every humiliating failure Scott had ever suffered.

The next two minutes were a frenzied blur as Scott and Larson went at each other like rabid dogs over raw steak, Larson's targeted punches more controlled, Scott raining down blows as if possessed by demons. By the end both men were staggering wretches.

"Feel better?" Larson manage to stifle through exhausted huffs, his hands on his knees.

"Damn....right...."

Twenty minutes later they were cooling themselves on stools in Fong's fitness café while a waitress blended fruit smoothies. Scott's arms were pure jelly, the lactic acid taking its sweet time evacuating his muscles. Every inhale was a cheesegrater across his throat, every exhale a xylophone wheeze. In spite of it all, he felt relaxed in the way only exercise could bring. Violence had somehow begotten inner peace.

The waitress put down milkshake glasses filled with green and orange concoctions. Larson slurped and asked, "So what's on your mind, man?"

Scott cleared his phlegmy throat. "Offshore companies."

"What about them?"

Scott drummed his fingers on the metallic bar and ordered his thoughts. He wanted to play this right. "I got this case," he said. "The details aren't important. But I have to find out who owns this particular company – let's call it company 'A'. It's a Hong Kong company, so I searched the Companies Register, which told me company 'A' was owned by another company – company 'B'. So I searched the Register for company 'B'...."

"And found company 'B' is owned by company 'C'?" Larson said.

"Right. Only company 'C' isn't a Hong Kong company. It's domiciled in the Caymans."

"Ah!"

"So the question is, how do I find out who owns company 'C'?"

"Easy," Larson said. "You can't."

"What?"

"Sun, sea and confidentialiteee, dude," Larson jived like he was laying down a blues track. "Joy and fun and secreceeee. That's the Caymans. One of the world's favourite financial hideaways."

Scott chewed his lower lip. "So I can't find out the shareholders?"

"Uh-uh. Shareholder details of Cayman companies aren't public record. And even if they were, it wouldn't do you any good."

"Why not?"

"Two words: bearer shares," Larson slurped his drink. "They're allowed in the Caymans. Bearer shares means ownership of the shares passes with possession of the share certificate. So whilst the existence of the shares is formally registered, the person who owns the shares isn't. Proof of ownership comes through possession of the certificate. Not registration."

Scott shook his head. "What about directors?"

"Same answer. In the Caymans, director and shareholder records aren't for public consumption."

"That's not helpful," Scott said.

"It's not supposed to be. Look," Larson explained, "you know why offshore companies exist? Because of tax. Pure and simple. If you're offshore, you don't have to pay any – or not much, anyway – so businesses do what they can to try to make it look like as much of their income as possible is made offshore. That's where offshore companies come in. The confidentiality regime just aids the process. Makes it easier to disguise income sources."

Scott made a face. Apparently being a punch bag for the evening had led him straight into a brick wall.

The waitress brought Larson a second smoothie. "Tell me," Larson said, "does your company 'A' – the Hong Kong one – have a name?"

"It's got many names." Larson frowned puzzlement, so Scott clarified, "I mean there are lots of companies. As in the case I've got. I was hoping to find out if they were connected in any way through their ownership."

"Why?"

There it was. The question Scott had been hoping to avoid. "I'm looking into a number of companies which were policyholders with a particular insurer," he trod carefully. "Each policyholder made a claim on the insurer which the insurer then denied. The policyholders then threatened to sue and then the claims were settled pretty quickly."

"That's a connection isn't it?" Larson asked the question as if the answer was obvious, but Scott shook his head.

"Not really. Denying claims, threatening to sue, quick and dirty settlements, they're part and parcel of being an insurer. Nothing unusual there. And these claims, they were all made at different times – sometimes years apart. I can't find a pattern, which is why I was hoping to see if the policyholders had common ownership somewhere down the line."

Larson asked, "Why's it so important to find a connection?"

Again with the 'why'. Scott took a breath. Time to see if his cover story had legs.

"The client I work for reinsures the insurer. The insurer's just filed a big claim, which my client doesn't want to pay. The claim is made up of amounts which the insurer has paid in settlements to its policyholders...the company 'A's, I mentioned. I figured if there was some sort of connection between the policyholders, it might point to some sort of fraud and...."

"And you could tell your client not to pay," Larson snorted. "Just another lawyer trying to help his rich client stay rich, huh? Well as a tax accountant, I can dig that." Scratching his forehead he said, "so some of these policyholders are ultimately owned by offshore companies."

"Not some," Scott said. "All."

"All of them?" Larson's voice was filled with surprise. "That's weird, man."

"Thought you just said it was no big deal. For tax reasons."

"Well," Larson moved his head side to side. "Put it this way. It's not uncommon. But to find a whole group of Hong Kong-based private companies being owned offshore? Got to ask questions, I'd say."

They sat thinking for a moment.

"What kind of fraud are you thinking of anyway?" Larson asked.

"Not exactly sure. But one of my colleagues mentioned something about money-laundering?" Scott wanted to dissociate himself from the idea in case it sounded stupid.

Larson sucked his teeth. "Could have a point, your colleague. The advantages that make offshore companies tax-saving vehicles mean that, on occasion, they're targeted for purposes which, let's just say aren't entirely legal. Money-laundering's a big one. An offshore company network really helps in the layering process."

"What?"

"The layering process."

Scott looked blank.

"Placement, layering, integration," Larson listed them off on his fingers, "the three stages of money-laundering."

"You seem to know a lot about it."

"I've got to in my job. For compliance reasons," Larson said. "Look, here's how it works. Let's say you're a drug dealer. You sell drugs for lots and lots of cash, right? But if you go around spending bundles of cash, you're going to draw attention to yourself. So somehow you've got to turn your cash into a form of money which isn't going to attract attention. Effectively, you've got to make it look like the money's legitimate. You've got to launder it."

"Okay," Scott said.

"So stage one of the laundry process is the placement of the cash into the financial system. Depositing it into a bank account, purchasing some sort of financial instrument, whatever. Placing's usually the most difficult stage because banks have to report large deposits and do identity checks on their account holders."

"Lawyers do too," Scott said. "I know that much at least."

"Same with most professions these days," Larson confirmed, "and if you forget, the regulators will chew you up and spit you out. Anyway, assume the money's been placed. Stage two is layering it – effectively putting as many layers as possible between the money and its origins, so it's virtually impossible to trace back. That's where offshore companies come in, because you can't find out who owns them. Plus, most offshore jurisdictions have secrecy laws which prevent banks from disclosing information on their account holders."

Scott thought for a moment, remembering something he had read. "Wasn't there a crackdown on laws like that after 9/11?"

Larson smirked. "Sure, new bilateral agreements were put in place. But laws are only as effective as their enforcement. And if the offshore authorities enforced them too well, they'd drive away business. Asset protection and tax avoidance – the legitmate reasons for going offshore – are underpinned by the confidentiality. So why screw yourself up? Plus the reporting obligations require a bank to have 'reasonable suspicions' about their customers. Your average criminal puts on a suit, hires an accountant or a lawyer, what's to suspect?"

It made sense.

"So how does this layering process work?" Scott asked.

"Simple. Our drug dealer sets up a load of different offshore companies, opens bank accounts for them all and transmits money from account to account, in different amounts, through as many different jurisdictions as possible, until the path is so complex, no one can trace the money back where it came from. If an investigator starts looking, he can't even find out who owns the companies. Just like you've found." Larson slurped his smoothie down till the glass rattled. "There was this Irish accountant called Shaun Murphy, he used to layer money for clients. One time, he set up forty different offshore companies and ninety different accounts. That's how sophisticated it gets."

Scott mulled this over. This was interesting stuff and it begged an obvious question. "So the situation I have," he said. "You reckon it could be a layering process?"

"That's a big leap, man. The policyholders could have gone offshore for any number of legitimate reasons – saving tax, protecting assets," Larson shrugged. "But on the other hand...." He didn't finish the thought.

Scott twisted his mouth. "So the three stages are placing, layering and....?"

"Integration," Larson said. "After hiding the origin of the funds, our drug dealer has to 'integrate' them back into his pocket by making it look like they came from a legitimate source."

"How does that work?"

"Many different ways," Larson scratched his muscular chin. "You manufacture a fictitious sale from one offshore company to another, so the money becomes sale proceeds. Another way is to consolidate the funds into one account, then take out a loan using the account holder as guarantor and the money in the account as collateral. The criminal gets his money through the loan and the bank's repaid through enforcing the collateral when the loan isn't repaid. They call that one a 'Dutch sandwich'. It used to be a favourite in the Netherland Antilles. What other ways are there?" – Larson looked off, reaching for ideas. – "Could buy property with the laundered funds and then sell it a few months later. If it's a rising market, you make a profit too. Could do the same with an investment company."

"How about an insurance company?" Scott asked.

Larson stopped, pushed out his lower lip. Nodded. "Yeah. An insurance company. That could work too."

They stayed quiet for a moment. Dance music pounded through from the floor above.

After a while Larson looked at his watch. "I got to get going. Got a spinning class in the morning. What's your email address, dude?"

Scott reached over for a napkin and wrote it down.

Larson pocketed it. "I know a guy who does consulting work for the Hong Kong police. He specializes in money-laundering cases. Real old school English, he is. Discreet and no bullshit. Talk to him. I'll send you his details."

"Cheers Larson, I owe you one," Scott said, regretting it as soon as the words were out of his mouth, but it was too late to retract

"Cool, I'll book the ring again for next week then."

CHAPTER TWENTY-ONE

"Thank's for staying late, gentlemen" Cyrus Kwan addressed the two men in his office. "How about a glass of Cognac to help stimulate the thought process?"

"Cyrus, you're spoiling us." Tyson Mok's apple face glowed with delight. Mok looked more like everyone's favourite uncle than the hard-nosed business veteran who had been Cyrus Kwan's deputy for twenty years. "Maria would kill me if she found out I was deviating from my diet again, but since you insist...." he reached for the snifter.

Kwan turned to the other man present. "What about you Simon?"

Simon Ng stayed standing, shifting his slight weight from foot to foot, his expression locked in the bitter-lemon grimace that came with the territory in risk management. "Not for me, Cyrus!"

"Come on, it will reinvigorate you." Cyrus measured out another glass and handed it to the number three in his organization.   Reluctantly, Ng acceded.

Cyrus Kwan settled back in his seat, swirled his Cognac under his nose and savoured the enchanting rich vanilla scent. As he sipped, he closed his eyes so nothing would interrupt the smooth taste caressing his palate. When he opened his eyes again, all hint of lethargy was gone. He was ready. "I need to give Leopold Chan an answer tomorrow. It's been less than twenty-four hours, I know, but I need your input, gentlemen. Should we take this deal? Or walk away?"

Mok put his glass down on the coaster and was the first to weigh in. "Who does this Leopold Chan think he is, giving us such an ultimatum? He should be happy we're even considering buying his company."

"I agree," Ng said. "This isn't how we negotiate."

Cyrus Kwan blew air slowly through his mouth. "I don't like it any more than you do, but there are special circumstances at play here. When we targeted AsiaRisk last year, its value far exceeded the price Chan has given us. It would be a shame to lose this just because of a tight timetable. Now I know we don't usually countenance walk-away ultimatums like this. I'm also conscious that it's Rupert who brought us this opportunity and that he's desperate to make amends for his recent behaviour. But I need you both to ignore those two factors for the moment. Look at the substance of the offer. Look at its fundamentals. Take all caveats as read and tell me what you think."

Mok puffed his flabby cheeks. Ng paced. Kwan waited.

"Well, the fundamentals suggest we should do it," Tyson Mok was the first to stick his neck out. It didn't surprise Cyrus. Mok was impulsive and emotional by nature, but more often than not his instinct was perfectly in tune with Kwan Holdings' requirements. "On paper AsiaRisk is a good prospect. That was the case when we looked at it last year. Nothing's changed since then. I've had my feelers out to see if there's any gossip on Chan which we should be aware of."

"And?" Kwan asked.

Mok spread his chubby hands. "No one has a bad word to say about the man. Chan seems well respected in the industry. Reading between the lines, his story holds up. He's in his sixties now and, apparently, there is no identifiable heir at AsiaRisk. So this has the hallmarks of a legacy move. I don't like the way he's trying to force it down our throats and I certainly don't like the way he's come to us through Rupert. But ...." He showed Cyrus open palms.

Cyrus Kwan nodded slowly. A legacy move. He could understand that, the deep-seated desire to build something worthwhile to leave behind. The same impulse was why he himself was so keen to see Rupert rehabilitated quickly despite his obvious faults. "What about you, Simon?"

Simon Ng paused his pacing and plucked nervously at his chin. "I took a look at the research we did on AsiaRisk last time round. Year-on-year turnover is healthy. Loss-ratios and combined-ratios hold-up well against their competitors. AsiaRisk hasn't chased the market down on premium rates in bad times, nor has it overcharged in good times, which to my mind is indicative of sensible management practices. They appear to have invested well, particularly with a number of project offices on the Mainland. Potential for growth is positive with the

Cooperation in Services Agreement on the horizon. I'd like to see their internal management accounts and projections, though, and talk to their risk people. But based on what I have seen, I agree with Tyson. On balance it's worth doing."

It was typical Ng. Analytical to the point of being anal and a conclusion caveated with a desire to see more of the facts and figures.

"I sense there is a 'but' in there somewhere, Simon." Kwan knew Ng far too well.

"There's always a 'but' with Simon," Mok chuckled.

"You pay me to watch both your backs." Ng defended himself.

"....and Tyson and I appreciate that. What are your concerns?"

Ng glanced between the two men. "I'm sorry, but despite the ultimatum, we have to do some more due diligence before making an unequivocal commitment."

Cyrus turned back to Mok. "Any views?"

Tyson Mok gave a heavy sigh. "I totally agree. At the very least we have to make sure AsiaRisk is as good a prospect as it was a year ago. I'm sure we could get someone who could do it quickly."

"And we'd want Chan to sign a non-disclosure agreement," Ng added. "None of this gets out."

"Agreed," Mok said.

Cyrus Kwan locked his fingers and stayed deep in thought. Not for the first time he was impressed at how two such uncomplimentary characters as Ng and Mok could arrive at such a commercially sensible suggestion with the help of some direct questioning and a little Cognac to get things moving in the right direction.

"I could give one of our panel lawyers a call," Ng suggested, "line someone up for the due-diligence. If Chan signs the non-disclosure tomorrow, the lawyers could get started and report back to us, Thursday. We could have the board meeting Friday morning, subject to obtaining agreement to the short notice, sign later in the day and announce first thing Monday. Can't see Chan complaining about that."

Cyrus Kwan nodded. "Yes, I think that timetable is do-able. But don't worry about the panel lawyers, Simon, I already have someone in mind for the due diligence."

"Who?" Ng asked.

Cyrus glanced at them both. "I think this may be one for Rainbow Choi's particular brand of expertise."

Silence. Then Ng and Mok nodded at the choice.

"Gentlemen, I have kept you away from your families long enough," Cyrus said. "If you'd excuse me, I have a couple of phone-calls to make before calling it a night myself."

After Mok and Ng had left his office Cyrus dug out Leopold Chan's business card from his desk drawer, but just as he was about to dial, a thought struck him.

Rupert.

Rupert had set up this opportunity. With any other analyst, there'd be no question of involving him fully in the deal and allowing him to see it through to its conclusion. But only a fortnight ago Rupert had visited near disaster on Kwan Holdings. Could he be trusted again so soon? Cyrus pondered the conundrum. If he let Rupert take charge, then it was questionable whether his nephew would have learned anything from his stupidity. But isolating Rupert risked damaging his confidence at a time when it needed nurturing.

After a moment, Cyrus made his decision and called his nephew.

"Hello?"

On the phone, Rupert sounded so much like his father. Cyrus sighed at the memory of his brother, but pushed it aside quickly. This was business. "Rupert, I wanted you to be the first to know that we've made a decision on AsiaRisk."

"Yes?"

Cyrus told him they were accepting Leopold Chan's offer, subject to a non-disclosure agreement being signed and satisfactory due-diligence being carried out by Rainbow Choi.

"I don't know her. She any good?"

"She's exactly what we need on this," Cyrus replied testily. He didn't like the knee-jerk questioning of his choice. "Now, I shall be taking charge of this deal personally."

"But I thought...."

"You'll be the prime point of contact with Leopold Chan on my behalf," Cyrus moved to head off the disagreement he knew was coming. "Learn as much about AsiaRisk as you can, Rupert and I *may* ask you to take an executive role in the new acquisition."

Seething silence bloomed on the line. "I see," Rupert said petulantly. "So I bring in the deal and you take all the glory."

Cyrus let go a weary sigh. "When are you going to learn that business isn't about personal glorification! It's about people working together in a team, trying to build something profitable and long-lasting!" Another lengthy pause followed. "Now I repeat, I will be in charge of this deal. You will perform a liaison role. You will report back to me directly on everything, Rupert. Do you understand? Everything!"

Rupert grudgingly gave his agreement.

Cyrus finished the call with a heavy heart, wondering how differently Rupert's character would have turned out had his father lived. The memories came flooding in then…their escape as teenagers across the border to Hong Kong, to the chance of a new life….their reliance on each other in the squatter camps….the bunk beds in their first public housing flat….pooling their pay cheques, working hard to further themselves and become self-reliant.

Desperate times they had been, yes, but somehow much simpler. Cyrus missed his brother.

A while passed. Then Cyrus reached for the phone and dialed Leopold Chan's number.

CHAPTER TWENTY-TW0

The high pitch of his mobile ring-tone jangled Scott awake. Pain jutted through his neck at his first attempt at movement. His muscles were stiff from the beating Larson Twain had served up the previous evening. Eventually his fingers found the phone. Drawing it to his ear, he croaked his name.

"Ouch, what happened to you?" The voice was definitely female and familiar, but through the thickness of recent slumber, it took Scott a moment to place it.

"Aloysia!" His voice was syrupy with phlegm. "How you doing?" Rolling onto his back, he sat up tenderly and massaged one eye with his palm.

"Obviously better than you. Good night, was it?"

"Something like that."

"You alone?"

"Yeah."

"Not that good then."

"Ha bloody ha."

"Want me to call back?"

"No, no. Now's good." Scott slowly got to his feet, mouthed a silent 'ahhh!' as his hamstrings protested. "This is to do with the AsiaRisk case I asked about, right?"

"Dragon Transport versus AsiaRisk," Aloysia confirmed. "At least that was the name you gave me."

"Hang on, let me get a pen."

"Forget it, there's nothing for you to write down."

"What?"

"We've never heard of the case, my friend" Aloysia said. "You've got the wrong firm."

Scott took a moment to process her words, then said: "Wait a minute!"

He tip-toed out into the sitting room, unable to extend his red-raw Achilles tendons down to the floor. Unwelcome sunlight hit him through the gap in the curtains. Shielding his eyes, he tottered unsteadily towards his study, the sauna-like warmth already sending his T-shirt into cling-mode. The AsiaRisk papers were arranged in alphabetical order on his desk, the pages on Dragon Transport easy to locate. He found the copy of the Jackson's pro-forma case summary, which he'd taken from Kimmie's office. Third line down was the name of Dragon Transport's solicitors. "You're with Lo, Tse & Hamilton, right?" Scott asked.

"That's the name of Daddy's firm all right."

"And there aren't two Lo, Tse & Hamiltons in Hong Kong?"

"Nope!"

A beat of silence

"And you're telling me you've got no records on Dragon Transport? You're certain?"

"Our litigation partner has never heard of it, Scott," Aloysia chirruped. "Neither has our court clerk. Both of them have been here for ten years plus. Trust me, they would know. I even asked the clerk to do a record search. Came up blank. Sorry, Dragon Transport's not one of ours."

Scott stared down at Conrad's case summary again. Re-read the name. 'Lo, Tse & Hamilton'. According to the dates this had all taken place last year, so even if the records were lost the lawyer would remember, especially a case like this where the client had extracted a decent settlement. This was one for the brochure, a notch in the win column.

Aloysia's voice cut in again. "Incidentally, I know a few firms who might be interested to know you're looking for new employment."

"Who says I'm looking?"

"I'm just saying, if you were....a lot of people know your true worth, Scott. And if no-one else wants you, you can come here and make me tea again."

"A hard-to-refuse offer," Scott smiled. Deep below the layers of high-maintenance cosmetics, Aloysia Tse was as genuine as they came. "Well, if I am looking, I promise you'll be my first phone-call."

"Cool," she said with the nonchalance of a French model. "I'll speak to you later."

They said their goodbyes and Scott rang off.

Lunch. Food. Sounded like a plan, but his mind was already trying to fit together the new information Aloysia had just served up. Charles Conrad's records could have been wrong, of course. It wouldn't have been the first time. But getting the wrong name of the opposing solicitors? Not even Conrad could have been that stupid. And in any case, the proformas were probably reviewed by his secretary, so there would have been a double-check.

Gingerly, Scott tip-toed through to the kitchen, clicked on the kettle, downed some water, splashed some more on his face, felt perhaps one percent better because of it, then went back to the study. He was still in his underwear, hadn't washed properly, but indulged himself in the thought that he didn't have to be in an office any time soon.

So Dragon Transport hadn't been represented by the solicitors named in Jackson's records. Turning the fact round in his mind, Scott flipped to the next AsiaRisk case in the pile and reviewed the case summary, this one a claim by Jaytech Limited, an electronics outfit which had threatened to sue AsiaRisk for not paying up on a business interruption policy. In the dispute which had followed, Jaytech's solicitors, Stephen Wing & Co., had wrestled a decent two million dollar settlement out of AsiaRisk. On the face of it, not too bad. Conrad had done the settlement agreement and charged a hefty fee. Everyone had come out of the deal a winner, it seemed.

Jaytech's solicitors were named as Stephen Wing & Co. Not a firm Scott had heard of before, but he located their details easily enough in his Law Society Directory.

Time to give the tree a shake and see what fell out.

Scott took a moment to run through an appropriate cover story, then took a deep breath and dialed. An efficient receptionist answered and Scott asked to speak to Stephen Wing, deciding to handle the call in Cantonese.

"Who is calling, please?" The receptionist asked.

"I am Mr Lee, from Jaytech company. We are a client of Lawyer Wing."

"Please wait one moment."

The music of Greensleeves entertained while he held.

"Hello!" The voice that eventually greeted Scott was a rich trust-me baritone. Scott pictured a Chinese version of James Earl Jones.

Scott cleared his throat. "You are Lawyer Wing?"

"Yes."

"I am Mr Lee from JayTech company. I am the new accounts department manager."

"Hello, Mr Lee."

"Lawyer Wing, I want to ask for your help. Our auditors have asked for a copy of the letter of retainer for the work you did for Jaytech last year in a claim against our insurer, AsiaRisk. Since I am new here, I have not been able to find our file on the matter. Could you fax a copy of the retainer to me for my records?"

There was a pensive silence. Then: "I am sorry Mr Lee, but I do not know the name of your company. I believe you must have the wrong firm." The words carried with them a certainty that demanded no argument. Scott made profound apologies and quickly extracted himself from the conversation.

When he hung up, his heart was thrumming in his chest. Independent corroboration, that's what they called this. Two different AsiaRisk claims; two different sets of opposition lawyers; but neither of the lawyers had ever heard of the clients they were supposed to have represented. So whatever it was that Charles Conrad and Leopold Chan were up to, it didn't take a genius to work out that it flew well beyond the line of legality. Scott rubbed a hand across his face, his skin felt oily and bristled with morning stubble. One by one, he listed the links in the chain of evidence he had so far.

One, the ownership of each policyholder named in the Jackson's files couldn't be traced because their lineage always ended up in an offshore tax haven. Two, the law firms named as having represented the policyholders had been plucked from thin air. Three, Kimmie Yang had told Charles Conrad that certain payments from AsiaRisk should have been reported to Jackson's Anti-Money-laundering Officer as suspicious transactions.

The three links drew Scott to a conclusion he was finding hard to believe, but harder still to discard. One that said the cases Charles Conrad had conducted on behalf of AsiaRisk were pure works of fiction, documented ruses created to provide a legitimate veneer for money-laundering. A truth which Kimmie Yang had stumbled on by doing exactly what any good lawyer should have done: asking questions and refusing to take 'no' for an answer. Obeying the rules.

And now she was dead.

Scott felt his throat start to close in on itself, as if choked by the ruthless chain of logic he had just constructed. The black abyss was coming, he could feel it, salt already flushing round his tonsils. Reaching out, he steadied himself against the edge of the desk and gulped deep, steadying breaths. Ice prickled his skin, but the coldness didn't last, as the heat of guilt and anger started to rumble through his soul, like a freight train careering down the tracks until, bam! it hit him hard and sure, knocking his mind off balance. He let the thoughts ride through without trying to stop them. How easy it would be to go back to Central Plaza now, wait for Conrad to leave for the night, follow him home and under cover of darkness exact a dark revenge. Rain down blows of anger the same way Scott had done with Larson Twain the night before when his rage switch had been flicked. Only this time there'd be no bell to stop him, no control, no mercy. He could imagine it, he could see it in his mind, hitting, kicking, stamping, stomping, being fueled on by Conrad's pathetic screams and breaking flesh.

Scott let the frenzy build and build and reach its conclusion. And when he was done, he allowed the inevitable sense of guilt and self-loathing to bring him back to where he needed to be.

He had loved Kimmie and his mission to make amends on her behalf remained his fixed intent. But knowing what he knew now heightened the stakes for which he was playing. A dark side of humanity was confronting him, men capable of going to any length to protect their greed. Every fibre in Scott's being made him question Kimmie's suicide. But if it wasn't suicide, the alternative explanation was one that made Charles Conrad and Leopold Chan something else altogether. Pure and bitter bile gripped Scott's stomach at the thought.

Kimmie had been silenced because of the dark secret she had stumbled on.

A dark secret, which Scott also now knew.

CHAPTER TWENTY-THREE

Everything was on target.

At precisely four minutes to nine the previous evening when Leopold Chan had heard his phone ringing, his initial reaction had been to leave it. His staff knew better than to disturb him at home and the only other person who ever called at that time was his ex-wife and he certainly wasn't in the mood to listen to Trixie's high-maintenance ramblings.

"This is Leopold Chan, I'm not available to take your call. If it's urgent, please try my office number or leave your message after the tone."

"Leopold, Cyrus Kwan here, I was hoping ...."

Leopold bolted the receiver up to his ear. "Cyrus, I do apologise. I was out of the room. What can I do for you?"

This one call he was prepared to take. Taken aback by the interruption, Kwan took a moment to gather himself.

"Sorry for calling at this late hour, Leopold, but you set me a deadline and I am a man who respects time-frames."

A tinge of excitement rose from deep within Leopold, but he suppressed it and asked the question which had been preying on his mind all day. "Well let's get to it then, Cyrus. Is Kwan Holdings going to buy AsiaRisk or am I going to have to take my offer elsewhere?"

Silence bloomed on the line, the kind of awkward silence that holds its own voluble negativity and for a moment Leopold thought he had overplayed his hand. Speaking to Cyrus Kwan in such overbearing terms was pure nectar to his spirit and fit with the strong negotiating position of a man apparently willing to sell away his life's work at a substantial discount. But Cyrus Kwan was a man who had already amassed enough of a fortune to be able to walk away from a deal, no matter how good it was, just because he found the other party objectionable. Leopold knew he was treading a particular fine line.

"Your offer is accepted in principle," Kwan said. Leopold let slip a slow breath. "But there are some conditions." – Kwan explained about the non-disclosure agreement and his intention to carry out a full due-diligence exercise. – They were entirely fair and reasonable requests, but then again Leopold had his own strict timetable to adhere to and no slippage from that could be countenanced.

"I can live with that, Cyrus," he said, "provided we can agree a time-limit to your enquiries. It's in both our interests not to leave things hanging, wouldn't you agree?"

"Forty-eight hours is all we need," Kwan had obviously anticipated the response.

Leopold was surprised. He had been willing go up to a week. "Forty-eight hours it is."

"Very well, my representative will be round to your office in the morning."

And so she was.

Leopold stared at Rainbow Choi through the CCTV cameras trained on AsiaRisk's reception. She couldn't have been more than five foot. Mid-thirties, Leopold guessed, and with her black hair boyishly cut short, clearly not one for whom hours in the salon were a priority. Nevertheless Leopold sensed a certain something about her. It was there in the way she just sat there so relaxed, absorbed in *The Herald Tribune*. A calm determination, definitely. A confidence about being able to complete successfully the task she had been sent there to carry out. If AsiaRisk's books and records held any nasty surprises, then Rainbow Choi would find them, that's what her whole demeanour told Leopold. She was going to make a formidable opponent, Leopold sensed.

Easing into his zone, Leopold went out to greet her.

"Ms Choi? Leopold Chan."

The Herald Tribune was folded up and put back on the coffee table. Rainbow uncrossed her legs; her hands smoothing her skirt, every movement deliberate and unhurried. Her handshake was as solid as any man's and when juxtaposed with her lack of height, was enough to throw the recipient off-balance.

But Leopold took it all in his stride. "Please," he said ushering her in the direction of the meeting rooms. "I thought you might like to start with our internal accounts and projections. Then I am in your hands. Anything you want will be at your disposal."

"Including access to your staff?" The question appeared conditional on her taking another step forward.

Leopold widened his smile. "Of course. But I would ask you to be sensitive to our business needs. The less disruption, the better."

"You won't even notice I'm here, Leo."

Leopold felt a shard of irritation. She had just called him Leo. Benny Wang called him Leo. He hated being called Leo.

They continued across to reception, Rainbow Choi's heels clicking as if to announce her presence in the building. Leopold was so focused on the sound that he didn't hear the hiss of the opening lift-doors.

"Leopold! Leopold! I need to speak to you. It's urgent."

Leopold turned to see Charles Conrad hurrying towards him, a picture of agitation, sweat plastering his fringe to his forehead, his breathing heavy and his tie askew. Anger pumped heat into Leopold's face "Charles. I'm sorry, but do we have an appointment? I'm in the middle of something important...."

"No....Sorry....I mean....this is really very urgent."

Rainbow Choi stood there with a look of suppressed amusement.

Forcing an easy smile, Leopold ushered Conrad off to one side. "I have another priority right this minute, Charles. Take a seat and I'll be out to see you in a second." He turned to the receptionist. "Jeneane, please get Mr Conrad a coffee and check if there's a room available."

"Yes, Mr Chan."

Turning back to Rainbow Choi, Leopold gave a little bow and they continued on towards the meeting rooms.

"I seem to have come at a bad time," Choi said when they were out of ear shot.

"Oh don't worry about Charles," Leopold parried. "He's my lawyer. Clever chap, but with a tendency to panic on occasion. I suppose that's what I pay him for."

"Yes," Rainbow said, the smile showing in her voice.

The room he had chosen for her was windowless. She took a seat at the head of the table. "So he's your lawyer," she said. "What was his name again?"

"Conrad....Charles Conrad. Of Jackson, Weiss, Macdonald? We've been using them for a number of years, I'm sure you'll come across the name in our files."

She laid pens out on the table. Nodding to the pile of paper in the centre, she asked, "Those are the management accounts you mentioned?"

"Yes."

"I'll start with those then. Give you a chance to speak with your lawyer," her voice was heavy with suggestion.

Leopold opened his mouth to say something, then thought better of it. "If you need to get hold of me, just call reception."

As soon as she was on her own, Rainbow Choi took out a make-up compact and checked for dark circles under her eyes, evidence of her overnight blitz of background-checking into Leopold Chan and AsiaRisk. The five-am layer of foundation was still holding firm. She touched it up for good measure.

Next out of the briefcase was an A4-notepad, half full with her scribbled chronology of AsiaRisk's history. Nothing too unconventional there. The company's profitability over the years had moved in sync with the Hong Kong market, although the shallowness of the peaks and troughs suggested a conservative underwriting approach of which Cyrus Kwan would have approved. Perhaps the only anomaly was that AsiaRisk remained a privately-run company. For years, Leopold Chan had resisted cashing in with a public offering so as to maintain complete control. And yet here he was now looking to sell out at a huge discount to Kwan Holdings.

The question was, why?

Cyrus Kwan had given Rainbow forty-eight hours to find the answer.

Kwan had told her of Chan's stated desire to pass on his legacy to a safe pair of hands. Perhaps it was the cynic in her, but Rainbow had found it hard to get comfortable with that explanation. It didn't fit with Leopold Chan's personality type and the more she had discovered about the man, the less convincing the explanation became.

She quickly reviewed the chronology of Chan's life. Sixty-two this year, Chan had been educated in England. On leaving university, he had joined a Lloyd's of London syndicate and quickly excelled as part of the underwriting team. Keen to tap the promise of the Asia market, the syndicate had posted Leopold back to his native Hong Kong to set up an underwriting agency on their behalf. Leopold had quickly rewarded his English bosses' faith by producing a decade and a half of outstanding profits. Nervous about the transfer of sovereignty back to China, however, his bosses had then looked to exit Hong Kong. Leopold had smoothed the way for this by suggesting the management buy-out which had seen him take sole ownership of the agency in 1990, obtaining a full insurance licence. And so AsiaRisk was born.

When Rainbow reached the end of her chronology, she smiled. The last thing she had written on the page was a three word summation of Leopold Chan based on his personal history.

Ambitious, individualistic, driven. And having met him in the flesh now, she was convinced her assessment was right. The way he had been so eager to please, yet keen to make her work to his agenda, guiding her straight to his internal accounts. The way he had put her in this windowless room, hoping she would soon get fed up and give Cyrus Kwan a quick all-clear. Leopold Chan was definitely the controlling type. Definitely a man used to getting his own way.

But clients expected much more than the usual due diligence from Rainbow Choi. Forty-eight hours wasn't long, but she had worked to tighter deadlines than this and experience had taught her it was never the tightness of the deadline that counted anyway. Getting to the truth was a matter of pressing the right buttons.

Leopold Chan was presenting a façade, she was sure of that. Her job was to get behind it by stirring things up, throwing him off-balance and seeing what fell through the cracks. Before she'd walked through AsiaRisk's doors that morning, she hadn't known what pebble to throw in to disturb Chan's tranquil waters. But then right there in reception an opportunity had presented itself. A weak spot which Leopold Chan had not meant her to see. She had caught the flinch in his eyes. *Now how to exploit it?*

She reached for her mobile and called back to her office. "Hi, it's me. Here's what we need. I want Chan followed. Full surveillance for the next forty-eight hours. Where he goes, who he meets, the lot. He passes water, I want to know where and how long, got it?" They got it. "Second, I'm going to need some digging done. Find me everything you can on a lawyer called Charles Conrad. He works for Jackson, Weiss McDonald. ....Good....call me when you're done."

She closed the phone and bounced the edge of it off her chin, picturing the panic in Charles Conrad's sweaty face as he had panted out of the lift.

A lawyer in a panic.

A definite weak spot to exploit.

*

Charles Conrad was halfway to his feet when Leopold entered the room. "Sorry about turning up unannounced like this but I really needed to...."

"Don't ever come to this office again without making an appointment!" Leopold clicked his fingers, pointing Conrad back into his chair.

Conrad appeared about to apologize again, when Leopold felt the itch in his throat. He knew what was coming. Seconds later a death-rattle cough exploded in his mouth. Then another. Grabbing the back of a chair, Leopold bent forward, his shoulders juddering as the fit took hold, rasp after violent rasp blocking his windpipe, his face furnace-hot, pain splintering through his ribs, the world moving round him, the tight control he had on events loosening.

Damn this disease!

"I say, are you all right?" Conrad's annoying voice came through a filter.

The door opened, Leopold didn't see who it was. He didn't need to.

Terrence O'Rourke poured out a glass of water and handed it to Leopold with a set of pills. Leopold drank....swallowed....drank some more. A well-practised routine. The world came to a halt as the pain subsided. Leopold dabbed away tears, signaled he was all right. O'Rourke made to leave. "No, stay please Terrence," Leopold said, his voice hoarse.

O'Rourke nodded as if to say 'as you wish' and leaned back against the wall by the door, folding his arms, stretching his massive biceps menacingly through his suit sleeves. A sight which made Charles Conrad squirm in his seat.

167

Control restored, Leopold thought. But the coughing fit had left its message, loud and clear. *One chance to pull this off, Leopold. No more mistakes.*

"What do you want, Charles?" Leopold asked.

Conrad's tongue licked his thin, dry lips, his eyes shifting from O'Rourke to Leopold. "It's about Scott Lee," he said.

Leopold made a face. "I thought the Law Society complaint had seen him off."

"It did. Or at least I thought it did. But now I...." Conrad swallowed.

"Well spit it out, man!" Leopold was losing patience.

"I...." Conrad stammered. "I think he's on to us."

Pins and needles pricked Leopold's skin. "On to us?"

Charles told him about his secretary finding Lee's fountain-pen under a cabinet in Kimmie Yang's old office.

"You're sure it's his pen?"

"It has his initials on," Conrad said. "It was his leaving gift from Jackson's, I remember. He must have got into the office and snooped around in Kimmie's old room and dropped it."

Leopold was puzzled. "Why would he do that?"

Conrad's eyes glanced down at his tremoring hands, his complexion grey and sweaty.

"Scott knew Kimmie." Conrad hesitated. "They were....close."

Leopold's breath stopped. He held it a moment, then told himself to let it go. *In....then out. That's it. Control.* Drumming his fingers, he weighed the significance of this new piece of information. *What did it mean?* Scott Lee, this young lawyer who had come to see him out of the blue to try to wrestle away AsiaRisk's business from his former boss, Charles Conrad. It appeared an enterprising move, Leopold had thought at the time. Entrepreneurial. Lee's intelligence had also impressed Leopold.

But had there been more to it?

Now here was Conrad telling him that Kimmie Yang and Scott Lee were 'close'. Kimmie Yang; that silly girl who had almost blown apart the whole operation, all because Conrad couldn't control his own staff.

"Tell me there was nothing to find in her office, Charles," Leopold said after a moment.

Conrad swallowed hard. "There was a box of old cases I handled for you."

The blood in Leopold veins dropped below freezing. "And you didn't think to mention Scott Lee's relationship with Ms Yang before now?"

"I didn't think it was relevant."

Leopold Chan stood and paced. *Another challenge, another situation to control. That was the key. Establishing control at any cost.* He turned suddenly and faced Conrad.

"Charles, I want you to do exactly as I say! Go back to your office. Find Scott Lee's personnel file and let Terrence here have Lee's home address. Do it now, please!"

Conrad's eyes darted between Leopold and O'Rourke. The man was clearly terrified, exactly what Leopold wanted. Terror and greed were the two greatest motivators for human beings. Greed had sucked Conrad into the scheme; terror would now be used to keep him on a tight leash.

Conrad finally got up to leave.

"Oh and Charles," Leopold said. Conrad let go of the door handle as if it was electrified. "If I hear from Terrence that you haven't phoned him within the hour, I'll ask him to pay your wife a visit!"

Whatever blood was left within Conrad's face quickly drained away. Eyes cast down in fear, he left.

"Want me to follow him?" O'Rourke asked as soon as they were on their own.

"Charles isn't the problem now. This fellow Scott Lee is."

Leopold pondered his next move. The next forty-eight hours were going to be critical.

Then turning back to O'Rourke, Leopold gave his orders.

CHAPTER TWENTY-FOUR

As soon as Gloria Koo sat down, the heat of the stone bench seared through her skirt to the back of her legs. Midday was the wrong time of day to be lazing out by Queen's Pier, the sun was at its peak, the air stuffy with grit. Normally at this time Gloria would be cooling her heels and exchanging idle gossip with colleagues in one of the *Tsa-Tsan Teng*s on Central's back streets. Today, however, that routine had to be broken. Today, loyalty to her country came first.

Gloria checked her watch.

Her contact was late. He was never late. Gloria wondered if something had happened, if something had gone wrong. When he had called for this rendezvous, there had been an urgency in his tone which she had never before detected and....

"Hello Mei Tsing." The voice came from over her shoulder. She turned to look at him.

There he was; dark-suited, hunched shoulders, wisps of white streaking through his black pate. And in his hand, as always, that jade laughing Buddha face on the end of his keyring, his fingers in constant nervous movement across its surface as if trying to wipe away a permanent blemish from the deep green.

He had never told Gloria his real name; only his job title. He was a Recruiter. And two years ago he had recruited Gloria to his network.

"Let us walk, Mei Tsing," he said to her. Gloria liked the way he always used her Chinese name.

They ambled over to the black railing overlooking the harbour, Gloria keeping one step behind him. He was looking older than usual, she noticed, his back slightly more stooped than before, the white streaks in his hair almost dominating what was left of the black. Here were the physical symbols of the great responsibility which this man bore, Gloria mused, a responsibility which Gloria was proud to play her little part in helping him discharge. This man had taught her to believe in the great future that was her country's for the taking. He had given her a role in fulfilling that destiny. And as they stood there in the baking sun, with the ships and boats ebbing across the polluted waterway before them, Gloria cast her mind back to that moment seven years ago when he had stepped into her life and changed it forever.

It was on a Tuesday morning, Gloria recalled, and she had been on her way to work, hurrying with the hordes along the underground corridor in Central's MTR station towards the exit for Kwan Tower.

Just before the long travelator, she noticed him standing off to one side turning a map this way and that, looking like any other befuddled, confused out-of-towner overwhelmed by the wave of humanity which made up Hong Kong's morning rush-hour. When he had stepped out in front of her to ask for directions, it seemed like a random choice and Gloria took pity – not many others would have done, just clicked their teeth and moved on. But Gloria had always been taught to offer help where help was needed.

Yes, right up until that moment it had seemed to Gloria like this was a perfectly random encounter. But as soon as they were shoulder to shoulder, he spoke words that shocked her to the core.

"Do not be alarmed, Koo Mei Tsing!" He knew her name. But before the instant jolt of fear could take hold, he said, "Yes, I know who you are. In fact, I know everything about you." And as if make his point, he rattled off her age, ID card number, home address and the names of her parents with whom she lived.

It was the tone of the man's voice which made Gloria's trepidation subside, as if his words carried a certain authority that made her realize no crime was being committed, that she was in no danger. So when he asked her to accompany him on a short walk, Gloria agreed because her instinct told her it was the right thing to do.

He led her out to the open area under the HSBC Building, and it was there, shaded by the two lion statues marking its entry, that he put his proposition. "Listen to me carefully, Koo Mei Tsing. China has made great economic strides in recent decades. Our economy has become the envy of the world and our government now benefits from a surfeit of financial reserves. If invested right, these reserves could provide the stability required to make China the leading power everyone expects it to be. Do you understand what I am telling you, Koo Mei Tsing?"

"I'm sorry, I'm not sure...," Gloria stammered, but he had held up his hand for her to stop.

"I know you are a careful investor with your own money, Koo Mei Tsing. Like I said, I know all about you. You pay additional contributions into your pension every month and contribute to a balanced fund run by your employer. This is very prudent. And you would expect the People's Government to be equally prudent when investing the reserves it holds on the people's behalf, would you not?" This time he wanted an answer.

"I....I suppose so," Gloria stammered. The fact that this man knew intimate details about her financial dealings, which she never discussed with anyone, sent a queasiness running through her.

"The People's Government agrees with you, Koo Mei Tsing. They wish to invest the people's money, only they do not wish the world to know about it. When you swim in a new ocean, you do not jump straight in. You test the temperature with your toe, so that if the water is too cold you can withdraw without catching pneumonia. This is the investment strategy the People's Government intends to adopt. Like a swimmer venturing into a new ocean, it should start with one toe in that part of the ocean with which it is most comfortable. That is why I am here in Hong Kong, Koo Mei Tsing. The Hong Kong stock market will be the place where the government dips its toe. Foreigners have always believed Hong Kong to be the gateway to China. But a gate swings two ways. Now Hong Kong will serve as China's door to the world. The People's money will be invested in companies listed on the stock market here. And that is why, Koo Mei Tsing, I have come to ask you to do your country a great service."

This time Gloria forced through her protest. "You must be mistaken, sir. I am just a personal assistant. I know nothing about fund management...."

"There is no mistake, Koo Mei Tsing. The investments of which I speak are not for you or me to decide on. It is only my job to monitor them. To make sure the companies entrusted with the People's money do nothing to cause embarrassment to our Government or its citizens."

Gloria allowed her focus to drift to the noise of the trams rattling across their tracks down Queen's Road; to the stop-start traffic edging its way through the streets around them; to the shouts of the newspaper vendor outside the nearby MTR exit; anything to remind herself that this conversation – the most surreal of her life – was actually taking place. "I still don't understand what this has to do with me."

The man turned to her, his dark eyes serious and set within deep wrinkled crevices of experience. It was then that Gloria first noticed the Jade Buddha he was pinching between his forefinger and thumb.

"What I am about to tell you must remain a secret," he said. "You must carry it to your grave, do you understand?"

Gloria gave a reluctant nod.

"Kwan Holdings is one of the companies in which the People's money will be invested."

The sounds of the trams and the traffic stopped dead and were replaced by a dull buzzing in Gloria Koo's ears.

"Did you hear what I said, Koo Mei Tsing?"

"I....I can't do this....I have to go."

Gloria made to turn away, but the man placed his hand on her arm. No force was applied, but it was done with such authority that Gloria stopped statue still.

"Your loyalty to Tyson Mok does you credit, Koo Mei Tsing. It is that same loyalty I am asking you now to give to your country." As if sure that she would not turn and run, he took his hand away. "Mr Mok's business skills are greatly admired by the people I work for. He has shown great support for Cyrus Kwan throughout his career. Mr Mok has helped build Kwan Holdings into the success it is today. Kwan Holdings is a company of which China can be rightly proud. This is why the People's money will be invested in its shares." She had felt his doleful eyes probing her for signs of a reaction. "You have worked for Mr Mok for almost five years now, Mei Tsing. He must be a good employer."

"Oh, he is." Mr Mok is very committed to his staff and to the company.

"What I am about to ask you to do does not break any loyalty you owe to Mr Mok, Mr Kwan or Kwan Holdings. It is important that you understand that." Gloria looked at him suspiciously, but he did not flinch. "The People's Government does not wish the world to know that it is using the Hong Kong stock market as a testing ground for investing the People's money. They must keep this venture secret. No one at Kwan Holdings will know that the People's money has been used to buy the company's shares. No one, that is, except you Koo Mei Tsing. This is a great responsibility I am entrusting you with."

"But....but I am sure if you told Mr Mok, he would understand...."

"No!" His answer was abrupt. Then he softened his tone. "We are investing in the business skills of Mr Kwan and Mr Mok. We do not wish those skills to be swayed in any way by the knowledge that they have been entrusted with the People's money. Can you understand that?"

"I....I think so."

"Mr Mok and Mr Kwan are high profile figures, whose every act is under close scrutiny from the news media here in Hong Kong. If we entrust this knowledge to them, there is a great risk the secret will be discovered and published, causing the people I work for to reverse the experiment, an act which would be detrimental to the entire nation. But at the same time, it is important that the investment of the People's money is protected. That is my task, Koo Mei Tsing. And that is where you come in. As Mr Mok's personal assistant, you are trusted with commercially sensitive information about Kwan Holdings' business strategies. All I ask of you is that you meet with me, like this, whenever I call on you to update me with anything you think I should know."

"You want me to spy?"

The man drew a deep breath. "As Kwan Holdings is to be entrusted with the People's money, enemies of our nation will wish to see the company fail. Political enemies. The realm of politics is not something with which either Mr Kwan or Mr Mok is familiar. But the people I work for are. By providing me with the information I am asking for, you will be enabling us to protect the Chinese people's investment and the company you work for."

It was then that he fixed her with his hard stare and in solemn tones he spoke the words which had changed Gloria Koo's life forever. "I am asking you to do a great deed for your nation, Koo Mei Tsing. I am asking you to serve."

Gloria would never forget how she felt at that moment. The dull buzzing in her head, the overwhelming sense of pride and privilege that he had bestowed on her. The sense that her life now had great meaning.

She had just been recruited.

As they stood shoulder to shoulder at the harbour's edge, Gloria looked down and noticed the rubbish, which had collected on the surface of the water, lapping up against the wall just before it fell below the waterline: a nasty collection of fast food cups and broken bits of Styrofoam stained with seaweed.

"I am sorry that I have been forced to ask you to do this again, especially so soon after last time," the man whom she knew only as her recruiter said. "But it is necessary that I have up-to-date intelligence from everyone in the network." Then he turned side-on and looked and Gloria. "So, Koo Mei Tsing, what do you have for me?"

"Only this," Gloria said, reaching into her handbag and handing him the memo addressed to Cyrus Kwan and Tyson Mok by Simon Ng. Tyson Mok had given it to her that morning and told her to shred it straight away. "I would be grateful if I could have it back, after you have read it," she said, keen to obey Mok's instruction.

As the man read the memo, his brow deepened into a frown under his salt-and-pepper hair. "Do you know anything about this company, AsiaRisk, Koo Mei Tsing?"

"I do not, sir. But I believe that whatever business Mr Kwan has with it will take place in the next few days. Mr Mok and Mr Ng have had many meetings in private with Mr Kwan and his nephew about it already. I sense there is an urgency."

"His nephew? Rupert Kwan is involved?" That piece of news appeared to surprise him.

Gloria nodded.

He blew through his mouth and the tempo with which he rubbed the jade Buddha increased, as if stimulating his thought process, layering implication upon implication. After a moment he handed her back the memo. "You have done well to bring this to my attention, Mei Tsing."

His words made Gloria blush with pride. "I hope it is useful."

"I sense," he said, "that it may be more useful than you realize."

As Huang Yi watched Gloria Koo walk back towards Kwan Tower, he felt an acid ball form in the pit of his stomach.

This last seven days he had been busy, setting up meetings with all the contacts in his network, asking them to provide him with up-to-date information. It had been tough-going. Many of them had taken considerable convincing to come forward this time. Huang Yi wished his masters in Beijing realized that implementing a Code Blue wasn't a question of just making a few phone-calls. The network which Huang Yi had built was entirely voluntary. It worked on persuasion and a deep-seated desire to serve the nation, not on compulsion.

And most of the information the Cold Blue had elicited this time round had proved to be entirely irrelevant. Just profit projections, restructuring proposals and internal accounts from which nothing could be gleaned.

But the memo which Koo Mei Tsing had just shown Huang Yi registered hard on his radar screen.

He hurried away.

He had to contact Beijing.

CHAPTER TWENTY-FIVE

Amongst the glittering skyscrapers of Wanchai's waterfront, the grey-pillared five-storey police station resembled a Disco-king who had just woken up after twenty years in the middle of a dance rave. Scott paused outside to admire the old edifice. One day, it would be up for re-development and there would be the usual round of protests about how Hong Kong was losing its heritage. But in the end money would talk – it always did in this city – and the building would disappear. Continual change was about the only constant in Hong Kong. Still, it would be a shame.

Scott's regret withered and died, however, as soon as he stepped through the entrance into the functional interior which was no match for the magnificent external façade. Grubby white walls looked down at him from all sides, decorated only with the occasional poster broadcasting obvious warnings about criminal intent. Vinegary disinfectant seemed to be absorbed into every surface.

Four individuals were slumped in varying poses on a set of uncomfortable gym benches against one of the walls. None of them looked like this was their first time in a police station. Scott quickly worked out they made up the queue for the three officers manning the desks behind the glass-windowed counters. That made Scott fifth in line. He took a ticket – it told him he was number eighty-two. Hoping there was some logic to the numbering system, he parked himself down on the bench next to a man with a face hardened by experience. Experience of what, Scott couldn't tell, but the man was in no mood for talking, which suited Scott fine.

Scott thought about going over the material in his briefcase again while waiting. But he knew it well enough already. Through the night he had boiled it down into the salient steps which he was here to present.

Fifteen minutes went by.

Eventually one of the counter-clerks, a woman with eyes that said manning reception wasn't the reason she had joined the force, called out number 'eighty-two'. Scott went over and told her that he was here to see Ian Wallingford. She tapped her computer, rang somebody, told Scott to wait another five minutes and Wallingford would be down. Scott moved back to the bench, placed the briefcase down beside him, leaned his elbows on his knees and interlocked his fingers.

Five minutes passed. Nothing. Scott glanced down at the briefcase. Doubts began to filter in. Taking this to the police was the only realistic way forward, he knew that. But it had taken a lot of self-convincing. At Yip & Siu, Scott had carved out a niche for himself by battling bureaucracy and government rigidity. His case-load had fostered his innate suspicion of authority. But experience had also taught Scott to recognize his limitations. He was no criminal lawyer and this was too important to go it alone.

Eventually a tall, thin white man came through a pair of double doors from up the corridor to Scott's left. The man had white hair and an assured composure. He spoke to the desk-clerk who pointed in Scott's direction. The man walked over and held out his hand.

"I'm Ian Wallingford." His accent was pure Yorkshire, his eyes a piercing blue. Scott felt the heat of their scrutinizing intensity. "Please come this way."

Wallingford led Scott through the double-doors, then up a flight of stairs. At the top, passing a water-dispenser, they walked along a corridor lined with doors on either side, each one labelled 'interview-room' with a slide underneath showing 'occupied' or 'vacant'. Scott felt guilty just being there.

"This one looks free," Wallingford said. He moved the slide rule to 'occupied', and ushered Scott in. A small table was positioned centrally in the room.They sat on either side of it. The noise of scraping chair-legs echoed off the dank walls. Scott slipped the briefcase down the side next to the wall. "How's Larson these days?" Wallingford asked. "Still disgustingly fit?"

"Disgustingly."

Larson had passed Wallingford's name to Scott as someone he should speak to about money-laundering. Now here Scott was. In a police interview-room.

"I was thinking more along the lines of a cup of coffee at Starbucks," Scott said looking around at the blank walls.

Wallingford took his glasses off, polished them with his tie and blew on the lenses. "Look Scott....mind if I call you Scott?" Scott didn't. "Pussy-footing around over a couple of lattes isn't going to help you and it's not going to help me. What will help is, if you just say what you've come to say. Leave nothing out. I come with no preconceptions and everything you tell me is off-the-record. I will take no notes and nothing leaves this room unless you want it to. You have my word on that."

Discreet and no bullshit. Just like Larson had promised.

"Did Larson say anything about what I wanted to talk to you about?" Scott asked.

"He said it had something to do with some money-laundering issues you were facing."

"Nothing else?"

"No."

Scott bit his lip. Somehow he wasn't ready. The interview-room, the way Wallingford had thrown it open just like that, no introduction, no nothing, had unbalanced him. This wasn't how he wanted to play it. "Can I ask you something?" Wallingford shrugged for Scott to go ahead. "What do you do here, exactly?"

Wallingford's narrowing eyes sized Scott up. "I've been a policeman for over twenty-five years. Started off on the beat in Hull, then moved to CID and got posted down to London, where I met my wife. A while later we moved out here, she being originally from these parts. Been with the Hong Kong police ever since. Seven years ago, I was asked to head the Financial Institutions Crimes Unit, to deal with white-collar crime – fraud, money-laundering; that sort of thing –   because no one else wanted the job. I retired officially two years ago, but they've kept me on as a consultant, to try to get the youngsters interested in spending hours going through financial reports. Not an easy task, I tell you. I'm working harder now than I did when I was full-time. That answer your question?"

Scott nodded. They sat in silence. A minute passed by. Scott counted the seconds off his watch, its tick the only sound in the room.

"Why don't you tell me what all this is about, eh?" Wallingford eventually said.

Scott leaned his elbows onto the table, locked his fingers and tapped his thumbs. "I used to work for a law firm called Jackson,

Weiss, Macdonald," he said. "They have a branch office here run by a partner called Charles Conrad. The office gets a lot of its work from referrals from other Jackson's offices round the world. But it does have one major Hong Kong-based client: an insurance company called AsiaRisk, run by a man called Leopold Chan."

"I don't think I know it," Wallingford said.

"It isn't a huge player in the industry," Scott continued. "But AsiaRisk does have a particular specialty in servicing the SME market – private companies with small-scale turnovers."

"Okay, I'm with you."

"So naturally SMEs make up a large element of AsiaRisk's policyholders," Scott said. "They pay premiums to AsiaRisk for insurance. In return, AsiaRisk is supposed to pay claims."

"I sense there's a 'but' coming."

Scott shifted in his seat. "When a claim is made on an insurer like AsiaRisk, the standard procedure is to examine the insurance policy to check whether the terms have been complied with. If they have, AsiaRisk pays. If they haven't, AsiaRisk declines the claim."

"Bloody insurers!" Wallingford disapproved. "When my wife pranged the car last year, we had to make an insurance claim. Like getting blood out of a stone."

"It can be difficult," Scott accepted. "And if the policyholder doesn't agree with the declinature, it can take legal action against AsiaRisk. Which is when AsiaRisk instructs my old boss Charles Conrad at Jackson's."

"I see."

"There's a bit of brinkmanship from both parties to start with. Then negotiations start and after that, the dispute is settled pretty quickly without getting anywhere near a court. Jackson's draft the settlement agreement. AsiaRisk pays the settlement amount into Jackson's client account. Jackson's pays the money on to the policyholder."

Three beats of silence.

"So what's the problem?" Wallingford asked.

Scott weighed his next words carefully. "The whole thing's a scam. That's the problem."

Wallingford's brow creased in two. "I don't follow."

"It's a way of laundering money through AsiaRisk, don't you see?" Scott said. "Dirty money comes in the front door in the form of premiums paid by the companies which AsiaRisk is insuring. The same money goes out of the back door dressed up as legitimate insurance claims, documented by binding settlement agreements, and given an added air of legitimacy from having been passed through the client account of a reputable law firm."

Wallingford took off his glasses again and sucked the plastic-covering of one of the arms. "Are you saying the policyholders that AsiaRisk insures don't exist?"

"No, they exist all right. Only they're not legitimate businesses. They're just shell companies, whose ownership is lost in a myriad of offshore shareholdings, so it's impossible to trace who controls them. My guess is that all roads lead back to Leopold Chan."

"The head of AsiaRisk."

"Correct."

"So he controls the policyholders, which his company insures?"

"Well, some of them; not all of them," Scott said. "Most of AsiaRisk's business is legitimate insurance. The legitimate business helps disguise the illegitimate business, which, like I said, is concentrated on AsiaRisk's SME line."

"So the SMEs which AsiaRisk insures...or some of them at least....are companies which you say this Leopold Chan has set up."

"That is my belief, yes," Scott said. "But he's hidden the ownership in an offshore shareholding structure."

Silence. Wallingford tapped the arm of his glasses against his teeth, testing the truth of Scott's synopsis. "So Chan fixes the amount of premium payable, when insurance is purchased by one of the policyholders he controls. That's the dirty money going into AsiaRisk's accounts. Then he manufactures an insurance claim to pay the money back out once it's been through AsiaRisk's books. And it's legitimate because it looks like the proceeds of an insurance claim."

"Exactly."

Wallingford cast his eyes up to the ceiling, then back down. "Clever," he said. "But why go through the charade of having these policyholders sue AsiaRisk? Why not just pay out the claim?"

"They don't actually sue AsiaRisk," Scott corrected him. "They only threaten to sue. It's the threat of being sued which enables Leopold Chan to involve Jackson's. That's how the money, when it's eventually paid out, is funneled through Jackson's client account and then back to the policyholder. It gives the payment added legitimacy and the protection of lawyer-client privilege."

Nodding slowly, Wallingford slipped his bottom lip up over his top lip. "Wouldn't the policyholders have to instruct lawyers of their own when they threaten to sue AsiaRisk?"

"They do..." Scott said, then stopped himself. "I mean, they don't, but it's made to look like they do."

"You've lost me!"

"When you look at Jackson's files for each dispute, the name of the opposing party's solicitor is listed. But I've checked with some of the firms. They've never heard of the policyholders they're supposed to have represented. Charles Conrad just made it up."

"So this lawyer – this Charles Conrad fellow – is in on it?"

The air in the room became still then, like a tranquil pond daring Scott to disturb its calm surface by tossing in a pebble. "Up to his neck," he said.

Wallingford held the stare, sizing up Scott's demeanour, searching out weaknesses.

"And he used to be your boss?"

"Yes."

"Leave on good terms, did you?"

Scott hesitated. "Is that important?"

Wallingford shrugged. "Might be suggested you have an axe to grind. That you're making this up to settle an old score."

Scott blew air through his mouth and readied himself to crush the notion. "I'm not going to lie to you. Charles Conrad was why I left Jackson's. But that's not why I'm here."

"Then do you mind my asking why you are here?" Wallingford's tone took on an accusatory sharpness. Outside a car-horn blasted above the constant monotony of the traffic.

"Because I believe that what Leopold Chan and Charles Conrad are doing is wrong."

That was good enough. Scott wasn't bringing Kimmie's name into this, not yet. The last thing Sally Yang or her parents needed was the police crawling all over them, stirring up the raw emotions which they were trying to deal with in the depths of tragedy.

Wallingford let the silence hang, waited for Scott to fill it, expectant of something more. Nothing came.

"Sounds like quite a neat scam," the Yorkshireman eventually admitted. "If it's true, that is. I assume you've got some evidence in that briefcase of yours."

Scott picked up the case, unzipped it, took out the blue wallet-file holding the key documentation that he'd put together. He placed it on the table, rested his fingers delicately on top.

"Doesn't look much," Wallingford said.

"It's enough."

Wallingford folded his arms. "Two things puzzle me. If Leopold Chan and Charles Conrad are laundering money, who are they laundering it for?"

It was a question Scott had anticipated.

"I don't know. I was hoping the police would find that out. What's the second thing?"

The senior police-officer turned his face towards the wall as if reading patterns in the paint-work. Then he swivelled back to Scott. "Why?" he said.

"Why what?"

"Why are two apparently professional men doing this? Take this Chan fellow. What's his position in AsiaRisk? Chairman? Chief executive?"

"He owns it and runs it," Scott said.

"A person in that position isn't going to be short of a few pennies. So what's his motive?"

Scott rubbed his forehead. It was slick with sweat. He hadn't noticed how hot the interview-room was. It felt like a pressure-cooker, a place where confessions were sweated out.

"I'm a lawyer, Mr Wallingford. I deal with evidence," Scott tapped the file. "You want to get inside a person's head and explain why he's doing stuff, find a psychologist."

"Fair enough," Wallingford gave a half-chuckle. "But motive is one thing they'll look for, if they decide to take this on."

Scott didn't like the sound of that. "If *they* decide to take it on? What do you mean, 'they'? I thought you were the one who...." Wallingford was already shaking his head.

"I used to be head of the Financial Institutions Crimes Unit. Not any more. I'm a consultant now. I can make sure this is seen by the right people. I can even make recommendations. But it's the full-time case officers who make the final decision. Not me."

Disappointment twisted deep within Scott. Wallingford was a straightforward man, Scott could tell. But the prospect of explaining it all over again to a case-officer smacked of a system which allowed ample opportunity for buck-passing, the very thing Scott had wanted to avoid.

"Leave the file with me, why don't you?" Wallingford said. "I'll look at it. If I think it's got legs, I'll make the strongest possible recommendation I can. These grey hairs still earn me some respect around here, you know," he tapped his head. "And I take it those are just copies. A cautious man like you wouldn't be handing over the originals now, would you? So what have you got to lose?"

It was a good question.

"How long will it take for a decision?" Scott asked. "More than a week and I'd feel I've wasted my time."

Wallingford appeared surprised at the sharpness of the comment. "I'll look at it this evening and speak to a case-officer tomorrow, if I think it's worth doing. How's that sound?"

Scott paused a moment, excitement prickling down his neck at the thought that he might be getting somewhere at last.

He slid the file over.

CHAPTER TWENTY-SIX

Benny Wang looked ridiculous in his pink Lacoste polo-shirt and knee-length eggplant-coloured knickerbockers. Teeing up a golf-ball was an effort clearly beyond his grotesque physique.

From the backseat of the golf buggie, Leopold swallowed down disgust. Why did golfers think it okay to dress up like sixteenth century court-jesters? It was such a stupid game, a pathetic excuse for grown men to spend a day away from the office. And Benny couldn't get enough of it apparently. *Why doesn't that surprise me?* Leopold thought. A hoodlum, craving acceptance amongst Hong Kong's social élite, was Benny Wang. Well, it would take more than just a slick fashion sense and a sub-eighteen handicap....

But distasteful though it was, Leopold knew he still needed to keep Benny on side, which was why he was here today, ready to offer reassurances that everything was going according to plan and to deal with those last minute jitters Benny always went in for.

While Benny took practice swings, Leopold took a quick mental audit of all his moving pieces. The takeover was proceeding sufficiently smoothly. Rainbow Choi's due diligence was the last hurdle and Leopold didn't foresee that posing any difficulties. He was confident that, within a matter of days, AsiaRisk would be part of Kwan Holdings. And despite Conrad's panic attack earlier that morning, Leopold couldn't see Scott Lee being a problem. O'Rourke was more than capable of handling that particular situation if it ever got out of hand.

But right now, it was the jig-saw piece, following the takeover, which was concerning Leopold most. The piece which made Benny Wang such a vital part of things.

Benny swung clumsily and sliced his shot into the undergrowth. Leopold rolled his eyes.

"Good shot, boss!" Benny's caddie dutifully commented, a lank-haired youth with acne scars and mirrored sunglasses, who looked like he'd be more at home with a Playstation. Benny handed the kid his club and, just when Leopold thought things couldn't get any more ridiculous, lit an inch-thick cigar.

"You should play, Leo. It's fun." Benny waddled back to the buggie and eased his bulk into the back seat next to Leopold. The buggie sank down on one side.

"Not my thing," Leopold was impatient to move the conversation on. "I'm only here to talk business!"

"Then talk."

Leopold cast an eye towards the caddie, now in the driving seat.

"Oh don't worry about Eric," Benny said. "He wouldn't understand anyway."

Probably true. The buggie jolted with a high pitched whir and they trundled unsteadily forward.

"You've spoken to the owner of the Chow Mei factory, I take it?" Leopold asked.

Benny gave him a sidelong glance. "That pig Eva Chow sold me the rights to her insurance policy without any problems. Not surprising, since you cancelled the damn thing the day before her precious factory burned down. Five million it cost me! You better know what you're doing, Leo!"

Leopold declined to comment, so Benny told Eric to stop the buggie. After they had ground to a halt, Benny swiveled his ample physique sideways until sour breath and smoke was blowing in Leopold's face. "So what did I get for my five million, Leo? Apart from a worthless insurance claim?"

Leopold gazed round the golf-course. Lush green turf as far as the eye could see, marred only by the occasional loudly-dressed idiot bellowing in Mandarin. Rarely had such prime real estate been put to such bad use. "I've told you what you get. Control of Kwan Holdings!"

Benny's rasping cackle came full with a cloud of nicotine-laced spittle, but it soon died when he realized Leopold wasn't joining in the joke. Benny stared with hard, sunken eyes, cheeks twitching, his mole bobbing rhymthmically. "Okay, I want to know what the plan is!"

Leopold met his gaze. "There you are, Benny, you only had to ask. Not so difficult, was it?" He could almost hear Benny's vast insides roiling with humiliation. There they sat, two men, one vastly superior to the other. Both possessed of ambition, but only Leopold had the intelligence to make it reality. "AsiaRisk fully intends to honour any claim made on Chow Mei's insurance policy," Leopold said. "Since the entire Chow Mei factory has been destroyed, I estimate that would be somewhere in the region of two hundred million Hong Kong dollars. And you own the right to that money, Benny. It's yours."

Benny's eyes narrowed into pips. "Hmm. So my five million turns into two hundred million. Not bad."

"No, Benny," Leopold explained, like he was talking to a small child. "That's not how this works. The two hundred million is already yours. It's money which I'm going to launder for you. This time, however, instead of cleaning it in a series of small payments like we usually do, I'm paying it out in one single legitimate insurance claim on a factory that actually burned down. It's the perfect disguise."

The thought took a while for Benny to compute. "How does that get me control of Kwan Holdings?"

"That, my dear Benny, is the brilliant part." A beat of silence. Then: "I'm selling AsiaRisk to Kwan Holdings."

"You're what?" Benny bellowed like a walrus.

"And if all goes to according to plan, the deal will be completed within the next forty-eight hours. At which time you will submit your insurance claim on the Chow Mei factory. I shall ensure the claim is paid out to you in full. And then you, Benny, will go to Cyrus Kwan and ask him to appoint you to the board of directors of Kwan Holdings."

From the look on Benny's face, he evidently found the suggestion incredible. "You can't be serious!"

"I'm perfectly serious, Benny. And trust me, Kwan will have no choice but to adhere to your demand; because you would have just successfully laundered two hundred million dollars through *his* new company. Or to be more precise, through Kwan Holdings. Think what would happen to Kwan Holdings' share price if that was ever made public? You see Benny, I'm giving you the power to blackmail Cyrus Kwan. You control Cyrus Kwan, you control his company. *That's* the return you get on your five million investment."

The embers on Benny's cigar died out. He relit it, settled back in the seat. "Don't see why we have to go to all this trouble. The current system works fine. Why take this risk?"

Leopold worked hard at keeping his features stoic. Inside, though, he was screaming at the spineless fat idiot sitting beside him. But then again, nothing had been more predictable than this late change of heart. It always happened with Benny and this time Leopold had come prepared. "Can we make a quick detour to the club house? There's someone I want you to meet."

"I'm in the middle of a round!" Benny said indignantly.

"It will be worth your while, I promise. Twenty minutes, that's all. Then you can come back and finish your little game." Like coaxing a recalcitrant school boy. But Benny finally agreed and ordered Eric to drive them.

On reaching the clubhouse, they disembarked. Leopold led Benny through the main entrance, then down a corridor to the players's bar, a light airy room with floor to ceiling windows opening out onto a picturesque patio. A waiter approached them but Leopold waved him off. He had already spotted the person they were there to meet.

Rupert Kwan sat by one of the windows in relaxed pose, wearing slacks and a sports jacket. His handsome face was turned side on as if searching out his perfect camera-angle.

"Nice of you to make it," Leopold caught Rupert's attention.

Rupert got to his feet, did up his jacket and flashed a toothpaste advertisement smile. "Thank you for inviting me." Then, turning his attention to the waddling Wang. "A pleasure to meet you at last, Benny. Leopold has already told me so much about you."

Benny Wang's jaw went slack. Starstruck, the only word for it. Just like Leopold knew he would be.

Cyrus Kwan's nephew played his part, offering Benny a seat, ordering him a drink, regaling him with tales of his hyped commercial exploits. Leopold looked on as all the doubts which Benny Wang had harboured melted to nothing. Here was living, breathing proof of the kinds of social levels to which Leopold's plan would give Benny access. All Benny had to do was do as he was told.

When their conversation was over, Leopold ushered Benny back to his buggie out front.

"You're okay with us going ahead then?" Leopold said. "No more jitters?"

Benny said nothing, but the look on his face gave Leopold his answer. The great oaf was drunk with images of his life to come, of his new social status, of the power he could exercise as a director of Kwan Holdings. Putting him in the same room with Rupert Kwan was pure genius.

"You've done well Leo," Benny drawled. "This plan, it's all happening in the next couple of days then?"

"It is."

"And nothing can go wrong?"

Leopold hesitated a moment as his recent conversation with Charles Conrad blasted into his mind. Scott Lee, the solicitor who had so impressed him; who had seemingly broken into Jackson's office, perhaps discovering more than he should have done. A potential wild card; an unexpected third party, over whom Leopold did not yet exercise control. But precautions had been deployed. O'Rourke was on the job now. And if Scott Lee stepped out of line....

"No, Benny. It's all under control."

Back in the bar, Rupert Kwan remained seated, his manicured hands clasped over his knee.

"You outdid yourself, Rupert, I must say," Leopold congratulated him.

"Who was that guy anyway?"

"Benny Wang? Oh he's one of AsiaRisk's biggest clients. That's why I thought you two should meet. You've certainly made an impression there. I can see my company will be in safe hands. How are things going with your uncle? Anything I need to know about?"

Rupert looked at the window and checked his reflection in the glass. "It's going to come down to whatever this Rainbow Choi has to say about things. I don't know her personally, but the board seems to worship the ground she walks on. Quite the little tigress apparently."

"Don't worry," Leopold said. "I have nothing to hide from Ms Choi."

Rupert turned his handsome face to Leopold. "And you're definitely stepping down after the sale goes through?"

Leopold smiled. This obnoxious neophyte's ambition was as naked as Benny Wang's. Physically, they couldn't have been more different. But in terms of personality, they were cut from the same mould. Well, they were welcome to each other as far as Leopold was concerned.

"Don't worry, Rupert. You'll be free to take on the management reins once this is over. Provided, of course, uncle Cyrus allows you to."

The comment stung Rupert, but Leopold didn't care.

He'd had enough of massaging egos for one day.

CHAPTER TWENTY-SEVEN

Some days Scott craved room to breathe, to find an open space where he could be alone with his thoughts. Today wasn't one of those days. Today, Scott needed Hong Kong to satisfy a different need, to absorb his restlessness and soak away his tension.

So he lost himself on its streets, walking as the mood took him, everywhere and nowhere. Past the local cafés on Percival Street, with their succulent roasted meats and whole crispy ducks hanging in the windows; where people huddled tightly around formica tables slurping noodles. Past jewelry shops, glittering with gold Buddhas and diamond-studded watches. Through Jardine's Crescent to the Sogo crossing – the busiest in the world – where, when the traffic-lights changed, two surging armies of humanity came together under the humid heavens.

Street vendors tried to sell him broadband services, horse-riding courses and mobile phone repairs. Chain stores showed off widescreen TVs in their windows. At a 7-Eleven, Scott bought a *South China Morning Post* and a bottle of water. Old ladies with trolleys shouted for people to get out of the way. Old men delivering Styrofoam lunch-boxes dodged across the road between Porches and BMWs. Mobile phones trilled. Music and air-conditioners blasted out from each shop entrance. Advertising screens with David Beckham, and metal washing-lines with damp clothing hanging on them filled the sticky heavens.

This was Causeway Bay, the crowded, constantly-fidgeting part of Hong Kong that Scott needed right now. Where the only way of not letting it get to you was to play ignorant to everyone else's presence. Solitude in a sea of millions; anonymity by immersion.

Just before midday, his pent-up energy exhausted, Scott caught a tram, heading south up Wong Nai Chung Road past the race course, back to his Happy Valley flat. The rest of the day stretched out before him like a depressing empty chasm. He should have been making plans for the future and looking for another job, but each time he turned his mind onto that idea, he stumbled on the same question: Should he stick with Hong Kong or return to London?

Neither option seemed palatable right then. He had lived in Hong Kong for eight years, long enough for it to feel comfortable, but not long enough to call it home, not really. At the same time, London had stopped being home for him a long time ago. Whenever he went back there now, it felt like bumping into a distant school-friend for an hour or two. So here he was, stuck in the hinterland between two worlds and unable to choose between them.

Scott thought of calling Yip, to see if they were missing him at work. Then he decided against it, as he might not like the answer.

He also thought of ringing Ian Wallingford, but realized there was little point in that either. No way Wallingford would have an answer for him yet; it was far too soon. The Hong Kong police didn't strike Scott as an institution that had the capability to move that fast. Government was, after all, government.

So in the end, Scott went back to the notes he had made on AsiaRisk, his current obsession.

The air-conditioner in his spare-room-cum-study was broken now and sounded like an Apache helicopter. Flipping through the pages, he soon realized there was nothing in these notes he couldn't recite with his eyes closed, so he turned back further through the note-pad; tracing the building-blocks of his thought process over the last few days, the random jottings following his conversations with Larson Twain and Aloysia Tse, information from the company searches he had undertaken, evidence of the many hours he had already committed to this project....

Steel fingers suddenly tightened around his ribcage. Project? Was that all this had become now? Just another case measured by the hours he had spent working on it?

Kimmie.

The dull, deep, empty ache came upon Scott hard and fast then. Most of his contemporaries were married with kids, settled in family lives, battling hard for their loved ones and completely content in the struggle. Scott looked at the room around him. Paint peeled at the edges of the walls and apart from his West Ham poster, their surfaces were bare. The broken air-conditioner drummed a steady, annoying beat. Somehow, that flat summed up his life. A life of selfish impermanency, with no one to care about but himself. And the one person who had ever come close to changing it all was Kimmie Yang.

No, this wasn't just another project.

Scott got up, walked around, cleared his mind, then went back to his notes and turned through the pages again, going back in time to the pitch he had made to Leopold Chan where this had all started. The preparatory notes he had made leapt at him off the pages, reminding him of the work he had put in. A comparison of charge-out rates, calculations demonstrating the saving AsiaRisk could make by moving its work away from Jackson's to Yip & Siu. It made Scott marvel at his own naivety. If he had known then what was going on, he could have ....

The thought snapped off,as his gaze snagged on the squiggled words in the margin of the page. Here was something out of place, something he had forgotten about. Scott swiveled the page to look the words straight on. A memory sparked of Leopold Chan coughing his guts up. Chan's assistant....what was his name....O'Rourke....yes   that   was   it....Terrence O'Rourke....helping Chan with his pills. During the coughing fit, Scott had stayed silent, not wishing to embarrass his host. For the sake of pretending to have something to do, he had noted down the names on the outside of the bottles containing Leopold Chan's medicine. Names which now stared up at Scott from the margin of the page.

Prednisone/ Percocet.

Was this something? A different angle to explore, perhaps?

Five minutes and a google-search later, Scott read the Wikipedia entry for 'Predisone'.

"A synthetic corticosteroid drug that is usually taken orally but can be delivered by intramuscular injection and can be used for a great number of different conditions. It has a mainly glucocorticoid effect. Predisone is a prodrug that is converted by the liver into prednisolone, which is the active drug and also a steroid."

Scott blinked a couple of times then read it again, but it was still meaningless gobbledegook. It might as well be in Russian for all the explanation it offered. He had better luck with Percocet, however. It was some form of pain-killer – prescribed, not over the counter – which meant Leopold Chan may have had health issues that went beyond just a nasty cold.

Scott wrestled with his thoughts. Did this change things at all? Was it relevant? The obvious and immediate answer was 'no'; what possible link could there be between Leopold Chan's health and the closely-guarded secret of his money-laundering operations? But Scott had always been cautious of letting seemingly unrelated details go so easily. Everything needed to be explored, dissected and understood before being rubbished, that was the approach he had always taken. And given the claptrap Google had just tossed him, Scott was far from being satisfied that he could let this information go just yet. Especially when all it needed was an email to the one person Scott knew who was qualified enough to address his question.

Just one quick email. Such an easy task, yet at the same time, for Scott, such a massive leap of faith.

Surfing to the Yahoo homepage, Scott opened up his email account and scrolled the pages of his inbox. He never cleared it out and hit page seven before he found what he was looking for. It was an e-card from Christmas two years ago, complete with fluttering snow and a reindeer in the sky. The message read simply: *"Scott, Hope all's well in HK. Have a great Christmas. John, Sandy, Beck and Tom."*

Scott had never replied to it, so those three lines represented his last communication with his brother, Doctor John Lee, oncologist at the John Radcliffe. Mr Impressive himself.

Scott felt all his teenage inadequacies filter back in then; about never having been a school prefect when John had been head boy, or being good at sport the way John had, or being able to rattle through equations with his eyes shut like John could. Scott had always had to work flat out to achieve even mediocrity while big brother John had coasted along effortlessly in his happy successful, blessed life. Adulthood was supposed to have seen the re-balancing of their respective fortunes, at least that was what Scott had always told himself. By now he was supposed to be able to look his brother in the eye as a partner in a top commercial law firm, not from the shadow of his own inadequacies. But here he was, having tossed away his career, having to go to big brother for help. Again.

What the hell. Scott hit 'reply' and spent an hour typing before he had something which he felt conveyed the right tone but without giving anything away about his predicament.

Hey Bro,

Apologies for the absence in correspondence, but you know how it is. Dad's been keeping me up-to-date with progress. Congrats on the promotion and glad to hear of Beck's straight A star sweep with his GCSEs. Chip off the old block. Tell him Uncle Scott says 'well done'.

Got a quick favour to ask. I have a colleague who has some health problems, but is reticent to talk about it. I'm worried about him. He's got this real bad cough. I mean real bad. And he's taking these pills called Prednisone and Percocet. I have no idea what they're for. Thought you might know. Any time you have a spare moment....

Love to the family, Scott.

He didn't expect an answer any time soon. John had always led his own life and Scott had always kept his distance. Thirteen thousand miles worth of distance, in fact. But when it came down to it, family was family and that was about all Scott had left now. He pressed 'send'.

The phone started ringing. Scott welcomed the distraction and answered it.

"Scott, it's Ian Wallingford."

Scott straightened in his chair.

"Ian. How are you?"

"Fine. Listen, can you come down to the station this afternoon, say three o'clock? Some of my colleagues want to have a chat."

As soon as Scott saw Ian Wallingford standing outside the station, he sensed something was wrong.

Wallingford was smoking. In itself that was strange, the Yorkshireman didn't seem the type. There was also a distraction in his manner which somehow seemed to border on annoyance.

"Nasty habit, I know," Wallingford said when he looked up and saw Scott approaching, "but it's about the only pleasure I have left these days. The top floor frowns on it. They can frown all they like, won't do any good. I'm already retired." Those last words were more pointed than flippant. A joke with bones. "Hope I didn't pull you away from anything important. Where do you work anyway? You never said."

Scott decided to go with a half-truth. "I'm in between things at the moment." He didn't want Yip & Siu being dragged into this.

Wallingford finished his cigarette in one draw, smoke flowing through his acquiline nose with a tension-relieving sigh. "Let's get you upstairs then."

Inside the station the air-conditioning was being rationed, no doubt part of the government's brilliant plan to be more energy conscious. Being green took priority, it seemed, over sweat-stained shirts. They walked up two flights of stairs, then down a corridor which trapped the echo of their footsteps. Wallingford stopped outside a door on the left. A conversation was going on inside. Two men, both Cantonese speakers, though Scott couldn't make out the words. Wallingford knocked and showed Scott in. The conversation immediately peeled into silence.

The man who had just been speaking sat behind a desk, collar open, tie loosened, shirt stretching over a beer-belly. His suspicious eyes looked Scott up and down. He had the beginnings of a moustache on a blubbery set of lips. His complexion was an overhang from an unfortunate adolescence.

From the visitor's chair, a second man turned to Scott. He was the polar opposite of the desk-jockey. Younger, shirt pressed, tie perfectly positioned, hair gelled to a strict side parting, clean skin taut over a bony face. The only commonality between the two was the suspicious eye-balling.

"This is Detective Chief-Inspector Shing and Detective-Sergeant Tam," Wallingford said. Shing was the specimen behind the desk, Tam in the visitor's chair. Damp handshakes followed. Tam gave Scott his card. Shing didn't bother. "I'll wait downstairs," Wallingford said, closing the door before Scott had the chance to ask why he wasn't staying.

"Sit down, Mr Lee!" Shing brushed two fingers on the spare chair. Tam handed Shing a file. Shing opened it and read the top page. "Quite a story you've come to us with." His tone was as friendly as a rusty chain-saw and about as subtle.

Scott felt heat in his cheeks at the word 'story'. It made him want to bang the desk and tell Shing to take his government salary and shove it up the body part which got most exercise. Casting up an image of ice-cubes clinking in fizzy water, Scott let the heat dissipate.

"Unfortunately, we can't take this further," Shing said.

Just like that, there it was, the big 'no', served up cold and devoid of sugar coating.

Scott's ice-cubes melted in an instant furnace. "I'm sorry, but I don't accept that!"

Shing looked like he'd just been slapped in the face by the response, but Scott didn't care. He knew Shing's type. Probably a twenty-year man who relied on promotion by longevity, not merit. Clearly not used to back-talk either. Well, Scott was about to throw him in at the deep end.

"I have a lot of experience with cases such as these," said Shing. "I can tell you the chance of a successful outcome is...."

"Did you even bother reading any of the documents, or don't my taxes which pay your salary even stretch to that courtesy?" Scott's words singed like caustic acid. Shing's blubbery lower lip fell open. A man used to dishing out orders had just been welcomed to a whole new world.

"Of course I've read your papers…"

"What's the name of the law firm at the heart of it then?" Scott was on him like a rash.

"I beg your pardon?"

"The law firm I'm accusing of money-laundering. What's its name?"

Shing's eyes darted to the folder on his desk.

"Ah-ah! Without looking!"

Shing swallowed and blinked, his embarrassment exploding in the silence.

"Jackson, Weiss & Macdonald," said Sergeant Tam, seated next to Scott. "That's the name of the law firm, Mr Lee. And you used to work for them." There was a deliberation about the junior officer that made Scott sense that here he was dealing with a different prospect. A man who, unlike his superior, did have a clue what was going on. "I've read your papers, Mr Lee. I understand your theory of how AsiaRisk is creating false insurance claims to launder millions of dollars and how

197

Jackson's is giving credence to the process by documenting imaginary settlement contracts. Perhaps you would permit me to elaborate on our decision not to take matters forward?"

A reasonable proposal, put in a reasonable manner to which Scott had no comeback.

"You understand, Mr Lee, that we have to be careful in how we allocate our resources. That is the way of modern policing. When we see a case like yours, our first task is to assess whether it is worth the cost of our investigation. We balance the chances of a successful conviction against the cost of obtaining it. I believe in the business world you call it a 'cost benefit analysis'."

Scott was getting a sense of where this was going.

"In any money-laundering case, the costs are always going to be high because the crime is difficult to prove." Tam continued, deadpan Mr Reasonable.

"So you don't bother prosecuting because it costs too much?"

Tam nodded like an understanding elder brother might. "It's frustrating, I know. But the truth is that sometimes it is better not to prosecute, than to prosecute and to lose. Nothing encourages crime more than a failed attempt at enforcing the law. And in this case, we do not believe that your evidence will stand up to scrutiny."

"What the hell do you mean by that?" Scott snapped out the words like gunfire.

Tam let go an imperceptible sigh. "The documents you have given us depend on a single interpretation proving to be correct. Your interpretation, Mr Lee. Which means your credibility will be central to the case. We do not believe you will make a credible witness."

"I beg your pardon!"

"Tell him what you found! Go on tell him!" Shing urged from behind the desk, like an excitable playground bully.

Tam ignored his superior and carried on, slow and deliberate. "In your interview with Mr Wallingford, he asked why you had started looking into this matter. He asked you whether it had anything to do with you leaving your employment with Jackson, Weiss & MacDonald. Do you recall that?"

Scott paused for a moment. "Yes."

"You indicated that, while you and Mr Charles Conrad did not always get on, this case had nothing to do with your seeking revenge for how he had treated you. But that is not how it appears, Mr Lee." Tam gave Scott a chance to respond. Scott stayed silent. "You see, I did a background check on you, Mr Lee. You are a solicitor, so I spoke to the Law Society and they told me about the complaint Charles Conrad has made against you in relation to the aggressive way you tried to convince Leopold Chan to stop instructing Jackson's and to instruct your current employers, Yip & Siu, instead. We have also found out from...." He looked down at his notes, "from a Mr Gordon Siu, a partner at Yip & Siu, that since the complaint, you have been placed on unpaid leave."

Scott tried to swallow down the sense of the walls of his life crashing in on him.

"So you see, Mr Lee, it could easily be suggested that this is a personal vendetta you are pursuing against Charles Conrad. That dents your credibility, which, as we have established, is central to a case like this. That is why we cannot risk taking any further action. I am sorry."

"This isn't a personal vendetta!" Scott said through clenched teeth.

"May be so," Tam said. "But that is not the point. What matters is appearance and for the reasons I have given, a defence counsel would have no trouble in making it appear like a personal vendetta. As a lawyer, I am sure when you look at it objectively you will agree with us." Tam gave Scott the chance to contradict him.

But Scott had nothing left to say.

Two floors down from where Shing and Tam were dropping their bombshell, Ian Wallingford leaned against a window-ledge, his keen eyes trained on the street below. Ten minutes later he saw Scott Lee leaving the station, the disconsolate droop in his shoulders unmistakable. It made Wallingford's blood boil, another member of the public being let down like this. Another opportunity to make a difference walking out the door.

"Damn!" The expletive rode through his clenched teeth. Seven years Wallingford had spent, building the Financial Institutions Crimes Unit into an effective force, convincing promising young officers that, if they really wanted to bust Triad rings and drug lords, then strangling their laundering outlets was the way to go. It wasn't glamorous, but it was damn effective and in his day Wallingford had shown how success could be achieved, success which had attracted talented juniors to join FICU. The team he'd built was hungry, open-minded and motivated to work like hell to get results. FICU's future seemed secure when he'd retired.

But then the top floor had appointed Detective Chief Inspector Shing as his successor and the whole thing had gone to hell in a hand basket. FICU wouldn't look at a case now unless a result was guaranteed. Well when was that ever going to happen!

So Scott Lee hadn't been forthcoming about his run-in with the Law Society, so what? Wallingford had seen enough in the documentation to know that what Lee had found merited further investigation. Shake the tree see what falls out, that's what Wallingford would have done. Instead, the lad had probably been served some lame excuse about the costs not matching the potential benefits, then sent on his way.

Wallingford had only agreed to come back to FICU as a consultant to try to salvage the unit's reputation before Shing's incompetence made it a backwater for cops looking to eek out their last few years before retirement, rather than a haven for talent. But what was the use? While Shing was in charge, things wouldn't change, the criminals would always have the upper hand and Hong Kong would return to the days when it had been just one giant money-laundry sink.

But there was always more than one way to carry on the fight....

That morning, after Shing and Tam had told him of their decision, Wallingford had contacted one of his old colleagues who was now working in the private sector. White-collar private investigation work paid well these days, it seemed. Wallingford had asked his friend to keep an ear to the ground on AsiaRisk, see whether there were any rumours or speculation doing the rounds.

Within the hour his friend had phoned back.

Someone else was making discreet inquiries about AsiaRisk, he told Wallingford; and left him the person's contact number. All day that number had been smouldering in the Yorkshireman's pocket. And as Wallingford watched Scott Lee walking away, the smouldering became a furnace.

It went against his instinct to go to someone outside the force with this.

But what choice was he left with?

Scott couldn't remember storming out of Shing's office, or walking down the stairs and out the building, but it must have happened because here he was in the street, traffic swishing by him on the Eastern Corridor by-pass, petrol reeking in his nostrils. His life in one holy mess.

He walked home on auto-pilot, his mind somehow fixating on the low points in his life: his mother's death; the phone-call from Richard Denham, kissing his Jackson's partnership goodbye because of Project Claret; the moment when Yip, his best friend, had forced him to look in the mirror and admit his drink problem. All of them were chiseled deep into Scott's subconscious, ready to emerge and kick him in the gut when he least needed it. Today had just added another event to that growing list of disappointments.

What was it Shing had said when Scott was half way through the door? *If you don't let this go, we'll prosecute you for wasting police time!* It was the cheapest of cheap shots. Payback for the way Scott had verbally picked Shing up by the lapels and rammed him against the wall.

Three years ago Scott had been on the verge of obtaining everything with Jackson, Weiss & Macdonald. Now he was jobless, shunned by the Law Society and had just been threatened with prosecution for wasting police time. *Way to go! Hate to think what you do for an encore!*

When Scott reached home, he didn't bother with the air-con. The sun and humidity had already cooked the living-room up to a thirty-five degree sauna, but even in that heat he felt a cold emptiness taking hold. Right on cue another thought lashed out a vicious kick.

Kimmie.

Scott was sure it wasn't suicide now. But the night after Sally had first told him, he'd asked himself some big questions. How could she have done that to herself? What desperate state did a person have to be in to make the decision to close the door on their own life?

Right then, as Scott sank down onto the sofa, he felt closer to an answer that ever before. Pulling his knees to his chest, he hugged them tightly, rocked back and forth, back and forth, eyes clenched shut, praying that when he opened them again the clock would be turned back to the moment the idea of coming out to Hong Kong had first been put to him. If only he hadn't said 'yes'. If only he had never met Charles Conrad.

If only....

CHAPTER TWENTY-EIGHT

The Preciousware Trading Company was revealed only by a discreet placard in the window of its third-floor premises in North Point. Trading companies had to be limited with their marketing; margins were low, budgets tight. Unless expenditure could be justified it had to be slashed; that was the life of small import-export businesses, everything cut to the bone.

It was a perfect cover.

When Huang Yi reached the top of the stairs, he held his Buddha charm up to the swipe pad and clicked the glass entrance open. He went through to his office and shut the door. Slumping down behind his desk, he breathed deeply, quieting his mind until it was as still as the surface of an undisturbed pond.

He waited.

He had already received his orders. The phone-call had come through from Deputy Controller Liuming himself. Liuming, that grandfather of Chinese Intelligence, the man who had personally overseen Huang Yi's training for this mission ten years ago, when Huang had first been dispatched to Hong Kong with the specific mandate of reinvigorating the Third Bureau's intelligence network in the territory. Back then, as a young crusader, Huang Yi had set about his task with passion and pride, recruiting people from the very community which the Third Bureau was seeking to understand, people in low-level clerical jobs with access to high-level information. People just like Gloria Koo, the asset Huang Yi had recruited from inside Kwan Holdings.

The piece of information which Gloria Koo had delivered up from the Code Blue had formed the subject of Huang Yi's phone-call with Liuming earlier on that day.

"So Kwan Holdings is looking to buy this AsiaRisk," Liuming's thin reedy voice had uttered down the line. "And our source says that Rupert Kwan is involved with the purchase?"

"He introduced the opportunity to his uncle." Huang Yi confirmed.

"Hmm," Liuming pondered. "We have not heard of this AsiaRisk before now. But our researchers have been working on it. They tell me it already has representative offices in the Mainland. Perhaps that is why Cyrus Kwan sees it as a favourable target. That is how it should be, Huang Yi. The People's money is invested in Kwan Holdings. Then Kwan invests it back in the People. Capitalism without selfishness."

Liuming was referring to the seven percent strategic shareholding the Chinese Government held in Kwan Holdings. Only a handful of people in the world knew about the investment, not even Cyrus Kwan or his fellow directors were privy to that secret. The Government did not want their day-to-day decisions clouded by such complications. The investment had been deemed necessary because Kwan Holdings had come to symbolize how the methods of western management could be taken apart and put back together in a Chinese way to produce a superior result. Kwan Holdings was the true manifestation of the socialist modernization doctrine. It provided a road map for the future, a tangible example for how the People's Republic could harness the global capitalist system to the needs of its citizens.

"You have done well to bring this matter to my attention."

When Liuming spoke those words, Huang Yi sighed, sensing the flattery to be a prelude to a set of orders which his overstretched resources were going to have difficult in meeting. His instinct was quickly proved right.

"Rupert Kwan's involvement gives me considerable cause of concern," Liuming said, "particularly as it comes so soon after the business with the container terminal. The last thing we want is another scandal, especially with the Cooperation in Services Agreement coming into force. We must keep a close eye on this. Huang Yi, you must put Zhong on it straight away."

"It will mean having to pull him off his current investigation, Deputy Controller," Huang Yi protested. "That investigation is of the utmost importance. It has already been delayed because of other priorities. The people in my network have shown the Third Bureau considerable loyalty. It is imperative that we return it."

"Ah yes," Liuming showed his understanding. "I appreciate your concerns. Believe me I do. But I am afraid the current situation demands immediate vigilance. Right now there are opposition forces searching for an opportunity to gain traction inside the government. I fear that any further adverse publicity involving Kwan Holdings will play into their hands. It is imperative we give this takeover priority. You will have to redeploy Zhong."

"He's not going to like it, Deputy Controller...."

"Neverthess those are his – and your orders – Huang Yi."

Silence.

"As you wish, Deputy Controller."

His orders. Ten years ago Huang Yi would have set about the task with relish. But sitting there that evening in Preciousware's office, he felt jaded by recent events and his meagre resources. He was letting down people who deserved his support.

Huang Yi shut his heavy eyes and immersed himself in the solitude of his own mind. Outside, taxis honked, laughter peeled, mobile phones trilled cantopop ringtones. All of it helped focus his thought process, like a gun to the head forcing a recollection from a hostage. Opening his eyes, Huang Yi checked his watch in the flicker-flicker of the neon lighting arcing in the window. Almost time. He passed the extant few minutes, wallowing in reminiscences of life before he had joined the Third Bureau. Before Hong Kong. Happier times, less stressful times.

The knock on the door when it came was hardly audible. A bare whisper of knuckles on wood. Huang Yi drew in a deep breath and called him in.

Zhong.

Huang Yi had always thought the counter-intelligence operative looked younger than his experience suggested. The stubble on his chin and cheeks looked like the patchwork attempt of a rebellious youth. His hair was upright and slanted, as though he had just got out of bed. His white untucked shirt was unbuttoned to his chest; his jeans were ripped; his workman's boots were laced half way up their eye-holes. Leather ties dangled from thin wrists.

The training provided by the People's Liberation Army aimed to break its recruits and remake them as part of a single efficient fighting unit. Soldiers did not need to think, only follow orders. But Zhong had been one of the few who had been impervious to the training. He had a mind of his own and viewed superiors with suspicion. His preference was to react to a situation as it arose. Not a man to be bound by the constraints of army life was

Zhong. Perfect for the Third Bureau's line of work, but hellishly difficult to manage, as Huang Yi had long ago discovered.

"Sit down," Huang Yi pointed to the chair opposite his desk.

Zhong took it and threw one booted foot over the opposite knee, pushing a lazy hand through his hair. "So what do you need now?"

Huang Yi was used to the lack of respect in Zhong's tone. "What progress have you made on the investigation?"

Zhong's eyes narrowed. "Progress? I have made no progress. If you don't let me approach the family or the police, how the hell do you expect me to find out...?"

"You know our mission here is secret!" Huang Yi snapped. He was not in the mood for insubordination, not tonight. But his words bounced off Zhong like Styrofoam off granite. "Anyway, I have orders to redeploy you to another project!"

"Another project? Just like that?" Zhong gave a derisory snort and shook his head. "Those people you recruit, they put themselves at risk every time you contact them. And for what? – Nothing more than loyalty to their country. And when it comes time for us to show them some loyalty, to show them they're not just dispensable pawns in some game, we do nothing. We just move on to the next thing!"

Each word was like a nail through Huang Yi's chest because, deep down, he agreed with Zhong. But orders were orders. And the mission came before everything else.

Huang Yi laid it out for Zhong, the details of the proposed buy-out of AsiaRisk by Kwan Holdings, and Deputy Controller Liuming's orders.

"There is some problem with this AsiaRisk, then?" Zhong asked.

Huang Yi didn't want to explain, but he knew Zhong needed to know the 'whys' not just the 'whats'. An irritating trait, yes, but a by-product of having someone able to think on his feet, which was a must in this line of work.

"We need to keep an eye on this takeover of AsiaRisk, make sure there is nothing wrong with it," Huang Yi explained. "Cyrus Kwan is leading the buy-out project personally, so he is the one we need to watch. You are to follow him, to his home, to his office, anywhere he goes. Don't let him out of your sight and report to me regularly. Particularly if his nephew comes to see him, understand?"

Zhong took out a pack of cigarettes from his pocket, lit one, drew in a lungful of smoke and exhaled slowly. "And if I see something that needs immediate action?"

Huang Yi leaned forward. "Then you take immediate action."

Zhong nodded and got up to leave.

"Remember the rules," Huang called out after him.

Zhong stopped and turned back. The hint of a sardonic smile.

"Anything happens, I don't know you," Zhong said.

Huang Yi thought about offering some final words, something aimed at filling Zhong with the same feelings of patriotism and nationhood that he imbued his assets like Gloria Koo with.

But there was no point. Zhong had already left.

CHAPTER TWENTY-NINE

The rap on the door ruptured Scott's head like a snapping tendon forcing him to consciousness. Flu-ridding, draining, sweat had soaked his clothes, leaving a coldness which had worked its way into his bones. Opening his eyes, he saw day had turned to night. He let out an acrid groan.

Bang, Bang, Bang, went the door again. It set off the chi-wah-wah upstairs. The yapping and yelping and the pitter-pitter of claws trilling across the ceiling were like a nail through Scott's skull. All he wanted then was to lie back down and block the world out. But the world had other ideas.

"Mr Lee, Mr Lee!" It was Kin-son, the Manchester-United-supporting security-guard from downstairs.

"Wait one moment," Scott called out in groggy Cantonese. Rubbing his palms across his face, he smudged a clammy film of oil and felt the way you feel when you touch chewed gum under a cinema seat. He flipped the light on and glanced in the mirror at his firework hair and the chiseled sleep creases in his face. His mouth was pure sludge. Insipid body odour layered the stuffy air. The window sucker-punched with relief as he opened it.

"Mr Lee? You have a visitor!" Kin-son called out impatiently.

Whoever it was, sure could pick their moments.

"No problem, I'm coming."

Scott made it to the door. Opened it. Kin-son was there, stooped over, face full of concern. Something about that made Scott feel a microscopic bit better. Here was a sixty-year-old man looking eighty-year-old frail, being paid the minimum wage by a cheap-skate landlord to protect the building as best as his stick-insect frame could manage. Most people would have coasted the job; come in, drunk tea, watched TV all night. But Kin-son had pride. No way anyone was getting in unless Scott gave his say-so. It was sad and good at the same time.

"This lady is looking for you," Kinson stepped aside to reveal her.

She was petite with short dark hair and a pleasant, no-nonsense smile. It was a smile that made Scott shake off some of the cobwebs in his head and try to flatten his hair.

"Can I talk to you for a minute, Scott?" She said his name confidently, like they'd known each other for years. Stepping forward, she profered her business card.

Scott glanced at the name on it. He hadn't a clue who she was, so he hit her with a line from his 'killer-openers' reportoire.

"What's this about?"

Her smile stayed pleasant, but in a way that suggested her answer was going to be a kick in the nuts. She was right about that.

"I want to talk to you about AsiaRisk."

Heat prickles danced on Scott's forehead. Something inside began to twitch, maybe a self-defence mechanism which, after years of dormancy, was being dragged kicking and screaming out of hibernation.

Forget her smile, he told himself.

"No," he said.

"No?"

"Whatever it is and whoever you are, I'm done."

He began to close the door but it stuck half way against the edge of the woman's shoe.

"Five minutes. That's all I'm asking."

The door held.

Scott's self defence mechanism screamed for him to tell her to get lost. But old habits die hard.

"Five minutes," he opened the door. "Then we're done."

The open window had done little to quell the vapour of recent sleep. Scott apologized for the mess and plucked random items of clothing off furniture. He pointed her into a heat-faded dining-room chair on his way through to the kitchen to make coffee.

"Sorry, there's no milk," he said, handing her a mug, "no sugar, either."

He sat down on the other partially acceptable dining-chair and looked at her business card again. "So why's a forensic accountant interested in AsiaRisk?"

Rainbow Choi didn't bolt out her answer, just held a confident pause as if suckering in Scott's curiosity before revealing her secret. "I have a client who wants to buy it."

A spasm of disbelieving laughter erupted from Scott's throat. "Someone wants to buy AsiaRisk?"

"You find that funny?" Her eyes narrowed.

Scott shrugged.

He felt her draw out the pause, waiting for him to give away more. Her eyebrows did a flirty tango thing when he didn't. It made him pay attention.

"My firm has been instructed by the interested purchaser to do the due diligence," she said. "Find out what skeletons AsiaRisk has lurking in its closet, if you know what I mean."

The smile she gave him made it sound like a double entendre.

"So what do you want from me?"

A beat of silence.

"Word is, you've found a skeleton." She pointed a finger and swirled it in a circle.

Scott took a large gulp of coffee. It was too hot and smarted going down, but the coppery after-taste helped jolt away any residual drowsiness. "How did you find me?"

Rainbow Choi did that eyebrow dance again, as if to ask: 'you really want to play that game?'

He did.

"Ian Wallingford contacted me. You're just back from Wanchai Police station, I understand."

Scott stiffened. "That's none of your business."

"It is if the reason you were there concerned AsiaRisk!" Her tone suddenly sharpened, but quickly the friendly, flirty smile returned, like a cat lashing out a warning paw one second and licking it the next.

"So you know Wallingford," Scott said.

"Not exactly," she swept a finger girlishly behind her ear. "We put word out that we were interested in any market intelligence involving AsiaRisk. Gossip, rumour, things that wouldn't show up on the balance sheet." She shrugged her shoulders. "Ian Wallingford got in touch."

"That's some due diligence service you supply."

"My clients always expect more. I give it to them." Again with the eyebrows

The answer amused Scott. He was feeling drawn to this Rainbow Choi in a way he found difficult to explain. "So who's this client?" he asked, playing it cool.

Her eyes stayed steady on him this time, as she held her lower lip gently with her teeth. Scott could see the debate going on in her head. Give up the information, or wait until he'd yielded something tangible? Eventually she let go a dramatic sigh. "I represent Kwan Holdings. Cyrus Kwan to be precise."

It was thirty degrees plus in the room, but her answer sucked the air into a frigid vacuum.

Cyrus Kwan. Scott had heard the name, of course. One of Asia's richest. "Kwan Holdings is buying AsiaRisk?"

"Thinking about it, yes."

"And Leopold Chan is okay with this?"

She nodded. Deadpan.

Scott stood up, his curiosity pricked, his mind moving through the gears.

"You find the notion of Kwan Holdings wanting to buy AsiaRisk surprising?" Rainbow Choi asked him. "Why? AsiaRisk seems to be a good company on paper. Kwan Holdings wants to get into the insurance game. With the CSA coming in soon, the timing seems perfect. So why the concern, Scott?"

The CSA. The Co-operation in Services Agreement. Scott had read the newspaper reports on the Financial Secretary's vainglorious speech. He had received the free summaries of the bilateral treaty's provisions from law firms looking to advertise their expertise. A great opportunity for the Hong Kong financial service industry, it was being heralded as. A headstart in the Mainland market for Hong Kong financial sector companies. They were being given the keys to the Middle Kingdom.

"What else did Wallingford say?" Scott wanted more before sharing.

"He said only that I should talk to you if I wanted information on AsiaRisk. So here I am." She held out open palms.

"Funny. His precious Financial Insutitions Crimes Unit kicked me to the curb this afternoon, so forgive me if I seem a tad reticent."

"Scott, come over here and sit down."

He was taken aback by the request. So taken aback that he obeyed it. He sat, leaned his elbows on the table and stared at her.

"I understand how you feel...." She reached out and touched his arm.

"Well, that's big of you."

"But I don't sympathize!" That sharp tone again.

Quiet knifed the room. Rainbow's hand softly stayed on his arm, her eyes drawing him in, her strength beginning to fascinate him.

Then it hit him. She reminded him of Kimmie. That same streak of fierce independence which he had found so stimulating.

The realization made him suddenly pull back from the table and adjust.

Rainbow Choi pushed ahead the advantage. "So, a couple of boneheaded policemen didn't give you the time of day! Big deal! Well, Scott, I'm here now and I'm telling you I'm prepared to listen. Why? Because I want to do right by my client. As a lawyer, you should appreciate that. I'm not here to judge you or give you a hard time. Just to hear what you have to say."

Scott took a moment to let his thoughts slow down from the snow-storm which was going right then. Some day it had been so far. Progress in the morning had turned to despair by mid-afternoon. Now, come nightfall, Rainbow Choi had shown up, barged in and sent him spiraling again. The roller-coaster of Hong Kong life. How Scott wanted to stop it, get off and leave it all behind. But then there was that nagging itch, the one telling him that the only thing worse than carrying on, was stopping, knowing that there was something more he could have done to make things right by Kimmie. Unexhausted avenues; the great 'what ifs' of life. Pure torture for the soul.

Scott had had enough of them for one lifetime. He looked Rainbow Choi straight on, took a deep breath, started at the beginning and didn't stop until he was done with every last detail.

O'Rourke bit into the new stick of gum and worked his jaw to a steady beat. Since two that afternoon it had been the same routine; a new stick every hour on the hour, its mintiness stimulating his taste buds for all of fifteen minutes, but he'd stay with it for the next forty-five, then spit and start afresh. Chewing helped him keep his focus and kill the boredom while he waited there in the garden.

Garden! What a joke that was. O'Rourke looked at the 'no dogs' sign. They weren't missing out on anything much. No grass to sniff, no trees to piss against. Just a sectioned-off, heat-absorbing piece of concrete with a couple of benches. An open air toilet minus the porcelain.

But at least it had a perfect view of the block where Scott Lee lived.

The lad himself had returned home at quarter-past four that afternoon looking as pissed off as a drunk with an empty bottle. Why? O'Rourke didn't care, that wasn't his job. But seeing Lee enabled him to make an assessment more pertinent to his line of work.

How tall was he? Five foot eight, five nine, O'Rourke guessed, and a hundred and fifty pounds in weight. He looked fit, but the kind of fit that only kept stomach muscles hard and cheek bones perky. That made Lee a piece of crepe paper for what O'Rourke had in mind. One firm smack would sit Lee on his arse then O'Rourke could finish him however he wanted.

O'Rourke chewed on the thought. Boredom like this was part of the job. It called for discipline, patience, an ability to know how to while away long stretches of nothing. Some people listened to Ipods, some ate junk. O'Rourke worked out the most efficient way of killing a man. Psychologists would have had a field day with that, probably talk about an abused upbringing or wonder if he dreamt about screwing his mum. But at the end of the day that was a pile of gobshite. He did what he did because he was the person he was. Everyone was born with some kind of talent. Taking life was Terrence O'Rourke's.

A firm smack in the mouth to paralyse him with fear. Then a boot to the temple, maybe, or a well aimed stamp. His skull would crack like an egg-shell. Problem solved.

But that wasn't what the boss wanted, not yet anyway. Follow Scott Lee as a precaution, Leopold Chan had told him.

Precaution. O'Rourke sneered at the word. Precaution was bullshit. Precaution meant the chances of action were slim. But if the opportunity arose, he'd be ready. So he would let time pass, let the anticipation build, savour it, taste it, and if his talents were called upon, the first bone would pop like a champagne cork and he'd love it.

Two hours slipped by. O'Rourke played with the thought some more.

And then as day turned to night, he saw her. Or was it her? O'Rourke leaned in for a closer look.

She paused outside Lee's building, checked to see she had the right place.

Yes, it was her all right. *Well, well, well.* Rainbow, that was her name. Funny name like that stuck easily.

The gum's mintiness had long gone. *Rainbow, Rainbow, Rainbow, thank you so very much!* O'Rourke sensed his chances of action had just gone up a few notches.

He dialed his mobile and smiled.

"I think we may have a problem, boss."

CHAPTER THIRTY

Rainbow's instinct had told her that Leopold Chan had been hiding something.

But money-laundering? Now, that was unexpected. But after she'd had time to think it over, somehow it all seemed to fit. A damn clever scheme it was too, Rainbow had to admit, creating false insurance claims to funnel funds through AsiaRisk's books. And if anyone asked questions, there was the proper legal documentation to back it up thanks to Charles Conrad, that jelly-fish of a lawyer she'd run into in reception.

This was big. As in big, big.

"Impressive," she said to Scott when he had finished laying it out. "And you found this out by yourself?" The look Scott threw her said she was being patronizing. She changed tack. "How did you get that documentation from Jackson's files?"

Another look. One that said *don't even go there.* Definitely the sensitive type.

"I mean it, Scott. This is impressive," she decided to go with flattery and this time got a neutral shrug by return. It was progress, at least.

"Well Wallingford's colleagues down at FICU didn't seem to think so." Scott collected up his papers and slipped them back in his briefcase. "And there are still a lot of pieces missing."

As she watched, for the first time Rainbow saw the real mix of east and west in him. He was handsome, but not the kind that smacked you in the face and made your jaw drop. Rather, it radiated out the more you got to know him. A handsomeness born of character. Behind his eyes, she sensed a soul strained with the experience of someone much older.

"What are these missing pieces then?" she asked.

He turned to her. "For one thing, who's Chan laundering funds for? Wallingford asked me that. Damn good question and I don't have the answer."

Rainbow pondered it a moment. "I might be able to help with that."

Scott stopped what he was doing.

"I've had someone following Leopold Chan for the last two days," Rainbow said.

"You've had somebody *following* him? What kind of due diligence service do you run?"

She shrugged. "Like I said, my clients always expect more."

Scott looked at her for more explanation, but none was forthcoming.

"So what did you find?" His curiosity was well and truly hooked.

"Yesterday afternoon, Leopold Chan decided to take some time off for a round of golf up at Fanling. I didn't think much of it at first. A businessman playing golf on a weekday is hardly a big deal, right? But it turns out Leo wasn't a member of the club. In fact, according to his staff, he hates golf. So I figured he must have been meeting someone there," she said. "My people couldn't get onto the course to see who it was, but they checked out the names who had signed in for eighteen holes around the same time. And one name jumped out like a slap in the face....Benny Wang."

Scott frowned. "Who the hell's Benny Wang?"

"Benny's a businessman," Rainbow said. "Of the very illegitimate kind. Pirate DVDs, knock-off designer wear, untaxed booze and ketamine; that's how he makes his money." She allowed the pause to drag out a little. "On its own, Leo Chan and Benny Wang being on the same golf course at the same time isn't much of a connection. But add in what you've just told me...."

"Could still be just coincidence," Scott said.

"Sure. Or it could be that Benny's a man who needs to clean a lot of cash and his buddy Leo knows just how to do it."

She saw the bead of sweat trickle down from Scott's hairline, saw the hardness appear in his eyes. Nagging doubts were disappearing and the lethargy she had seen when she had first walked through the door that evening was well and truly gone. That someone else believed him seemed to strengthen his resolve and she could see him gearing up for something.

"What happens now?" Scott asked, his voice a deep whisper. "You tell Cyrus Kwan and he walks away from AsiaRisk. Is that how this works?"

"No. Not quite." Rainbow said.

"Then what 'quite'!" His tone seeped with irritation.

She slung an elbow over the back of the chair. "As soon as I report back to him, Cyrus will call off the takeover, I'm sure of that. But that's not going to be enough for a man like Cyrus Kwan. He'll want to know more. Always does. That's why he hired me."

"What else is there?"

Rainbow Choi raised her eyes to the ceiling before leveling them back to him. "First he's going to want to know how much his nephew knows about all of this."

"His nephew?"

"Rupert Kwan. Or as the press have dubbed him 'Public Enemy Number One'. You read the stuff about the Lantau container terminal a couple of weeks ago?"

Scott's eyebrows puckered up, as he grasped for the recollection she'd hit on. "Yeah, I remember that. He tried to sell the terminal outside of Hong Kong, right?" He shook his head, the frown eased down to an irreverent smile as another memory took hold. "Rupert Kwan," his head shaking, "that guy's always in those gossip magazines you see on the news-stands, usually with some cutie-pie cantopop model hanging off him. What's he got to do with all this?"

"It was Rupert who brought Chan and his uncle together," Rainbow said. "He thought AsiaRisk was a good opportunity, found out Leopold Chan was interested in selling, so put him and Cyrus in the same room to talk terms. Given what you've discovered, Cyrus is going to be asking some serious questions about his nephew's judgement and the company he's been keeping!"

Scott was quiet for a moment. Then: "You think Rupert Kwan knows about the money-laundering?"

Rainbow stuck out her bottom lip. "Put it this way. When Leopold was at the golf club with Benny Wang yesterday, guess who else turned up? Rupert Kwan."

"So Leopold Chan, Rupert Kwan and Benny Wang all know each other?"

She shrugged. "It would seem so, yeah."

Scott puffed out his cheeks. This was moving quickly. Too quickly. Rainbow Choi was feeding him more new information than his brain was up to processing right now.

Think, Scott, think!

He got up, switched on the air-conditioner and let its drawl plunge his hot flat into a hard silence. There was something he was missing, something in the documentation that may have seemed irrelevant at the time, but in light of these new facts needed to be looked over again. It was in the depths of his memory-bank somewhere. Close, but agonizingly still just out of reach.

The briefcase with his papers sat on the dining-room table. He grabbed it and fingered through the documents, pulling out his handwritten notes, searching for a spark to pin-point his recollection. Half names of false companies were scribbled on the pages in no particular order. Figures, dates, solicitors' names, nothing that he didn't know already, nothing that he hadn't turned around in his brain a hundred times already ....

The memory spliced through the greyness into technicolour, like a scalpel renting skin. The night he had been in Kimmie's office....Charles Conrad coming back... having to hide on the floor to avoid being caught....Carmella Lo saving him when Conrad was about to open the door....the reason Charles Conrad had come back to the office that night.

Scott bolted to his spare-room-cum-study. Piles of documents lay on the floor and desk, ordered in a way to which only he held the key. What he was looking for was in the third pile. The print-out of the email which Charles Conrad had sent out that night. The conflict-check on his new urgent AsiaRisk case.

He went back to the living-room and asked Rainbow, "Do you know anything about an insurance claim just filed against AsiaRisk by the Chow Mei factory?"

She gave him a poker face.

"Come on, Rainbow! It's a two hundred million dollar claim against a company your client is looking to buy. Leopold Chan instructed Jackson's on it last week. You must have seen it in the due diligence?"

She took her sweet time with an answer. "Yes, I know about the Chow Mei claim. Chan was quite the Boy Scout about it, in fact. The claim was highlighted in the first set of management accounts he gave me. AsiaRisk have reserved in full for it."

Just then something set off the chihuahua upstairs again. Machine-gun-fire yaps and the sound of scuttling feet flew across the ceiling. The owner's voice cut in. The dog stopped.

"You think the Chow Mei claim is part of this money-laundering scam?" Rainbow asked.

"I don't know." Scott pushed a hand through his hair.

"Well let's see." Rainbow drummed her fingers on the dining room table. Unmanicured nails, Scott noticed. Not the kind of girl to put fashion ahead of function evidently. He liked that. "If I've understood you correctly, Leo Chan's scheme relies on false insurance claims which are made to look real. Not claims which are actually real. The Chow Mei claim's as real as they come," she said.

"You're sure?" Scott asked. "Just because there's a policy and a completed claim form...."

"It's real," she cut him off. "The Chow Mei fire made the news and AsiaRisk insured it."

He screwed his eyes up tight.

"And that isn't the only mismatch with your theory, Scott. Look at the size of the claim. Two hundred million dollars. The false claims you've been talking about haven't been any where near that size. My guess is that keeping the amounts low on the false claims was deliberate. The bigger the amount, the more attention it draws, so the harder it is to hide when you're putting it through the accounts. I'm not seeing any connection with Chow Mei here."

Scott coughed into his hand. The buzz had taken hold. Debating details on a case, throwing around ideas, pounding them into submission until you got the answer, he used to live for it, back in the days when his career was going somewhere, before being stranded with Charles Conrad out in Hong Kong. *'Uh, that sounds about right, but you might want to check with someone in the London office'* was about as far as his former boss would ever venture in putting his neck on the line.

Rainbow Choi, though, this due-diligence accountant who had come to his door out of the blue, she was good at this. She grasped things quickly, saw logical links and weaknesses for what they were and was prepared to test them, through some give and take. Yes. It reminded him of the way he and Kimmie used to work, how they hammered out a strategy on cases. There was always that tension in the debate. But it was part of their passion for each other. Like electricity coursing through your veins.

It had been a while since he had felt anything like that. But there was a hint of it creeping in now with Rainbow Choi. She had a certain something, for sure. His mind was buzzing. And he was ready with his comeback.

"You missed two connections," he said.

"And what might they be?"

"AsiaRisk instructed Jackson's on the Chow Mei claim, just like all the others."

She didn't buy it. "So AsiaRisk use Jackson's on their insurance claims."

Scott gave a half chuckle. "Rainbow....You want to money-launder you use a lawyer like Charles Conrad because he's desperate and, frankly, stupid. If you've got a real claim that needs defending, you go to someone who is good. But Leopold Chan hasn't. With a two hundred million dollar claim, he's gone to Conrad."

Rainbow moved her head left and right in a 'so-so' kind of way. "Or from time to time he throws Conrad a real instruction to hide the false ones."

"A two hundred million dollar instruction? That's an expensive cover-up"

Silence.

"What's the second connection?" she asked

"The timing."

"The timing?"

Scott paced, mentally rehearsing the right way to put it. "If you were in Leopold Chan's shoes, why sell AsiaRisk to Cyrus Kwan at the exact same moment that your company is about to incur a huge two hundred million dollar liability? Surely it depresses AsiaRisk's value and the purchase price takes a hit? One answer could be that AsiaRisk's desperate for Kwan's capital to stay afloat."

"No," Rainbow said. "Definitely not. AsiaRisk's capital position is fine. We've run the numbers. Even if it ends up paying out the full two hundred million on Chow Mei, AsiaRisk will still be healthily solvent."

"There you go. So why sell to Kwan now when there's no need to? Why doesn't Chan wait, settle out the Chow Mei claim, re-build AsiaRisk's equity base, boost the value of the company, then go to Kwan?"

Rainbow shrugged. "Chan says he's more interested in his legacy being looked after than the price. He's looking to secure its future under Kwan Holdings and step aside. That's why he's pushing it Kwan's way at a discounted price."

Scott stopped. Turned. "And you buy that?"

This time the poker face wasn't able to mask her suspicion.

"I think there's something going on with the Chow Mei claim," Scott said.

Rainbow Choi drummed her fingers again. Her eyes focused on nothing, as she worked out her next move. Then after a moment she got up and headed for the door.

"Hey, where are you going?" Scott asked.

She looked over her shoulder. "To find out if you're right." A few more steps then she turned again. "Well, come on then!"

CHAPTER THIRTY-ONE

Rainbow Choi lurched her two-seater Mercedes SLK through the Cross Harbour Tunnel to Kowloon side, punchy on the accelerator and brake, refusing to let the gap with the KMT double decker bus in front grow to more than a metre. She barked instructions into a Blue-tooth and within seconds someone back at her office had an address for the SatNav. A false marketing call to the address verified someone was home.

"You don't mess about!" Scott muttered from the passenger-seat.

In response, Rainbow flashed another flirtatious smile at him. It caught Scott unawares. Something thudded in his chest, the same way it used to, those times when Kimmie came into his office and looked at him in a certain way that made him think, for a split second anyway, that the rest of the world didn't exist.

He looked out of the passenger window. Exhaustion had taken hold, and that was probably partly responsible for the way he was feeling. How much time had he wasted on his pathetic excuse for a career, to the detriment of all other aspects of his life? Opportunites missed. The great 'what ifs'. He blinked away the thought and forced himself to reach for the cold spot where his emotions couldn't get to.

"You going to be okay?" Rainbow sensed something was up.

Her concern bolted Scott back to his senses. "Just peachy."

Exiting the tunnel, they headed north, the concrete mire of Kowloon ending when they crossed Boundary Street, ushering in an expanse of the mountainous landscape known as the New Territories. 'New' because in 1898 the British had forced the Chinese to lease it to them as an add-on to what they'd already forcibly extracted in 1842 and 1860 in the treaties ending the first and second Opium Wars. Ironic then, that ninety-nine years on, when the lease expired, the British were forced to hand back the whole lot and kiss colonialism goodbye forever.

They headed up the Tolo highway, the main coast-road going north-east, sticking to the fast lane, turning off after Shatin, skirting round the back of the Chinese University campus. Eventually, the SatNav led them to the countrified development they wanted.

The quiet hit Scott hard when they parked up and got out. It was a silence louder than any sound. This was the side of Hong Kong tourists never knew. No overflowing pavements here, no sense of the walls constantly pressing in. Even the air tasted different.

"South View Villas," Rainbow said looking up at the white-façaded house. "Must be a great view in the day time."

The house had a ground-level garage and three spacious floors on top of it. On the first floor, a retracted awning framed full-length windows, which sat back behind a large patio that doubled as the garage roof. Inside, Scott saw high ceilings and sparsely-decorated walls which conjured up a sadness he couldn't quite place.

Rainbow was definitely in her zone. Fact-finding was in her blood and she couldn't wait. She headed straight for the stairs up to the front door. "When we get in there, let me do the talking. Whatever I say just look serious and nod."

"Yes ma'am!"

She ignored his sarcasm and pushed the electronic door-bell, which sounded out a painful version of *When the Saints Go Marching In*. The echo of footsteps approached. A lock clicked. The Filipino maid stared up at them through reticent brown eyes.

"Is Ms Chow home?" Rainbow asked.

The Filipina told them to 'wait please' and snapped the lock shut. Scott and Rainbow exchanged glances. A few minutes later the door opened again.

"Ms Eva Chow?" Rainbow took the lead. "We'd like to talk to you about the fire at your factory."

Three beats of silence.

"Who are you?"

Rainbow raised a business card. Chow looked at it, bemused.

"I'm appointed on behalf of AsiaRisk to look into your insurance claim." Rainbow told the lie with such impressive certainty, even Scott had to catch himself.

Definitely not someone to be messed with.

Chow took a step back, as if punched in the stomach. Rainbow pushed forward. "Mind if we come in and talk for a moment? It won't take long. I'm sorry about the late hour, but we're keen to verify things before our month-end."

Eva Chow's eyes debated. Then she turned. They followed her inside and through to a kitchen, white-tiled, spacious and sparkling, but somehow short on contents. Rainbow took a bar-stool at the breakfast bar. Scott did the same.

Eva Chow stood, arms folded. She was the human equivalent of a bowling-ball. No neck between her shoulders and head. Her face was not a soft one. It was brutish and spiteful at God for having made her that way. "What do you want?" she glared.

"You've filed a large claim, Ms Chow. We want to make sure that all the policy conditions have been met before making payment."

Chow gave a contemptuous snort.

"Is there a problem with that?" Rainbow challenged.

"I don't want to talk to you."

The answer was off and Scott knew it. He'd seen insurance claims turn nasty, he'd taken many to court, so he knew how claimants acted to get their money. They screamed bitter complaints about how insurance companies dragged their feet and whined about how much premium they'd paid over the years. They lied through their teeth to make themselves look whiter than white. Money stimulated great emotion. Yet here was Eva Chow, owed two hundred million dollars by AsiaRisk, not even wanting to talk to the people who owed her. Scott wanted to grab Rainbow out of there, give her his views and work out a strategy to shake the truth from the tree.

But he should have expected that Rainbow Choi had her own way of doing things.

"Ten years!" She said. "That's how much prison-time you're looking at for insurance fraud, Eva. So we can leave, and you can talk to the police. Or you can tell us what's going on. Your choice."

That wasn't so much shaking the tree as throwing up a hand grenade and blowing off the branches.

Several emotions played out on Eva Chow's face in a matter of seconds. Shock, irritation, anger, fear, then stoicism.

"Who did you pay to burn down the factory?" Rainbow forced things on.

"What? You're crazy!"

"Come on, Eva, the place wasn't making money, your only asset was the insurance. So you torched the place to access it."

"What?"

"It was the only way you could get enough to retire on!" Rainbow bulldozed away. "A fat cheque from the insurers. You didn't care about your staff, Eva. As long as you were okay, it didn't matter...."

"How dare you!" Eva Chow exploded, fists balled tight, face rage-red. "You people did this!" she yelled. "You took away everything my father and I had worked for! You are the ones who have left those people without jobs! You cancelled the insurance! Not me! And you dare to come into this house and accuse me of...."

There it was. The truth.

Chow's eyes suddenly filled with the fright.

Ice-cold silence spilled through the kitchen.

AsiaRisk had cancelled Chow Mei's insurance. Not something Scott had been expecting and, although her face remained a mask, he could see the confusion at work in Rainbow's eyes. His mind slewed with questions. If AsiaRisk had cancelled the insurance, why pay the claim at all, why reserve for it in full? Why not just decline and walk away?

Unless. A moment of clarity clicked.

Ignoring Rainbow's instructions, Scott ran with the half-formed idea. "You're not making the claim are you? Someone else is!" he asked Chow,

Eva Chow's face was stone. "I want you to leave." Neither Scott nor Rainbow moved. "I mean it!"

"What are you going to do, Eva? Call the police? Go ahead, I'm sure we'll have plenty to talk about." Rainbow twisted the knife.

Eva Chow turned her ugly face to the window and stared without looking. It was a stare that played out the regrets in her life, of bad decisions made and of acceptance of a final reckoning she had somehow been expecting. "I thought my father would be ashamed of me for what I have done." Eva said it out loud, but it was a comment directed more to herself than anyone else. "But it is he who owes me forgiveness. I never wanted his factory, I never wanted his life. But he made me take it anyway. And look where his legacy had ended up. It is nothing now! Nothing!" She let spill a brutal cackle, which quickly subsided into heavy sobbing.

Scott and Rainbow waited while the pent-up emotions siphoned out of Eva Chow like air from a tyre. When the time was right, Rainbow turned to Scott and nodded for him to continue.

"Someone paid you not to say anything," Scott said. Eva Chow didn't answer, but that was confirmation enough. "Whoever paid you was responsible for burning down your factory, Ms Chow. They put your staff out of work. If you care at all about them, you'll tell us who did this."

Although she didn't move Scott knew his words had touched a nerve. Her large face showed guilt and shame digging into her like painful splinters. Then a look of resignation grew in her eyes, now red-raw from her crying.

"A man came to my office just after it happened," Chow eventually said. "He promised me five million dollars in return for giving him all rights to the insurance claim against AsiaRisk. He said I wasn't to tell anyone."

"What was his name?" Rainbow asked

"He never told me," Chow's voice hitched. "He said I didn't need to know."

In the silence that followed, tears slipped down the contours of Eva Chow's heavy cheeks again. Her lower lip trembled. She wiped her face on her sleeve. Composure returned, but she was no longer challenging, no longer ready to fight.

Scott and Rainbow looked at each other and understood what they had to do. Together they had found the key and opened the door. Time to bring it home.

"Eva," Rainbow said softly. "What did this man look like?"

Eva breathed through her lips. "Big like a mountain," she said, "with tattoos. I remember them here and here." She touched her forearms. "I didn't know who he was. But I knew what he was. I thought I had no choice. But I was wrong." Eva Chow threw another blank stare at the window. "Everyone has a choice. Everyone does."

Satisfaction stirred in Leopold Chan's breast when he saw his creation at the bottom of the stairs.

Thirty-five years ago he had seen the real thing in Belgium. Waterloo. It had left its indelible mark on his soul. For hours Leopold had stood on the grassy Lion hillock, overlooking the magnificent vista where the world's course had changed forever, when the Duke of Wellington had defeated the Emperor Napoleon. The idea of the immense power resting in the hands of the two men that day had obsessed Leopold ever since, and after his divorce, when he had finally rid the house of Trixie's meaningless trinkets, he had given into his obsession, transforming his basement into a re-creation of the final stages of the Battle of Waterloo. Each tiny military figurine, each canon, each horse had been lovingly assembled to replicate the final formations, just before Napoleon's Imperial Guard had made its last stand. Years it had taken him to assemble it. And then there was Alfonso, the Filipino artist whom Leopold had persuaded to give up selling landscapes to tourists, in favour of a steady income painting the figurines to exact specifications. Hadn't Alfonso done well? It was perfect. There was the ridge behind which Wellington had masterfully hidden the strength of his forces. There, the Union Cavalry unflinchingly charging into the teeth of the French artillery. Opposite, the ranks of the Napoleon's Imperial Guard – stalwart veterans, before that day undefeated – resolved to die rather than surrender.

Today, it seemed, economic forces held sway over life and death. History was no longer dictated by the decisions of great men. But Leopold had never been convinced of that. History was past, but what was it that Confucius had said? *To understand the past is to divine the future.* Indeed. The valiant armies ranged before him may have been replaced by currency flows and stock-market rumours, but these were still instruments which great men used to change the world.

Leopold loved this basement. Apart from Alfonso and his two maids, no one else knew about it. Not even O'Rourke. This was his haven.

He was close, he could almost taste it. General Zhao would have been pleased, had he known of the progress which had been made. But it was Zhao who had insisted on no communication until the moment was right. That suited Leopold just fine. Everything was on schedule, Cyrus Kwan and Benny Wang positioned exactly where Leopold wanted them, the first taking the bait to buy AsiaRisk, the second indulging himself with the prospect of gaining long-craved-for respectability. Yes, it was perfect. *Almost.*

For in the midst of the moving pieces, a potential obstacle had now emerged. Somehow Rainbow Choi and Scott Lee had found each other. O'Rourke had seen them and followed them all the way to Eva Chow's place. Wang would have told Chow to shut her mouth. But betting on her silence was not a chance Leopold could take.

This wasn't the first time Leopold had arbitrated over life and death. Scott Lee and Rainbow Choi were getting too close for comfort. They were two individuals of remarkable talent.

It was a shame their lives had to end before reaching their full potential.

But end they must.

Leopold called O'Rourke back and gave his instructions.

CHAPTER THIRTY-TW0

"Benny Wang, that's who paid off Chow," Rainbow Choi was still a dynamo of excitement as they headed back to the car.

"How do you know that?" Scott just about shut the passenger door as they screeched away from the curb.

"My people got a photo of Wang at the golf club. Man mountain. Tattoos. Just like Chow said back there. We're going to see Cyrus Kwan with this, right now!"

Rainbow stuck her foot down, the force of the acceleration slamming Scott back into his seat. He fumbled the seatbelt into its slot and grabbed the overhead handle. "You know what time it is?"

"Trust me, he'll to want to see us," Rainbow insisted. "How did you figure Chow wasn't making the claim?"

Scott's knuckles went white on the handle as they hit a bend at speed. "Let's just say I've read enough about money-laundering in the past few days to know that buying legitimate insurance claims is a favourite technique. Hey, take it easy will you!"

"Sorry!" Rainbow eased off the pace. The engine slowed down a little. She was breathing rapidly with the excitement of having hit on what seemed to be the truth. Something about that made Scott smile. He started to wonder what it would be like if he had met Rainbow in other circumstances, whether it could have been the start of something....

"What was that you just said about buying legitimate insurance claims?" Her question broke off his thought.

He took a moment to arrange what he wanted to say in his head, then hit her with his theory. "Okay, here it is. Say there's a flood at a warehouse reported in the newspaper. The warehouse owner is insured for flood damage, but it can take months for the insurer to pay up. Meantime the warehouse owner's out of pocket, but that's just the way it goes. Now let's say you're a criminal looking to launder money. You read about the warehouse flood in the paper, go to see the warehouse owner and offer to help.

You'll invest in the business in cash right now, to help the warehouse owner out with his cash flow. Then when the insurance money comes through, the warehouse owner will buy you out. So our criminal transforms his cash into clean money using the warehouse's insurance claim."

"And you think that's what happened with Chow Mei?"

Scott shrugged. "Could be. If Benny Wang needed to launder a large amount of cash in one go, Leopold Chan would have known enough to tell him they couldn't use a fake insurance claim. That only works with small sums. For this, they needed a real insurance claim. That was the only way it could work."

Rainbow picked up the thought and ran with it. "So Benny and Leopold make sure one of AsiaRisk's policyholders – Eva Chow in this instance – suffers an unfortunate accident. Then Benny goes in and offers her cash in return for the insurance pay out."

"Yeah, but there's a twist," Scott said. "Remember Eva Chow said AsiaRisk had cancelled the insurance. So with her factory in ashes Chow thinks she's finished. With no insurance, she's got nothing. Then, out of the blue, in walks Benny Wang with an offer of five million dollars. Eva takes the offer because it's better than nothing. Now all Leopold Chan has to do is lose the cancellation notice from AsiaRisk's files and a two hundred million dollar legitimate insurance claim from the Chow Mei factory can flow through AsiaRisk's books straight to Benny Wang."

Rainbow shook her head. "What a pair of sweethearts."

Scott looked over at her. The green glow from the dashboard lights played on her face. Her eyes held a burning intensity which made him want to know more. He liked the way she was going about the task which had been set her, so concentrated, so determined....so damn like Kimmie.

"What?" she said, catching his eye.

He looked away, part embarrassed, part pleased he'd been caught.

A sign flashed by, announcing they had two kilometres to go before arriving back on the Tolo highway. It triggered Scott back into the moment. "There's something I still don't get," he said.

"What that's then?"

"The timing."

"We're back to that?"

"Well think about it. If we're right, Leopold Chan has manufactured a massive insurance claim against his own company at precisely the same time he's selling it. It doesn't make sense."

"You know what Scott? It doesn't really matter. We've got enough to convince Cyrus that buying AsiaRisk is a big mistake. That's all I'm interested in right now."

They swished round another corner.

"Can't this wait till tomorrow?" Scott asked.

"Uh-uh. The Kwan board meets at eight tomorrow morning to make a final decision. After that, the lawyers will document the deal, get the contracts signed, then it's done. We've got to do this now! And anyway, Cyrus is at his house in Fanling tonight which isn't far away from where we are now."

Scott rested his head back and closed his eyes, but his mind was still working busily.

A thought hit him through the darkness like a sniper's bullet. "Is Charles Conrad representing AsiaRisk on the takeover?"

"Yes."

Scott felt his throat thicken with anger, an image of Kimmie in his mind. Her smile, a swish of black hair. Such a damn waste and Conrad was up to his neck in it.

"Do me a favour," Rainbow's voice pulled him out of it. "I need my Bluetooth again. It's in my handbag behind my seat. I need to tell Cyrus we're coming."

Scott swiveled round, saw the bag, tried to reach but couldn't make it, so he released his seat belt and tried again. Just then, lights from a car behind shone through the rear window. Scott saw the bag caught in their glow and brought it forward onto his lap. The car pulled out and overtook, its headlights dazzling for a moment before plunging them back into darkness. A BMW, Scott noticed as it swung back into the lane ahead.

"Thought your driving was bad!" he said.

"Just shut up and find the earpiece!"

He heard the smile in her voice again.

"Which pocket?"

"Oh give it here."

Rainbow snatched the bag onto her lap and had the earpiece in place within seconds.

Cyrus Kwan ran the numbers in his head again and came to the same conclusion.

On paper AsiaRisk was as good a deal as any he'd seen, a company with a proven performance in its market, a name associated with good value, with a respectful attitude to risk management and a low staff turnover: the key building blocks Cyrus always looked for in an investment and AsiaRisk had it in spades. So why did he feel like there was something missing? A certain genuineness, may be. It just seemed too good to be true and long experience had taught Cyrus that nothing should ever be this easy. But neither Tyson Mok nor Simon Ng had been able to find any material holes. So Rainbow Choi was the last big test.

Rainbow had always been a cynic. When Cyrus had called her earlier that day for an update, she'd been her usual ebullient self, questioning Leopold Chan's stated motives for the sale. *Legacy, Cyrus? He's sacrificing making money for his legacy? Come on!*

She had a point. As justifications for selling a business like AsiaRisk went, Leopold Chan's was hard to believe. As yet, however, she hadn't delivered up anything to contradict it.

Mok, Ng and the other directors whom Cyrus needed for a quorum were on call for an eight am board meeting the next day. He had given Rainbow until then to come up with something tangible.

Cyrus slotted his reading glasses into their case and poured himself some ice-water, touching his fingers to the condensation on the glass, then using his forefinger and thumb to pinch the top of his nose. It offered some relief to his tired eyes. He had been reading all day, every memo, every profit projection and bar-chart which his analysts had produced on AsiaRisk. With a head stuffed with figures, Cyrus decided to sleep on his decision, see where it got him by morning.

Reaching for the light-switch on his banker's lamp, his hand paused on the electronic game embedded into the mahogany base plinth. It was the hand-held version of *PinTec*, the electronic tennis game which had made Cyrus his first fortune, this one the first to have come off the factory line. It symbolised where it had all started for Cyrus and Kwan Holdings all those years ago. Hong Kong had been good to him. The risks, the hard work, it had all paid off. Only in Hong Kong, where individual responsibility and entrepreneurialism were worshipped, could it have been possible.

Shutting off the light, Cyrus took his ice-water and started on up the stairs. He'd dismissed the staff hours ago and he knew that his wife, Stephanie, would be asleep by now. She turned in early these days. No longer the fashionable socialite of old. More like a life-long companion. Cyrus liked it that way and part of him longed for the day when he could let go and hand over the reins. But his only son was a doctor and had no interest in the business. That left only Rupert.

The thought of his nephew filled Cyrus with an odd mix of exasperation and admiration. Rupert was a long way from being ready; still a young man trying to buck the trend. But spotting AsiaRisk and going after it was an impressive move, Cyrus had to admit. Or was that the nagging doubt which was troubling him? Was it too early to trust him after that container terminal business? Pausing at the landing half-way up the staircase, Cyrus stared out of the window into the darkness. He loved the solitude of the night.

His mobile vibrated in his pocket, disrupting the peaceful moment. Rainbow Choi's name flashed up on the screen.

"Cyrus, it's Rainbow," she said in clipped tones, when he answered. "We need to talk!"

"Have you found anything?" Cyrus asked, ignoring pleasantries. Part of him wanted her to have discovered a flaw, something that would give AsiaRisk the genuineness he was searching for. The thought tailed off when he realized her answer was taking too long. "Rainbow?" He took the phone away from his ear, looked down at the screen. "Damn!" They'd been disconnected. He waited for her to call back, his ice-water turning tepid in his grasp.

Three minutes went by. He called her number. It cut straight to voicemail. He hung up, tried again. Same thing. "Rainbow, it's Cyrus. We've just been cut off. Give me a call as soon as you get this." He stayed where he was, ruminating a while. What had she found? Anything? Nothing? Eventually, Cyrus continued his long journey up the stairs.

CHAPTER THIRTY-THREE

It was over in seconds. But at the precise moment Scott braced for the impact, time hit the slow-motion button and the tragedy he was about to be part of played out frame-by-frame.

Rainbow's hands were at ten-to-two on the wheel, earpiece in place, eyes peering with intent at the dark road ahead. "Cyrus, it's Rainbow. I need to talk to you!" Just as she said it, she hit the bend. And in a flash there it was. The BMW which had left them only seconds before was now stationary in the road, its tail-lights coming towards them at a horrifying rate. No way Rainbow could avoid it.

"Watch out!" Scott heard himself scream. Pure instinct made him reach over and grab the steering wheel. They jolted hard right, missing the BMW by a paper-cut, but now they were on the other side of the road, heading straight for a line of metal barriers. Rainbow pulled the wheel right, screeching tyres beneath them as they fishtailed. The sickening sound of metal folding in on itself spliced the air as the SLK's backside smashed against the barriers.

Scott felt his body whip forward and in a flash, an awful thought. *No seat belt!* He'd taken it off to get Rainbow's handbag. Marshmallow airbags slowed his fall but his head smacked the windscreen. Stars burst behind his eyes, but no pain, not then because there was no time to feel it as the car hurtled down the bank beyond the barriers, wheels jolting beneath them as they picked up speed.

Warm stickiness filled Scott's eyes as he fought the deflating airbag. A glance at Rainbow. Her body flopped like a rag doll. He wanted to reach out and steady her but then....

Whump!

They smacked something solid. More sickening metal on metal. Glass shattered all around. Scott smashed the windscreen with his elbows, went airborne and hit the ground with a vicious thud. Over and over Scott flipped, stones piercing his flesh.

The movie ended there. The shutters came down.

Darkness reigned.

*

The sky had never been so blue, nor the clouds so white.

Fields of differing greens and browns stretch out below in a never-ending patchwork quilt. The glider sweeps down at an exhilarating tempo, the fields now a kaleidoscopic rush. Houses on the horizon; rows and rows of them, terraced with gardens behind and trees in front. The glider circles, chooses one and comes to rest outside. Beyond the red gate, a stone pathway leads up to the front door. Laughter and joy spill through the windows.

Scott wants to join the happiness, but a voice cuts him dead.

"No! Not yet!"

His mother. Standing defiantly, all five-foot-four of her, pointing him back the way he came with that don't-argue-with-me look he knows so well. The riposte kicks the glider into hard reverse, above the houses and the fields, the sky still blue but the clouds soon closing it out to nothing.

That's when Scott opened his eyes and the darkness and heat enveloped him. Snatching gasps clogged his throat. Then the pain came, creeping up through his body, wincing and brutal.

What the hell....

He remembered. The car crash. It flooded back into his mind, those few seconds of violent confusion re-playing: swerving to avoid the BMW, smashing through the barrier, dropping into nothing, the smack at the end tossing him into oblivion.

Light cut through from his left, shimmering through rising steam. Scott tried focusing on it. Slowly the swaying halted. The SLK's headlamps, that's what they were. The car's rear concertinaed into a splintered tree trunk, smoke hissing from the engine, shattered glass all around.

Somehow Scott had ended up outside and ten feet away. Stones and glass shards pierced his fingers as he made fists. A pain in his shoulder sharpened, stabbing him like a knife.

Move, Scott told himself, but something deep inside urged him to take things slowly. His shoulder had taken the worst of it. Ah yes. He winced as he moved it in its socket.

Then a thought.

Rainbow!

Getting gingerly to his feet Scott peered back through the smoke towards the car.

And when he saw her, his insides went cold. Rainbow Choi wasn't moving. Her head lolled unnaturally to one side.

A sound. A cracking twig, a crunching of leaves, uneven footsteps coming down the bank towards them, a torch-beam dancing in the headlights, shadows disturbed by the beams.

Scott saw the man in black outline, towering in height, with shoulders that could have formed the foundations of a skyscraper. The man peered at Rainbow through the missing driver's window.

A hint of recognition stopped Scott from shouting out to him. Nothing much, but enough to stop his voice. A misty light danced off the man's face, the chiseled jaw-line plain even from that distance. Then it caught; the memory of Leopold Chan's right-hand man helping his boss swallow pills and adding a general aura of menace to their meeting. *Terrence O'Rourke. That was his name.*

The connections came quickly then, one after the other. The BMW disappearing past them up the road, reappearing stationary round a blind corner, forcing them to swerve....

And then it happened

In one fluid movement O'Rourke's right arm was raised, the barrel of the gun glimmering in the pale light, levelled at Rainbow Choi, aim straight and true, nothing showing on his face, no hint of emotion.

Phut! Phut!

Scott saw her body jolt as the bullets ripped into her, the speed of it surreal.

Cold terror kicked in like a shot of pure adrenalin through Scott's blood stream, choking him with fear, making him lose control, making him take that step back, even as his foot moved Scott knew it was a mistake, but the sheer horror of what he had just witnessed had taken hold and there was nothing he could do.

Glass crunched. O'Rourke's face turned and met Scott's eyes. Nothing showed on the Irishman's face, no hint of regret at having just taken a life. Only a small sick smile.

The gun started to move.

Scott was no longer in control, just along for the ride. He couldn't remember pushing with his legs but it must have happened because he was airborne, horizontal, diving to his right, no thought, just reflex.

Phut! Phut! The gun blinked through Scott's consciousness. Pain knifed his shoulder as he hit the ground, instantaneous but oddly relieving and disappearing quickly as he rolled down the bank, splaying bushes and bamboo which pierced and stabbed their revenge. When Scott came to rest, the vegetation provided some cover but leaves and twigs were no match for bullets. *Phut! Phut! Phut!* Bamboo stems cracked and splintered around him, bitter smoke trails sparking in his nostrils. *Move!* Scott's head screamed, adrenalin pushing him to his feet. He ran for his life, down the slope, pumping his arms, tripping, hitting the ground, getting up, pushing forward, further and further into his dark abyss, not knowing where it would end.

The snooker club was quiet, like only a snooker club could be.

O'Rourke loved this place. It was the little piece of Belfast he could hold onto in this Chinese city, snooker the one constant in his life. Hanging round the clubs back home when he should have been at school, running errands for the big hard men at the tables in return for small change, that was how he'd been introduced to the life. Now the game served as a way of clinging on to who he was. Playing it was a deep-seated need, like going to church on Sunday, only without the self-loathing.

O'Rourke chalked his cue, took another shot. The white ball smoothed across the baize, the click with the red as pure and cathartic a sound as there was in this world. A trigger-pull was the only thing that came close. O'Rourke reached for his Jameson's. The glass had that just-so heaviness, the glowing whisky it held as precious to him as gold. His tongue savoured the peaty taste.

Only then did he notice Chan's shadowy outline in the doorway. O'Rourke put down his glass, settled in and took another shot, but this time his cueing was off, the ball ricocheting in the pocket, spinning out and colliding with the pack.

"What interesting places you frequent, Terrence," Chan said.

O'Rourke thought about explaining, but a man like Chan wouldn't understand. He lined up another shot. "You won't be havin' any more trouble from that Rainbow Choi."

He heard Chan's breath pause. It was all his Chinese boss gave away. *Cold bastard*, O'Rourke thought, but he was respectful of that. All his life, O'Rourke had known men for whom death was just business, a means that justified the ends. Usually they were hard types who had spent years being de-sensitized behind bars, steeped in bitterness at family members getting swept aside as collateral damage. But Leopold Chan brought coldness to a new level. Chan was pure ice, lost in his twisted world of money and power. Brains and brutality made for a lethal combination. But O'Rourke didn't care, so long as his pay-cheque was regular.

"What about Scott Lee?" Chan asked.

O'Rourke downed the rest of his Jamesons. "Didn't manage to get the lad."

Flashing back to the moment when the gun was levelled at Lee's chest. He'd shot. He'd missed. Emptied the rest of the magazine into the darkness, but a quick search told him the effort had been wasted. Lee was gone.

Next time, he wouldn't be so lucky, though. Next time it would be personal.

"Soon as he turns up, I'll finish the job."

Out of the corner of his eye he saw Leopold Chan nodding. "How did you do it? Rainbow Choi, I mean."

O'Rourke looked up from the table. *Now wasn't that funny.* Men like Chan had no problem giving the order. But talking about it, even mentioning the word 'kill'....

"I put two bullets in her. Then torched the vehicle."

The lack of response on Leopold Chan's face sent a chill through the room. Even O'Rourke felt it. There they stood, facing each other in hard silence, while Chan worked it through and O'Rourke waited for the order.

"Do you still have the gun?" Chan eventually asked.

O'Rourke nodded.

"Okay then Terrence, here's what I need you to do."

Chan went through it twice to make sure it was clear. It was a strange set of instructions and O'Rourke didn't get the reasoning behind this new strategy.

But then again, he didn't need to.

He just put down his cue and went to take care of business.

CHAPTER THIRTY-FOUR

The harsh burr of the entry buzzer lifted Kinson from sleep.

Napping wasn't strictly permitted when he was on duty, but the building management never complained. So what if a security-guard dropped off at the reception desk for a few minutes? That and the prospect of watching TV were the only real benefits of doing the night shift.

The buzzer sounded again. Kinson yawned then shifted his eyes to his digital clock which told him it was 1.35 am. Shuffling at a speed which would have given a snail a chance at victory, he made his way down the marble stretch to the front entrance. Through the glass doors he saw the two policemen, one tall and young, the other chubby and older. Kinson pulled the door ajar.

"Sorry to disturb you," the chubby one said. "We need your help. Can we come in a moment?"

Kinson glanced from one to the other.

So what to do? Ring management and cause a fuss? There seemed little point; probably they would just tell him to deal with it himself. With a laconic shrug he opened the door. The policemen followed him at his arthritic pace back to the front desk.

On the television, an advert was airing for a new luxury development in Shatin. A Gwai-mui – a western woman – was horse-riding on a beach, an Italian prince amorously looking on. Always this advert, it seemed, and Kinson never understood how it related to the property on sale. Every year the world became that little bit stranger to him. But so long as his job gave him enough to gamble on the football, Kinson was content with his little corner of it. "So, Ah-sirs, what do you want?"

"Have you seen this woman here today?" The chubby one pushed a photograph over the desk.

Kinson squinted. His eye-sight wasn't what it used to be. But he recognised her immediately. "Yes. She was here," he said, adding quickly "Not a resident. A visitor."

"Who did she visit?"

Kinson hesitated. "What's this about?"

"Please," Chubby said. "I wouldn't be asking if it wasn't important. Who did she visit?"

Sweeping a bony hand through his whispy hair, Kinson thought for a moment. This job may not have been much, but it was all he had. "People here trust me," he said.

"You think you can talk to us like that!" The younger policeman suddenly came to life. "Let me see your ID card...."

"Officer Cheung!" Chubby cut him off. "Please radio the station and tell them we have found the building!"

Sulkily, the younger officer went back down to the glass doors. Chubby turned back to Kinson. "Look, this lady," he pointed to the photograph. "Her name is Rainbow Choi. We need to find out where she has been today."

"Why?"

Chubby sighed. "Because she is dead."

Kinson's hand dropped from his head. "Dead?"

The policeman nodded. "A sad business, I know. And I'm sorry to have to ask you these questions. But please. Who did she come to see?"

Still Kinson said nothing.

"Was it Scott Lee?"

Kinson made a face. Well if they knew already why were they asking him? Was it some sort of test? Ah, the police and their strange ways. "Yes," he admitted.

"And did they leave together?"

"Yes."

"What time?"

Kinson shrugged. "Around seven-thirty may be."

"Has Mr Lee returned?"

"I didn't see him come back. I've been on duty the whole time."

"But he could have come back, without you seeing, yes? He may have just been waving her off, or something. You're not at the desk all the time are you?"

Kinson frowned. "I guess not. But most of the time"

"Can we go up and see if he's in?"

Kinson wasn't sure about that, given the lateness of the hour. But Mr Lee would understand, it was the police after all. "I'll take you up, but please try not to wake anyone."

"We'll be quiet, I promise," Chubby said. He called down Officer Cheung and all three of them rode the lift to the seventeenth floor. When they got out, Kinson rang Lee's doorbell. Nothing. He rang again, then knocked. Still nothing.

"He's not in," Kinson whispered.

"He usually stays out this late?" Chubby asked

Kinson shrugged. "Not often. But he's a Gweilo, a young man. Not a crime to enjoy yourself, is it?"

Hands on hips, Chubby let his eyes glide slowly up and down the hallway. When he saw the shoe-locker next to the front door, his gaze was grabbed by something. The shoe-locker door was slightly open. Something was glistening inside. He took a pen out of his pocket and shifted the door outwards to get a better look.

"Hey, what are you doing?" Kinson asked. But the officer ignored him as his eyes came to rest on the shiny implement which the door had partially hidden.

"What is it?" Officer Cheung asked his older colleague.

Chubby stepped aside and all three of them stared in horrible silence at the gun lying flat next to a pair of running-shoes.

Divorced and with a career long in stagnation, the night shift suited DI Kam Sing-Yeung.

A tall young officer opened the door when Kam held his badge up to the glass. The kid looked surprised. It was the toothpick, probably; a nasty habit Kam had picked up since he'd given up smoking three years ago. He'd work it round his mouth to absorb the nicotine craving then let it sit behind his gums and forget it was there.

Ignoring the young officer's judgemental eyes, Kam rode the lift to the seventeenth floor. It had just gone 2.30am.

A fat officer met him there. Kam recognized him – one of the old brigade who liked to use their heads rather than the rule book to get the job done – couldn't recall his name, though. Next to the officer on a chair in the hallway sat an old man wearing a security-guard's uniform. The old man was so frail it looked like a gust of wind had knocked him on his backside.

"Where is it, then?" Kam asked. The officer pointed out the shoe-locker. Kam saw it. He took out a pencil and lifted it by its trigger protector. An NP 42, 9 millimetre. Hard to get hold of unless you knew the right people. He sniffed at the barrel, his nose flexing away at the smell.

So the tip-off had been right.

At midnight a 999 call had reported a car crash on a side road off from the Tolo highway, the caller identifying himself only as a passing motorist who had stopped to help, but on hearing what he thought were gunshots and seeing a young man running off into the undergrowth, he had got back into his car and driven on. Only later did he decide to be the good citizen and call in every detail except his name.

A patrol car was dispatched and found the crash sight at the bottom of a slope. Kam, on duty, had caught the case and set to work on the number plate which told him the car belonged to one Rainbow Choi. By all accounts the plate was about all that was left of the car, except the charred remains in the driver's seat. There were certainly no immediate signs of gunshots, though the autopsy would tell them more.

Gunshots. Kam had wondered about that. How would your average 999 caller know what they sounded like?

Turned out Rainbow Choi was some hot-shot accountant. Kam managed to track down her secretary, roused her out of bed and asked about her boss's movements that day. The last thing the secretary had heard, Choi had been on her way to a residential address to speak to someone called Scott Lee.

Now here they were, outside Lee's flat. With a recently-fired gun in his shoe-locker.

Kam placed the gun back down carefully. If Lee had shot this Choi woman, why put it in the shoe-locker? And why go out again?

Whatever! He needed Lee in custody. Quickly.

"Wait here!" Kam said to the officer. "Someone will take prints, then get that thing bagged and down to ballistics. Who's this?" He pointed with his jaw to the old man.

"Security-guard," the officer said.

Kam stared disdainfully. *Security-guard.* A six-year-old could have got past him. Not out of the question then, that Lee had come back and gone out again without being noticed.

"What's your name?" Kam asked the old boy.

"Kinson, ah-sir."

"Let's go back downstairs, Kinson." They got into the lift and started to descend. "So what do you know about Scott Lee?"

"Not much."

"Live on his own?"

"Yes."

"Girlfriend?"

A shrug.

"Many visitors?"

"No."

"Talk to you much?"

Another shrug. "More than others do. He likes football. He's from England so knows a lot about the Premier League."

The lift doors opened. Kam told Kinson to take a seat and phoned the station on his mobile.

"We'll need a warrant for this guy's flat. You got the address? Good. Also call Choi's secretary again. I want to know what business Choi had with Lee. And his ID card picture. Get it circulated. We need to find him. I'm going to stay here, talk to the security-guard some more. My guess is Lee will have to come home at some point and....hang on."

The phone on the front desk was ringing. Kinson looked at Kam, his eyes asking for permission to answer. Kam nodded.

"Hello," Kinson said into the receiver. A pause. A nod. Then his bony hand went up to the mouthpiece: "It's Mr Lee."

Kam closed his mobile. "Ask where he is and when he's coming back. Don't tell him we're here."

Kinson looked serious, cleared his throat, used both hands to lift the handset back to his ear. "How are you Mr Lee....you lost your keys?....yes, I have a spare set....no problem....no problem....yes, yes, I'm fine....only three hours till my shift ends, so I feel good....but not as good as you did when West Ham beat Man U away, you remember that night, Mr Lee? You were so funny when you came back, so happy....yes....yes....okay....I see you later."

Kam lifted his palms and waited for an explanation.

"He says he's been out drinking in Wanchai and lost his keys. Wanted to know if I had a spare set. He's on his way home now. He'll be here in fifteen minutes."

Kam slipped the toothpick out from his gums and started chewing.

CHAPTER THIRTY-FIVE

O'Rourke was out there. Somewhere.

Taunting him, ready to step out of the darkness any moment, flash that horrid little smile and pull a trigger. In the blackness Scott gasped for oxygen. How long he'd been running he didn't know, but he sensed it wasn't long enough. That it would never be long enough. The image of Rainbow Choi – a woman he had known only for a few hours, but with whom he had made a connection – jolting, as the bullets tore into her, sparked in his mind.

The first time he had seen a human life ended. A life, a whole life. Birth, school, work, friends, love, hurt, relationships. All gone in a trigger pull.

It sickened and numbed Scott like nothing before.

Keeping moving was his only option. Half-jogging, half-running, he let the physical effort absorb him, stop his mind becoming overwhelmed by a situation it wasn't equipped to deal with. He found a road and followed it back towards the Tolo Highway, ducking in the shadows every time a car passed by.

Tai Po was the nearest place he'd been to around here. Years ago he'd ridden the cycle path, crammed between Tolo harbour and highway, which led straight into the market town. About as picturesque a ride as watching concrete solidify, Scott remembered thinking at the time, and – next to the traffic on the highway – about as healthy too.

But finding the route again was the plan now. And thankfully, it wasn't too difficult.

It was past midnight. The cycle path was dark. The kind of dark that makes you sick with fright every time a shadow flickers. Scott passed a public toilet still with its lights on. Inside, it stank from a full day's usage. But today, Scott was willing to bet he'd been through more shit than it had. Staring back in the clouded mirror was someone different to the person he'd woken up as that morning. Someone long past his breaking point. It was only a matter of time before his brain caught up to that fact, then the disintegration would begin. *Black abyss, here we come!* For now, though, he'd rely on the numbness to put off what he'd have to cope with later.

He washed blood from his face, the result of a cut above his hair-line. The bruising to his shoulder was already a healthy shade of blue. His shirt was a soaking, sweat-stained dish-cloth. He ran it under the tap, wrung it out as best he could, and stuck it under the hand-dryer until it was passable. Putting it back on added to the list of unpleasant experiences that day, the fresh dampness forming goose-bumps on his back and arms.

Right then Scott felt brittle and ready to rupture. He grabbed the sink edge and gulped deep, steadying, breaths. *Just keep it together a little while longer.* Home, he had to get home. Thankfully, his wallet was still in his pocket; his keys too.

Leaving the toilet, he branched off the cycle path through a network of pedestrian walkways and underpasses until he made it to Tai Po Market station. The platform was deserted and he rode the train to Tsim Tsa Tsui, all the while keeping his head tucked in, his eyes shut and his arms folded. At Tsim Tsa Tsui he caught the last MTR of the night back to Central, then changed for Causeway Bay. He arrived just before one am.

Stepping out into the familiar polluted air of Hong Kong Island brought a sharp relief Scott had never thought possible. But not as much as a shower and a few hours with shut-eye would. Sleep would be too much to hope for, but a chance to re-group, get his head together, was the next best thing.

The walk up Wong Nai Chung Road was an endless torture and when he finally turned into the entrance of the street where he lived, the fatigue had left him punchdrunk. But the sight of the policeman outside his building was like a bucket of iced water in the face.

Scott slipped quickly back round the corner, his breathing low and shallow, iron panic-bands tightening fast round his chest.

It could be someone on one of the other twenty-four floors the police were there to see, he tried to rationalize. *The hell it could!*

Calming himself, he reviewed his options, which right then made for a pretty short list. He could carry on, go home, see what the police wanted, take his chances. Or he could get the hell out – probably make himself look as guilty as sin, but at least it would buy time to think.

An idea burst like a firework through the haze of panic. A long shot, but worth a try, just to check whether this was just a bad case of paranoia. One of the few phone-boxes left in the area was on Wong Nai Chung Road. Scott hurried to find it, fumbled some change into the slot and dialed. Kinson answered on the third ring.

"Hi Kin-son, it's Mr Lee from the seventeenth floor." Scott tried to keep his Cantonese lilting and care-free.

A long pause. A scratching sound on the mouthpiece. Scott was about to hang up when Kinson said: "Mr Lee, how are you?"

One breath out.

"Oh I'm a bit drunk. Too much beer with friends in Wanchai. I lost my keys."

"You lost your keys?"

"Yes. I don't want to go back to the bar to find them. Do you have one I can use?"

"Yes, I have a spare set."

"Oh great, I'll be there in fifteen minutes."

"No problem, no problem."

Scott swallowed. Here went nothing. "So how are you? Okay?"

"Yes, yes I'm fine." Pause. Then: "Only three hours till my shift ends, so I feel good. But not as good as you did when West Ham beat Man U away, you remember that night, Mr Lee? You were so funny when you came back, so happy....Yes....Yes....okay....I see you later."

Click. Dialing tone.

The ba-bump of Scott's heart thundered through his head. He knew little about the wizened old man who sat at the front desk day after day. But he did know one thing. Kinson could recite every score line and scorer, for every one of his precious Manchester United's games. And back in August, West Ham had been handed a lesson in football at Old Trafford. Manchester United 4, West Ham 1. A bad night that had been for Scott. Not as bad as this one but bad all the same. A strange way to pass a warning. But Scott had received it loud and clear.

He looked down at his wallet. Buried within the copious receipts was a green fifty dollar note. Next to it, his Octopus card probably had another fifty on it. The ATM was too risky, but a hundred bucks didn't go far in this town. He needed help and as ever there was only one person to whom he could turn when his life was in a mess. He stuffed the slot with coins and dialed, praying it wouldn't cut to voicemail

Twenty minutes later, Scott was at the top of a concrete staircase connecting the residential solitude of Shu Fai Terrace to Stubbs Road fifty feet below. Through the trees the red AIA sign advertised a monstrosity of an office block sandwiched between an impressive Sikh temple and the vast Happy Valley Protestant and Catholic graveyards. Only in Hong Kong, where space was so limited, could such a strange juxtaposition have evolved and become permanent.

Philip Yip's car eventually came into sight and pulled up, Yip wearing a yellow Lacoste polo-neck, the collar turned up. Not even a situation like this could dent Scott's old friend's unique sartorial standards. Scott stepped out of the shadows and opened the passenger door.

"What's going on?" Yip didn't waste any time.

"I can't tell you."

"What's that supposed to mean?"

"It means what it means," Scott said impatiently. Yip was his best friend. There was no way he was going to involve him in this mess. "You got the money?"

He felt Yip's probing eyes on him, searching him for some clue as to the level of trouble he was in. "You been in a fight or something?"

"Phil, do you have the money!"

Yip stayed still a moment, then reached into his chest pocket and pulled out a roll of notes. "That's all I had in the house." It was more than enough.

"Thanks," Scott said. A glance passed between them. A silent bond.

"Scott let me help you, just tell me...."

"Go home, Phil."

Before his friend could say anything else, Scott shut the passenger door and started down the staircase.

CHAPTER THIRTY-SIX

Dawn was easing its fingers round the tip of the Peak, tempering the rugged, rocky outline blue and red. A warning to early risers to get their exercise in early, before the sun turned up the temperature to unbearable levels.

Detective-Inspector Kam rang the doorbell of the house on Plantation Road, a two-storey villa with a terracotta roof and a beige, granite finish. Big-Ben chimes sounded. A light flicked on. Kam was ready with his badge as keys rattled in the door. It was a man who answered, a thin Filipino, not the usual robust type Kam associated with domestic work. Kam asked if Leopold Chan was in.

"He asleep," the Filipino said.

Kam worked his toothpick. His patience was a commodity in short supply that morning.

"What's your name?" he asked.

The Filipino eyed him suspiciously. "Alfonso."

"You work for Mr Chan, Alfonso?"

"Yes."

"Doing what?"

"I paint for him."

"You're his decorator?"

"No I am painter. Artist," Alfonso swished his hands as if brush-stroking his way to a masterpiece.

Kam's toothpick stopped. Leopold Chan had his own personal artist? Kam had lived in Hong Kong all his life, so he knew how the eccentricities of the filthy rich were laid bare for all those at the other end of the economic spectrum to see. He'd often wondered how healthy it was, people being constantly confronted by a world which most of them would never be able to attain. Did it create false hope or just an eternal sense of resentment that led to crime?

"Who is it, Alfonso?" A voice called from back in the house. Alfonso opened the door some more and the owner of the voice bustled into sight.

Leopold Chan. It had to be. Some people just had a presence that made you involuntarily step backwards and adjust. Chan's hands laced up a silk dressing-gown which looked like it had been cut by the gods. His face suggested that five-thirty in the morning wasn't his usual waking time, but he was ready to take whatever the world had to throw at him all the same. Kam took note.

"Mr Leopold Chan?"

"And you are?"

"Detective Inspector Kam," Kam flipped his badge. Leopold Chan took it, inspected it and came up with a smile that would have made a cockroach feel welcome.

"What can I do for you, Inspector?"

Kam decided to dive straight in. "You know a lady called Rainbow Choi?"

Chan's smile stayed in place. Not a flicker. "Yes, I know Ms Choi." Then something on his face changed. "Oh please tell me this isn't part of the due diligence. I'd heard her methods were unorthodox but this is going too far, really!"

Kam had no clue what he was talking about, so just hit him with it.

"Rainbow Choi is dead."

Leopold Chan straightened, his eyes widening with shock. "Oh my goodness. That's ....that's awful." He steadied himself on the door frame. "How? When?"

Kam assessed the reaction. "She lost control of her car on a tight corner. Sometime last night, around ten o'clock. Maybe I can come in and we can talk?"

Chan took a moment to answer. "Please," he said – his voice a breathy whisper – and led the policeman through to an immaculate living room. He sent Alfonso off to make coffee. Alfonso opened the curtains, revealing a superb garden through a set of double patio windows.

Rich people, it really was a different world.

"Did Ms Choi have any family?" Leopold Chan asked,when they were both seated.

"She was single. Mind if I ask how you knew her?"

Chan didn't seem to hear the question. He was staring off into the distance. "I can't believe this." The words seemed aimed at no one in particular, just voicing thought.

"Mr Chan?"

Chan snapped back in. "She's working on an important transaction involving my company."

"What sort of transaction?"

Chan sighed heavily. "It's a buy-out. I'm the managing director of an insurance company which someone's looking to buy, Inspector. Ms Choi represents the purchaser on the due-diligence. She's been in my office for the past two days. I...I can't believe this has happened."

"Your company would be AsiaRisk?" Kam needed to press on, throw out the results of the little homework he'd managed to do in the few hours available.

Chan paused, perhaps in surprise that Kam already knew his company's name, but he was quick enough to recover. "That's right."

All genuine reactions so far, Kam concluded. He took the tooth pick out of his mouth, looked for an ashtray, but couldn't find one. So popped it back in to give it more mileage. "Mind if I ask who's buying your company? The party that Ms Choi was representing?"

Chan moved in his seat. "Is this relevant, Inspector?" He asked, but followed up quickly with an apologetic gesture. "I'm not really sure I can tell you without first obtaining legal advice. I signed a confidentiality agreement, you see."

Kam mulled on that. When there was a crime involved, a confidentiality agreement meant zip as far as he was concerned. But he didn't want to play that card yet. "Does the name Scott Lee mean anything to you?"

Chan's face switched to confusion. "I know that name from somewhere....but...." Then it dawned. "The lawyer who came to see me looking for work." His voice was disapproving. "He suggested I wasn't getting the proper representation from my current lawyers and that he could do a better job. Yes, I remember him. What's he got to do with this?"

"Your current lawyer would be Charles Conrad of Jackson's?"

"That's right," Chan said. "Inspector Kam, would you mind telling me what this is all about. Why are you asking me about....what was his name again?"

"Scott Lee."

Kam stayed stoic except for the toothpick, searching for signs of something out of the ordinary in Chan's reactions. So far there had been nothing and it had reached the stage in the conversation where he had to make a decision. Usually, when questioning someone, Kam would hold back on as much information as he could until he was sure he had dragged the truth out of the person. But there was far more at stake here and time wasn't on his side. He needed to find Scott Lee. Fast. That was priority number one right now. Everything else could wait. To do that, Kam realized he had to give information to get it back.

Decision made.

"We think Scott Lee had something to do with Rainbow Choi's death," he said, feeling like he was crossing some sort of rubicon.

"But…you said she died in a car crash?"

"Her car crashed, yes. But we're not making any assumptions yet about how she died," Kam corrected. "We think Scott Lee might be connected. And we think it might have something to do with a personal vendetta he is pursuing against you, Mr Chan."

"Vendetta?" Chan's confusion continued. "What are you talking about?"

"Look, Mr Chan. I need you to listen and cooperate!" Kam reached into his jacket pocket, flopped open his notebook. "Here's how it is. At eleven-fifteen pm yesterday night, a 999 call was made reporting a car crash. The caller reported hearing gunshots. He also said he saw a man fleeing the crash scene."

"Gunshots?"

"Gunshots," Kam confirmed. "Uniformed police were dispatched to the site within the hour and found a Mercedes SLK belonging to Rainbow Choi down the side of a slope. There was a body in the car, a woman, Ms Choi we believe. The car was incinerated…"

"Oh God!" Chan winced.

"….there were no signs of any one else in the car," Kam continued. "But broken vegetation around suggests there may have been a passenger who left the scene." Kam turned the page. "I've spoken to Ms Choi's secretary. Last she heard, Ms Choi was on her way to Scott Lee's flat around seven o'clock yesterday evening. Said it had something to do with the matter she was working on. I'm guessing it was the transaction you just

251

mentioned, Mr Chan. Any idea why Ms Choi would want to speak to Lee about that?"

Chan bit his lip. "None at all. The only people who even know about the buy-out are myself, the purchaser and our respective advisers."

Kam looked back down at his notebook. "Officers were sent round to Lee's flat. He wasn't there. But we found a gun in the shoe-locker outside. Ballistics will tell us more on that. We waited around to see if Lee returned home. He hasn't, not yet anyway. And we don't know where he is. So you see, Mr Chan we need to find Lee. Fast."

"Well I don't where he is!" Chan said. "And I know nothing about any personal vendetta!"

Kam rubbed his eyes with his fingers. It had been a long night but things had fallen quickly into place. When they'd run Lee's name and ID card through police records they'd come up with a direct hit. "Scott Lee met with detectives from the Financial Institutions Crimes Unit yesterday afternoon," Kam said, recalling his conversation with the head of the Unit, Chief Inspector Shing who'd been pissed off at the early morning wake-up call. "He made some allegations about you and Charles Conrad being involved in some sort of money-laundering scheme."

"What?!" Leopold Chan snapped forward in his armchair. "That's totally outrageous!"

Again Kam took note of the reaction. Anger, shock, a soupçon of defensiveness. All genuine. "When the FICU officers looked into Lee's background they found out about a complaint Charles Conrad had made to the Law Society about Lee. About certain comments Lee had made to you about Mr Conrad."

Leopold Chan's expression twisted then. "Yes," he said. "Yes I remember now. When he tried to poach my work for the law firm he now works for, he said some absolutely outrageous things about Charles."

"Because of that, FICU told Lee they didn't take his allegations seriously. This was only yesterday afternoon, Mr Chan."

Leopold Chan screwed his eyes up. "So what exactly are you saying, Inspector?"

"Bear in mind, we don't have a full picture yet. But, it seems that Scott Lee was angry at you and Charles Conrad for the Law Society complaint. We know that Lee is single; so I guess his career is very important to him, maybe it's all he's got. And here you were trying to ruin it."

"It was never my intention to..." Leopold began; but Kam interrupted him.

"I'm just telling you how I think Lee's mind could be working. He was upset, angry, wanted to get his own back on you, to lash out. So he goes to FICU, makes some allegations to stir up trouble for you and Mr Conrad. FICU tell him to get lost, which leads to more frustration, more anger. Then all of a sudden, Rainbow Choi turns up on his doorstep and Lee finds out about AsiaRisk being bought. He figures the transaction must be important to you," Kam shrugged. "So he tries to make trouble for you that way, by killing the purchaser's representative, right in the middle of the process."

Leopold's mouth dropped open. Nothing came out.

Kam needed to hurry this along, but he also needed Chan to digest the information. He paused a moment to let Chan think.

After a while, Chan said, "I can't believe this! All this because I didn't give him any legal work? So he...what...kills an innocent woman, just to get back at me? Do you know how ridiculous that sounds, Inspector?"

Kam wet his lips. "Right now, all I care about is finding Scott Lee. Do you understand?"

"Yes," Chan said.

"If Lee's intention is to ruin a transaction involving your company, Mr Chan, I need to know who else is working on it. They could be potential targets. We don't know how much Choi told Lee."

Just then there was a knock on the door. Alfonso stood there holding a silver tray with freshly-brewed coffee. Chan beckoned him in with two fingers. Alfonso pressed down the plunger on the pot, poured it out into the bone china, gave a little bow, then left.

Another world, Kam thought, reaching for his cup and taking a sip. The sensation of real coffee almost overloaded his tastebuds, dulled by years of drinking the muck that came out of the station vending machine. "I take it this transaction is important to you, Mr Chan?"

Chan got up from his chair and rolled his shoulders in a stretching motion. "Yes, Inspector, this transaction is very important to me and to the future of my company. Too important to let some lunatic ruin it. I know that may sound callous, but ...."

Kam kept his face straight. There it was. The key to obtaining this kind of life. Everything else came second to chasing money. Sometimes Kam hated the city he helped to protect.

"Who else does the transaction involve?" Kam said. "They may also be in danger."

Leopold Chan nodded, his face betraying a decision to let Kam in on the secret. "Kwan Holdings. That's the company which is looking to buy AsiaRisk."

Kam lifted his eyebrows. "Kwan Holdings is the buyer?"

"Yes."

Kam considered that. "Forgive me, Mr Chan. But how exactly does it work? How does one company buy another?"

"Well," Chan shrugged. "In this particular instance, first we fixed a price for the shares. Now Kwan Holdings is doing its due diligence on what it's buying. That's why Rainbow Choi was in my office. After that, Cyrus Kwan will make a final decision. If he still wants to proceed, we sign contracts. Apart from a few regulatory approvals, which should be a given as its Kwan Holdings, that's really it."

"Sounds pretty straightforward."

"It has gone smoothly, Inspector. Up until now, that is," Chan let out a sigh of frustration. "Cyrus Kwan rang up yesterday to tell me his board of directors are meeting at eight-thirty this morning to make their final decision. This really is the last thing I need!" He rubbed his wrinkled forehead with his fingers.

Kam checked his watch. Eight-thirty was just over two hours away. "Where does this meeting take place?"

"At Kwan Tower. Oh my goodness, you don't think...." Chan said, but stopped himself.

"What is it, Mr Chan?"

Chan stared straight at him.

"Rainbow Choi would have known about the meeting. You don't think she would have told this Scott Lee about it?"

Kam ran into the same thought at the same time. There it was, what he had come for. The next place where Scott Lee might turn up.

Kam got up to leave. He'd have other questions for Chan later. After they'd got Lee locked down tight.

"There's going to be a police car positioned outside your home, Mr Chan. I want to take the necessary precautions. Just in case."

Chan nodded. "What about Cyrus Kwan?"

"I'll make sure we've got people on the ground," Kam checked his watch.

"Thank you, Inspector," Chan said, then asked Alfonso to show Kam out.

As Kam left the living room, he glanced back. He could have sworn Leopold Chan was smiling to himself. What about, he didn't know. Too much money had a strange effect on the human psyche. Kam had seen enough of life to know that.

Rich people, they really did live in a world all of their own.

The 999 call had been a master stroke, placing Scott Lee at the scene of Rainbow Choi's untimely demise. And O'Rourke had certainly redeemed himself, planting the gun in Lee's shoe-locker for the police to discover. With a few well-positioned brush-strokes, Leopold was satisfied that he had created a devastating masterpiece.

He'd worked out that if Lee was going to turn up anywhere, it would be at Kwan Tower. Now the police would be waiting for him. And so would O'Rourke, who would be keen to make amends for his earlier mishap. Next, he would need to call Cyrus Kwan, give full disclosure about the visit he had just received from the police concerning the dreadful news about Rainbow Choi. Of course, he would understand if Kwan wanted to call off the whole transaction. But the old tycoon wouldn't want to stop now, Leopold was sure. Kwan would struggle with the decision, but ultimately he would go through with it. Probably see it as a way of assuaging his guilt over Rainbow Choi. Make sure her death hadn't been for nothing.

Well, Cyrus, it certainly won't have been for nothing.

Once again, Leopold felt in control, like a chess-master already several moves ahead.

Today he was ready to make his own piece of history.

CHAPTER THIRTY-SEVEN

A night was a long time in business. Markets were active twenty-four hours, momentum was continuous, the global money-machine never stopped.

Sometimes, though, none of it mattered.

Rainbow Choi hadn't called Cyrus back. When he woke to find there had been no further contact from her through the night, he knew something was wrong. He felt dreadful. Age was supposed to bring with it great wisdom, but all it had seemed to deliver Cyrus that morning was weary bones and a horrible sense of foreboding.

Half way through his *Wall Street Journal* at breakfast, his mobile rang. Still it wasn't Rainbow. It was Leopold Chan with the news that she was dead. Gone. Just like that, a puff of smoke through a key-hole.

Shock took hold of Cyrus, as Chan explained what he had learned from the police about this being the cruel result of some crazy lawyer's personal vendetta. "I'm so sorry, Cyrus. I can't help feeling responsible. If I wasn't selling AsiaRisk to you, none of this would have happened. Ms Choi would still be alive. I don't know what to say. I know your board is due to meet this morning. I want you to know that I completely understand if you want to call the whole thing off in light of this terrible tragedy."

Cyrus heard the words without taking them in. He mustered the effort to thank Leopold. One way or the other he promised to get back to him during the course of the morning. His inclination was to conference call Tyson Mok and Simon Ng, get them up to speed, take their soundings. Neither of them had known Rainbow that well so they could give an objective assessment. But that was the coward's way out. Objectivity had its place, but it wasn't a holy grail.

Cyrus thought back to the one thing which had been stopping him from committing to this transaction, the residual doubt that AsiaRisk appeared too perfect, that it needed some bumps in the road to make it appear genuine. Careful what you wish for, wasn't that how the saying went? Cyrus wasn't normally given to emotion, yet he felt the loss of Rainbow Choi as holding a mirror up to his own mortality, bringing with it the echo of guilt. He, along with his aged bones, was still alive. Rainbow Choi was gone before her time. That was not how it was supposed to be. And all because of some insane lawyer who was driven by a crazed desire to harm Leopold Chan. Yes, Cyrus had found his bump in the road.

He thought of his own son then, working his way through the ranks of the medical profession. He thought about his brother too, snatched away at too young an age. Inevitably his mind then turned to Rupert, in many ways so like his father, eager to the point of recklessness, constantly overreaching. How Cyrus had hoped the AsiaRisk deal would mend their strained relationship.

Finally, he thought of Rainbow Choi. The tenacity with which she had gone about any task he had set her was something to behold, like a terrier sinking teeth into flesh and not letting go until she came away with an answer. A rare quality; yet probably the very trait which had caused her downfall. If she hadn't been so damned determined, she would never have stumbled across the twisted individual who had ended her life.

If he walked away from this deal now, Rainbow's death would have achieved the very end which that lunatic wanted, Cyrus realized.

There was no way Cyrus was going to let that happen.

The drive from Fanling to Central was usually a pleasant experience, one that Cyrus passed chatting idly with his chauffer or quietly examining paperwork. But today, the car journeyed south in heavy silence. Cyrus had made his fair share of enemies down the years, such was the price of success. Hard decisions had to be taken which impacted livelihoods often for the worse. Behind every staff cut, lay a family put under pressure. But sometimes hard decisions had to be made to save more jobs being lost. Often life was like that, shaded grey, not black and white, the lesser of two evils often prevailing. Yes, there were those in the world who probably cursed his every waking moment, Cyrus realized. But no one had gone so far as to take a life just to harm him. Leopold Chan had that unenviable edge over him now.

Cyrus didn't like Leopold Chan much. He possessed the kind of arrogance which Cyrus had seen in so many successful businessmen down the years, perhaps even himself on occasion. But, personality aside, there was no denying the fact that Cyrus had had his instinctive suspicions about this deal.

Well, not any more.

The traffic in Central was not yet at standstill point. Before eight in the morning it was possible to zip along the streets, stopping only for the traffic-lights. Cyrus glanced at his watch. Still an hour to go until the board meeting convened. As the car slowed on its approach to Kwan Tower, he knew what his decision was going to be.

This deal would go through. By the end of the day AsiaRisk would be part of Kwan Holdings. A testament to Rainbow Choi, the lady who had made it happen.

He was too wrapped up in that thought to notice the young man in the baseball-cap approaching the car as it glided to a halt.

The hotel was a dive. Grubby rooms by the hour and damp mattresses. But they took cash and asked no questions, so Scott wasn't complaining. Still, come morning, he was glad to get out.

By seven am he was in Chater Gardens, a concrete oasis in the heart of Central Distrct, hunkering in the shade of a concrete overhang at the Garden's southern edge, hidden by a line of bushes that looked out onto Queen's Road. North of him, intermittent palm trees stretched out from straight-edged grass patches. Water from a fountain misted the morning humidity and beyond, the MTR exit showed slim signs of life.

Poking up above the treetops to Scott's east he could just make out out the dome of the old Legislative Council building, its sandstone-archwayed porticos a welcome hangover from a past colonial century. Scott's main focus, however, was directed south through the bushes, to the other side of Queen's Road, where the old Bank of China building vyed for attention with the triangular silver-and-black verticals of its modernist counterpart. Inbetween the two bank buildings, completing the miracle of the Hong Kong sky-line, lay the magnificent Kwan Tower.

Another time, that hotch-potch of architectural extremes would have taken Scott's breath away. But not today. Today, fear was Scott's constant companion. Every person glancing down from the trams which rattled past him on Queen's Road, every car that stopped at the lights, every flickering shadow put him on edge. The police were out there, O'Rourke was too, he was sure of it. And all he had to shield himself was a baseball-cap and a pair of sunglasses he'd picked up from a Wanchai market-stall opening up for the day.

He had a plan too. Well, sort of. Hang around, wait for Cyrus Kwan to turn into the underground car entrance of Kwan Tower, then sprint across the road and somehow gain his attention. *What could possibly go wrong?* The thought made Scott want to laugh. – Or was it cry? – He wasn't really sure which, he was so far outside his comfort zone now.

The slow drip from the MTR exit was showing signs of becoming a stream. In front of him, trams going east and west crossed each other, blocking his view, the ka-klump across the rails slowing as they came together. Then they parted like curtains.

And that's when Scott saw it. The black Mercedes waiting at the lights and indicating left into the Kwan Tower entrance, one figure in the driver's seat, one in the back, his head bowed, but the white flock of hair unmistakable. Cyrus Kwan was about to enter his building.

Scott felt the adrenalin surge and went with it. On his feet, he jumped the wall and padded up to the road's edge. The green man had turned red, but he made it to the island in the middle of the four lanes, pausing for a gap in the traffic, watching the Mercedes as it sleeked down into the entrance. Hurrying across the road, Scott's gaze followed the Mercedes into darkness. Down a short ramp he saw a turning circle for vehicles. He spotted three cars, engines growling in the enclosed echo. Doormen in white gloves and peaked hats were guiding the vehicles to drop-off points. Kwan's Mercedes was third in line.

Scott waited. When Kwan stepped out of the car, that was when he'd make his move.

One of the doormen was looking in his direction. Scott turned away, trying to look natural and probably failing miserably. But his eyes were drawn straight to the massive figure not fifty yards up the pavement, moving towards him and closing fast.

Terrence O'Rourke was coming for him.

O'Rourke's dead unrepentant eyes bore into Scott with one aim in mind.

Scott glanced back down the ramp at Kwan's car. The back door was opening, a foot stepped out, a head of white hair appeared. Swivelling back, Scott looked at O'Rourke closing the distance between them at an unrelenting pace.

No time, damn it! No time!

Only one thought, now....

Run!

Well, would you look at that, the lad was right there, just like Leopold Chan had said he'd be, poking around outside Kwan Tower. Once again, O'Rourke found himself impressed at his boss's ability to call it right. But then that was what made them such a winning combination. Chan the strategist, O'Rourke the executioner. The perfect mix.

The police were there too. O'Rourke hadn't seen them, but Chan had somehow made sure of it. And if they picked Lee up, then O'Rourke wasn't to worry. But if O'Rourke got to Lee first, then he was to finish the job. Those were his orders.

O'Rourke was going to make damn sure he got the gobshite lawyer this time. No mistakes. Since the early hours he'd been waiting, watching, spotting Scott Lee sitting there in Chater Gardens bold as bloody brass, the hat and sun-glasses a pathetic disguise, but what could you expect from an amateur.

An amateur who already got the drop on you once before!

O'Rourke bit down the piercing shard of ire. It was time to put matters right. But where Lee was sitting, there was no way of getting the jump on him. Too many places for him to run. So O'Rourke bided his time, waited until Lee made his own move, then he'd take care of business.

He didn't have long to wait, it turned out. As soon as Lee was on his feet, O'Rourke picked up his trail. Crossing the road, O'Rourke reached into his pocket for the blade, the calmness of the kill descending as his fingers touched steel. The anticipation, the tautness of every sense. Tingling fingers snaked down his spine. This wasn't his training kicking in, this was his nature, the way he'd been hardwired. A predator finally closing in on his prey; the natural order about to be restored. A simple 'swipe and go' was all it would take, a casual collision with a fellow pedestrian. No one would notice him plunging the knife into Lee's chest, the beautiful rasp of cauterizing flesh, the hiss of a lung puncturing. O'Rourke would be long gone by the time the first passer-by screamed.

Up ahead, Lee slowed to a halt at the mouth of the car-park entrance.

Perfect. This was going to be easy. *Enjoy the moment, but finish him quick....*

Scott Lee turned, saw him. Froze.

Now!

O'Rourke closed in, the hunter bearing down on the hunted, Lee a fragile deer in headlights. But fear was also the great motivator.And now Scott Lee was running. Running for his pathetic little life.

Garden Road skirted round the edge of Kwan Tower and rose vertically up to Mid-Levels.

Scott took the hill at a sprint, his lungs at their limit, the activity absorbing him into the moment. Through the adrenalin dump, he focussed on keeping his feet soft and his turnover fast.

Landmarks leapt out like snapshots to trace his ascent; an escalator on the left heading to an overhead walkway; a sign for Battery Path; a waft of cigarette smoke from a group smoking by a bus-stop. Passing St John's Cathedral on his right, he recalled that the ecclesiastical landmark was the only freehold land left in Hong Kong, he'd learned that in his qualification exam, his mind inexplicably dredging up the useless fact now his lungs were on fire and his life on the line. He hit the junction with Lower Albert Road, just as the lights changed. Cars moved off the white line, but Scott didn't stop. Brakes screeched, horns screamed as he threw himself into their path.

As the pavement jolted left, he risked a glance back down the slope and saw the group of smokers at the bus stop splinter apart as O'Rourke shouldered through them, juddering relentlessly on like an automotan, no sign of fatigue in his awkward gait.

Scott pushed on, his calves and thighs burning, his lungs well beyond their limit.

A blue sign-post for the Hong Kong Zoological and Botanical Gardens descended into his line of vision like a film credit, causing another memory to blast like a wave against the shoreline. He'd been there once with Kimmie, a myriad of confusing winding concrete paths amidst vegetation and exotic animals. And it had at least ten exits over which they'd argued.

Through growing fatigue, the memory sparked something of a plan and galvanized Scott to keep going. He pushed on. Past the large, silver lettering for the American Consulate, the pavement disappearing into a staircase. Scrambling up the steps two at a time, Scott bounded across the slip-road at the top. Another staircase hit him, this one switching back on itself and affording a second uninterrupted view back down the road.

O'Rourke. Still there. Still running hard. The gap closing.

At the top of the stairs, the entrance to the Botanical Gardens appeared, an archway memorializing the war dead, either side of it one stone lion throwing each other a grin. Scott sprinted on through. Once inside the park, trees quickly closed out the light overhead. Paths sprouted in different directions like veins on an arm. Scott headed left and was hit by the mist of a power-fountain. A sea of old men and woman were smoothing their limbs through tai-chi routines. Scott stopped, hands on knees, sucking in whatever oxygen the humidity could spare. *Okay, now what?*

A hiding-place, that's what he needed. In this sanctuary the possibilities were endless. He headed right, into the Garden's massive exotic aviary. Walls of black and green netting towered either side of the path, Scott's eyes catching flashes of flamingo-pink and parrot-green. Cawing and crowing filled the air, an unusual soundtrack for a city's heart.

At the end of the netting, sectioned off by waist-high green fencing and flower beds, was a stretch of grass that was off-limits. Scott stopped by it. Checked left and right, vaulted in, then flopped prostrate onto the grass, rolling in towards one of the flower-beds till a spider-plant's spines was tickling his skin.

As he lay there, he focused on getting his breath back. Sweat cascaded down his face, salt stinging his eyes. His heart pounded into the ground beneath, the cool moisture of the grass offering an ounce of respite. He listened for footsteps. But all he got was strange bird-calls cutting across the fountain's distant hiss.

One hundred and eighty-seconds. He counted it out in full then got to his feet. Staying in a low crouch, he padded over to a clutch of bamboo for cover.

He looked up and down the path. Nothing

The park was split into two parts, he remembered; the aviary section, which he was in; and up the hill was the zoo, where old orang-utangs looked miserable and a grotesquely overweight soft-bellied leopard lounged without room to run. He and Kimmie had spent an afternoon walking around there. After debating the issue till it was dead, they'd chosen an exit which brought them out into the heart of Mid-Levels.

Now if he could only find his way up there unnoticed, Scott hoped he could ....

"Don't you bloody move!" O'Rourke's voice cut in from over his shoulder.

All hope ended right there.

CHAPTER THIRTY-EIGHT

Five officers. How the hell was he supposed to catch a fugitive in Central with just five officers?

Not for the first time in his less-than-illustrious career, Detective-Inspector Kam felt short-changed by his superiors. "Sir, the man we want for murder may be in the vicinity of Kwan Tower within the next hour. This could be our only chance!"

"Be that as it may, five officers are all I can spare," the superintendent told him. "Now take it or leave it."

Reluctantly – after negotiating a squad-car to be thrown into the bargain – Kam took it.

The five officers, each of them about to head off from the night-shift, were none too pleased at being held back, but the promise of overtime put them in a better mood. In a ten-minute briefing, Kam showed them a map of Kwan Tower and the surrounding streets, pointing out the three pedestrian entrances and the sheltered vehicle-drop-off zone. He wanted one officer inside each entrance. The fifth would drive Kam in the squad-car, circling Kwan Tower.

"This is the man we're looking for," Kam handed round a copy of Scott Lee's identification card. "He's a western male, in his early thirties, slim build. He's been out all night so unlikely to be looking his best. His name is Scott Lee and, according to the doorman in his building, he understands Cantonese."

"Handsome," said one of the officers, the only female.

"Well if we find him, I'll let you in on the interrogation," Kam said.

"Your husband won't be too happy about that. Thought you only used the cuffs on him!"

Hearty chuckles all round. Nothing wrong with banter between colleagues, but Kam needed to get on, so dismissed them, and by seven-thirty they were all in position.

From the squad-car, Kam kept a watchful gaze as they circled Kwan Tower. After completing each circuit, he radioed the other officers to check status. Following their tenth go-round, and with not even the hint of a sighting, Kam began to lose heart. Central District was waking up. Soon, he realized, there would be no chance of spotting Lee in the crowds of commuters on their way to work, not with such a small team. He shook his head. This situation was a nightmare in the making. Yesterday, Scott Lee had voluntarily walked into Wanchai police station and been told to get lost. Less than twenty-four hours on, Lee was on the run and wanted for murder. The press would have a field day if the story ever got out; and Kam could see questions being asked at the highest levels, questions which would filter down to the officer unlucky enough to have caught the case. Wrong place, wrong time. The story of his career.

The toothpick in Kam's mouth poked hard into the inside of his cheek as the officer driving pumped the brake with too much enthusiasm.

"Hey watch it!" Kam said.

"Sorry sir."

The car had just entered its eleventh circuit.

That's when Kam saw him.

A man, base-ball cap flying off his head, sprinting past them up the hill and disappearing out of the back windscreen as they drove down Garden Road.

"There! It's him!" Kam shouted, swivelling to follow the runner's trajectory.

"Sir, someone's chasing him."

Kam flipped back round, just as the second man fizzed by his side window. He was tall and western and all awkward power. That was all Kam could make out.

"Pull over!" Kam shouted. A cacophony of impatient car-horns burst out as they screeched to a halt on double-yellows. "Call for back-up. I'll follow on foot!"

"But sir..."

"Just do it!"

Clambering over the metal barrier, Kam felt a trouser leg tear. His knees jarred with pain as he landed awkwardly on the pavement in front of St John's Cathedral. He recovered and started running up the hill, grimacing in the sticky air. Ahead, he glimpsed Lee disappearing up a staircase. Lee's massive pursuer was labouring two hundred metres back, passing the Helena May Institute.

"Move!" Kam wheezed to a group of smokers by a bus-stop, his mind desperately trying to work out the pursuer's connection to all this.

Eventually Kam made it up the switch-back stairs and across the slip-road to the entrance to the Botanical Gardens. He carried on up the steps and straight through, but stopped abruptly as the pathway broke off into four separate arteries. There was no sign of either man.

Damn, now what!

Kam's hands dropped to his knees, his cigarette-laden lungs heaving for mercy. The shrill cawing of birdsong pierced the air. He looked up. Trees met overhead, the psychedelic trickle of light and dark playing in his eyes, disorientating him, making him want to sink down and give up.

A sign pointed him straight ahead to the aviary. When his wheezing had eased to panting, Kam followed the path. If his driver had done his job, back-up wouldn't be far away. They could close the exits then. Meantime, his only option was to keep looking.

As he hit the aviary's edge, there was a meltdown of cawing and chirping. Black netting sectioned off the massive exhibits either side of the path. Inside the exhibit to his left violent-pink flamingoes with S-shaped necks preened and posed around a man-made lake. On his right, in a tree above a waterfall, birds with glow-in-the-dark red feathers nested. The cooling mist from the waterfall offered Kam some temporary relief from the suffocating humidity.

Something in the midst of the birdcalls made him stop dead.

Voices. Male. Indistinct. Kam traced their direction to where the netting ended and a waist-high fence began. Keeping his footfalls light, he crept up to the edge and risked a look.

There they were. Two figures facing off against each other across the short expanse of fenced-off grassland. Scott Lee with his back to a bamboo clutch, cornered by his giant pursuer. Sun glinted off a knife in the pursuer's meat-cleaver hand.

Oh my God!

Kam went for the holster on his hip. It had been years since he'd drawn his weapon in anger and his fingers fumbled desperately with the unfamiliar clip.

The big man cocked the knife and started to advance on Lee. Lee screamed something indistinct and for a moment they seemed to pause and stare at each other like two boxers waiting for the bell.

Then all hell broke loose.

"Don't you bloody move!"

The voice was gravelly and laced with menace.

Terrence O'Rourke was standing there. Back to finish the job.

Scott's eyes gravitated immediately to the blade. A dull buzzing filled his ears. He didn't want to look, but a horror-movie-like fascination drew him back to the sheen of the steel, its edge honed and ready to slice.

O'Rourke started towards him.

The buzzing disappeared as Scott suddenly became conscious of everything around him, his dripping sweat, the dryness of his lips, the taste of salt on his tongue, the high-pitched calls of the macaws in the aviary, the look in O'Rourke's eyes, somehow dead and excited at the same time.

"Don't do this!" Scott said, taking a step back. It was a stupid statement, he knew, one born of pure desperation. But he was working on instinct, and somehow, trying to draw the brute into conversation seemed his only hope. O'Rourke advanced across the grass, footsteps sinking into the turf, slowly and deliberately as if drawing out his pleasure and heightening Scott's terror. Scott stepped back again but this time he felt the bamboo clutch press against his back. He glanced left and right. The green fencing on either side seemed to grow tower-high.

There was nowhere left to run.

Moulten fire suddenly lit up Scott's veins, his muscles stiffening like iron bars. He pushed himself off the bamboo, leant forward onto his toes. Rainbow being shot, Kimmie choked by charcoal fumes, the look on Sally Yang's face as she had told him about it. All three, people whose lives had been destroyed by the brute with the knife standing in front of him. Each image steeled Scott's psyche for what he was about to do.

Time slowed down to an eerie calmness.

O'Rourke stopped as if he had sensed the change in Scott and welcomed it, that sick little smile playing on his face.

The next few seconds seemed like minutes. Scott could smell the scent of orchids, taste the tang of sweat, feel his nostrils flare and his veins explode. This was it, this was what it came down to. *Go!* his mind screamed. He churned his legs, tucked his head down and led with his shoulder. Not as quick off the mark as he would have liked, but charging all the same, conscious of nothing and everything, a strange detachment descending, as if he existed outside time, outside space, outside of life itself. O'Rourke was a blur in front of him now, but the blade sparkled in ghastly technicolour.

And then it happened.

A speck of movement gnawed at the corner of Scott's vision. It quickly transformed into a tangible moving force. A person, running hard down the concrete path, vaulting the green fence, hitting the grass at speed, eyes fixed only on O'Rourke.

For Scott, the detachment ended there and he was suddenly back in himself, horrified at what he was doing. Instinct made him slow and slant his run.

The third figure who had just vaulted the fence was now bolting towards them at a terrifying rate.

Seeing Scott veer made O'Rourke sense something amiss, his face turning to where Scott was looking, but too late to evade the interventionist who was airborne now, flinging himself with complete abandon, smashing into O'Rourke's midriff. O'Rourke went down hard, the impact forcing an explosion of wind through clenched teeth. Skidding across the grass, he and his assailant were a mass of muscular out-of-control limbs.

Scott swerved to avoid them, then looked back. O'Rourke was down, but certainly not out. The assailant glanced up from the ground. Scott noticed his Chinese features, his stubbled chin, his hair that of a teenager in rebellion.

Scott nodded a 'thanks' to the stranger, whoever the hell he was, then turned and sprinted for the fence.

One leap and he was up, over, and gone.

Physically, he was shaken by the tackle.

But for Terrence O'Rourke the biggest wound was to his pride. Rage broke through the surface, as he rolled away from the assault. The knife was still in his hand, still a part of him, still begging to be used on whoever the bastard was that had denied him his pleasure.

"I'm going to mess you up, fella!" O'Rourke sneered, rounding on the stranger, not caring if this Chinese thug understood English.

The man was on his feet too, standing in a posture that suggested he was trained to fight. O'Rourke, desperate to work out his adrenalin, was thankful for the challenge.

Then a voice called out: "Get your hands up! Police!"

O'Rourke looked over and saw the cop, plainclothes, gun leveled in one hand, badge visible in the other.

"Drop the knife!"

O'Rourke swallowed his rage, but made his calculations quickly. There were two of them the cop needed to arrest and that gave O'Rourke his chance. Hand still holding the blade, he took a step back.

"Don't move!" the cop screamed.

But O'Rourke ignored him, stepping back again.

It did the trick, forcing the cop into the fatal mistake which O'Rourke was banking on. Putting his badge away the cop looked for a way over the fence. And whilst his eyes were diverted, O'Rourke made his move. It was nothing spectacular, nothing fancy. Just a fast spin and breaking into a run, then five steps of pure power diagonally across the grass and behind the bamboo clutch using it as cover ....

"Halt!"

But O'Rourke was already in mid-hurdle across the fence. He brought his lead leg down fast onto the tarmac path, then snaked round the next bend and out of sight, keeping going, not looking back, the distant sound of sirens proving enough of an incentive for that.

No way he was going to be taken down in this menagerie. He was going to live to fight another day.

Scott Lee could bloody bet on it!

CHAPTER THIRTY-NINE

"Wei, wake up you! Get out of the way! Get out the way!"

The voice was loud and coarse and sounded like it was well used to being that way. Scott bolted out of his stupour and into the surroundings of the nullah. Rotting bags of rubbish festered around him, their putrid stink assaulting him like an army on a blitzkrieg. That he had fallen asleep here at all said a lot about how far his fortunes had descended.

The grating voice belonged to the old crone looking down on him, her face chiseled deep with a seventy-year-old's wrinkles, but her body suggesting life had aged her well beyond her years. Her wiry arms flexed on the handle of a metal trolley, laden with damp cardboard, paper and scrap metal. "This is all mine!" she croaked in Cantonese, waving a veiny hand at the rubbish pile. "Hands off!"

Feeling the edge of the crone's trolley against his shoes, Scott hugged his legs to his chest. The crone picked up whatever sodden newspaper and cardboard she could find and went on her way.

Scott's head fell back against the wall. Above him, the top edges of the buildings framed a brilliant hot blue sky, one of those rare days in Hong Kong when the pollution had taken a break from irritating the city's occupants. And here he was in this stinking nullah, his life an impossible mess. Part of him began to find amusement in the symbolism. Former partner material, now part of life's rubbish heap. Quite literally.

Ten hours had passed since he had seen Rainbow shot at point-blank range by that Irish thug. Two hours since his own desperate escape from the same man in the Botanical Gardens.

Somehow, Scott had found an exit out a side gate, taken a moment to get his breath, then jumped the first mini-bus to wherever it would take him, through the tunnel under the harbour, it turned out. Getting out somewhere east of Nathan road, he'd walked and walked until he was done, until he needed to find a place to rest, to recoup. To forget.

So now here he was.

The tranquility of the nullah made it seem like days ago. Time meant nothing any more. So far his mind had blocked and parried it all, but he was coming off the adrenalin dump now and his body's defence mechanism was easing down its protective shield.

It hit Scott fast and hard then: that image of Rainbow dead in the car and the realization of how close he himself had come to death. – Twice. – It swept his mind like an overpowering tidal-wave pulling him under. Leaning over, he vomited hard on the concrete. Guttural, uncontrollable sobs erupted from deep within his core, catching in his throat. He let the wave of emotion drain him until there was nothing left.

Shutting his eyes, Scott let his mind wander in whatever direction it wanted to go. It hit on a memory, one from his London days as a trainee when he had sat and watched the chief executive of an IT company collapse at the prospect of a client suing him for fraud, confessing that he didn't have the stomach for a legal fight. The partner Scott worked for at the time was called Mark Whiting, a man with the stalwart temperament of a seen-it-all, done-it-all litigator. Whiting had told the chief executive not to worry, that the worst thing he could do was think of the magnitude of what faced him. Think only of the immediate steps, Whiting said, bite-size targets, for the next minute, the next hour, the afternoon, the next day. Meet those targets and when you're done, keep on going. 'Manageable chunks of forward motion', Whiting had called it.

Right there and then, Scott forced himself to embrace that advice. Manageable chunks of forward motion. He opened his eyes, blew through his mouth.

New clothes; the first manageable chunk. His shirt was streaked in dirt, buttons missing, trousers ripped at the knees, shoes smattered in his own puke, everything sodden with perspiration. His hand shot to his pocket. A relieved sigh, as he felt the familiar shape of his wallet with the money Yip had given him. Somehow it had survived all the mayhem, his keys too for all the good they did him.

Another memory snagged then, of all the evenings he'd been too drunk to remember getting home. Somehow, no matter how obliterated he'd been, he'd always made it back in one piece with wallet and keys intact. That drinker's primal survival instinct. Today, it had served him well. *Not as well as finding his passport and a ticket out would do....*

Sardonic, graveyard humour had always been Scott's last resort when he was in a tight spot. And they didn't come much tighter than this. But it quickly hit him that even his damn passport would be useless to him now. As soon as it got scanned, his name would start flashing red on a screen somewhere and they'd know where to find him....

Easy now, Scott told himself circling back to Whiting's principle. *Manageable chunks of forward motion.* He pushed himself to his feet. As he stepped out of the nullah, the sun lazered his eyes. Homantin Street was in a quiet exclusive suburb of Mongkok where trees stretched half way across the road and plush residences with large semi-circular balconies retreated behind iron-gated entrances. It was the last place anyone would think of looking for him, even though it was only pure panic which had led Scott here.

Rumblings of traffic and life wafted over from a few blocks away. Scott retraced his steps in their general direction. Crossing a road. Passing under a flyover. Past a Buddhist Temple he caught a sweet waft of joss-sticks. Soon he was back in the thick of it: Mongkok. Crowds came at him like an asteroid storm. Multi-coloured overhangs jutted out over the top of the pavement advertising foot massages, cameras, restaurants of every kind. Snippets of irritable Cantonese fired in from all angles. And best of all no one gave a damn about his ramshackle appearance.

When Scott hit the chaos named Argyll Street he found his bearings and went with the momentum of the crowds till he reached the turn-off for the Ladies' Market. Tarpaulin-covered stalls towered on either side of the tight thoroughfare, selling clothes of all kinds. Walls were covered with T-shirts declaring their love for Hong Kong or displaying Bruce Lee in various war-like poses. Base-ball caps and Maoist hats hung on tree stands. One stall displayed only knickers and bras on unerotic polestyrene half-torsos.

Scott settled on a shirt, something half-blue, half-white and totally sleeveless up to the tops of the shoulders. He managed to bargain with the stall owner to throw in a black baseball cap for free. A couple of stalls down, he picked up a grey pair of combat trousers with pockets on each thigh. In a darkened shop around the back, he purchased some cheap trainers.

His next stop was a Mannings chemist for some deodorant. Then he ducked into a Macdonalds to wash and change and when he was done, he hardly recognized himself. The clothes weren't his usual style. They belonged to a typical Hong Kong teenager, the attempt at rebellion so ubiquitous it produced a kind of conformity parents were secretly pleased about. The cuts on his face added to the image of youthful exuberance. With the cap on, he looked like an over-aged brat, who had tumbled off his skateboard attempting a docile trick that any ten-year-old US kid would have nailed with his eyes shut.

On Dundas Street, Scott found a local café where the waitress made room for him at a round formica table by shouting for people to shift round and squeezing in another wooden stool. Scott ordered a baked pork-chop with rice and iced lemon tea and virtually inhaled them when they came. The woman at the till didn't give him a second glance when he paid.

That was it. Manageable chunk one complete. Scott tossed a silent thanks to Mark Whiting. Discarding his old clothes in the nearest bin, he walked some more and tried to rationalize his options.

Jumping on a plane was out of the question, he had already figured that out. Instead he began toying with the idea of a boat. He could find a captain looking for cheap labour and prepared not to ask too many questions, or who would be prepared to turn a blind eye for cash in return for a passage out. Scott liked the idea. In the space of a few days his life had been destroyed and, sure, maybe it was his mind moving back to block-and-parry mode, but right then the idea of a few anonymous months at sea felt liberating. It needed some research and planning too. But right then the thought of a new life away from it all offered a speck of light in the darkness.

Leopold Chan was in his garden on the Peak. For the last time. On this, his last day alive.

Such a luxury to own a piece of land like this in Hong Kong, where he could just wile away the hours in greenery and peace. He was going to miss it for sure. Casting round a steady glance he drank in the personal touches which had proved an outlet for his creative mind down the years. The enchanting rockery of quartzes and jades, each piece carefully hand-picked and positioned to his own specification. The immaculate lawn, like green velvet. The kaleidoscope of flowers, selected by Alfonso's artistic eye, produced a spontaneous sense of rapture. Leopold shut his eyes and breathed in their sweet scent. The painkillers had dulled his olfactory system, but the flowers' natural perfume still broke through, his pleasure enhanced by the soft burbling of the fountain.

The soul lived on after death, so some people believed, and if that was true, Leopold knew that, although he was leaving it, this haven would never be lost to him....

The thought stopped hard like a hand tightening on his heart. It was nothing more than a disturbance in the air around him, but still he sensed it. His eyes flared open.

"Sorry if I scared you boss." Terrence O'Rourke was standing there.

Leopold felt an instinctive waft of disgust. Something of the night had just entered his haven. A pollutant introduced to purity. He wanted to order O'Rourke out, but control, as ever, was the touchstone by which Leopold lived his life. Calmness descended once again.

"What can I do for you, Terrence?" There was no hint of surprise that O'Rourke had managed to get into the garden without recourse to legitimate means, no concern that he had managed to elude the watchful eyes of the police-car which Detective-Inspector Kam had stationed outside.

"This morning,'" O'Rourke said. "It didn't go according to plan."

"You mean Scott Lee?"

O'Rourke nodded. "The police didn't get him either."

A beat of silence.

"I see."

"Some stranger stuck his nose in as I was about to finish things. Lee got away and the police turned up. I had to make myself scarce."

The fountain burbled its soft melody. Leopold realized he was beyond disappointment, beyond anger. Yesterday, a surprise like this would have presented a fresh challenge, which the machinations of his strategic mind would have delighted in overcoming. Today, however, it was too late.

Just before coming out to the garden, Leopold had made his final arrangements. Two hundred million dollars of Benny Wang's laundered money, which Leopold had been building up in his offshore company network, had just been collected together and paid in a single lump sum into AsiaRisk's accounts. Later that evening, Leopold was due to meet with Cyrus Kwan at Jackson's offices to sign the agreements that would formalize Kwan Holdings's purchase of AsiaRisk. Following that, the two hundred million dollars would be paid straight out by AsiaRisk to Benny Wang in settlement of the Chow Mei factory fire claim. At that moment Cyrus Kwan, the embodiment of the Hong Kong spirit – some might say of Hong Kong itself – would be tainted with the payment and the set-up would be complete.

The rest would be up to General Zhao.

It was strange. All his life, Leopold had been repulsed by the kind of leftist, neo-conservative dogma which Zhao and his comrades worshipped. But here Leopold was, at the very end of his life, using Zhao's destructive doctrine for his own objectives. Zhao, like the two Kwans and Benny Wang, were just pawns in his game. Leopold was giving Zhao the crisis he had promised, a crisis that would justify the General's immediate seizure of Kwan family assets. But unlike Zhao, Leopold knew how a society as purely capitalist as Hong Kong worked. He knew the extent of the panic that bringing a company like Kwan Holdings to the brink of destruction would cause in the markets, in the newspaper headlines, and in the streets.

Yes, today, Leopold Chan was about to make history.

In the peace of the garden, the panic he was about to unleash seemed so distant. But there was no doubt it would ensue; there was no stopping the momentum now.

Alive or dead, it was too late for Scott Lee to interfere.

Leopold looked at his watch. It had just gone midday. Six hours until he signed away his company. Six hours, only. Yes. Too late for interference.

"This is the last time we'll probably be seeing each other," O'Rourke said to him. "The cops. They'll be looking for me. Better get out while I can."

Terrence O'Rourke, ever the professional.

Leopold felt strangely moved. "Do you need anything? Money? I have cash in the house you can take."

O'Rourke raised a meaty hand. "I'm fine."

Something crossed Leopold's mind then. Six hours until the signing. A lot could happen in six hours and it always paid to have all the bases covered.

"Perhaps, there is one last favour I can ask of you, Terrence?" Leopold asked. "Or would that be too much?"

O'Rourke's face showed no emotion. "You're still the boss."

Leopold told him.

"Shouldn't be a problem," O'Rourke said.

Leopold thanked him. "Well, I guess this is it?'

O'Rourke nodded.

"Look after yourself, Terrence."

Leopold turned and breathed in the heavenly fragrance.

When he opened his eyes again, Terrence O'Rourke was gone.

CHAPTER FORTY

The sign read 'fifteen minutes max' and requested that consideration be shown to others who wanted time on the computer, but the kid with dyed blond hair and his i-pod cranked up high had been on the internet for half an hour already and didn't show any signs of moving.

If Scott hadn't been trying to keep a low profile, he would have taken delight in throwing the kid off, but as it was, all he could do was sit close by, stew in frustration and make sure he was next in line.

The café was a floor up from street level. Definitely not Scott's type of place, with its black and white nonsensical photographs and plastic purple seating. He was a decade older than most of the other clientele there. The offer of free internet access was about all the place had going for it.

A sickly sweet Mochacino sat half finished in front of Scott, its sugary first half turning his arteries to stone. At a table nearby an American-born Chinese girl with big frizzy hair and a voice built for volume was talking on the phone, her annoying conversation about as deep in content as a fast evaporating puddle.

"So you think, like, Frankie will ask you out, do you think you guys have chemistry? You should totally know by now. I was at this Radiohead concert, and this guy, he just, like, came up to me, and asked if I wanted to share his weed, and I was like 'Oh my God!'" On and on it went, like a slow-drip water torture. "Okay, mom, I'll be, like, home in an hour. Wanna check my emails, but some bozo's totally hogging the computer."

Her mother. Scott made a face. The next generation was out of hope.

When Frizzie started calling someone else, Scott finally decided enough was enough. He got up and tapped the blond kid on the shoulder. Blondie looked up from the computer, but kept his headphones on. His glare aimed for tough but wouldn't have made an ice-cream melt. Scott pointed to the fifteen minute sign and signaled for the kid to move it. The kid clicked his teeth, packed up his ruck-sack, hitched his trousers down his backside and muttered something derogatory as he left.

"Whatever!" Scott said, adopting the rap *du jour*.

"Oh-my-God, some guy's just totally queue-jumped me!" Frizzie bellowed from over Scott's shoulder, but she quickly flipped on to another subject to the poor unfortunate on the other end of the line.

Scott clicked on the internet icon, pulled up the Google home page and searched for information on boat passages out of Hong Kong. Ten minutes on, the best he'd come up with was an advert for crew members on a cruise liner, but they wanted qualifications which Scott had never heard of. There was nothing on stowaways or on how to cadge a casual lift on a fishing trawler, not that he expected there to be, but some encouragement would have been helpful. Beyond that, as with everything else in Hong Kong, the only information on boats fell under the broad heading of 'luxury': gin-palace yachts, berth charges in the Aberdeen Marina, a CNN piece on a family who actually lived on a boat moored at the Royal Yacht Club.

Soon his fifteen minutes was almost up and he sensed Frizzie's dagger-eyes boring into him. He decided to spend the rest of his time-limit on a side-trip back to normality, logging onto his yahoo email account. Most of it was just unopened spam from an investment website he'd signed up with, replete with testimonies of how he could make millions if he was willing to pay for some once-in-a-lifetime opportunity.

One email, however, jumped out and slapped him hard across the cheek.

John, his brother.

A reply to the veiled inquiry Scott had sent about the medicines he'd seen Leopold Chan take. Scott clicked it open and was surprised by its length:

Bro, Great to hear from you. Glad all is well in Hong Kong. I guess you've decided to stay out there permanently? Don't blame you, mate. Not much excitement back here in Blighty.

Beck was asking after you the other day. He's considering visiting you on his year off before he starts at Oxford. He's going to be eighteen in a few weeks time! Doesn't seem like five minutes since I was changing his nappy!

Tom was captain of Colt's Cricket last year and has just been selected to represent the county. Sandy is on at me to take him shopping for a new bat. Says I know more about that sort of thing than she does.

Anyway, we all miss you and send our love. I know you're busy but we really should make the effort to have Christmas together one year. I'm sure Dad would love it. Any plans in December? You're welcome to stay and it would be great to see you. If you've got a lady in your life, bring her along too. The more the merrier.

Scott felt the words ball into a fist and slam into the pit of his stomach. He wanted to cry, to let it out, to break down just so he could re-make himself from scratch. His family. Since Mum had died he'd seen less and less of them, always thinking there would be time later when he was more settled, when work calmed down. *Stupid, stupid, stupid!* The odds were that he would never see them again now. That was going to be hard to accept. But accept it, he had to. Forward motion was his only hope. He went back to the email.

Well that's all the personal stuff. Now for this business about your colleague and his meds. Obviously, I can't give any sort of proper diagnosis without seeing the guy. But I can give you my "best-guess".

You said he was taking Percocet. That's a pain-killer, a strong one. It's a morphine-based non-steroidal anti-inflammatory. It's relatively high up on the "pain ladder". I prescribe it when the over-the-counter options aren't sufficient.

Prednisone helps with breathing. It's usually given to people with respiratory issues.

If your friend is taking a combination of the two, my guess is that it could be quite a serious respiratory problem. It could be very severe asthma (although if you didn't see an inhaler, I would doubt it). Or it could be cancer. If it was cancer, you would expect your friend to be receiving chemo or radiation therapy as well, unless it had progressed to stage

IV, where the only thing left is to prescribe drugs to control pain and assist breathing. Of course, I'm not saying it is cancer. I'm just giving you an idea of the range we're talking about.

Do you know how many pills he took? As a rule of thumb, the higher the dosage, the more serious it is likely to be.

I would have a frank talk with him if I were you get it out in the open. If there is something wrong, just give him what support you can.

Anyway, let me know if there's any other questions. And think about what I said about Christmas. It would be great to see you. Take care. John

"Hey! Do you know you've been on there, like, forever?" Frizzie was on the war-path now. Scott felt a flush of heat and it was all he could do to stop himself turning round and slapping her across her obnoxious mouth. But he got it under control and politely apologized. Then he let her have her damn computer.

Half an hour passed.

Scott was wandering the streets, oblivious to the Mongkok crowds, lost in a deep blue ocean of fluid thought, the Whiting principle having served its purpose. Nothing about his predicament had changed, but his mind had recovered its edge now and was immersed back in the subject which had been his recent obsession.

AsiaRisk.

Deep down, Scott knew he couldn't just walk away. It simply wasn't within his make-up. Not after what had happened to Kimmie, what he had seen happen to Rainbow Choi and what he himself had been through.

Reading that email from his brother had been the trigger. It had reminded Scott of who he really was. A lawyer and a damn good one at that, who searched out the truth and didn't let go until he found it. And his brother had just served up a new piece of information which cast a new light on this whole thing.

Leopold Chan was ill. Seriously ill

Scott thought back to the coughing fit he had witnessed that day, Chan's face a mask of pain as he spluttered out of control;

then O'Rourke handing Chan water and pills in a practised routine.

Cancer. Terminal. John had mentioned it as a possibility and somehow it all fitted, whilst at the same time being complete nonsense.

Scott suddenly stopped walking. Here on the hot Mongkok back-streets wasn't the place to work it out. He needed his tools of the trade: a pen, some paper, a desk, some quiet. Pulling his cap down over his eyes, he headed for the MTR station and twenty minutes later he was back in Causeway Bay, hurrying up the stairs towards the Hong Kong Central library.

The library building was of suitable grandeur, standing there against the multifaceted skyline. Dwarfed by surrounding tower-blocks, its sparkling beige and glass façade housed an Athenian-colonnaded Parthenon at its apex, capturing perfectly the image of modernity, experience and knowledge to which its architect had aspired. None of that, however, mattered to Scott as he sped through the revolving doors and into its cool air-conditioned interior.

Picking up some scrap paper and a wayward biro from an empty counter, he hurried to the escalator and on up to the higher levels which housed the never-ending rows of books. On the first floor, a familiar smell hit him, the subtle mustiness of ageing paper, the true herbs and spices of knowledge. He found an empty booth on the fourth floor and sat down. Shutting his eyes, he took deep breaths, calming his mind, getting his head to where it needed to be.

Then he began, sketching notes on everything he knew about AsiaRisk, pouring it out, fact after fact, emptying himself, his hand writing furiously, his thoughts like liquid, smooth and fast. Twenty minutes later he stopped, looked up, eased his neck one way then the other. Then he took up the biro again and went through the notes, crossing off items which were clearly irrelevant, connecting others with arrows and marking them with asterisks, narrowing them down into a series of key points. When he was done, he looked over what he had written and tried to boil it down further into its pure core.

What he came up with were three building-blocks, on the face of it seemingly irreconcilable, but Scott knew that, together, they held the key to it all, from Kimmie's and Rainbow's deaths and his own ruination, through to Kwan Holdings' impending buy-out of AsiaRisk. Everything was connected. The only questions were how and why.

The first building-block was the theory that he and Rainbow had hammered out with a little help from Eva Chow. Leopold Chan was trying to launder two hundred million dollars of Benny Wang's dirty money in a single transaction, disguising it as a legitimate insurance claim relating to the incineration of the Chow Mei factory. Chan had instructed Jackson's on the claim, so clearly Conrad would be documenting the settlement to give it the façade of legitimacy, like he'd done with the false claims AsiaRisk had processed down the years.

Second, there was the takeover. Rainbow Choi had been hired by Kwan Holdings to do due diligence on AsiaRisk and Leopold Chan's background. The Kwan board of directors had been due to meet that very morning for its final decision.

These first two pieces of the puzzle didn't seem to fit, not in isolation as far as Scott could tell. And the missing link was the 'why' question. Why was Leopold Chan doing it? Why was he selling AsiaRisk at precisely the same moment that he was passing a vast and very illegitimate transaction through its books, a claim that would only serve to depress the value of the company at the wrong time?

Now there was this new third piece in the ill-fitting jigsaw: the email Scott had received from his brother John. If John was right – and Scott had never known an occasion when his damn near perfect brother had ever been wrong – Leopold Chan was a very ill man.

So here they were, three very different sides to Leopold Chan: the Machiavellian money launderer; the man selling his company to the biggest business in Hong Kong, Kwan Holdings; and the man in failing health. Each aspect of Chan's character seemed irreconcilable with the others. But there had to be a connection, Scott was sure of it. And that connection held the key to the truth of what was going on here.

As his mind whirled like a typhoon, Scott folded his arms in irritation. He needed to slow things down, concentrate, wrestle out a theory which cemented it all together. Getting up from the booth, he started to walk past the lines of hardworking students, then turning down a random row of book-shelves, allowing his eyes to run across the Chinese characters on the book spines without taking them in. Back out into the middle section of the floor, he passed more students tapping on their lap-tops and old men studying the racing form. At the water-fountain, Scott took a long, cleansing drink.

By the water-fountain was a notice-board pinned with flyers about community events. Scott allowed them to distract him away from his conundrum for a moment. The special events for that month included a talk on an archeological find out at Lantau and an exhibition on calligraphy. Other posters advertised a range of extra-curricular activities – ball-room dancing, fencing, tae-kwando – each poster vibrantly coloured to hook the interest of mothers seeking to build their children's CVs with something out of the ordinary. In the centre of the notice-board was a list of the special-subject reference libraries, most of them down at the City Hall branch. Business and finance came first, as it always did in Hong Kong. Then there was a special subject for industry and environment – another of the territory's main priorities. Third on the list was the Basic Law library, set up as a joint venture between the Cultural Services Department and the Basic Law Institute; its aim, to enhance the public understanding of Hong Kong's mini-constitution.

Scott liked that idea. A whole library section dedicated to constitutional law. It had been his favourite subject, back in law school. The English with their unwritten constitution, the Americans' enshrining their right to pursue happiness, the French sticking with the more cynical right to pursue property. Back in his student days, his constitutional law tutorials had always stimulated the most interesting debate. Scott wondered if Hong Kong law students of today would ever have the chance to argue like that or whether they were destined to be driven by their parents to concentrate on money-making subjects like corporate and commercial.....

The thought stopped hard and fast, the recollection crashing through like a sudden tsunami, thundering Scott back to his first meeting with Leopold Chan, Chan collapsing in a coughing fit as Scott had pitched Charles Conrad's bad points. But there had been something else too, something which Scott had totally forgotten until now, something embedded deep within the recesses of his memory, just now triggered to the surface by the information on the notice-board.

Article 109 of the Basic Law, Leopold Chan had asked him, *What does it say?*

At the time, Scott had thought it a test of his legal skills, one he had passed, telling Chan that Article 109 required the Government to maintain Hong Kong's status as an international finance centre, that the territory's continued existence depended on it.

Hurrying back to his cubicle, Scott planted himself down and looked at his notes. Slowly the pieces of the jig-saw started moving into place.

Leopold Chan had told Rainbow Choi he was selling AsiaRisk to secure his legacy. Both Scott and Rainbow had thought it thin justification at the time, one which had all the hallmarks of misdirection on Chan's part. But what if Chan had been telling the truth? To a dying man, legacy was all-important. And here was Leopold Chan, in failing health, engineering the sale of his company, AsiaRisk, to Cyrus Kwan at precisely the same moment he was laundering two hundred million of Benny Wang's dirty money through its books.

Scott swallowed hard as the implications fell into place.

Cyrus Kwan, Asia's richest man, well-connected on the Mainland – the pinnacle of probity in Hong Kong and China – was about to be sucked into a money-laundering scandal. A scandal like that involving a company like Kwan Holdings, would rock Hong Kong's reputation as an international finance centre to its very core. Hong Kong's continued existence as guaranteed by Article 109 of the Basic Law was about to be brought into question by Leopold Chan.

Some legacy for a dying man.

A moment passed.

Desperate to slap himself with a reality check, Scott hurried to the washroom, splashed cold water on his face and stared at himself in the mirror.

This wasn't some tutorial where he could mess around with wild speculation. This was life, *his* life, which right then lay in tatters. And all because he couldn't let things go, couldn't let things lie, couldn't walk away because he was too stubborn to admit that he'd been wrong all along; that he, Scott Lee, was the one who had thrown it all away, undone by his own arrogance in viewing Charles Conrad as somehow inferior to himself, when the opposite was true. Charles Conrad had worked out how to survive in the world of law-firm politics, and that was all that mattered to get ahead, not being proved right.

Scott's image in the mirror wasn't a pretty sight. Stubble had massed on his top lip and chin, his face was scratched. He was a mess, both outside and in. And yet, he still couldn't bring himself to let it go.

If he was right, then Leopold Chan was a man with nothing left to lose. Scott could relate to that. Thanks to Chan, his own life had hit rock-bottom. But in many ways hitting rock-bottom was freedom in its purest form. Caution didn't matter any more. There was no downside to taking the one final risk he had in mind.

Scott thought of Kimmie, of Rainbow too, and felt his resolve rising.

One last throw of the dice.

Twice now he had failed to get into see Cyrus Kwan. That avenue had to be considered closed. But Cyrus Kwan wasn't the only person Leopold Chan was setting up for a fall. There was someone else – someone who could help Scott stop Chan before it was too late.

Scott sped back down to the ground floor and shot over to the row of public phones. Grabbing a Yellow Pages directory, he flipped to the law-firms section. He fed coins into the mechanism and punched in the number.

"Roger Farley and Co., how may I help you?" The sickly sweet receptionist's answer sounded like one she repeated a hundred times a day.

"Is Roger there?" Scott asked.

"Who may I say is calling?" Scott gave his name. "One moment please."

Scott was put on hold to Bob Marley's 'I shot the sheriff' and felt a shard of a smile creeping in. Roger Farley was a larger-than-life Australian to whom, eight years ago, Scott had lent his lecture notes for the Overseas Lawyer Qualifications Exam. Now the unscrupulous champion of the criminal fraternity in Hong Kong, Farley was the kind of lawyer who got by on a big breakfast and his native wit, not caring about the morals of the people he defended.

"Scott Lee, what the bloody hell do you want?" the receiver bellowed. Being polite had never been Farley's strong point.

"I need a favour, Roger."

"Only bloody calls I get these days. What's up?"

Here went nothing. "I need to get in touch with a guy named Benny Wang. Dabbles in soft drugs and piracy. Figured you might have come across him in your professional capacity?"

A loud huffing. Then: "Someone called Wang into soft drugs and piracy. You've just described half my client-base, mate. Any distinguishing features you can think of?"

Scott thought back to the description Eva Chow had given them. "He's a big guy. Mountainous. Quite old. Tattoos on his forearms."

Farley gave a grunt of recognition. "Yeah, I know him. Represented a couple of his cohorts a few years back. This the number you're on?"

"Yes, but it's a pay-phone."

"Ring me back in ten, then. I'll see what I can do."

Scott stayed by the phone, and virtually counted off the six hundred seconds in his head. When he rang back the hold music had moved onto Bon Jovi's 'Dead or Alive'.

"There's a bar called Atmosphere on Kowloon side, just off Kimberly Street," Roger told him. "Go there today. Ask for Jimmy and mention my name. He's expecting you."

Scott thanked him.

"No problem, mate. Just promise me I'll be your one phone-call should whatever it is you're up to go tits up! Sounds like it could be a nice little earner."

Farley was all heart.

CHAPTER FORTY-ONE

Detective-Inspector Kam eye-balled the man sitting across the table from him. Time was ticking down on his decision of whether to charge or release.

Kam had witnessed the whole thing. Scott Lee and that giant *gweilo* facing off like two rutting stags, testosterone at boiling point as they'd hurtled towards each other. Then, out of nowhere this third man, now seated across the table, had appeared, and without an ounce of fear, had flung himself into the *gweilo's* path, shouldering him off-balance. Lee had run; the *gweilo* too. Only this stranger, lying winded on the ground, was left for Kam to arrest.

Obstruction of justice was Kam's pretext for bringing him in, but it would never stick. If anything, this man had foiled a crime, intervening in a knife-fight with nothing but his bare hands. But who was he? Some bystander who just happened to be in the Botanical Gardens at that time of morning? Kam's instinct told him there was more to it than that, and the fact that the man had not uttered a word since his arrest had served only to heighten his suspicion.

So there they sat in frustrating silence, the air-conditioning turned down low to increase discomfort, but Kam the only one affected, the dark patches on his shirt almost meeting in the middle. The suspect, by contrast, appeared completely unruffled. His fair skin and narrow eyes suggested a northern Chinese, someone not used to humidity, but there was no sign of discomfort and thus far he hadn't responded to any questions in Mandarin or otherwise. Hair, clothes and physique put him in his mid-twenties, Kam guessed, but the gaunt face and wispy stubble was of someone much older. And evidently police custody held no fear for him, his whole demeanour was part contempt, part amusement and totally disrespectful.

"You know it's a crime not to carry an ID card?" Kam decided to have another crack. "Tell me who you are; I could have you out of here in no time."

The man gave back flat eyes. Gnawing on the toothpick in his mouth, Kam led him again through the familiar round of questions. What had he been doing in the Botanical Gardens? Did he know Scott Lee? Why had he helped him? Silence after frustrating silence.

"The man you helped escape is a suspect in a murder case! Does the name Rainbow Choi mean anything to you? She was killed yesterday evening! Where were you yesterday evening?"

Nothing.

"You want me to charge you for perverting the course of justice?" Kam banged his fist on the table. The pitying look he got by return made him feel impotent. Frustrated, Kam rocked back in his chair about ready to give in.

The door to the interview-room opened.

Kam swung round, ready to let rip. Never interrupt an interview without knocking; didn't they teach these imbeciles anything these days? But when he saw the superintendent, Kam held his tongue and got to his feet.

A man followed the superintendent through the door. He was short and stooped, his face etched hard with wrinkles and he took in the room with tired, doleful eyes. White streaks interspersed his black hair.

Kam's heart sank. He had an inkling of what was coming next. This was probably some lawyer, or may be even the rich benefactor of the policeman's retirement fund who just happened to be a relative of the man in custody. Pulling strings, calling in favours, it didn't matter how you dressed it up, it amounted to the same thing. Sometimes Kam despised this job, the way it held a mirror up to society and revealed the truth about Hong Kong; that the only checks and balances which mattered were those on people's bank-account ledgers. Money talked and the law walked.

"Inspector Kam," the superintendent said when the door closed. "This interview is terminated. All recordings are to be wiped. This man is free to go."

Kam snorted and shook his head, a mixture of frustration and resignation thudding in his chest. He decided some push-back was necessary; but even as the words left his lips, he knew it was pointless. "This man is the only clue we have to what happened this morning!"

"Please do not argue with me, Kam!"

Twenty years in the job and this is what it always came down to. Kam threw a nasty glare at the man who had accompanied the superintendent into the room, then shaking his head, made to leave.

"Wait! We need him!"

It was the suspect.

The words threw Kam off-balance. *They need me?* But he wasn't in the mood for any more games. All he wanted was a hot shower and some home time....

"Please, Detective-Inspector. Come back and sit down." This time the request came from the man who'd walked in with the superintendent. Kam sensed the soft drip of authority in his voice. The superintendent gave Kam a nod to obey, but Kam stayed where he was. "My name is Huang Yi, Detective-Inspector," the stooped man continued. "Please come and sit down." Then turning to the Superintendent. "And, perhaps, we could be left alone?"

Kam expected the line to be drawn there, for his superintendent to launch into a speech about how this was 'his station' and how nobody could give him orders on his own turf. But to Kam's utter astonishment, there was no word of protest. "Give these men whatever cooperation they need," the superintendent said; then left the room.

Now it was just the three of them.

"Please, sit down," the man who had just introduced himself as Huang Yi said.

Kam's frustration suddenly gave way to trepidation. He sat.

Huang Yi stepped to the edge of the table and it was then that Kam noticed the fingers on his left hand fidgeting with something. A deep green jade charm. A laughing Buddha-face.

"So who the hell are you, Mr Huang Yi?" Kam decided to go on the offensive, see if he could gain some traction. "His lawyer?" He signaled with his chin to the suspect.

The suspect snorted a laugh.

"I suggest," Huang Yi replied. "That we deal with the questions which I have for you first, Detective-Inspector."

Kam's toothpick stopped in his mouth.

Huang Yi's doleful eyes went round the room, before falling back on Kam's sweat-drenched shirt. "Turning the air-conditioning down low, to make a suspect more conducive to answering questions. A neat trick, Detective-Inspector. But unfortunately such games are meaningless here." Huang Yi signaled with his eyes to the suspect. "Zhong here has been trained to resist interrogation techniques far more onerous than this."

Zhong. At least Kam now knew his name.

"Don't feel too bad," Zhong said.

Kam stiffened. Their Cantonese was good but heavily accented. Mainlanders for sure, Beijingers probably, he guessed. And with enough pull to instruct the Hong Kong police what to do in their own backyard!

"Have you ever heard of the Third Bureau of State Security, Detective-Inspector Kam?" Huang Yi asked. Kam shook his head. "It is an arm of the Chinese Intelligence Services, responsible for internal security in Hong Kong, Macao and the Special Economic Zones in China. That's who we are, Detective-Inspector. I am head of the Third Bureau's Hong Kong operation. And it appears that you have just arrested one of my operatives whilst he was on a job. So we have ourselves a situation, wouldn't you say? One of your creation, Detective-Inspector! So I would like you to tell me exactly what happened!"

Kam felt both sets of eyes on him. The tables had been turned. He was now the one being interrogated.

By Chinese Intelligence....

"I was investigating a possible homicide!" Kam heard himself say.

"What homicide?"

Kam took deep breaths to calm himself, then gave them the basics: Rainbow Choi's death, the anonymous tip-off, finding the hand-gun outside Scott Lee's apartment and their subsequent surveillance of Kwan Tower because that's where they thought Lee would turn up. "I sighted Scott Lee on Garden Road. He was running away. I gave chase and followed him up to the Botanical Gardens. Then you turned up!" He jabbed a finger at Zhong. "The man you saved this morning. That was Scott Lee. That was our murder suspect."

Zhong's eyes narrowed. "Who was the monster with the knife?"

Kam worked the toothpick. "I don't know. He was just there. He was the person that Lee was running away from."

A cold, hard silence hit the room. Huang Yi's face deepened in thought and Kam saw his fingers increase their tempo across his jade charm.

"So you thought this suspect....this Scott Lee would be at Kwan Tower. Why?" Huang Yi asked "And what is his connection to the Kwan organization?"

"The woman we think he murdered," Kam said, "Rainbow Choi, she was an accountant carrying out some work for Kwan Holdings."

"What work?"

"Due diligence on some takeover."

Huang Yi looked hard at Zhong before turning back to Kam. "You mean Kwan Holdings' takeover of AsiaRisk?"

"Yes," Kam said.

"Tell me what you know about it."

Kam paused. He had deliberately held back on giving AsiaRisk's name, just in case he could turn the situation around and trade information. But these men seemed to know a lot more than they were letting on, so Kam decided it was best to come clean.

"I know only what Leopold Chan told me. He's the managing director of AsiaRisk."

"You've already spoken with Leopold Chan?"

"Yes."

"When?"

"This morning. About five-thirty."

"Why?"

"Because of the investigation! Like I just told you, the victim – Rainbow Choi – was doing due-diligence on AsiaRisk for Kwan! She turns up dead. And the last person who saw her alive was Scott Lee."

Huang Yi took a moment to consider the information. Then: "Why would this Scott Lee want to kill the person carrying out the due diligence on AsiaRisk?"

Kam sighed. "Look it's nothing solid, but there's a suggestion that Lee is pursuing some sort of personal vendetta against Leopold Chan. He's gone on record as making some pretty wild allegations about AsiaRisk. So we figured, maybe he was trying to sabotage the takeover of AsiaRisk, just to get back at Chan."

"So he kills the woman carrying out the due-diligence?" Huang Yi didn't seem to get it.

"Look, it's just a theory." Kam went on the defensive. "We've been working on this for just over twelve hours so...."

"Tell me about the allegations Scott Lee was making!" Huang Yi interrupted.

Kam twisted his mouth. He didn't want to go down this route but had left himself little choice. "Lee says AsiaRisk is some sort of money-laundering vehicle. But there's no truth to it. He's acting crazy, the Law Society has already censured him and...."

"The Law Society?"

"Scott Lee," Kam replied, "he's a lawyer. That's how this whole personal vendetta thing with Leopold Chan got started. Look, Lee wanted a piece of AsiaRisk's legal work. So he went to Leopold Chan and told him that AsiaRisk's current lawyer was totally useless. Chan thought it was a lot of rubbish because he's known his lawyer for years and has never had any problems. So he showed Lee the door and told his lawyer what Lee had been saying about him. It turns out there was already bad blood between Chan's lawyer and Lee. They used to work together and had fallen out or something, I don't know the exact details. Anyway Chan's lawyer complained to the Law Society about what Lee had said. And Lee appears to have gone crazy, making these money-laundering allegations against Leopold Chan and his lawyer. Next thing we know, Rainbow Choi, Cyrus Kwan's due diligence expert on the AsiaRisk takeover, turns up dead. And Scott Lee, who like I said was the last person we know who saw her alive, has a gun outside his apartment."

The slow hum of the air-conditioner became the only sound in the room. Zhong sat there eye-balling Kam. Huang Yi ambled up and down by the desk, digesting Kam's words, assessing the areas he needed to probe further. After a while he stopped and turned to Kam. "What's the name of Leopold Chan's lawyer, the one Scott Lee used to work with?"

"Wait a minute," Kam fumbled in his pocket and came out with a notebook. Wetting his thumb, he turned pages. "It's in here somewhere....yes....here....Jackson, Weiss, Macdonald is the firm's name. The lawyer is Charles Conrad."

Zhong's chair scraped on the floor.

Kam looked up and saw that Huang Yi's haggard face had gone a translucent white.

That piece of news appeared to have smacked them both hard.

"We have to go now, Detective-Inspector," Huang Yi told Kam, his tone suddenly hard-edged with urgency.

"What? I don't understand...."

"Please give me one of your business cards."

Kam paused a moment, shrugged, handed a card over. Huang Yi handed him one by return.

"Now listen to me carefully, Inspector. I want you to leverage all of your contacts. We need to find this Scott Lee and we need to do it fast. Do whatever it takes, but tell no one why you are doing this, understand. We must find him! And make sure you keep your mobile on so we can contact you if we need you!"

Before Kam could answer, protest or ask what the hell was happening, the two men were heading for the door, leaving the policeman slack-jawed and more confused than he had ever felt in his twenty years on the force.

CHAPTER FORTY-TWO

'Atmosphere' was the name of the bar Farley had given Scott.

It looked about as welcoming as a shark pit. Outside, two Chinese pit-bull types, heavily muscled and with enough tattoo ink between them to open a gallery, were exchanging idle banter. Scott strode straight past them, ignoring their 'you-gotta-be-kidding-me' eyes, and in through the door.

The bar was a dump. A scrap-heap for those with good reason to drown their sorrows in the middle of the day. There was a time when Scott would have felt right at home here. A dozen pairs of hardened eyes turned in his direction, every look bitter with regret and intimidation, but they all quickly turned back to their drinks and private despairing thoughts.

"What you want!?" It was the shaven-headed specimen tending the bar, less a question than a challenge.

"San Mig," Scott eased himself onto a barstool.

The bartender banged the open bottle down in front of him, no coaster, no glass. That kind of place. "Twenty-two dollar!"

Scott held out a pair of pink hundreds. "I want to see Jimmy."

The bartender smiled in an unpromising way and shook his head. He took one of the hundreds and turned to the till. "Hey Jimmy! That *gweilo's* here!" He shouted to no one in particular. As he slid the change across the bar, Scott felt like the idiot he deserved. The San Mig looked tempting. He had told himself he wasn't going to touch it but temptation was a strange mistress and the salt taste was already dancing on his tonsils.

Something tapped Scott on the arm. He swiveled round.

The man standing there was rat-like and wiry. He had black hair separated by a bald strip down the middle. His hands were stuffed into his jeans, his eyes fidgeting all over.

"Are you Lee?"

"Yes. You're Jimmy?"

Jimmy gave him the kind of smile that made you want to have a wash after being on the receiving end.

"Lawyer Farley said you want to meet with Benny Wang."

Lawyer Farley. *Nice crowd you're running with these days, Roger.*

"That's right."

Jimmy's eyes shifted up and down him. Scott felt like he was being violated.

"Please follow," Jimmy turned and scuttled back into the bowels of the bar like a cockroach.

Suspending caution, Scott slid off the stool, followed Jimmy through a door, past the toilets, then down a short corridor which stank of stale urine and sweet beer. Another door led them outside. There, a white van was waiting, its back sliding-door open, revealing a dark cavern inside.

Before Scott could say anything, his arms were gripped from both sides. He was dragged forward and off his feet. Panic surged as the two tattooed pit-bulls from out front went about their day-time job, heaving him up and into the van. Scott's backside clanged against the corrugated floor, the impact shooting pain up his hip. The pit-bulls climbed in after him, lifted him onto the seat, and sandwiched in on either side of him.

"You shut up!" Jimmy said, framed by the square opening, before clunking the door shut and plunging them into darkness. Scott heard the driver's side-door open and close. The engine gunned and they were away.

Jimmy was a fidgety driver, all accelerator and brake and nothing in between; but each time Scott felt himself jettisoning forward, one of the pit-bulls shouldered him back into place. It gave Scott little chance to control his thoughts and soon he was back in that flow of unconsciousness that served as his defence mechanism, so far out of his comfort zone he needed a map to get back.

How long they drove for, Scott couldn't tell. Could have been ten minutes, maybe half an hour. Time meant nothing anymore. He tried to listen out for identifiable sounds, but it was no good. The two pit-bulls made for silent companions, one chewing gum, the other emitting the occasional belch, filling the van with the stench of gastric air.

After a while the van started turning round tight corners, throwing them one way then the other. Eventually they skidded to a stop. The engine cut, the driver's door opened, the sound of footsteps followed, then the back door clunked and slid open. Sunlight burst through the square, lazering Scott's eyes.

"Out!" Jimmy commanded.

The pit-bulls did the work for him, shoving him out into the open. Scott squinted through the sun.

A grey tenement block leered over them. A fifty-year-old lowrise, probably dating from when the original squatter sites had been turned into public housing, back in the fifties. Rusting air-conditioners lurched out from every window, washing hung draped from iron bars that looked like they'd once been part of illegal-structure add-ons. The whole place was decrepit and decaying. Part of the front was covered in bamboo-scaffolding which seemed to be holding the place up. Green netting was drapped over the meshed pieces of wood. The pavement was full of dust and the black plastic ties they use to fasten the bamboo poles into place. Oddly though, there was no sign of any workmen.

The nearest door had a sign in English and Chinese, saying it was for authorized personnel only. Scott was given a helping shove through it anyway, stumbling into a wall on the other side, the cold concrete offering stark comfort.

The corridor inside was white, the walls bubbling and cracked. Scott was shoved in the shoulder again, an action he was getting increasingly used to. Jimmy led the way. Scott followed with the pit-bulls as his shadows. They turned into a stairwell that stank of smoke, went up one floor, then down another dilapidated corridor. They reached a door. Jimmy pointed Scott in.

"Where am I?" Scott asked.

This time the shove was harder. Scott hit the floor with a hard smack, wind releasing through his lungs like a broke piston. Somewhere a switch clicked darkness into light.

Scott made it to his feet. A table and two wooden stools were the only furniture.

"Sit!" Jimmy pointed to the stool on the left.

Scott did as he was told. "What am I doing here?" He managed to unleash just before Jimmy shut the door. Receding foot steps turned to nothing. Scott was on his own.

It was windowless. Less a room than a prison cell. *Was this it,* Scott wondered, *the end?* Concentrating on the drawling air-conditioner, Scott drowned out the thought and peered round. Something was smudged on the surface of the wall at face-height next to the door. He focused on it, then wished he hadn't. It was blood.

Seconds passed. Minutes too. Fear built in his chest. Then the sound of footsteps approached. Scott held his breath. The door opened and one of the pit-bulls stepped in.

There was a pause before the next person entered the room. When he did so, no introductions were necessary. Benny Wang, just as Eva Chow had described him. Man mountain, jabba-the-hut-like fat, tattoos on his arms which ended in thick slabs for hands. But what Chow hadn't described was the plain sinister aura of the man. It was as if the temperature in the room had dropped ten degrees when he walked in. His meaty face was filled with folds. A mole sat accusingly on his right cheek, daring people to look at it.

Scott wanted to run, but his legs were already jelly. The second pit-bull followed Wang in and closed the door.

Benny Wang stared at Scott with an empty look. Then he took the opposite stool, not an easy task for a man of his bulk. One of the pit-bulls waited by the door, the other took up position at Wang's shoulder.

Silence again. Wang continued to stare at Scott then reached into his pocket and placed something on the table between them. A mobile phone. Scott glanced down at it then back at Wang who was waiting until he had Scott's full attention.

The second thing Wang took from his pocket made Scott's stomach disappear.

It was a hand-gun, an automatic. In Wang's hand it looked like a toy, almost benign. Wang snapped a magazine in place, a practised move that showed familiarity with the instrument, and handed it to the pit-bull at his shoulder. Then he cleared his throat, all sand-paper and phlegm, leaned over and spat on the floor. The smacking globule echoed off the walls.

"Jimmy said you understand Cantonese. Is that correct?" Wang's voice was corrosive..

"Yes. I understand," Scott said.

"I remember a time when the *gweilos* in the police spoke Cantonese, before the handover. They were forced to learn it. Hardly any of them left now. It's unusual to meet a foreign devil who bothers to learn." Wang's faced scrunched into a frown, eyes peering steadily. "But maybe you are not a foreign devil? Maybe you are *xap xong*."

Scott felt the slow burn of anger light in his chest at being called *mongrel*, literally 'a mess of all races', by this hideous ogre; a man who sold ketamine to kids; a man who thought nothing of bringing a hand-gun to a meeting. What part had he played in Kimmie's death? Had he ordered one of his men to snuff out her life? How Scott wanted to say, 'to hell with it', reach over and stab his thumbs into Wang's eyes, tear at his fat flesh, cause him pain. Half a metre was all that separated them. Time enough to cause damage before a bullet severed his brain stem.

But there was too much at stake here. *Shake it off. Treat this as just another negotiation, that's all it is! Roll with the insults, keep your eye on the prize*! Scott took a breath.

"My mother was local," he said. "She taught me how to speak!"

"And then you became a lawyer. Like Farley? But you are worse than Farley. You are a mongrel lawyer." Disdain dripped from fat man Wang's waxy lips. "I hate lawyers! Twisted-tongued serpents. Eunuchs, that's what they used to be in the old days, advisers without the balls to make tough decisions. Nothing changes. Farley is a whore. I pay him when I need a release." Wang twisted a vile smile at his own joke. He picked up the phone, checked it, then placed it back down. "So what do you want Mongrel Lawyer Lee. Make it quick! I do not have time to waste on your kind."

Scott hadn't given any thought on how to approach this moment. The plan had been to obtain an audience with this thug and take it from there. But here he was now, sitting with Benny Wang, a man who bore responsibility for Kimmie's death. Quite how far that responsibility extended, Scott wasn't sure, but it was this man's dirty money that Leopold Chan was laundering. That was the secret which Kimmie had learned, the secret which Chan, Wang and Conrad had been so desperate to keep quiet. Her blood was on this brute's hands. Her's and Rainbow Choi's. – Just collateral damage in Wang's sick world. – And here Scott was, trying to obtain his help. The thought sickened.

"What's this?! A mongrel lawyer who has nothing to say?! Has there ever been such a thing in this world. A lawyer whose tongue is so twisted he can no longer speak!"

"I know about the Chow Mei insurance claim!"

Wang's face gave way under a heavy frown.

Scott had attracted his attention. Now to give it a twist. "Mr Wang, you bought the rights to Chow Mei's insurance claim against AsiaRisk so you can 'launder money'," the last two words he said in English, not knowing the literal Cantonese translation. "Two hundred million dollars you want to clean! I have spoken to Eva Chow!"

The taut silence which followed strained every sinew in the atmosphere.

"You know nothing, you sniveling pig!"

Scott soldiered on, interspersing with English when he couldn't find the right word. "I know that Leopold Chan is selling AsiaRisk to Cyrus Kwan. I know that immediately after the sale is signed, Chan will launder your money through AsiaRisk, just so he can implicate Cyrus Kwan in an illegal, criminal transaction."

Wang's eyes held a look of pure fury. It was too late for Scott to stop now.

"What has Chan promised you, Mr Wang? A way of blackmailing Cyrus Kwan, is that it? A way of controlling Kwan? If I am wrong, Mr Wang, just tell me and I will walk out of here!"

"No!" Wang's face contorted with rage. "You will never walk out of here!" He turned on his stool and held out his hand. The pit-bull handed the gun to him. Wang checked and cocked it.

Fright blurred Scott's vision. *He had to keep going! He had to make him listen!*

"Chan has lied to you, Mr Wang! He is setting you up! He is going to destroy you. Are you hearing what I am telling you, Mr Wang? He....will....destroy....you!"

The gun was pointed at Scott now. Heart thundering, Scott fought down nausea. *Keep going!* "As soon as the takeover is completed you will be arrested, Mr Wang! Chan will give information to the police about your money-laundering activities. Not just the Chow Mei claim. All of it. The information on all the laundering Leopold Chan has ever done for you, the police will have it!"

The gun stayed rock-steady. Scott's breathing went shallow as he waited for the snap of the trigger, the spark, the crashing noise, the bullet scything through him. The blackness.

"What did you say?" Wang asked.

Drops of Scott's sweat smattered the table. "Leopold Chan is going to tell the police everything!"

A hint of confusion mixed in at the edges of Wang's fury.

"Chan wants you to be arrested, Mr Wang! He wants to destroy you!"

Wang shook his head. "If he does this, he knows I will kill him. You don't know Chan, like I do. He is a clever man, just like a lawyer. But like a lawyer, he is also a pathetic coward. He fears me! No way will he do what you say!"

Scott kept his voice calm and steady. "Mr Wang, Leopold Chan is not scared of you. He has cancer. Here!" Scott pointed to his ribcage. "Soon he will die anyway. *You* cannot scare him! That is why he is doing this! Because a man with nothing to fear is the most dangerous kind of man, am I not correct?"

Two beats of silence.

"How do you know this?"

"Because I have seen the medicine Chan takes and my brother is a doctor. I asked my brother why a man would take such medicine. He told me what I am telling you. Leopold Chan has cancer. He is dying. You have seen him coughing? You have seen him take medicine?"

Imperceptibly, Benny Wang's face changed as it snared on exactly the memory Scott's words aimed at. Wang lowered the gun and placed it next to the mobile phone. "Chan wants to buy off his sins by giving me to the police, is that what you are telling me?"

Scott bit his lip. "It is not like that. Yes, Chan wants to destroy you, Mr Wang. But you are not his target. Cyrus Kwan is. That is why he wants to make Cyrus Kwan complicit in your money-laundering scheme. He is using you to get to Kwan. And after Chan has laundered your two hundred million he will have achieved this aim."

A shadow seemed to pass across Wang's face then. "So I am being used to destroy Cyrus Kwan."

Scott was about to push home his advantage, when somewhere a mobile phone started ringing. It belonged to Pitbull number one who answered it and handed it to Wang.

"Yes....okay...." Benny said before hanging up. "I have to go now!"

Scott wasn't sure if he had heard him right. "What about what I have just told you?"

"What you have just told me, mongrel lawyer Lee?" Benny picked up the gun, released the magazine, checked it, snapped it back into place, his movements now fast and deliberate. "I do not believe you! And since I have no further time to waste...." He signaled with a nod to the pit-bulls, who stepped towards Scott, put him in a half-nelson and rammed his face down onto the table.

Scott's heart went into overdrive as his cheek blossomed with agony.

The cold metal of the gun barrel pressed into his temple. Stars burst behind his eyes.

"No more lies, lawyer Lee!" Wang barked. "I want the truth about why you are here!"

The hand pressing down on Scott's face was released enough for him to speak.

"I've told you the truth...." the words tumbled from his mouth. "I swear it. I've...." Scott stopped.

All of a sudden a strange calmness descended as the taut strand of hope which had kept him going all this time finally snapped. *What was he doing pleading for his life from this man, this brutal thug who had taken Kimmie from him? This was not how it was going to end!*

"Hurry up then!" Scott relaxed, his voice flat as the doldrums. "It takes three of you and a gun to kill me, huh? How many of you did it take to kill Kimmie? It is you who is the eunuch, Mr Wang! You can pull that trigger! But don't ever forget my face! Because every time you stare at your prison walls, you will remember it!"

Scott shut his eyes.

Thoughts of his mother and of Kimmie wrestled in.

CHAPTER FORTY-THREE

Charles Conrad sat alone in the conference room of Jackson, Weiss & Macdonald's Hong Kong office on the sixty-second floor of Central Plaza. Correct that. This was *his* office. He had been the one they had sent out to set it up. What was it the partnership had said? *Five years, Charles, and you'll be back in the London office, probably be worth a seat on the management council when you return.* Yeah right!

A decade on, he was still here. Ten years and the time hadn't flown. It had crawled, forcing Charles to experience every nuance of the train-wreck his life had become. From respected solicitor to Leopold Chan's whore; the sum total of his career achievements. The money had been good, but it hadn't brought with it the status he had so craved. For a long time now, Charles had suppressed his feelings of disgrace, told himself that the means justified the end. But at the very core of his being, Charles Conrad was disgusted with what he had become, and that sense of self-loathing had been brought starkly into focus over the past few days.

Representing AsiaRisk on the Kwan Holdings takeover had been the catalyst. For too long Charles's job had been nothing more than glad-handing at the right cocktail parties, showing London he was out and about making the right contacts. Except for the settlement agreements he topped and tailed for Leopold Chan, he never did any real legal work.

But the AsiaRisk buy-out had changed all of that. This was something Charles knew he had to handle himself. Because in a life littered with mistakes, Kimmie Yang's death was his worst.

There it was, finally, the truth he'd buried for so long.

It was my damn fault!

Charles had never learned the complete truth of what had happened to Kimmie, but he knew Leopold Chan and that vicious psycho, Terrence O'Rourke were behind it. The suicide story was a joke. Kimmie lived for work. No matter how much pressure Charles piled on her, it would never have driven her to take her own life. Never!

But Charles knew deep down he was complicit. Not overtly, but if he hadn't panicked when he'd found out about Kimmie's threat to involve Jackson's Money-laundering Reporting Officer. If he hadn't picked up the phone to Leopold Chan ....

Guilt was a strange mistress. It wormed away inside, exploring the corners of the soul, until ignoring the truth was no longer an option, and some act of defiance was necessary to break free from its clutches. Not redemption, it was too late for that, and really that wasn't what Charles was searching for. What he needed was a way out. If he could get away and start again, he could live with the guilt. It would fade eventually and he could forget.

And today was the day, Charles had decided, to exercise his get-out clause.

At five-thirty pm Charles heard the chime of the bell at the main office door. His secretary rushed to open it. "Please come this way Mr Chan, Mr Conrad is waiting for you in the conference room."

When Leopold Chan appeared, Charles took a deep calming breath and extended his hand.

"Charles," Leopold said a little testily at having to waste his effort. A needless gesture of false amity, Charles agreed, but one he wanted to start with to ensure this conversation went on his terms. "So," Leopold seated himself at the head of the conference table, "you wanted to see me before Cyrus Kwan and his entourage turned up?"

"I thought it would be a good idea to take you through the documentation in advance."

Leopold looked amused, as if humoured by having to go through the charade of pretending this was a real lawyer-client relationship.

Charles cleared his throat. "I've structured the deal in two agreements." He picked up the agreement on the top of his pile and slid it across. "This is the share purchase agreement, by which you'll be transferring your entire one hundred percent shareholding in AsiaRisk to Kwan Holdings for the consideration price. Both the money and shares will be held in escrow pending regulatory approval and stamping. That's perfectly standard, but can I ask you to have a look at clause two. This makes clear that the share purchase agreement will become effective only when the second of the two agreements is executed. It's what's called a condition precedent and...."

"I know what a condition precedent is, Charles. I've been in the insurance business for thirty years."

"Yes. Of course." Charles cleared his throat. "But given the importance of this particular transaction, I just wanted to make sure you understand the implications. Anyway, if you turn to the last page of the share purchase agreement, you'll see I've marked with a pencil cross where you have to sign."

"How very efficient of you."

"The second agreement," Charles soldiered on, sliding across the second document, "transfers ownership of AsiaRisk's office in Central to Kwan Property Limited. This needs to be done by separate agreement because the Kwan organisation holds all its properties in a subsidiary separate from their operating companies. So AsiaRisk and Kwan Property Limited will be the counterparties to this second agreement. Now, like I said, because it's such an important element of the deal, Kwan Holdings has made the first agreement – the share transfer – contingent on the second agreement being entered into. It's a moot point, because you're executing both agreements at the same time anyway, but I just wanted to make it clear. Again if you turn to the final page I've marked where you need to sign."

Leopold flipped the pages, nodded and slid the agreements back. "No outstanding issues from Kwan's lawyers then?"

"No, everything's been checked and we're good to go. There is, however, one outstanding issue from my end, Leopold."

Leopold fixed Charles with a glare. "Yes?"

"After tonight, I will not be accepting any further instructions from you. I'm out. Finished. And if you...."

"My, my, Charles. Do I detect you growing a semblance of a back bone?"

"If you..."

Charles tried to go on, but Leopold cut him off

"Are you just about to threaten me, Charles? What are you going to do, go to the regulators? The police? The Law Society?"

The silence which followed stretched into a tight garrot around Charles Conrad's neck.

"Well, let me save you the trouble, Charles. Nothing would give me greater pleasure than never having to deal again with a jellyfish like you! After tonight, consider yourself discarded. Like a used condom."

Charles Conrad felt anger spark as Leopold fiddled with his gold cufflinks. How he wanted to reach across and punch the man. Just one single act to demonstrate he was no longer under Chan's control. But insult or no insult, Charles had said what he had needed to say, and ultimately, he had received the response he wanted. After tonight, his life could begin again, free of Chan's clutches. He could take Cathy back to England.

He was done with Jackson's, done with Leopold Chan. Done with Hong Kong.

Conrad muttered some excuse about having to make some last minute preparations and left the room.

Pathetic! Leopold thought as the conference-room door closed. Charles Conrad, Rupert Kwan, Benny Wang, they were all the same, merely manipulated pawns in his unfolding drama. None would be permitted to avoid their come-uppance. By tomorrow the Hong Kong financial markets would be in meltdown and all three would be at the heart of the storm; the lawyer, the spoiled tycoon brat and the criminal, each of whom had let his greed rule his judgement. An old, old story. Centuries of progress, yet still things stayed the same. Tragic, pathetic figures, all three of them and, thanks to Leopold, they were each about to be pilloried as symbols of public hatred.

But after the storm had past, after it was over, all three of them would be just wisps of smoke in the wind. Gone, forgotten and disregarded.

Only the true genius would be remembered, the architect of the whole cataclysmic downfall. History was about to be made, and long after today, it was his name, Leopold Chan, which would live long in everyone's minds.

Just a shame he wouldn't be around to witness the unraveling, Leopold mused.

But then immortality did have its price.

CHAPTER FORTY-FOUR

The crack exploded through Scott's head.

His legs gave way, he started to fall. By the time he hit the concrete he knew he'd be dead. This was his last moment. No pain, no coldness, just a kaleidoscopic rush towards oblivion. The flick of an off-switch and then blackness, as he'd always imagined it to be.

"Get him up!" A distant echo. Then something gripped him under the arms and pulled him to his knees, transforming the expectation of impending death into utter confusion. Snatching inhalations, a desperate hollowness in his chest, one that made him hit on the realization that he was still here, that he was still alive.

Staring up, Scott made out the door, swinging on its hinges. Two figures shimmered through watery fingers, both of them men, one of them moving to the table to collect something, his features magnifying and sharpening, as he squatted down to Scott's level. "Sorry we put you through that, Mr Lee, but time is short. We needed to be sure you were telling the truth. So I had Mr Wang place you under stress. But you are safe. For now, anyway."

Scott felt the man's voice lifting him back to consciousness.

"We heard your conversation." The man held something up in his hand. It took all of Scott's effort to focus on it, but when he did, he saw it was the mobile phone which Benny Wang had put on the table. A call was still in progress on the florescent screen. The man looked up, tossed the phone back to Wang and said, "Leave us!"

Wang and the pit-bulls went out without a word.

"I suggest you sit and take a moment, Mr Lee. I have some more questions for you."

Much had changed about Scott's life in forty-eight hours, too much for him to cope with right now, so he just let it wash over him with a strange sense of detachment. Seated back at the table where a gun had been pointing at his head only moments before, he looked hard at the man who had just addressed him, searching for some hint of recognition. The man, now sitting across from him, showed no emotion on his experienced face. On the table-top, his fingers toyed with something. It drew Scott's attention.

Looking down, Scott saw the key-ring with the jade emblem. The man's fingers rolled back and forth across the green surface, like a smoker in the process of giving up, all nervous and fidgety. Seeing the trinket seemed to trigger something in Scott's mind, some distant memory lurking deep in the grey recesses. But Scott couldn't grasp it, not just yet.

When Scott looked across at the other man in the room, however, recognition was immediate. It was his impromptu guardian from earlier that morning, the man who had wrestled O'Rourke to the ground in the Botanical Gardens.

Scott tried to put it together, but his mind was too fluid, images of Kimmie and Yip and Rainbow pinging around in a confusing rush, none of it making any sense.

"Mr Lee!" the man seated opposite said, his tone flat and commanding no argument. "I shall summarize your story and you will tell me if I have it correct. Leopold Chan is selling AsiaRisk to Cyrus Kwan. As soon as the transaction is complete, AsiaRisk will pay an insurance claim to Benny Wang, a payment that will constitute money-laundering. Cyrus Kwan will be implicated in this criminal act, as he would have just bought AsiaRisk when the payment is made. This will damage Kwan, as it will Leopold Chan. But Chan does not care. He is dying and a dying man has nothing left to fear. Is this accurate?"

Scott tried to focus, but it was as if the man's words were being filtered through a dull murmuring, the calmness with which they were delivered a surreal juxtaposition to what had gone before.

"Why is Leopold Chan doing this, Mr Lee? What does he stand to gain from ruining Cyrus Kwan?"

Scott told himself to get a grip, but his journey back to concentration wavered as a tide of dizziness hit. Two minutes ago he could have been dead, his body on the floor bleeding out, his brain stem severed by a bullet; and now this man expected him to....

"Please, Mr Lee, you must answer!" The man's voice became moulten steel.

Scott straightened, took a deep inhalation. *Okay, okay, you can do this....*

"This isn't about Cyrus Kwan," Scott began. "It's about what he represents."

The man's face became heavy with confusion. "I do not understand."

Scott blinked hard, dispersing the grey clouds, forcing clarity to the surface like a self-imposed caffeine injection. A moment later, the dizziness had gone. He was ready to lay it out. "When news hits, that Cyrus Kwan is a money launderer, what do you think is going to happen to Kwan Holdings' share price?" he asked.

The man considered the question. "Are you saying Chan stands to make money if Kwan Holdings' share price falls?"

"No, this isn't about money," Scott shook his head, "this is about Kwan Holdings being one of the biggest companies in Hong Kong, involved in practically every sector of the economy." He scraped his teeth across his lower lip, tasted the gunge of dehydration, pushed his hand through his hair, pulling the skin tight across his face. "What's going to happen if Kwan Holdings becomes embroiled in a money-laundering scandal? Take Kwan's banking arm, what if you had your savings there, what would you do if you heard this rumour about Kwan Holdings could be awash with criminal cash?"

Something changed on the man's face. He understood where Scott was going with this. "I would take my savings out."

"Yeah, you and the rest of the population, before the regulators moved in to freeze all the accounts. Before you know it, you've got a bank run. And if you're a business partner with any other Kwan Holdings business, you're probably going to distance yourself, cancel contracts, exercise whatever termination clauses you can to limit your exposure."

"So Leopold Chan wants to ruin Kwan Holdings," the man said.

Scott shook his head in frustration, an action which pushed away the residuary grey blanket and allowed his thoughts to cascade out of him. "Kwan Holdings is Chan's target because of what it is to Hong Kong. It's *the* major blue chip, *the* pinnacle of

309

propriety. Think how many people in Hong Kong own its shares. And now suddenly it's embroiled in money-laundering? Think of the panic. Rumours will be pinged around like contagion. The Hang Seng will collapse. Money will be transferred overseas as fast as companies can extract it, confidence sucked out in a matter of hours. Hong Kong is an international financial centre, it relies on confidence and reputation. With those gone, what's left? Nothing but the kind of chaos, which it could take years to recover from. And all because of one man. One man who'll probably be dead by then, but who we're not going to forget in a hurry!" Scott took a breath. "That's what Leopold Chan wants!"

Silence gripped the stale room. Scott felt an odd sense of relief wash through him, as if finally finding his voice had hissed out a pent-up pressure.

"You used to work at Jackson, Weiss, Macdonald, Mr Lee. You knew Yang Kim Yee, didn't you?"

The question stunned Scott like a sucker-punch, forcing air up from his stomach into his lungs, turning it to lead.

Yang Kim Yee. It had been a long time since Scott had heard Kimmie's Chinese name.

"Answer the question!" The second man, leaning against the wall barked.

"I...I used to work with her," Scott heard himself stammer. *These men knew Kimmie.* He struggled to work it out, but nothing made sense. "Look, who the hell are you people?"

The two men looked at each other for a moment, then the man who was seated turned to Scott and spoke. "My name is Huang Yi," he said. "This man is my colleague, Zhong. We work for the Third Bureau of State Security. We work for the Chinese Intelligence Services, Mr Lee."

The murmuring filled Scott's ears again. He drew the back of his hand across his face, tried to push out the sound and get a strangle-hold on the rising tide of confusion spilling through. He stared at the man seated across from him, stared at the jade Buddha still moving rapidly through his fingers, reaching for the memory through his confusion.

Slowly things started to fall into place.

The man called Huang Yi cast him a look of pure ice. "I run a network, Mr Lee. A network made up of ordinary hardworking civilians – patriots every one – who, by reason of their profession, are in a position to provide vital information. Information which protects certain strategic investments which the Chinese Government has made."

A moment went by. The atmosphere in the room remained sticky and thick, but the blood turned to crystal in Scott's veins. Cold needles prickled down his back. A bead of sweat hit the edge of his eye, stinging salt when he blinked it out.

Then the memory finally kicked in.

"I've seen that before," Scott pointed down at the jade Buddha. Huang Yi's fingers stopped. He held up the charm for Scott to take a closer look. "Kimmie had one," Scott said, recalling the visit he had made to Kimmie's flat with Sally; the collection of necklaces from around the world draped over the photo-frame. Trinkets Kimmie had collected on her travels. And in the midst of all the paraphernalia, a small laughing-faced jade Buddha, the size of a thumb-nail, hanging on a leather tie.

"Yang Kim Yee – the woman you knew as Kimmie – she was part of our network," Huang Yi said. "An international law firm like Jackson, Weiss, Macdonald has many clients round the world. Having someone like Kim Yee was useful to our cause."

Scott reached down and gripped the sides of his seat to save himself from falling off the roller-coaster.

Kimmie Yang. A spy for the Chinese government.

God!

"We were deeply saddened by her death," Huang Yi continued, his tone suddenly hushed and resonating with a deep-seated bitterness. "It was a sad loss to China, to whom Kim Yee rendered great service in her life. It is our responsibility to put it right!" He looked over at Zhong before turning back to Scott. "You see, Mr Lee, just before she died, Kim Yee wanted to pass me some new information which she had learned about. Vital information, she said. But she never got the chance."

Three beats of silence.

"We have never believed this ridiculous suicide story, Mr Lee," Huang Yi continued. "And when something happens to one of the people in our network, it is our duty to make it right. That is what we have been endeavoring to do, Mr Lee. We have tried to investigate the matter. But our resources in Hong Kong are limited. Myself and Zhong here, we run the entire network on our own. We have been placed under significant pressure with the demands of other projects recently. Projects like the proposed takeover of AsiaRisk by Kwan Holdings. But this, Mr Lee, has led us straight to you! And you have led us straight back to the matter of Kim Yee's death!"

Thoughts and images snapped through Scott's mind, their rapidity bringing at first confusion, but then inexorably landing at a conclusion of diamond clarity. "Why is Chinese Intelligence looking at the AsiaRisk takeover?" he asked.

"Because one of the strategic investments the Chinese government has made is in Kwan Holdings itself," Huang Yi said. And then, "Your life relies on you keeping that a secret, Mr Lee!"

The comment pierced a shaft of anger through Scott's skin. "You know how many times I've been threatened in the past twenty-four hours. Believe me the novelty's wearing thin."

Huang Yi's eyebrows lifted. "That is fair comment in the circumstances, Mr Lee." He waited a beat before continuing. "To answer your question, there are certain....let us say....conservative sections within the Chinese government who are interested in seeing a company like Kwan Holdings – one in which the government has invested – become engulfed in scandal. They wish to use such a scandal as the basis on which to move against the assets of all major companies that do business in Hong Kong."

"What? That's crazy!" Scott couldn't believe what he was hearing.

"It is the Third Bureau's task to try to prevent that from happening, Mr Lee. To stop any scandals before they occur. That is why we were running a precautionary surveillance on the AsiaRisk takeover. And now here you are, Mr Lee, confirming that our worst fears are about to be realized. That Leopold Chan is about to do something that will give the hard-line elements in our Government the justification to launch their intended crackdown."

The room powered into silence again as all three men assessed the implications.

"Who was the man chasing you this morning?" This question from Zhong.

Scott swallowed hard at the memory. *Was it only this morning?*

"His name is Terrence O'Rourke. He works for Leopold Chan."

Zhong looked down at Huang Yi.

Huang Yi grimaced. "Then it would seem, Mr Lee, that you have knowledge which Leopold Chan wants kept secret."

"How did you find me?" Scott asked.

"The man who brought you here is a police informant."

Scott nodded. The rat-like Jimmy appeared to fit the bill. Another time it might have concerned him that the two men with whom he was speaking could exercise the kind of influence which extracted police favours. But right then, Scott was beyond surprise.

"Kim Yee's death and AsiaRisk," Huang Yi said. "As I say, you appear to connect the two, Mr Lee."

Scott swallowed hard.

"Did Benny Wang kill her?" It was Zhong who asked. He took something out of his pocket, an electronic device. Pressing a button, he released the high-pitched sound of fast-forwarded voices into the room. When Zhong pressed the button again Scott heard his own desperate voice cut in.

"It takes three of you and a gun to kill me, huh? How many of you did it take to kill Kimmie?"

Words he had uttered with a gun against his head only minutes before.

Zhong stopped the recording. "Did Wang kill her?"

Scott held his stare. "I don't know if it was Wang. But whether it was Wang or not, Leopold Chan was responsible. Kimmie found out Chan was using Jackson's to help launder Wang's money." Turning to Huang Yi, Scott added. "That's probably the information she was going to give you before she died. Leopold Chan somehow found out she knew and ...." He was unable to finish the thought.

Zhong and Huang Yi looked at each other again, their faces communicating silent thoughts in a way that made Scott uncomfortable.

"We need to stop Kwan buying AsiaRisk!" Scott said then. "I don't know where the deal's due to be signed, but we need to...."

"It's being completed this evening at Jackson, Weiss, Macdonald's offices," Huang Yi said. "We got that from the police."

Cold fingers tightened round Scott's throat. Of course, Charles Conrad was acting for AsiaRisk. Rainbow had told him that.

"We've got to get down there! We've got to stop this!"

Neither of the men moved.

"Please, Kimmie wasn't *just* my colleague!" Scott pleaded. "She meant more to me than that...." He stopped then and remembered his mission. Where it had all started; with Sally Yang's words. *I remember what Kimmie told me about you, Mr Lee. You always know the answer. You always know what to do, she said. I trust my sister's judgement.*

Scott stood up fast then, his stool clattering on the floor behind. He was done pleading. "Look, I've been through too much, to stop here. So either you get Benny Wang back in here with his gun to finish what he started. Or you let me do this!"

Zhong snorted contemptuously. Huang Yi's face was cold.

"Impertinence is not an attractive quality, Mr Lee," Huang Yi said. "But I believe in this instance, our interests are aligned." He stood up and made for the door.

Scott didn't need a second invitation.

CHAPTER FORTY-FIVE

Tom Benton, the lawyer whom Kwan Holdings had retained to handle the buy-out, was a serious man with a serious manner. "You should have let me draft the first cut of the documentation rather than leaving it to Jackson's, Cyrus. This Charles Conrad fellow really isn't up to much."

Neither Cyrus Kwan nor Tyson Mok were in the mood.

"Forget about word-smithing, Tom," said Mok. "Do the agreements do what they're supposed to?"

"Well....yes.... But it's just the way it's been drafted, it's so unclear and...."

"Then that's the end of it." It was typical Mok. Abrupt and to the point. Unfortunately, not abrupt enough to shut Benton up, who launched into a detailed clause-by-clause exposition.

Cyrus Kwan shut out his lawyer's dreary ramblings and stared out of the window as the people-carrier dawdled through the traffic on its way to Jackson, Weiss, Macdonald's office. It was the miracle of land-reclamation, which held Cyrus in captivity. Virtually every building they passed stood on parts of the harbour which had been filled in to create the necessary space. It was a truly amazing feat of engineering. Like many Hong Kongers, Cyrus hoped a line would be drawn one day to preserve what was left of the harbour. But the ingenuity and sheer boldness of the skyscrapers were simply breathtaking.

His own contribution to the skyline, Kwan Tower, shimmered behind them in the evening light. Cyrus remembered the opening ceremony; the suckling pig feast, the Feng Shui consultants who had been paid to okay the building's design and positioning, the whole thing a wonderful occasion. One day the Tower would be outdone, he knew, but that was what he loved about Hong Kong, its capacity for constant reinvention and progress, respecting tradition only in intangible form, never letting nostalgia prevent the forward motion of the money-making machine.

As the car bucked down towards Wanchai, Kwan caught sight of the Convention Centre. There it stood, like a beached whale, its grey and black contours somehow amusing. Then a memory sparked of the last time he had been there. The celebration of the Cooperation in Services Agreement; when Leopold Chan had first introduced himself.

That's when it hit Cyrus. Chan had planned this whole thing, timing his introduction for the celebration of the cross-border agreement which underpinned why AsiaRisk would be such an attractive acquisition for Kwan Holdings. God, Chan had probably planted the seed in Rupert's head the same day.

Yes indeed, he and his nephew had been played. Victims of a skillful piece of strategic manoeuvering. But what did it matter now? The end result was to his company's advantage, so it was worth the price of a bruised ego....

Then Cyrus remembered.

Rainbow Choi.

This deal had resulted in the young woman's death. If he hadn't pursued it, she would never have been killed by that mad hoodlum who was still out there. Somewhere.

Cyrus stopped his mind wandering any further. Effecting this deal was the right thing to do by Rainbow, he had already made his mind up on that. All he wanted now was to get it done and integrate AsiaRisk into the Kwan corporate structure as quickly as possible.

"What are Rupert's movements today?" Cyrus suddenly asked, interrupting Benton's legal monotone.

"I've arranged for him to have one-on-ones with each of the heads of division," Mok said. "Thought it best to keep him busy until everything's been signed, sealed, and delivered."

"Good. We could do without any distractions. But remember, Tyson, I've promised him an executive role in this new venture. The responsibility will do him good....provided he's kept on a tight rein."

Eventually, the car drew into the dropping-off point outside Central Plaza. The doorman tipped his cap as the triumvirate got out. Cyrus Kwan buttoned his jacket. He was ready for business.

The air-conditioning chill hit them as they entered the split-level marble cavern of Central Plaza's lobby. On the way up the long escalators to reception, Cyrus noticed pairs of militaristic security-guards posted at each of the main entrances to the podium level, conspicuous in their red berets and khaki uniforms.

Two had greeted him at the bottom of the second escalator. Two more waited at the top.

"Someone's tipped off the building management that you were coming!" – Mok had the same thought.

Leopold Chan, Cyrus realised. The flagrant breach of confidentiality jarred, but he thought again of Rainbow and how Chan had been the ultimate target of that young lawyer's anger. He couldn't blame him for wanting to take additional precautions.

They got into the lift.

"We change at the sky-lobby on the forty-sixth floor," Mok said, as their ascending speed made their ears pop. "Jackson's are on floor sixty-two."

When the doors opened on forty-six, Mok and Benton searched for the correct transfer. Cyrus ambled over to see what the the sky-lobby view was like. But half way to the window a shadow jumped out and accosted him.

"Mr Kwan, my name is Eve Fung, I'm a reporter with the *Economic Times*," a young woman, a good head shorter than him, with big glasses and a smile that didn't reach her eyes, rattled excitedly. "Can I get your comment on your takeover of AsiaRisk?!"

The sight of the tape-recorder sparked Cyrus's anger. It blossomed further when he recognized Eve Fung as one of the reporters whose amoral articles on Rupert had sought to keep the the Container Terminal incident firmly in the public consciousness long after it was dead. It was the type of journalism Cyrus so detested – gossip dressed up as serious business analysis – and judging by the look in Fung's eyes, authored by an ambitious reporter determined to write whatever she wanted to gain the limelight.

"I have no comment to make to you, Ms Fung!" He walked away briskly, searching for Mok. Fung followed, her determined heels echoing in the enormous sky-lobby.

"AsiaRisk is the first insurance company you are buying isn't it, Mr Kwan? You must be pleased?"

Cyrus quickened his pace.

"It's this way...," Mok appeared.

"Don't you think your shareholders have a right to know?"

Mok stepped in to intervene. "Go away, Eve! You've no right to be here!"

They reached the bank of transfer-lifts. Benton was already waiting, but Eve Fung wasn't ready to give up. "Is it true that you've asked Rupert to run AsiaRisk for you? Have you two made up, then? Will Rupert take over from you one day, Mr Kwan? Have you a message for your shareholders?" Each question was barked out with pure prejudicial acid, made worse by the horrible painted smile with which they were delivered.

"My client has no comment!" Benton said in his serious manner. The lift doors opened. Kwan, Mok and Benton stepped inside. Mok hammered the close button.

"I'll be here when you come out, if you change your mind about a statement, Mr Kwan!"

Sighs of irritation passed all round after the doors came together.

"Increased security! Now she's here! What's going on, Cyrus?"

"Leopold Chan," Cyrus said. He was being played again. "This is his doing."

"He signed a confidentiality agreement!" Benton jumped straight to legal recourse. "Cyrus, if you want to walk away, we can. I can take injunction proceedings to quash the story and start an action for damages...."

"Forget it, Tom. If Chan wants to play games, let him. Let's not lose sight of the prize. I want this deal. So if Eve Fung wants a comment, she can have one, but on my terms. In the meantime let's get this meeting over with. We have your briefing. So just show me where to sign and then we can leave."

The lift opened onto the sixty-second floor.

Zhong hurled the car in and out of gaps, slamming accelerator, brake, and horn successively, desperate to make headway. "Too much traffic!" He muttered in cool irritation.

Next to him, Huang Yi shut off his mobile phone and turned to Scott in the back seat. "That was my contact in Kwan Holdings. It's confirmed. The completion meeting is on for six-thirty. Cyrus Kwan has already left for Jackson's offices."

"Can't we phone ahead?"

Huang Yi looked at Scott with dead eyes. "Mr Lee, the police are looking for you. And Zhong and I have no official presence in Hong Kong. A phone-call to Jackson's is out of the question."

"But we'll never make it in this traffic!" Scott shouted. "Let's take the MTR! From Wanchai, there's an exit straight into Central Plaza. We'll do it in ten minutes!"

Huang Yi nodded to Zhong. Rubber screeched beneath them as Zhong threw the steering wheel right and U-turned into on-coming traffic. Vehicles swerved, mini-van drivers hit their horns, taxis tried to cut them up, but Zhong wasn't intimidated. He hit the fast lane, then headed for the next exit. Scott got his bearings. They were on the Hung Hom backstreets, swishing past the funeral parlours heading for the Colliseum. Zhong found an entrance for Tsim Tsa Tsui East Station and guided the car up to the curb.

"I'll stay with the car," Huang Yi said. "You two take the train! Whatever Zhong says, you do, Mr Lee!" Handing Scott a business card, he added, "If you get separated and you need help, call this number!"

"Come!" Zhong jumped out and broke into a run.

Scott hesitated a moment, his head still full of questions he wanted answered, but Huang Yi's hard glare told him this was neither the time nor the place, so Scott set off in pursuit.

They headed down the stairs and into the underground station. Two long, straight, connection tunnels followed, thankfully easy to negotiate, as the pedestrians stuck to the motorized walkways, oblivious to Zhong and Scott tearing down the side-channels. But when they hit the turnstiles, crowds of passengers blocked their momentum. Snaking down the escalators, they eventually hit the platform as a train pulled in.

"That's the one!" Scott shouted. The doors beeped to close. Zhong leapt aboard, slammed his shoulder into the gap, allowing Scott to sneak in. Tuts of disapproval came from all around as the train pulled away.

"Put your hand over your face!" Zhong whispered.

"What?"

"Police are still looking for you, remember!" Zhong moved in front of Scott, blocking people's view.

Scott felt the panic rise and subside. A manic desperation had taken hold in his bones. Here he was both captive and aid to the Chinese Intelligence Services. Here he was a fugitive from the police. And all that mattered to him now was stopping Leopold

Chan; stopping him, because when all was said and done, that man had been responsible for Kimmie's death.

"Did you know her? Kimmie, I mean?" Scott asked Zhong, as the train was halfway under the harbour.

"I met with her a few times! Her work for us was good!" Zhong's eyes moved to Scott. "When one of our own is harmed, we make it right. However limited our resources and however long it takes."

Those deadpan words filled Scott's veins with steel.

They left the train at Admiralty, charged with the hordes across the platform and had a frustrating wait for the Chai Wan line train. It couldn't have taken more than sixty seconds to arrive, but it seemed like an age. One stop later they were in Wanchai.

"Keep up!" Zhong ordered and barreled off the train as the doors hissed open, tugging Scott with him.

"Head for Exit A!"

Shouts of derision followed as they clipped and barged their way through, up one escalator, then another, through turnstyles, ignoring the station attendants telling them to slow down please.

They careered out into the open and onto the hot walkway which led across to Central Plaza, snaking through the crowds of commuters and the trapped heat, reflecting off the concrete. At the end, they hit the wall of air-conditioning inside the ground floor lobby of Central Plaza, Zhong skidding to a stop on the marble, Scott sprinting straight past.

"This way!"

"No!" Zhong shouted.

But it was too late.

An arm shot out from nowhere and stopped Scott like an iron gate, flipping him at the waist. He hit the marble with a bone-jarring smack, red agony blossoming in his skull, stars bursting through his vision. The red-bereted security-guard loomed over him, large hands reaching down to get a grip.

There was no thought in what Scott did next. Instinct driven by a surge of rage made him bring his knee up sharp into the guard's groin. The guard made an "ooff" sound, back-peddled and folded in two. Someone screamed and that was the cue for all hell to break loose.

Suddenly the lobby was pure movement, people hurtling in different directions, shouts echoing in the enclosed cavern, a mad cacophony of footsteps.

Scott caught sight of more red berets approaching fast, to aid their fallen colleague. Beyond, a policeman was barking instructions into a radio.

Damn it!

A hand reached out and dragged Scott to his feet, slapping him out of his stunned state. "This way!" It was Zhong.

They launched into a scrambling run, confusion providing camouflage and obstacles as they pushed people out of the way, no pretence at politeness now, rounding one corner, then another, hitting the outside, sprinting through the thick humidity of another external footbridge, this one with fewer people on it. Staircases went down to street level either side. Zhong took the first one on the left. Scott went with him. U-turning as they hit road level, they darted into the shadow beneath the angle under the staircase.

A minute passed.

Zhong risked a look, but his head shot straight back into the shadows, pointing upwards with his right hand, holding his left hand up in a 'V' sign and then moving his index finger over his lips.

Two of them right on top of us. Don't say a word.

Scott tried to hold his breath, but his lungs needed oxygen so he set about the next best thing – trying to slow the intake. *What the hell had just happened!* his head screamed. *You just assaulted a security-guard, that's what!* Scott left the thought behind. No time for regret. He was along for the ride, going wherever his reactions took him.

Another minute passed. Zhong checked his watch. They were running out of time.

"Jackson's is on what number floor?" Zhong whispered.

"Sixty-two."

"Wait here. I give a signal! You go up there. You stop Chan!"

"What? Wait!"

But Zhong was already on the move.

CHAPTER FORTY-SIX

The team from Kwan Holdings took their seats down one side of the board-room table. Cyrus Kwan sat in the middle, Benton and Mok flanked him. Leopold gazed slowly at the triumvirate and allowed himself a smile. Weary titans hurrying for shade, they seemed.

"Are the agreements ready?" Kwan kicked things off in an efficient Hong Kong tone, his question directed to the lawyers in the room. But this was Leopold's coup-de-grace and he wasn't going to let the head of Kwan Holdings have it all his own way.

"Anyone would think you were in a hurry to get rid of me, Cyrus."

Tyson Mok took the goad. "We were accosted by a reporter from the *Economic Times* downstairs, so we need to move quick! Someone," he eyed Leopold suspiciously, "seems to have tipped them off."

"I hope you're not suggesting it was anyone on this side of the table," Leopold pretended mock outrage. "Maybe it was someone on your end, Tyson? Someone, perhaps, with a history of opening his big mouth when it's better left shut?"

Mok erupted like a volcano. "How dare you! If you think...."

"Can we move on, please!" Cyrus Kwan coolly cut off his deputy.

Leopold drank in the growing tension, savouring every taste. "I think you know my representative, Charles Conrad. Charles perhaps you would be kind enough to take us through the agreements."

"Tom's already briefed us on the way over and I'm comfortable with everything, if that's any help, Leopold," Cyrus Kwan was clearly keen to get this over with.

"Well that's nice for you, Cyrus. However, I would like to be sure that when I sign my company over to you, it is done properly." Leopold was enjoying being disruptive. "So Charles, if you wouldn't mind?"

Having put everyone on edge, Leopold felt a warm glow inside. Soon he would never have to see or hear from any of these people again and the sense of liberation was feeding his outrageous rudeness. This was indeed the most fun he'd had in years.

The next fifteen minutes, however, were anticlimactic. Although Conrad stammered like a pupil on his first day at school, it was a far more assured performance than Leopold had hoped for. Not that it changed anything. It was far too late for Conrad. Lawyers always made good scapegoats and there was nothing in his entire plan which Leopold enjoyed more than the thought of his jellyfish of a legal representative finally getting what he ....his Blackberry vibrated in his pocket. Leopold took it out. An SMS was at the top of his in-box.

Just spotted our young friend. Seems he has company. I'll take care of it.

Leopold closed the message. So Scott Lee had made it to the party after all. And he had help now, it seemed.

Fun though this was, Leopold knew it was time wrap things up. "I think we can move to the signing formalities, Charles, I wouldn't want to hold up our illustrious guests any longer than necessary."

Zhong sprinted fifty yards across the open square, then ducked for cover behind a large ornamental flower vase.

Back under the stairs Scott held his breath and waited to see if the move had caught the attention of the security-guards hovering on the walkway above. Nothing stirred. He saw Zhong move again, another darting run behind a parked car, pausing a moment, then off and sprinting down a side road. Scott lost sight of him after that.

Great, what now?

Wait for a signal, Zhong had said, then get up to Jackson's offices and stop the deal. Who the hell did Zhong think he was, a one-man SAS team? And what was this signal supposed to be?

Scott wiped his face on his shirt, pulling his cheeks down and stretching his eye sockets, hoping the fleeting coldness would trigger some ideas. He needed to think, to absorb himself in the moment, quash the rising panic and adapt as the situation played out.

A plan; he needed a plan.

Glancing out from under the staircase, he tried to consider his next move. Getting to the sixty-second floor of Central Plaza meant either sixty-two flights of stairs or using a lift. The lift would definitely be easier, he figured, but he couldn't just waltz in past reception, not with the heavy security presence deployed. There had to be another way.

Think, Scott, think!

A memory jolted him like a thread caught on the jagged edge of a finger nail.

The goods-lifts. Central Plaza had them and he knew where they were. In earlier days at Jackson's, Scott had used them to transport trial bundles to and from court. He shut his eyes, let his mind drift back in time, tracing the journey from the loading bay on the sixty-second floor to ground level. Where the hell had the lift let him out?

Yes. The underground car-park, that was where. Its entrance was on the north side, he remembered. *Okay, okay, this is good, you can run with this, you can....*

The explosion threw Scott back against the wall, its physicality jolting through his chest. A nanosecond later his ears were ringing, his heart pounding like a bongo drum.

What the hell....

He risked a glance. A tower of smoke was rising from over the road. A car in flames, stunned onlookers running in all directions, searching round in disbelief for what had happened

Zhong. The signal.

Scott gave his head a clearing shake. The ringing lost an octave and rose two notches in volume. Sprinting footsteps on the walkway above. Guards running towards the action. Car alarms breaking the air.

Move! Now! Scott pushed himself out into the open, the panic caused by the explosion serving as his cover. Screams, sirens, car alarms, horns honking, footsteps, the full cacophony of pandemonium, building to its height around him. He rounded the corner, now on the north face of the Central Plaza podium, a mere mosquito on a wall, he hoped. Jutting out, twenty yards ahead was a wall. Beyond the wall, a ramp dropped down to the car-park. Cars were already backing up from the exit, security-guards speaking to drivers, gesturing reassurances, trying to instill calm.

Scott approached the wall, keeping his footfalls soft, followed it to its edge, then paused. Two deep breaths. He stepped out and began walking down the ramp along the queue of cars, keeping his pace expeditious but deliberate as if he belonged there. Slack-jawed drivers talked with the guards and stared past Scott towards the explosion site, no one giving him a second glance.

The ramp leveled off into the open underground space, rumbling engines echoing off low grey ceilings; the air was thick with heat and exhaust fumes, the whole place lit up in sterile fluorescence. Scott broke into a jog against the direction of the large white exit arrows under foot.

A sign pointed to the goods entrance. *Perfect!* – The goods-lift twenty yards ahead, its metal doors like the jaws of hell. – Then, a second later, *Damn!* – Opposite the lift was a booth manned by a red-bereted security-guard, with an uninterrupted view.

Slipping behind a pillar, Scott waited, trying to work out what to do next. Each time he risked a glance the guard still had the lift dead-centre of his field of vision. Sweat dripped off Scott's chin, turning the ground grey to black, the puddle growing with every passing second. He was wasting time.

Then the sound of a ringing phone. Scott took another glance. The guard had a receiver to his ear and was spinning in his chair, his back to the lift.

Scott didn't hesitate. Twenty strides and he was at the metal doors pecking the call button hard, heart thrumming, sweat soaking his clothes. *Come on, come on*, he willed it. He could hear the guard winding up the conversation and the dinosaur-like droaning of the lift's internal mechanism crawling ever closer.

"Hey!"

Sweat turned icy down Scott's back.

"Hey, you!"

The lift was taking too long. *What now? Bluff it out or just ignore him!?* Scott consciously relaxed his shoulders, slowly turned and went with the bluff, throwing the guard a casual wave. "Sorry, you were on the phone. I was here earlier today making a delivery to the tenth floor? Forgot to get them to sign for it. I'll be out before you know it." Turning back to the lift, he fingered the button again.

"No! You can't! Hey! I'm talking to you."

This time Scott went with ignoring him. He heard the guard leave the booth. The lift oozed to a halt, light appearing under the metal doors.

"Wait you! Stop!" The guard yelled.

Scott leapt in as soon as the doors were wide enough apart, hammering the close-button for all his life was worth, as the guard broke into a run. The doors started to come together. But just before they met in the middle, a hand reached out and stopped them.

Terrence O'Rourke stood there like a warrior from hell, grimacing with sick pleasure.

Panic flooded in, blurring Scott's vision and pinning his legs to the spot.

The Irishman's fist shot out like a piston. Scott felt his feet leave the floor. He hit the back of the lift, crashed down, flashes of light sparking behind his eyelids. Another crack, and this time the security-guard swam into Scott's view, crumpling on the ground outside.

O'Rourke stepped into the lift, pressed a button then knelt down. Hot, whisky-sour breath moistened Scott's face.

"Third time unlucky," O'Rourke grimaced.

Zhong saw the whole thing but was too far away to stop it.

The left sleeve of his shirt was gone, having served its role as a makeshift fuse dangling from the car's petrol tank, giving him enough time to get the hell away and enmesh himself in the panic when the vehicle ignited.

He went back to find Scott, but the lawyer had already vacated the cubby-hole under the stairs.

Without stopping, Zhong skimmed round the edge of the building, it seemed the most obvious route for a novice to follow, away from prying eyes and covered by shadows. At the building's corner, he saw the ramp down to the underground car-park. With no time for reflection he flew down it, ignoring the querying looks of the confused drivers. In the expanse below, he glanced right and left searching for Lee, his eyes watering against the condensed fug of petrol fumes.

"Hey you!" An urgent voice called out from somewhere. Zhong followed its direction.

Then Zhong saw him, Scott Lee, pecking the button for the goods-lift, ignoring the remonstrations of an approaching security-guard.

But in the next nanosecond, there was that man again, the one Zhong had tackled to the ground only that morning, barreling in from the right like a bulldozer. Lee's eyes were in the wrong direction, he didn't stand a chance.

Zhong accelerated, but he was too far away and could only watch helplessly as the man slammed Lee into the bowels of the lift and put the security-guard down with a single punch.

The lift doors closed. Zhong slapped them hard in frustration and let rip a guttural scream. Then turning to the prostrate security-guard, "Stairs, where are they?"

Dazed and bleeding, the guard pointed at a fire-door. Zhong shouldered through it and hit a stuffy stairwell. He started up the stairs two at a time, footsteps echoing to the heavens. Each floor he passed had a fire-door with a window at head-height through which he could see the digital display above the lift doors, the flashing number tracing Lee's ascent. The lift moved far faster than Zhong could run even though he was military-fit. For every floor Zhong ascended, the lift went up four. By the time he'd hurtled past floor sixteen the digital display had stopped on sixty-two.

The discomfort of oxygen-debt hurt Zhong's throat as he continued to climb. *Nineteen, twenty, twenty-one....*Hauling himself round corners on the banister, using the momentum to fling himself upwards, his calves and quads burned. *Twenty-seven, twenty-eight....*

Glancing through the glass window of the door on floor twenty-nine, Zhong suddenly stopped. Panting hard, his eyes went wide with concentration. Sweat beads tickled his face.

The goods-lift was on the move again.

Only this time, it was heading down.

Sixty-two floors up, silence stretched taut through Jackson's board-room, Mok and Kwan paging through the agreements, Conrad and Benton reviewing the other party's board resolutions.

Leopold Chan's Blackberry vibrated again. He checked it under the table. *Goods-lift Fl 62 come now.*

"Charles, do you mind if I use the facilities? Don't get up, I know where they are."

Out of the main door of Jackson's offices, Leopold walked down the hallway towards the washrooms, but instead of following the sign right, he headed left, glancing over his shoulder to check no one saw him pushing through the double doors marked "EXIT". The doors brought him out into a yellow-tiled area piled high with cardboard and other rubbish. Wrinkling his nose at the stench, he went on through another set of double doors which took him through to the goods-lift. There, he waited, listening to the sound of the lift straining upwards to its destination, the noise magnifying off the blank walls around him. Goose-bumps of excitement twinkled on his skin. New challenges were presenting themselves right up to the end, requiring him to pivot and twist the unfolding events to his advantage.

In the time it had taken Leopold to walk here from the office, he had worked out exactly how he was going to handle this.

Scott Lee was certainly proving to be resilient. But Leopold comforted himself with the thought that he had always been one step ahead, always able to predict Lee's next move and put in place the necessary precautions to manage any risk. If Scott Lee was going to try to effect a last chance attempt to stop him, then Leopold knew it would have been here at Jackson's offices, where Lee used to work. Rainbow Choi knew the completion meeting would take place here. Chances were she had shared that information before being silenced.

So the last favour Leopold had asked of O'Rourke was that he be ready and waiting.

O'Rourke had been only too happy to oblige.

And now it had all come together nicely.

The lift halted. The doors parted. A frisson of adrenalin jettisoned down Leopold's spine.

Terrence O'Rourke stood there, face taut, hands and fingers flexed like an animal fresh from another kill.

"Thank you for this," Leopold said to him.

They exchanged a nod which betrayed the bond they had built up down the years. Then Leopold searched beyond

O'Rourke to the figure on the floor, tucked up into the foetal position. It was pitiful. Leopold found it hard to believe that this same pathetic creature had been the cause of so many problems.

When Scott Lee looked up at him, Leopold saw his eyes burning with defiance. Blood snaked out the side of his mouth.

"Get him up!" Leopold said. He didn't have long. They were waiting for him back in the board-room. But he wanted to savour this moment of unexpected triumph. O'Rourke lifted Lee by the scruff of the neck, like a dog with one of its pups.

"You've certainly tested my strategic abilities, Scott," Leopold said. "You have my admiration for that. But in this situation, you are still the loser. And I am the winner."

Scott's eyes blazed fury. "Did you kill Kimmie?"

The question made Leopold smile with curiosity. "There," he wagged a finger, "that's why I win and you lose. You have talent, Scott. But talent is nothing when you let emotion rule your judgement..."

"Did you kill her?!"

O'Rourke let fly with a peremptory smack across Lee's face. Leopold watched in fascination as Lee winced with pain and struggled to hold it together.

"Ms Yang threatened to expose something which I wanted kept hidden," Leopold said coolly. "I wasn't prepared to let that happen. So, yes, I extinguished the threat. Or more to the point, I asked Terrence here to do it. He is far better at that sort thing than I am, as I am sure you are finding out for yourself."

A guttural scream tore out of Scott. He lunged out a kick, but O'Rourke was equal to it, tugging him back like a puppeteer, and landing a well-placed kidney-punch. Scott folded in two, a quivering, coughing wretch.

"Your continued hounding of me means that you've earned the right to the same fate as your girlfriend. Somewhat poetic don't you think? Tragic, certainly, but poetic."

As Leopold spoke, he could feel the power rising inside him. The power over human life, the power to make history; it was all his. The fates were moving into position for his glorious moment. Here, in this grubby lift area, his final threat was being snuffed out. The way forward was smooth and inevitable. "Another suicide, I think, Terrence," he said to O'Rourke. Then turning to Scott, he added: "The lawyer who told the truth, but who no one believed. That is to be your fate, Scott. Perhaps, in your final moments you may realize it is one worth having."

Back in Jackson's offices, Leopold watched the red seal and supporting signatures of the two Kwan Holdings directors go down on the agreements and felt the weight of history clawing at his insides in a way the cancer never could anymore. The disease hadn't beaten him. He was going out on his own terms in the knowledge that immortality had just come within his grasp.

No one else would have sensed the magnitude of what was being accomplished today, but such was the way with events that disturbed the world's spinning equilibrium. Their arrival was unexpected, their effect unnoticed right up until the moment when the pillars on which the establishment was structured toppled down in the eye of the storm.

"I suppose that's it then," Leopold turned to the Kwan trio as Benton gathered up the paper work. "Cyrus, you've made the right decision here and I'm sure Rupert will do you proud in running things."

Cyrus Kwan baulked at the mention of his nephew's name. "Perhaps I could ask one last favour, Leopold? The reporter downstairs....Fung, I believe her name is. She will be eager for a comment from you and me in particular. Perhaps we can agree to refrain from saying anything to the press until I have had my communications people work up a joint statement? It's important we strike the appropriate tone, don't you think? Pay compliment to the past and look forward to the future."

Typical Kwan. Diplomatic and silver-tongued. Impressive, Leopold thought.

"I shall say nothing until you give the all-clear." Leopold clapped his hands together. "Well, I for one have my retirement to think about. So if there's nothing else, gentlemen, I shall be on my way."

Handshakes and farewells followed all round, replete with false sincerity. Especially, when it came time for Leopold to shake Conrad's soggy palm.

"Charles, thanks for all your help. You've done well."

Conrad showed him to the door, a peremptory 'thanks' was all he could muster by return. Leopold could see utter relief in his lawyer's eyes. Again that amused him. For a moment, he felt tempted to say something, a final insult, a caustic comment, something just to smash that opening of hope which Conrad had evidently convinced himself existed. But at the last moment Leopold decided it wasn't worth the effort. In itself, that was insult enough.

And he still had work to do.

In the lift on the way down, Leopold took out his Blackberry and placed a call to the AsiaRisk accounts department. The account manager he had designated for the task answered. "The instructions for paying the Chow Mei factory claim. I assume they've been processed exactly as I requested?" Leopold asked.

"Yes Mr Chan. The money has been wired."

Satisfaction glowed in Leopold's chest. Two hundred million Hong Kong dollars. The biggest amount of money he had ever laundered in one shot. Another challenge surmounted. Another achievement ticked on his way to greatness. It was a complete thrill. Leopold enjoyed the sensation, then put it to one side. By the time the lift hit the sky-lobby, he was ready to move on.

"Mr Chan, Mr Chan. Did the deal go through?" Eve Fung teetered determinedly on her heels towards him, bristling with annoying excitement. "Can you comment, please?

Leopold thought of Cyrus Kwan's request to refrain from saying anything to the press, by appealing to his integrity. *How pathetic.* When occasion suited, Leopold could deploy integrity in abundance. This was not, however, one of those occasions. The bigger picture demanded something far more disingenuous. Which was why he had tipped Fung off in the first place. Eve Fung was exactly what he need; an ambitious reporter with a thing for the Kwans who was prepared to use innuendo and sensationalism to blow a story as wide as possible.

"Remind me what your name is?" he asked her, even though he knew full well.

"It's Fung. Eve Fung." Her smile remained painted on.

"Do you have an email address, Ms Fung?"

"Yes I do."

"Then let me have it please. There is something I want to send you."

Leopold worked his thumbs on the Blackberry, pulling up the prepared email from the 'drafts' file, making ready to implement the last act in his forty-year career. Fung excitedly dictated her address. Leopold typed it slowly. He checked it, then checked again and pressed 'send'. "There we are," he said.

"What have you just sent me, Mr Chan? Any comment?"

Leopold smiled. The story of how Rupert Kwan had convinced Uncle Cyrus to purchase a money-laundering outfit and proceeded to clean two hundred million dollars for a criminal thug named Benny Wang, was the answer. Facts, times, dates, names, money transfer amounts; the complete picture.

"The story of your life, Ms Fung," Leopold said. "I suggest you go to find a computer and write it."

With that, Leopold Chan turned and went to catch the lift to the ground floor. On his way he sent his final message. It went to an email account he had strict instructions to use just once and only at this moment.

'*It is done*', the message read.

General Zhao would know what it meant. The rest was up to him.

CHAPTER FORTY-SEVEN

O'Rourke's steel toe-cap caught the edge of Scott's ribs. Pain exploded through Scott's midriff. He crumpled like a piece of cardboard under a grand-piano leg. Eye-bulging gasps clogged his lungs as he tried to push out the whirling black spots turning his vision to water.

O'Rourke hit a button and jolted the lift into action. He knelt down to Scott, his granite face replete with the calm of an impending kill.

"Tall buildings like this," O'Rourke said, "they have these mechanical floors in them. For all the stuff they need to make things work. Ventilation, air-conditioning, all that crap. Thing with these floors is they don't have windows, just nice open side vents. Let's the breeze in, see, keeps everything cool. I saw it on the Discovery Channel once and guess what? Central Plaza, floor forty-four, was the example they used. Funny how information like that sticks in your mind. Think about that. Forty-four floors," he balled a fist, smacked it against his opposite palm and gave a low sinister giggle. "You'll be a piece of mush when they scrape you off the pavement!"

Scott was beyond fear now. Anger had pierced the terror, deflated it to nothing leaving only the purest of rages hurtling through his airways. These people had taken Kimmie's life for nothing more than greed. Adrenalin swept his body, its bitter taste absorbing through the sides of his tongue, but he caught it before he lost all control.

And in that aperture of clarity, he told himself to keep the pretence up.

Make him think you're down. Make him think you've got nothing left.

The lift shuddered to a halt. O'Rourke grabbed Scott up by the arm in a blood-cutting grip and dragged him forward, out of the lift into a hot windy expanse of machinery and metal-tubing. Yammering wind mixed with throbbing turbines filling the place with a deafening cacophony. Scott coughed and groaned and played jelly-legged so O'Rourke took the full weight of his drag.

Without even a pause, O'Rourke yanked Scott into the wind, wanting to get this over with. No more mistakes this time.

Through the blurred vision of panic, Scott made out the criss-cross reinforced struts through which the black sky beckoned him into nothing. O'Rourke, dragging him straight towards it. Scott's stomach fell through his shoes. O'Rourke would toss him through into oblivion, he realized, wouldn't even pause to think. An act as natural as a cobra spitting venom.

No more time. Act now or die.

His elbow still locked in O'Rourke's vice-like grip, Scott fell in mock stumble, tucking his head into his chest, bending his knees as he went down, bracing himself for what was to come. O'Rourke slowed for one second only. But that was all Scott needed. He exploded into action, whipping his head up, pushing hard with his feet. The back of his head hit something solid which gave way in a sickening crunch, loosening the grip on his arm.

O'Rourke span away, lost his balance and went down hard, hands flying to his blooded nose. Scott turned to run, but he wasn't quick enough. O'Rourke had recovered and reached out a massive hand to pull Scott's legs from under him. Scott's elbows crashed to the concrete. Adrenalin pushed the pain out but O'Rourke was just getting started. Scott felt the massive hand tighten round his ankle.

The Irishman, now back on his feet, continued to drag him towards oblivion.

"No!" Scott screamed, arms scrambling, finger-nails desperately trying to get purchase, his chest and face lacerated to shreds on the concrete. Yards to go, yards from nothing.

An AC unit hooked Scott's vision. Rolling left he reached out, caught its edge and tried to pull himself away. O'Rourke took an almighty tug and Scott lost his grip, but then caught the handle of the AC's door, his shoulder almost leaving its socket as O'Rourke hauled away and roared his frustration.

Scott held on for life as O'Rourke wound up a kick. He glimpsed O'Rourke's foot coming towards him and in that nanosecond lashed out and up with his free leg, his heel catching the Irishman firmly in the groin. O'Rourke let go of his ankle, stuttered back and bent double.

Scott could have got up and run then. He could have made it.

But the time for running was over. Anger and adrenaline were his master, now. The bursting dam of rage and frustration let rip with the thought that this man had killed Kimmie and Rainbow.

O'Rourke's face was turning upwards, but Scott didn't hesitate. Even though he was still on the floor, his kick was true, an upward diagonal trajectory, the connection with the sole of his trainer pure, catching the Irishman firmly in the side of his face.

O'Rourke's head snapped back, the momentum of the blow back-pedaling him to the edge of the gap, his massive frame now silhouetting the space where oblivion lay beyond. His arms wind-milled forward as he struggled to keep his balance and his life. Desperately reaching forwards, O'Rourke's fingertips hooked the edge of the nearest strut. It was just enough to allow him to start pulling himself back to safety.

Another kick caught O'Rourke firmly in the chest.

O'Rourke flew backwards into the night, his desperate scream disappearing through the gusting wind. Then nothing.

Scott looked up from the floor at Zhong. For the second time that day, the Chinese agent had come from nowhere and ended O'Rourke's threat.

This time permanently.

Two minutes passed.

Scott didn't feel sorry, not even a bit. O'Rourke had killed Kimmie. He had killed Rainbow Choi. Now O'Rourke was dead. That was how it was supposed to be. Period. Forty-eight hours ago he couldn't have countenanced such a thought, but now nothing seemed more logical.

"Come, we must go!" There was ice in Zhong's voice. "Floor sixty-two!"

Pain racked Scott's body; grazing burns down his chest, his arms like fire, the tendons in his shoulder twisted in agony, the right side of his face a slab of tenderized meat. None of that mattered. O'Rourke may have been Kimmie's executioner. But Leopold Chan had given the order and he needed to be stopped before more innocent lives were destroyed to sate his twisted god-complex.

They headed back to the goods-lift and up to the sixty-second floor. Limping, Scott led the way along the familiar route to Jackson's offices, triggering memories of coming back from lunch with Kimmie, of heading off to court with her, discussing cases, enjoying the banter, her smile, her intelligence. Normal times not that long ago which had ended because of Leopold Chan.

Scott rang the buzzer. He and Zhong stood back from the glass door.

Charles Conrad opened it and Scott saw it immediately in his erstwhile boss's eyes. Shock, yes, but also the realization that he was about to be undone. Zhong's foot went over the threshold just in case.

"What are you doing here?" Conrad stammered, his eyes widening with shock at the extent of Scott's injuries. "What's happened to you?"

Scott limped forward past Conrad. "Where's Leopold Chan, Charles?"

Conrad was about to argue, but Zhong slammed him against the wall.

"Answer him!"

"What's going on out here?" A stocky, full-faced man stood in the doorway of the conference room. Scott had seen his picture in the newspapers, some big-shot from Kwan Holdings.

"Don't buy AsiaRisk!" Scott said to him.

"What? Who the hell are you? I'll call the police...." The man fumbled in his pocket.

"Tyson, what's going on....?" Cyrus Kwan stepped out from the conference-room, eyes darting from Zhong to Scott, trying to compute what was happening.

"Mr Kwan, my name is Scott Lee. Please, I have to talk to you urgently about AsiaRisk. There are things you don't know about Leopold Chan which you need to know. If you buy AsiaRisk it will destroy you and it will destroy Kwan Holdings."

Silence hit like the aftershock from a hurricane. Cyrus Kwan's eyes darkened. "I know who you are, Mr Lee. Leopold Chan is not here and this deal is going through." His words were reinforced steel. "I suggest you calm down and wait for the police to arrive. Tyson, call them please."

"What? No!" Scott heard himself plead. "Mr Kwan, listen to me...."

He stepped forward. Kwan stepped back, his face etched in terror.

Then Scott realized. Cyrus Kwan was afraid of him.

The fat man called Tyson had the phone to his ear. In a blur, Zhong dropped Conrad from the wall, pivoted right, took Tyson by the wrist, released the phone from his hand and hung it up. "No police!" he said.

Silence again.

Kwan swallowed nervously. Over his shoulder, another man appeared from the conference-room, papers in his hand. The man froze and said nothing.

Scott kept his voice calm. "Mr Kwan, whatever it is you think I've done, it's not true."

Kwan seemed to straighten.

"Did you kill Rainbow Choi?" Again steel touched Kwan's words.

"No!" Scott blurted out, the shock of the suggestion contracting his stomach to nothing. But then he put it together. That's why the police were after him, because of what had happened to Rainbow. And now here Scott was, standing before Kwan, bruised, battered and bleeding, looking the part of the thug who had taken her life. "Mr Kwan. I didn't kill Rainbow. I swear it. It was a man called O'Rourke. I saw him do it. O'Rourke works for Leopold Chan. It was Chan who ordered her death."

Three beats of silence.

"Rainbow came to see me about AsiaRisk," Scott pushed on. "She told me she was doing due diligence on AsiaRisk for you. That's why I was with her. We were on our way to see you, when O'Rourke ran us off the road. We were going to warn you."

Kwan took a moment to process it. "Warn me of what?"

Scott held his breath a moment. "Warn you that AsiaRisk is being used as a money-laundering vehicle for a man called Benny Wang. Wang is a criminal, a drug dealer. As soon as you sign the papers to buy AsiaRisk, Chan's going launder two hundred million dollars of Wang's money through AsiaRisk's books. Then he'll go public with the news, make out that your nephew Rupert has implicated you in some sort of criminal scheme. Chan wants to destroy your reputation, Mr Kwan. He wants to destroy Kwan Holdings. He's setting you up."

"This is absurd!" Tyson chimed in. "I'm calling the police!"

"Chan is dying!" Scott shouted the response. "He is dying and he wants to make an impact!"

"I've never heard so much rubbish in all my life!" Tyson strode over to the small side-table in Jackson's reception-area and picked up the receiver from the land-line phone. Zhong stepped forward to stop him, but Scott put a hand up.

Scott Lee and Cyrus Kwan stared each other out.

"Mr Kwan, look at me. Three times in the last forty-eight hours someone has tried to kill me because of what I know. Rainbow knew it too and is already dead! You think I'm lying, go ahead, call the police. But if you have any doubts at all, then listen to me, because as soon as the press gets hold of this, the storm will start and you won't be able to stop it."

Tyson had the phone to his ear and was dialing.

Cyrus Kwan stayed ice-like still. "Tyson, put the phone down."

"What? Cyrus, I am not going to...."

"Put the phone down!"

Tyson did as he was told.

"We've already signed," Kwan said to Scott.

The sudden hush in the room took on an unnatural density.

"Cyrus, you don't think...." Tyson began, but then his whole body sagged to nothing. "The reporter downstairs!"

Kwan nodded. "Chan's already released the story."

Leopold Chan twizzled the tumbler of brandy – his second glass – around his hand, warming the contents to the correct temperature before taking a sumptuous sip and letting the after-effects ripple through him.

Waterloo stretched out before him, the battle which had been a turning-point in history. A personal contest between the Emperor Napoleon and the Duke of Wellington; the upstart commoner and the protector of the establishment. How Leopold admired the former and despised the latter. Napoleon's self confidence had driven him to conquer an empire, to lose it all and have the sheer hubris to try to regain it all over again with a bold call to arms. At Waterloo he had come within a whisper of success. On the fields of faraway Europe, the future of the world had been dictated by the decisions of two men.

Today the venue had been different – the sterile board-rooms of Hong Kong were a far cry from the sodden fields of Belgium – but the confrontation was equally immense. And on this occasion the upstart commoner had prevailed.

Leopold felt the inebriation taking hold. The end was close. Immortality beckoned.

On the stereo, the martial tones of Wagner's *Ride of the Valkyries* invoked the passion that came with making history. Leopold loved this piece, it was so uplifting, so right for this moment.

The Blackberry vibrated in his pocket. He took it out, pinned in his code.

Dear Mr Chan, Thank you for the information. Awesome! Eve Fung.

Leopold smiled. The pillars of the establishment were toppling as the storm unleashed itself. Napoleon wouldn't fail this time.

Leopold took a deep breath and ambled to his easy chair. Leopold had asked Alfonso to bring it down here to the basement, where he had done his best thinking over the years, watching his replica slowly develop into the masterpiece it now was. Alfonso and the rest of his staff had been told to take the night off. Leopold wanted to enjoy this, his last moment alone. Thoughts of greatness were best that way.

Settling back in the chair he used the remote-control to turn up the volume on the music. His glass was fully charged with brandy. Another sumptuous sip rolled round his mouth.

The pills sat on a silver coaster on the side-table. One by one he swallowed them, each with a large gulp. Leopold knew exactly how the cocktail would work. As with everything in his life, his death had been meticulously planned. Within moments he would start to feel drowsy, then he would fall into the deepest of sleeps. Death, when it came, would be painless.

He cast one last longing glance at his battlefield, his project for so many years.

Then Leopold Chan shut his eyes for the last time, settled back and looked forward to immortality.

CHAPTER FORTY-EIGHT

Cyrus Kwan introduced Tyson Mok and Tom Benton and they all proceeded quickly into feverish activity, Benton working through the agreements, Mok rattling instructions during a conference call with the Kwan Holdings communications department, Kwan separately phoning back to one of his personal assistants, asking her to work with the other three to convene the board as soon as possible. When Kwan had finished, he asked Benton for their legal options. Benton puffed out his cheeks. "We can sue for fraudulent misrepresentation, get a declaration the contracts are void...."

"How long will that take?"

Benton lifted his eyebrows in answer.

Scott reached over for the agreements and started to look through them, thinking a second pair of eyes might assist.

"Those are confidential," Benton pulled them away.

"Let him look!" Kwan snapped. Benton let go.

"Damn!" Mok slammed the phone into its cradle. "Eve Fung has the story. Chan gave her a complete dossier, apparently. She's already linking you to this Benny Wang person, Cyrus. She wants you to comment, even asked if you've ever taken drugs yourself! She's got one of Rupert's girlfriends to go on record about his antics with all sorts of substances. Communications told her to go to hell. I think we should call the police...."

"Tell her I'll provide her with an interview!" Kwan clicked his fingers and pointed at Mok. "An exclusive, tell her. We'll meet her at our offices in an hour!"

"What?" Mok was shocked.

"Tyson, if she thinks she'll get a comment, she'll hold the story. And get hold of Rupert, tell him not to say anything to anyone until I've spoken to him. I want him back at the office and secluded. Tell Fung that Rupert will be with me and we'll give her a joint interview if she holds the story until she's heard our side of things. That should buy us some time."

Mok worked the phone again.

Cyrus Kwan pushed a hand through his silvery hair and rubbed his temples. Scott could see the pressure building in the old tycoon's eyes, betraying thoughts about the mistake he had made in getting involved with Leopold Chan, a mistake that was about to cost him everything.

Scott sensed the whole effort slipping away too.

But he hadn't come this far to fail.

Gathering up the agreements, he made for the door. "I'll be in one of the offices."

"Suit yourself," Benton offered. "But I can tell you now, a case in fraudulent misrep is our only option. That's what you can tell the press, Cyrus...."

Scott let Benton blather on and walked out into reception. Zhong was standing there leaning coolly against the wall, staying out of the way, this particular mess beyond his niche skill set.

Scott went straight into Kimmie's old office and sat down behind the empty desk. Sadness still hung there like condensation in a bathroom after a slow, hot, shower. Scott tried to push it out, forcing himself to remember the cuddly toys which Kimmie had lined up by her computer. *Cuddly toys. Working for Chinese Intelligence.* He shook his head in disbelief.

Concentrate, Scott, concentrate!

He whipped through the agreements. Ten minutes was all he needed to get to grips with the key terms of the deal structure. The first agreement would automatically transfer all shares in AsiaRisk to Kwan Holdings when the regulatory approval came through. This first agreement, however, was made subject to the title in AsiaRisk's offices also being properly transferred, a matter which was addressed in the second agreement, a deed passing ownership of the property from AsiaRisk to a Kwan Holdings subsidiary.

Scott checked the execution provisions carefully; this was usually where mistakes were made with deeds. They had to be executed in accordance with AsiaRisk's articles of association, the company's constitutional document. AsiaRisk's seal was firmly imprinted next to the execution clause, and below the seal, Leopold Chan had signed his name.

Scott turned to AsiaRisk's articles of association, a copy of which was in the closing pack. It took him seconds to find the correct clause. A deed could only be executed by two directors, *or any person so authorized by the board.* Which meant, for Leopold to have executed the deed on his own, he needed the authorization of a board resolution. For an inkling of a second, Scott felt there might be a chance that.... but there it was. The next document in the completion pack which Jackson's had provided to Kwan's lawyers was a certified copy of the board resolution authorizing Leopold Chan to sign on behalf of AsiaRisk.

Scott blew air through his mouth. Benton was right. On the face of it, the agreements were unimpeachable unless they went with a case in fraudulent misrepresentation which could take months, even years to sort out. He slapped the certified resolution on the desk in frustration, rested his forehead on his palms, let his gaze drift across the files bulging in the cabinets, the boxes stacked high against the window wall, the dark lines flowing through the laminated wooden desk-top, then finally back to the certified copy of the board resolution.

He absorbed the words on the piece of paper, words authorizing Leopold Chan to sign all the transfer documents on behalf of AsiaRisk, then looked down to the certification given by a solicitor from a different firm on the next floor down in Central Plaza. That was the rule; certifications had to be made by a lawyer who wasn't involved in the deal, hence the need to go down to the firm on the floor below to do the certifications.

The certifying words confirmed that the copy was indeed a true copy of the original board resolution, just like they were supposed to do.

Scott stared at the solicitor's squiggled signature. The name was utterly indecipherable. He searched it closely, trying to work out if he knew the person, if he or she was one of the solicitors he had made small talk with in the lifts, back in the days when Scott had worked in Central Plaza.

Something caught. It was nothing much, just a whisper of familiarity, a vague memory that he had seen that indecipherable signature somewhere before. Picking the resolution up, he stared long and hard at it, trying to stir the recollection which had fish-hooked in his mind. There was something about that handwritten scrawl....

A cold bony palm reached out from the past and smacked him on the side of his head. *It couldn't be, surely.* His eyes screwed into tight pips, his fingers clenching stiffly on the paper. Looking at the signature, he let the memory form and take hold; and when it did, the connections and implications rattled into place at Formula-one speed.

*

The light in Charles Conrad's room was on, the door closed. This was Jackson's offices, but no one had noticed that Conrad was still here, skulking like an animal in his cubby-hole.

Scott didn't bother knocking.

"Why did you do it, Charles?"

Conrad looked up from his desk, then glanced back down at his hands, his fingers picking nervously at the loose flaps of skin on his thumbs.

"I don't know what you mean!" The reply fell as flat as a fish in the wet-market which had flipped away its last bit of life.

Scott placed the certified copy of the board resolution on the desk, slid it across, pointed out the squiggled signature, supposedly of the solicitor from the firm downstairs, confirming that it was true copy of the original. "That's your signature, Charles."

Conrad's jaw slackened. No words came out.

"Five years, I worked for you. The first two you wouldn't even let me sign my own letters. You think I don't know what your signature looks like? Think it's not burned on my memory?" Scott turned to the filing-cabinet, picked off a random file, leafed through its contents. "There," he slapped the file down, two fingers locked onto a photocopy of a letter and Conrad's squiggled name at the bottom. "Look at the signatures. They're identical. That's your signature, Charles! You signed as someone else. You pretended to be a solicitor from the firm downstairs, and certified that document as a true copy. What the hell were you thinking?"

Conrad's face hardened at the question and squeezed out a bitter stare. "You think you're so clever, you work it out!"

The response surprised Scott. He drew away, worked hard on keeping his temper even. "You're a lazy bastard, that's what I think! Too lazy to bother making the journey down one floor to get someone to sign their own name. So you just went ahead and scrawled it ...." He pulled up short as another idea suddenly twisted fast through his growing rage. "No, that's not it, is it?"

He searched Conrad's face for a tell. The bags under Conrad's eyes creased out another line. It wasn't much, but it was there. "This was deliberate wasn't it?"

Defiance leaked out of the edges of Conrad's eyes. Scott's mind moved up through the gears, grabbing pieces of the jig-saw and slotting them in place. "There's a warranty in the purchase agreements, isn't there? A requirement for all the supporting documents being provided – like that resolution – to be either originals or properly certified copies." He waited for Conrad to butt in and contradict him, but all he got was hard silence. "Leopold Chan has set up a breach of warranty, hasn't he Charles? A deliberate breach of warranty which means this whole deal can be unraveled at any time."

This time Scott got a reaction.

Charles Conrad started to laugh. A controlled chuckle at first, but it soon gave way to a hysterical cackle.

"What's so damn funny?"

The cackle subsided. Conrad's eyes blazed with blackness. "That's the trouble with you, Scott. You've always assumed I'm so damn stupid!"

Scott dropped a step back from the desk, unsettled by Conrad's answer. But it took him only a few seconds to put it all together. He'd been right about the breach of warranty being a deliberate set-up, no doubt about it. He'd just got the wrong person. "So this is your idea then. Leopold Chan doesn't know anything about it, does he?"

Conrad didn't answer straight away, but when he did his words were cold. "That's my insurance," he tapped the certified resolution with his fingers, "my protection."

"Protection against what?"

"Protection against that bastard ever sucking me into another of his sick schemes!" Conrad hissed. "I'm through with Chan. I'm sick of being his bloody tool. I've told him as much too. But I need to make sure he stays away from me. That's why I've done it. A breach of warranty, which only I know about. Now I can unwind Chan's precious bloody takeover deal any time I want. One phone-call to Kwan's lawyers, that's all it would take. And if that bastard ever comes near me again...!"

"You'll be struck off!" Scott said. "Prosecuted too!"

"That's a risk I'm willing to take," Conrad said. "And anyway, Chan wants this deal so badly he'll walk away and find some other sap to get his claws into, rather than risk my taking this to Kwan!"

They stayed where they were for a moment, letting the tense silence tighten to breaking-point. Scott could feel the anger working away under his surface, but he pushed it into a compartment and locked it up for later. Right now, he had to remain cool and think clearly.

"Want to know the ironic thing, Scott? It was you who gave me the idea, golden boy." Conrad jabbed his pudgy finger at him.

"What the hell are you talking about?" But as soon as the question left Scott's mouth, it hit him. "You mean Project Claret, don't you?"

Conrad's sick smile told Scott he was right. Scott looked away and shook his head in disbelief. Project Claret. When Scott had ruined his career at Jackson's by signing Conrad's letter of advice on the effective execution of a deed. That mistake had cost him everything, destroyed his chances of partnership and started him on a downward-spiral of alcohol and self-pity.

"The proper execution of a deed," Conrad drew his hand across his sweaty mouth. "I got it wrong back then and you paid the price. So I thought I'd better get to grips with the law this time round. For one director to sign a deed, the signature needs to be authorized by board resolution. Amazing what ideas you get when you bother to find out what the law is."

Again, Scott reached inside himself for the cold spot, pushing down his anger.

So Conrad had finally found out what it was to be a real lawyer, to wrestle with a grey-area problem and tease out a solution. But he was playing on Scott's turf now. And Conrad's scam had given him an idea. This was Cyrus Kwan's way out of the AsiaRisk deal. All Scott needed was one document to make the solution work. One missing vital ingredient, which Conrad wouldn't be willing to yield, because it would mean giving up his precious insurance policy. But Scott knew how to play his old boss's arrogance.

"You're wrong Charles. You are an A-one idiot. Always have been. That fake resolution gives you nothing. All Chan has to do is produce the original board resolution, prove he had the proper authorization to sign the agreements on his own and that's it," he clicked his fingers. "No breach of warranty and the agreements are effective. AsiaRisk remains part of Kwan Holdings and there's nothing either you or Kwan can do about it."

Conrad let out a sigh of satisfaction, shaking his head and smiling. "You see, there you go again, Scott, thinking I'm so stupid. Chan hasn't got the original board resolution," he pointed his thumb at his chest, "I have. I've made sure of that. I drafted it. I got it signed and...."

Suddenly Conrad stopped, his smile falling to nothing as he realized he'd given too much away.

"Where is it Charles? Where's the original?" Scott hit Conrad with the question while he was off-balance. Conrad's eyes flitted to the drawer under his desk. An instinctive reaction, another mistake on his part, but it told Scott all he needed to know. "Give it to me, Charles, or I'm bloody well taking it."

Charles looked down at the drawer again. His tongue came out to lick his thin, purple lips. "No," he said. "It's my only protection. My only chance of ensuring I get a new start. Is that too much to ask?"

Scott felt a little of the rage seeping through the seams of its compartment. "What about Kimmie's family, Charles? What new start do they get?"

The fight hissed out of Conrad then, like a punctured tyre. His eyes sunk into dark circles.

"He killed her, Charles! Leopold Chan ordered Kimmie's death. Kimmie, your colleague, who used to sit in the office over there!"

Conrad's hands fidgeted nervously on the desk top. "I didn't know he was capable of that. Not before it was too late." The words were breathless. "But don't you see, that's why I need this!" He tapped the certified-copy resolution again. "To make sure he can't screw me again."

All those years, Scott had hated this man. But now the time for payback had come, the past seemed irrelevant. "You still don't get it, do you, Charles? That resolution's useless. It doesn't give you any protection!"

"You're wrong!"

"Work it out, Charles!" Scott kept his temper stoic. "You've heard what's happened. Leopold Chan has already leaked the whole thing to the press!"

"So," Conrad remained defiant. "Big deal, Chan's told the press about the takeover. All the more reason why he needs the agreements to remain effective!"

Scott stepped forward, pressed his palms down on the desk and leaned into Conrad's sweating face. "Listen to me Charles. It's not just news of the takeover which Leopold Chan has leaked. It's the whole damn thing. Details of every single one of AsiaRisk's money-laundering transactions. A full dossier. The *Economic Times* has it all, every fake claim which you documented," Scott lifted a hand and pointed a finger. "They know about it and they know about your part in it."

Charles Conrad blinked steadily, his eyes widening every time they opened. "You're lying!"

"You know I'm not, Charles. Just ask yourself the question. Do you really think Leopold Chan would have left your name out of this? He's already screwed you Charles. That insurance policy of yours means nothing!"

Conrad took a moment to process it and when he finally did, his face drooped like a sock sagging over an egg. Suddenly a hideous cackle, laced with bitterness, rode through his lips. Tears ran down his deflated cheeks as he gave way to stuttering sobs, a loser through and through.

Scott let Conrad have his moment, let the sobs rise and fall into nothing. It was a pathetic sight. There were times when Scott had prayed for this moment, to see Charles Conrad finally crash in the flames of humiliation. But now it was just dust in the wind.

"Give me the original resolution, Charles."

"Why?"

"You know why," Scott's mouth was desert dry, but he spat his words out. "The certified copy's flawed. So the deal can only be made effective with the original, because that's the only proof that Chan had the authority to sign the deal. We destroy the original resolution, Chan will never be able to reverse the breach of warranty which you set up, which means the takeover's ineffective. Cyrus Kwan can back out of the deal straight away!"

Charles expression was blank, but Scott didn't have time to waste. "Damn it, Charles! For once in your life do the right thing! Take Chan down with you! Do it! Do it for Kimmie's family, if nothing else!"

Conrad's eyes shifted in hesitation. But only for a moment.

He opened the drawer and took out the original resolution. He looked at it, held it up for Scott to see. Then pincering the edges of the resolution he tore it in two. Then again and again, until thumbsize fragments of paper drifted like snowflakes to the carpet.

Scott hurried back to the conference room.

"The deal's off!" He announced it with a certainty that commanded no argument. Kwan, Mok and Benton looked at him through a daze of confusion, mouths half open. "The documentation's flawed, so the transaction was never completed properly ...."

"What!?" Benton tore off his glasses and was about to launch a broadside, but Scott cut him dead.

"Look I don't have time explain it all right now, but I'm telling you there's a problem with the agreements so the deal's off! Go and speak to Charles Conrad if you don't believe me. He's in the next room and knows all about it. Trust me, the deal's off!"

Benton was still for a moment. Then he pushed off his seat, hitched up his trousers, and went to find Conrad.

Scott turned to Kwan. "That reporter, what was her name?"

"Um," Kwan shut his eyes, shook his head trying to liberate himself from the confusion. "Fung....Eve Fung. Of the *Economic Times*. I have an appointment to see her ...."

Scott was already sprinting back to the privacy of Kimmie's office, fumbling for the business card in his pocket. Her phone was still connected. He dialed the number.

Huang Yi answered immediately.

"Do you have anyone in your network at the *Economic Times*?" Scott asked.

Pause.

"Yes."

"There's a reporter called Eve Fung. She has the story. We need to stop her from..."

"It shall be done."

Dialing tone.

Scott's heart was pumping so hard he could feel his ribs distending.

The door to the office opened. It was Zhong. The Chinese agent said nothing, just stood there in silence. Scott hardly noticed him; his mind was so filled with questions, trying to catch up on itself. Was it over now, the nightmare of the past two days? Suddenly he became conscious of things he'd been ignoring. The pain in his shoulder, the grazing wounds on his chest sticking to his shirt, the scabs on the edge of his hairline.

Yes, it was over, he tried to convince himself. It was bloody over. And yet, there was something left undone. One loose strand. One last thing he needed to do.

*

Leopold Chan was drifting off, the exultatory music lifting him up and out of this world.

What a life he had led, so many challenges overcome. And now it was ending with everything complete. His name everlasting, as the man who had torn down an international financial centre.

In his mind, blue skies were fluid with rolling clouds, perfection in his death as there had been in his life, everything under control, everything planned just as Leopold wanted it. Tomorrow everyone would know his name. One man could change the world. He had proved it was possible .....

Through the music, he sensed the Blackberry vibrating with a new message. Ah yes, he had left it on to obtain confirmation of the panic he had unleashed on Hong Kong. A triumphant response from General Zhao perhaps, or messages from Kwan complaining, or Charles Conrad trying to get hold of him to ask what was going on, or maybe more reporters.... The toxins were at work but the morphine had numbed the pain. Leopold felt himself drifting enticingly towards nothing. The sense of awesome bliss could be heightened further if he could drift into oblivion having glimpsed the start of the carnage he had let rip.

The message. Yes the message. That would give him his glimpse.

The room was spinning him towards darkness. He felt weak, but he was still able to raise the Blackberry and punch in his password. Through watery vision he looked at the screen, and read the words.

It was the last thing Leopold Chan saw before he passed out and died.

Later Alfonso would find his boss's body slack in the chair, his arm dangling over the side, the Blackberry on the floor where it had fallen from his hand; and Leopold's face, his death visage – replete not with the complete satisfaction with which he had wanted to leave this world – but wracked in doubt, perhaps even a spark of astonished rage.

The SMS message on the Blackberry came from a phone-number which wasn't listed in Leopold's address book.

But Leopold Chan would have known who its author was. That two-worded message could have come from only one person. From the constant thorn in his side.

From Scott Lee.

Two words which changed everything.

You lose.

EPILOGUE

As the masseuse's thumbs dug into the meat of his shoulders, General Zhao groaned with pleasure. The ordeal of the past month was over. He could finally relax.

On learning of Leopold Chan's suicide, Zhao had keenly awaited news of how Cyrus Kwan had let himself be manipulated by his wayward nephew into becoming a cheap money-launderer, a crook who lived in riches on the back of other people's misery. After that, it would have been so easy. Zhao would have called an emergency meeting with Secretary Wu, told Wu how he had been right all along and then demanded the authority to freeze and confiscate the Kwan family's assets.

And it wouldn't have stopped there. Investigations against all of the other so-called great tycoon families of Hong Kong would have followed – Zhao would have made sure of it – preventing their assets from leaving the territory and then moving swiftly to enforcement. He, General Zhao, would become the strong-man capable of taking the tough steps necessary to re-establish control over the corrupt Hong Kong tycoon-ocracy. He would be the pride of the Chinese nation. Promotion up the ranks of the party would have been inevitable after that.

That was how it was supposed to play out.

But no stories about the Kwan family hit the news in the days following Chan's suicide. And after the first week, Zhao had faced the awful truth.

Leopold Chan had failed.

The fear following on from that realization was worse than Zhao could ever have imagined. Paranoia became his constant companion, every minute he expected the knock at the door, arrest, public humiliation and imprisonment. He had only met face-to-face with Leopold Chan once in Hong Kong. But once was enough.

What was it that old buzzard Liuming had said about the Third Bureau's surveillance network? – It was so deeply ingrained in Hong Kong society, no one noticed it. – When Zhao had first heard that description, he had sneered. But after Chan's death, Liuming's words had haunted Zhao's every waking hour, made him vomit his meals, ensuring that the only sleep he obtained was of the pill-induced kind.

Yes indeed, these had indeed been the worst weeks of Zhao's career.

But now his ordeal was over.

Zhao had avoided discovery; the meeting he had attended that morning had confirmed it. And as the skilled masseuse worked her strong fingers down his spinal chord, Zhao comforted himself with the memory of the exchange.

"So," Secretary Wu had begun the meeting promptly, "Deputy Controller, I need to report to the Minister on the situation in Hong Kong following the implementation of the Cooperation in Services Agreement. Perhaps you could give the General and myself an update?"

Liuming looked as frail as one of the orchids in the river scenes depicted in the room's wall paneling. Before speaking, he gently cleared his throat and cast a doleful glance at Zhao.

The General's heart started to gallop. *Did the old bastard know anything?*

"The situation is stable, Secretary," announced Liuming. "In the first month following the signature of the CSA, the Registrar received over one-hundred and twenty applications from financial companies wishing to commence business on the Mainland. Our sources have told us that the treaty has stimulated much interest in Hong Kong."

Wu scribbled busily in his notebook. "And what of Kwan Holdings, no more problems I hope?"

Zhao held his breath. Liuming's baleful eyes were on him, searching him, torturing him. Slowly Liuming's face moved back to Wu. "On the contrary, Secretary, Kwan Holdings is the CSA's leading success story. It has recently acquired the staff of a defunct local insurance company and used them to set up a new insurance unit. The talk of the market is that Kwan Insurance will be Cyrus Kwan's platform for launching into China under the protections of the CSA. It is a move which has impressed the local press as an example of how cooperation between Hong Kong and the Mainland can create jobs and benefit all concerned. Rupert Kwan is the new CEO of Kwan Insurance and he reports directly to the board which is chaired by his uncle. The rapprochement between the two men should mean we will have no more trouble from that particular family."

Again Wu noted down Liuming's comments. Neither man noticed Zhao releasing a long-held breath.

"Do you have any questions, General?" Wu eventually asked Zhao.

Zhao cleared his throat. "I do not."

"It would seem then that the Third Bureau has everything under control. I shall report as such to the Minister. I'm sure he will be pleased. Thank you, Deputy Controller." Wu got up to leave. Zhao did the same, casting a token nod in Liuming's direction before heading for the door.

"I hope our respective departments can co-operate like this more in the future, General," the seventy-year-old Liuming said.

Zhao stopped, turned back. All he could do was respond with another nod. He couldn't wait to get out of there.

The elixir of sweet relief swept through Zhao as he left the building. The Third Bureau didn't know. He was safe. A massage was the perfect way to put the tension of the last few weeks behind him, so he allowed himself a detour on his way back to the office.

The masseuse moved onto his feet, running her knuckles down his sensitive instep, sending electric pulses of satisfaction through him. When she was done he enjoyed the rest of his lemon-grass drink before showering and toweling off. His whole body felt turgid, like a puppet with his strings cut. He had been to the brink and made it back. Now it was time to move on, to work on his next strategy for advancing up the echelons of power. By the time he made it back to the Military Affairs Commission, Zhao had already latched onto the beginnings of a new idea. What was it Liuming had said? Kwan Insurance was trying to launch into China. How interesting. Now the Kwans would be playing in Zhao's own territory and with Rupert Kwan heading up Kwan Insurance, it was only be a matter of time before that wayward idiot put a foot wrong and when he did, Zhao would sieze the chance to ....

As soon as the door to his office opened, Zhao sensed it. Something was off key.

Then he saw it.

The brown envelope on his desk. Waiting for him. The tension flooded back, the massage a distant memory, his new-found confidence evaporating to nothing.

Zhao picked up the envelope, fingered its edges, looked around as if expecting someone to step out from behind the curtains. Nothing moved. He was alone.

The blank envelope offered no clue as to where it had come from. But when Zhao opened it and saw the single photograph it contained, he knew immediately. It was black and white and slightly grainy, but there was no mistaking the two figures talking to each other outside Hong Kong's Chep Lap Kok airport.

I hope our respective departments can co-operate like this more in the future, General, that old buzzard Liuming had said to him. Looking down at himself and Leopold Chan in the photograph, Zhao knew Liuming's parting shot had been a statement of future intent and not a request.

He, General Zhao, had just become the Third Bureau's latest recruit.

Scott sat down on the stone bench under the shade of a pine tree overlooking the church.

He had been in already, taken a seat in a pew at the back and experienced part of the memorial service. It was a far cry from what he'd been expecting. Today wasn't about lonely vigils or sad goodbyes. Today was about giving thanks for the life of a wonderful young woman.

There was a lot about Kimmie that Scott hadn't known until that moment. Like how big an extended family she came from. Father, mother and sister aside, there were dozens of aunts and uncles, cousins and old classmates a-plenty, the church packed full with people whom Kimmie had touched, in a life so cruelly cut short.

But there was one thing about Kimmie Scott did know and had known from the moment he had set eyes on her that first day in Hong Kong.

He knew he loved her. And for that he was thankful.

When the service was about half-way through, Scott decided to make his exit. He wanted time alone. And on that bench under the pine tree, with the hymns spilling out of the open doors of the church below, he found it.

This was where he wanted to give thanks for Kimmie's life. Right here, on his own.

Much had happened in the past month.

A policeman called Detective-Inspector Kam had opened an investigation into Kimmie's death. Word was he'd been tipped off anonymously about new evidence. Huang Yi and Zhong, Scott guessed, must have been behind it. The Third Bureau looking after its own.

Kam's investigation was focusing on Terrence O'Rourke who, in a past life, had been James Higgins, an old-style member of a terrorist paramilitary outfit from Northern Ireland, forced to reinvent himself after peace had broken out in that province. Interpol had never found Higgins and were as shocked as anyone when he turned up dead on the top of the Convention Centre, having taken a headlong dive off Central Plaza, the same Hong Kong skyscraper in which Kimmie Yang had once worked.

It was a tenuous link at best, but enough for Kam to give credence to the suggestion that Kimmie Yang's death hadn't been the result of a stressed-out lawyer taking her own life, as the original inquest had concluded.

As conclusions went, it was far from ideal. But at least it gave the Yang family the beginnings of something which, Scott hoped, would one day allow them to find peace in their hearts.

Charles Conrad had resigned from Jackson, Weiss, Macdonald. His wife, Cathy, had returned to the UK without him. The last Scott had heard, Charles, no longer practising as a solicitor, was helping Inspector Kam with his inquiries into Benny Wang, tracing significant amounts of money which had been laundered through AsiaRisk's accounts.

AsiaRisk was now in liquidation, its portfolios and staff, including those in the rep offices on the Mainland, having been transferred to Kwan Holdings. The new business unit, Kwan Insurance, had been set up to take advantage of the Cooperation in Services Agreement and the regulators on both the Mainland and in Hong Kong were expediting Cyrus Kwan's licensing applications.

Leopold Chan had been cremated, his funeral organized by one of his hired staff, Alfonso, who had donated Leopold's replica of the Battle of Waterloo to a local children's charity, so the kids could play with the soldiers. A reporter called Eve Fung had written a short story on page ten of the *Economic Times* about how Leopold, the founder of a medium-sized insurance company called AsiaRisk, had taken his life, rather than face the pain of dying from cancer.

Yes indeed. A lot had happened in the month.

But not for Scott. He had pressed the pause button on his life, recovered from his injuries, been running every day and hadn't touched a drop of alcohol, although there were some nights he'd been sorely tempted. He'd had long telephone-calls with his dad and his brother John and listened to how his nephew was thinking of going into the law after Oxford.

He'd thought about leaving Hong Kong. He still hadn't reached a decision.

The church began emptying out, the congregation full of smiles and joy and tears.

"You lost the ability to answer a phone?"

Scott turned, looked up and saw Phil Yip silhouetted against the sun.

"I've been trying to reach you. In fact, for the last five minutes, I've been wondering whether to come over at all."

"All of a sudden you think I bite?" Scott said.

"I've long since given up trying to predict what goes on in your head." Yip sat down on the plinth beside him, rested his elbows on his knees. "Just wanted to know you're okay, that's all."

Scott felt the question ignite a comforting warmth.

Philip Yip. Still his go-to-guy in times of trouble after all this time. In the past few weeks, Yip had sent his maid round to Scott's flat with a hot meal every day, referred him to the right doctors to treat his wounds and emailed him regularly with news from work. But Yip had also known to keep his distance, like only best friends do.

They hadn't spoken much about what had happened.

"I still owe you some money," Scott said after a moment.

Yip looked down between his feet, shook his head and smiled.

"What, Phil, you want a hug or something?"

Yip looked at him, the smile instantly replaced by senior-partner mode. "What I want is for you to come back to work. Partner. Full equity. Straight off the bat."

Scott swallowed. All his career he'd been wanting an offer like that. But right here, right now, the very idea of it made him sick. "Bet Gordon Siu's got something to say about that," he parried.

"Who cares if he has? I promised that if you had your own client-base, we'd ignore Gordon. And since Cyrus Kwan's instructed us on the Kwan Insurance licensing, Gordon counts for zip. You're the man, now, buddy."

"Gee Phil, you're all heart."

"Amazes me as much as anybody, but Kwan wants you, Scott. And thanks to your rainmaking, we're swamped. I've taken on Carmella Lo from Jackson's to handle things for the moment...."

"She's good...."

"But she's going to need your guidance. We're talking about a major restructuring, absorbing AsiaRisk into the Kwan organization. AsiaRisk's staff are really up for it. Carmella keeps getting asked when they can launch the new branding. Gonna be a lot of work. And Cyrus wants you, Scott," Yip jabbed a finger. "Said he's seen what you can do with a takeover agreement, whatever that means."

Scott said nothing, kept his eyes firmly on the church. He didn't want to talk about this, not here, not now. Below, the crowds were thinning out and cars were leaving. The weather had turned cool. The whole city had an autumn feel to it. Across the road a woman with two labrador dogs came out of a building, their pink tongues flapping with eagerness at the start of a walk. Traffic-lights made that ticking noise. Taxis buzzed too and fro.

"Tell me you'll at least think about it?" Yip said cautiously after a while.

Scott turned to him. "I need some time, Phil."

Yip gave him a warm grin, no longer the senior partner. "You need anything, just call me, okay?"

"Always do."

Yip got up, patted him on the shoulder and made his way down the stone stairs to the church car-park.

Scott leant back on the bench, draped his arm on the back, and lost himself in a stream of thoughts and emotions which he just let ride through him, not caring where they took him. He thought a lot about Kimmie. About opportunities lost. About Hong Kong.

About what came next.

Seconds and minutes passed. The crowds below eventually cleared into emptiness. The labradors came back from their walks, tongues still flapping. Taxis still buzzed too and fro.

The afternoon sun came round and the shade disappeared. A warm Hong Kong glow descended. And after a while, Scott Lee realized it was time. Time for his new beginning.

ABOUT PROVERSE HONG KONG

Proverse Hong Kong is based in Hong Kong with long-term and expanding regional and international connections.

Proverse has published novels, novellas, fictionalized autobiography, non-fiction (including autobiography, biography, history, memoirs, sport, travel narratives), single-author poetry collections, children's, teens / young adult and academic books. Other interests include diaries, and academic works in the humanities, social sciences, cultural studies, linguistics and education. Some Proverse books have accompanying audio texts. Some are translated into Chinese.

Proverse welcomes authors who have a story to tell, wisdom, perceptions or information to convey, a person they want to memorialize, a neglect they want to remedy, a record they want to correct, a strong interest that they want to share, skills they want to teach, and who consciously seek to make a contribution to society in an informative, interesting and well-written way. Proverse works with texts by non-native-speaker writers of English as well as by native English-speaking writers.

The name, "Proverse", combines the words "prose" and "verse" and is pronounced accordingly.

THE PROVERSE PRIZE

The Proverse Prize, an annual international competition for an unpublished book-length work of fiction, non-fiction, or poetry, was established in January 2008. It is open to all who are at least eighteen on the date they sign the entry form. Unusually for a competition of this nature, there is no restriction based on nationality, residence or citizenship.

The objectives of the Proverse Prize are: to encourage excellence and / or excellence and usefulness in publishable written work in the English Language, which can, in varying degrees, "delight and instruct". Entries are invited from anywhere in the world. Semi-finalists to date include writers born or resident in Andorra, Australia, Canada, Germany, Hong Kong, New Zealand, Nigeria, Singapore, South Africa, Taiwan, The Bahamas, the Peoples' Republic of China, the United Arab Emirates, the United Kingdom, the USA.

359

FOUNDERS: Verner Bickley and Gillian Bickley. To celebrate their lifelong love of words in all their forms as readers, writers, editors, academics, performers, and publishers.

HONORARY LEGAL ADVISOR: Mr Raymond T. L. Tse.

HONORARY ACCOUNTANT: Mr Neville Chow.

HONORARY JUDGES: Anonymous.

HONORARY ADVISORS: Bahamian poet Marion Bethel; UK translator, Margaret Clarke; UK linguist & lexicographer David Crystal; Canadian poet and academic, Jonathan Hart; Swedish linguist Björn Jernudd; Hong Kong University Librarian, Peter Sidorko; Singapore poet Edwin Thumboo; Czech novelist & poet Olga Walló.

HONORARY UK AGENT AND DISTRIBUTOR: Christine Penney

HONORARY ADMINISTRATORS: Proverse Hong Kong.

PROVERSE PRIZE WINNERS WHOSE BOOKS HAVE ALREADY BEEN PUBLISHED BY PROVERSE HONG KONG

Laura Solomon, Rebecca Jane Tomasis, Gillian Jones, David Diskin, Peter Gregoire, Sophronia Liu, Birgit Linder, James McCarthy, Celia Claase, Philip Chatting.

Summary Terms and Conditions
(for indication only & subject to revision)

The information below is for guidance only. Please refer to the year-specific Proverse Prize Entry Form & Terms & Conditions, which are uploaded in April each year onto the Proverse Hong Kong website: <www.proversepublishing.com>.

The free Proverse E-Newsletter includes ongoing information about the Proverse Prize. To be put on the E-Newsletter mailing-list, email: info@proversepublishing.com with your request.

The Prize
1) Publication by Proverse Hong Kong, with
2) Cash prize of HKD10,000 (HKD7.80 = approx. US$1.00)

Supplementary publication grants may be made to selected other entrants for publication by Proverse Hong Kong.

Depending on the quality of the work in any year, the prize may be shared by at most two entrants or withheld, as recommended by the judges.

In 2015, the entry fee was: HKD220.00 OR GBP32.00.

Writers are eligible, who are at least eighteen on the date they sign The Proverse Prize entry documents. There is no nationality or residence restriction.

Each submitted work must be an unpublished publishable single-author work of non-fiction, fiction or poetry, the original work of the entrant, and submitted in the English language. School textbooks and plays are ineligible.

Translated work: If the work entered is a translation from a language other than English, both the original work and the translation should be previously unpublished. The submitted work will not be judged as a translation but as an original work.

Extent of the Manuscript: within the range of what is usual for the genre of the work submitted. However, it is advisable that novellas be in the range 35,000 to 50,000 words); other fiction (e.g. novels, short-story collections) and non-fiction (e.g. autobiographies, biographies, diaries, letters, memoirs, essay collections, etc.) should be in the range, 80,000 to 110,000 words. Poetry collections should be in the range, 5,000 to 30,000 words. Other word-counts and mixed-genre submissions are not ruled out.

Writers may choose, if they wish, to obtain the services of an Editor in presenting their work, and should acknowledge this help and the nature and extent of this help in the Entry Form.

KEY DATES FOR THE PROVERSE PRIZE IN ANY YEAR
(subject to confirmation and/or change)

Receipt of Entry Fees / Entry Documents	14 April to 31 May of the year of entry
Receipt of entered manuscripts	1 May to 30 June of the year of entry
Announcement of semi-finalists	July-September of the year of entry
Announcement of finalists	October-December of the year of entry
Announcement of winner/ max two winners (sharing the cash prize)	December of the year of entry to April of the year that follows the year of entry
Cash Award made	At the same time as publication of the work(s) adjudged the winner / joint-winners of the Proverse Prize
Publication of winning work(s)	In or after November of the year that follows the year of entry

NOVELS, SHORT STORY COLLECTIONS
AND OTHER FICTION
Published by Proverse Hong Kong

If you have enjoyed *Article 109* by Peter Gregoire, you may also enjoy Peter Gregoire's *The Devil You Know* (2014).

You may also like to read the following (all titles in English unless otherwise stated):

A Misted Mirror, by Gillian Jones. 2011.
A Painted Moment, by Jennifer Ching. 2010.
An Imitation of Life, by Laura Solomon. 2013.
Article 109, by Peter Gregoire. 2012.
Bao Bao's Odyssey: from Mao's Shanghai to Capitalist Hong Kong, by Paul Ting. 2012.
Black Tortoise Winter, by Jan Pearson. Scheduled 2015 / 2016.
Bright Lights and White Nights, by Andrew Carter. 2015.
cemetery miss you, by Jason S Polley. 2011.
Cop Show Heaven, by Lawrence Gray. 2015.
Death has a Thousand Doors, by Patricia Grey. 2011.
Hilary and David, by Laura Solomon. 2011.
Instant Messages, by Laura Solomon. 2010.
Man's Last Song, by James Tam. 2013.
Mila the Magician, by Zhang Jian. 2013. (English / Chinese bilingual)
Mishpacha – Family, by Rebecca Tomasis. 2010.
Odds and Sods, by Lawrence Gray. 2013.
Paranoia (the Walk and Talk with Angela), by Caleb Kavon. 2012.
Red Bird Summer, by Jan Pearson. 2014.
Revenge from Beyond, by Dennis Wong. 2011.
The Day They Came, by Gérard Louis Breissan. 2012.
The Devil You know, by Peter Gregoire. 2014.
The Monkey in Me: Confusion, Love and Hope under a Chinese Sky, by Caleb Kavon. 2009.
The Monkey in Me, by Caleb Kavon. Translated by Chapman Chen. 2010. E-book. 2010. (Chinese)
The Perilous Passage of Princess Petunia Peasant, by Victor Edward Apps. 2014.

The Reluctant Terrorist: in Search of the Jizo, by Caleb Kavon. 2011.

The Shingle Bar Sea Monster and Other Stories, by Laura Solomon. 2012.

The Snow Bridge and Other Stories, by Philip Chatting. Scheduled 2015.

Tiger Autumn, by Jan Pearson. 2015.

The Village in the Mountains, by David Diskin. 2012.

Tightrope! A Bohemian Tale, by Olga Walló. Translated from Czech by Johanna Pokorny, Veronika Revická & others. 2010.

Tightrope! A Bohemian Tale, by Olga Walló. Translated by Chapman Chen. 2011. (Chinese)

University Days, by Laura Solomon. 2014.

Vera Magpie, by Laura Solomon. 2013.

OTHER GENRES

We also publish in other genres, including autobiography, biography, children's illustrated books, educational books, Hong Kong educational and legal history, memoirs, poetry, teenage / young adult books, and travel. Other genres may be added.

WRITE TO US!

We are interested to read **your** response to
Peter Gregoire's *Article 109*
and any other of our publications.
Please write to our email address, proverse@netvigator.com,
giving us a few sentences which you are willing for us to publish,
giving your comments on this book.
If what you write is chosen to be included
in our E-Newsletter or website,
we will select another title published by Proverse
and send you a complimentary copy.
Please include your name, email address and mailing address
when you write to us, and state whether or not we may cut or
edit your comments for publication.
We will use your initials to attribute your comments.

FIND OUT MORE ABOUT OUR AUTHORS AND BOOKS

Visit our website
http://www.proversepublishing.com

Visit our distributor's website
<www.chineseupress.com>

Follow us on Twitter
Follow news and conversation: <twitter.com/Proversebooks>
OR
Copy and paste the following to your browser window and follow the instructions: https://twitter.com/#!/ProverseBooks

Request our E-Newsletter
Send your request to info@proversepublishing.com.

Availability
Most titles are available in Hong Kong and world-wide from our Hong Kong based Distributor, The Chinese University Press of Hong Kong, The Chinese University of Hong Kong, Shatin, NT, Hong Kong SAR, China. Email: cup-bus@cuhk.edu.hk

All titles are available from Proverse Hong Kong and the Proverse Hong Kong UK-based Distributor.

We have stock-holding retailers in Hong Kong, Singapore (Select Books), Canada (Elizabeth Campbell Books), Principality of Andorra (Llibreria La Puça, La Llibreria).

Orders can be made from bookshops in the UK and elsewhere.

Ebooks
Most of our titles are available also as Ebooks.

www.ingramcontent.com/pod-product-compliance
Lightning Source LLC
Chambersburg PA
CBHW072025020726

47501CB00006B/1958